DARKER THE SHADOWS

By

Susan M Cowley

Edited by John Parker

DARKER THE SHADOWS

DARKER THE SHADOWS

Introduction

It was a cold, autumn morning, as Marcus Alexander Stephenson stood at the loch side looking across to the mountains beyond. The gentle waves lapped the pebbles and a soft breeze whispered in the pine trees. Marcus sighed: if only he could see into the future, the momentous decision he was about to make would surely be easier. But then what man hadn't wished for a crystal ball at some point in his life?

Where the big issues were concerned one had to be bold, follow one's instincts and strike while the iron was hot. What was it his old headmaster used to say? Fortune favours the brave - that was it.

On the cliff above the loch stood his beloved Braeside, the grand and ancient house that his late father Alexander had bought when he made his fortune before the Great War.

Growing up in Braeside, with its magnificent, imposing rooms, fine library, sprawling corridors, endless enchanting nooks and hidey holes and a retinue of obliging servants, set on the estate of small farms, forests and the loch, had, for Marcus and his younger brother MacKenzie, been truly idyllic.

After their father's untimely death in February 1914 Marcus took over the Merchant Shipping business and moved it to Liverpool. He had avoided the war, for which he was quietly grateful, but his friend and accountant John Bamford had not. John had returned a changed man. He had contacted Marcus shortly after coming home, asking to resume his position. Though Marcus had been happy with John's replacement he had agreed without hesitation that his friend should return to the fold as soon as possible. He had not regretted the decision. Particularly since the dinner party three months ago, when John had introduced him to his sister.

"Marcus, may I present Clarissa." The pride in having such a ravishingly beautiful girl for a sibling had been evident in John's manner. Marcus, so struck by her beauty, had been unable to speak. With great courtesy he had taken her hand and placed a delicate kiss upon it.

"Thank you, sir," she had murmured softly.

Her words had been like sweet, infinitely seductive music in his ears. For the remainder of that evening he had been unable to take his eyes off her; her raven hair glistening in the candlelight, her dark eyes, black, like pools of deep mysterious, tantalizing water - how he longed to bathe in them. Her perfect, moist lips – how he longed, ached to kiss them! Never before had he felt such intense and overwhelming desire burning within him.

The decision he was now wrestling with had seemed simple enough when he was in Liverpool, amid the noise and bustle of the city, seated in his office, where he made a dozen confident decisions a day and issued orders and directives to all and sundry. There, the habit of command came naturally to him.

He knew he wanted Clarissa – body and soul. But now, not uncertainty exactly, but a strange unease had begun to affect him, which he was at a loss to define. Was it that part of him was unsure that Clarissa would like the life he was about to offer her? Or was there some deep unsolved riddle about Clarissa herself, something in those dark, mysterious eyes that unsettled him?
Perhaps it was simply an inner amazement that such a glamorous and beguiling woman would actually fall for him, as he so patently had for her!

Unable to settle these qualms in his own heart, it was to Braeside he had returned. In the shadow of the great house by the water's edge, in the beautiful, untamed landscape of his childhood, he felt sure he would find his answer.

CHAPTER ONE

1919

"Is she a quiet lassie Marcus," his mother asked him, her eyes wide with surprise, and a degree of anxiety, when, on his return from the loch he entered the drawing room of the family home, and finding his mother at her embroidery, announced his intentions.

"And what about her family. What do they do for a living? Are they our sort of people?"

Although Constance knew John Bamford she did not know anything about his family.

Marcus smiled at her. "My dear, Mama," he said, gently taking her hand. "Clarissa is all that you could wish for in a future daughter-in-law."

"That's your opinion" his mother replied briskly, darting her needle deftly into a nearly completed thistle design in her tapestry. "We have yet to meet her - and you haven't answered my question about her family."

"Yes mama, they are our sort of people," laughed Marcus shaking his head good-humouredly as he left the room.

His mother always worried, he reflected, she worried about everything and everyone, especially him. He realised one thing though; that she knew him well enough to know this girl must be very different from the others he had courted. He realised too that the announcement of his intended proposal must have unsettled his mother; she was after all facing for the first time the prospect of demotion, of being only the second most important person in her son's life. And that meant his brother Mackenzie would also shuffle down one place in the pack. And speaking of whom, he thought, where was Mac?

He found his brother sitting in his wheelchair by the fishpond watching the gardener gathering the fallen leaves and twigs and throwing them on to the bonfire. The wood smoke drifted towards him, he smelled the air joyously; he loved this time of year.

His thoughts like the wood smoke drifted to happier times when he and Mackenzie would find any number of adventures in the forests, would take the small rowing boat from the boat house and row out into the middle of the loch and spend all day fishing, the very best of friends. Mac had always been the wild one, the dare devil, the fun loving son They had wanted for nothing; whatever their father's money could buy had been theirs. But Mac had always wanted more; a shinier, even faster bicycle, or later, when he became conscious of his appearance and young girls' eyes upon him, another trip to the most sought-after tailors in Edinburgh. Then it was a car - but not just any car.

"We should have one of these, Father." Mac had shown him the picture in a magazine, of a sports model, a Bugatti no less, in gleaming red, a godlike machine. After much prolonged pestering Alexander had succumbed and bought the magnificent vehicle.

When it arrived, Mac of course, immediately took full control, finding some excuse why Marcus couldn't or shouldn't drive the splendid machine.

It had been raining heavily on the day the accident happened. Mac had been in an even more jovial mood than usual. He was going out that night with his beloved Edith, intent on proposing marriage.

"I'm taking Edith out tonight," he had announced with great pride. "And I hope, that she will accept my proposal. What do you think?"

Following his initial surprise, Marcus had replied, "You've been walking out for sometime now. It's the natural progression of things. I wish you luck. But take it slow, in every respect."

Mac had then laughed loudly. "Marcus, you old fuddy duddy. You know, it's about time you had a girl of your own, then you wouldn't be bothered about me so much."

"Well, you just be careful, you hear?" Marcus had replied, following his brother to the front door.

Mac jumped in the Bugatti and started the engine, which roared like a mighty beast.

Above the noise Mac had shouted back to his brother. "I'm always careful!" The next minute he was gone.

The police brought the devastating news. Mac hadn't seen the motorcyclist until it was too late. Swerving to avoid it, he drove the Bugatti off the road and head-on into a tree. He was unconscious and not expected to live.

Six weeks later, Mackenzie, to the amazement of the doctors, regained consciousness. He was however unable to move from the waist down. Edith visited for a while, but her appearances became less frequent. Eventually she stopped coming altogether. Mac was brought home to his family, a broken man.

Marcus remembered every detail of the hours he had spent quietly in Mac's room, just listening to him talk – about what he was going to do, about his plans to build a sports car he could drive with his hands alone, and win races, and climb mountains and go to America and god knows what other fantastical schemes.

And when Mac had exhausted himself with these dreams, Marcus would stay, sitting beside him, both men silent, simply being there with and for his brother, the adventurer no more, the hero fallen to earth.

"Hello Mac!" Marcus called.

Mac turned his wheelchair around to greet his brother. "Hello old chap," he said, reaching forward to shake hands as Marcus came close. "I'll not get up if you don't mind."

The two men laughed. Mac always said the same thing. After the first two years, this bluff, ever so slightly bitter humour was still his modus operandi. To those that didn't know him, it could be unnerving.

"So Marcus! What brings you here? Liverpool too quiet?" He quipped. "No, something tells me that you have troubles. I wonder what …I know," he grinned, "It's a woman!"

Marcus's face reddened. His brother could still read his mind, as well as make him embarrassed about the most normal of things.

"Sorry old man, forgive my ribbing. So it's an affair of the heart then – come, tell your brother all," said Mac, slapping Marcus's arm affectionately. Marcus pushed Mac's wheel chair to the bench beneath the oak tree and sat down.

"Her name is Clarissa Bamford, she is the daughter of a bank manager in the village of Crosslands. Her brother is my accountant and her mother's name is…."

"She has a dog, a pet rabbit," Mac interrupted loudly, "and a goat and three elephants, and likes butter on her toast - Marcus, stop jabbering nonsense and tell me about *her*."

—

7

Marcus looked at his brother's grinning face. Hidden deep behind the pale blue eyes that, in the animation of this moment between them danced with expectation, there was a feeling of remoteness, a sense of ineffable melancholy. I must share my joy with him, and my doubt, thought Marcus – I must not deny my brother the access to my heart.

"Well come on then - spill the beans. You do intend to marry her I presume?"

"I might," said Marcus laughing now. "Very well, I do, but I feel that she, that she might not..."

"Shall I say it for you?" Mac said archly. "She might not be able to cope with your life style – and your social standing in the community. I'm sorry old chap, but if that's all you can think about, then you'd better let her go to someone who loves her for what she is, not what you want to turn her into."

"It's true she does not have money, and her family are, well...but it's not like that at all Mac, really." Marcus replied defensively.

"Well it seems like that to me. You don't want a wife, you want a trophy, a beautiful thing that you can take out for social gatherings and then return to the cabinet until the next event." Mac seemed annoyed with his brother now.

This prevarication he felt was so unlike Marcus, and he sensed something more was bothering him.

"What's wrong Marcus?" Mac almost shouted the question.
Marcus turned away. "All right, I'll tell you what's wrong," he said in a voice tremulous with emotion. "It's because I love her so much it hurts - and if I should ever...ever lose her..." His words tailed off.
Mac moved his wheelchair closer. "Marcus, why would you lose her? If you are thinking of my situation with Edith, please, I beg you not to. This is you we're talking about."
Marcus turned back to face his brother, his eyes moist now.

"I'm so sorry Mac," he said, "for everything; I blame myself for what happened to you. I should have stopped you going in the car. I should have."
Unable to contain himself, he fell at Mac's feet and sobbed bitterly. Mac placed both hands on his brother's shoulders. His voice was soft now, gentle.

"Everything in life is a risk, and what can you lose? Does she love you?"

—

8

Marcus nodded, wiping his eyes. Mac smiled and took hold of Marcus" arms. "I lost Edith because of my stupidity, my arrogance. You have none of these, qualities."

"But I..." began Marcus.

"Now listen to me," Mac forestalled him. "Marry her do you hear, marry her and love her with all your heart, your body and your soul. Love her with a white heat of passion, of desperation, of tenderness - and don't ever let her go."

"So do you have an answer?" Marcus looked at his beloved across the table. Clarissa stared down into her napkin. He observed the colour rising into her cheeks. Oh god, he thought, this is what I dreaded. She is embarrassed and doesn't know how to let me down gently. The waiter discreetly topped Clarissa's glass up with champagne.

"Gosh Marcus," spluttered Clarissa under her breath, her eyes still averted, "this must be costing an absolute fortune."

"I have an absolute fortune." Marcus immediately regretted the remark. Now I sound like Mac he thought; she'll think me impossibly conceited, or that I'm trying to buy her affections. Oh lord - perhaps I am!

"I didn't mean that to sound in any way..." he began.
Clarissa took a hasty gulp of champagne. "No, no, and nor did I imply – its just that I'm not used to..."
They both laughed. Then Clarissa looked up and stretched both her hands out towards him. "Of course I will marry you darling," she said. Her dark eyes were now luminescent, her beautiful face beneath her raven hair radiant with joy.
Marcus gripped her hands tightly. "You won't regret it Clarri, I promise, I'll make you the best husband you'll ever have."
Clarissa laughed "I wasn't thinking of having another one; you do say the silliest of things."
Marcus smiled at her – at his fiancée.

"You are perfect," he said, "and I love you so very, very much."

Drawing her right hand towards him he placed a kiss gently on her milk white fingers. "When shall we make the announcement?" he said. "Oh no, of course, I shall ask your father in the right and proper way. I don't want him to think ill of me now do I?"

"There you go again," laughed Clarissa, "saying those silly things. You know my father thinks very highly of you."

"And what about you, my sweet," he whispered, gently pulling her closer to him. "Do you think a lot of me?"

Her cheeks reddened again. After a momentary pause, a mere heartbeat she replied, " I love you Marcus, and I always shall."

CHAPTER TWO

An Angel standing by his side

1920

It was summer the following year when Clarissa became Mrs Marcus Stephenson. The wedding, a very grand affair, had been agreed should take place in the small Kirk on the Stephenson's estate in Dunfallon followed by a reception for over two hundred guests at Braeside.

Several capacious, adjoining marquees had been erected on the lawns and Marcus had spared no expense for his dear Clarissa, everything she wanted, she had received, down to the finest silk for her wedding dress, imported from China.

Mackenzie was honoured and delighted to serve as his brother's best man, and Constance, very pleased with her son's choice of lassie, wept throughout much of the ceremony.

"What a delightful child she is Marcus," she had whispered to him as they waited for Clarissa to arrive.

And when she did - Marcus stood transfixed. He couldn't believe his good fortune all over again, as he watched her walking slowly towards him on her proud father's arm. For truly she looked like an angel, an angel standing by his side, and on taking their vows - to love honour cherish and obey, for richer, for poorer, in sickness and in health, Marcus pledged his love and faithfulness to her with all his heart and all his soul, for as long as they both should live. Every word spoken rang true in every fibre of his being.

As they turned to face the beaming congregation and the rousing strains of the wedding march began, he silently added one more vow of his own – that nothing, and no one would ever come between them.

After the speeches, and with the dancing underway, the guests began to relax into groups around the tables, sub-dividing and merging from time to time as introductions were made, old friendships renewed and new friendships – and in some cases more – were embarked upon.

The scramble for Clarissa's bouquet as it descended on the steps of the church had been performed in earnest, and several of the girls who had taken part were now to be seen either taking the floor, or receiving the attentions of one or other of the unattached male guests.

Clarissa herself was still the focus of much of the attention, and had already taken several obliging turns around the dance floor with an assortment of the Dunfallon men folk.

Taking his own eyes off her for a moment at last, Marcus went in search of brother, finding him holding forth to one of Clarissa's bridesmaids about his exploits with river salmon.

"That big it was, I swear!"

"Don't believe a word he says Beth," said Marcus, grabbing his brother's outstretched arms and pushing them together. "You know what fisherman's tales are!" Beth laughed and skipped away.

"Sorry, didn't mean to spoil your tête-à-tête."

"You didn't," replied Mac, "she was looking for an excuse to get away from me, poor lassie."

"Mac I can't thank you enough for – well, everything"

"For making you see sense, eh? Clarissa's wonderful and you would have been the all time fool if you had let her get away. I've only one regret."

"What's that Mac?"

"That I could not have the honour of dancing with the bride today."

Marcus looked down into his glass. Mac had once been a superb dancer.

"But on the bright side," said Mac, "I can now drink to my heart's content and not have to worry about making a fool of myself and falling over yon lassies!"

He threw back his head and began laughing heartily, Marcus soon joining in. Mac then spun his chair round full circle, as if in salute, slapping Marcus vigorously on the back as he came to a halt.

"Everyone can see she loves you man!" he said forcefully, "it's in her eyes - those jet black eyes, they must have broken many hearts, but captured only yours."

"Alright, alright Mac, you can stop now." Marcus gently clipped his brother's ear. The two men laughed again.

From a few tables away, their mother Constance looked on. It is good to see my boys laughing together again, she thought – laughing, as they used to do. She knew, only too well the darkness that had periodically threatened to engulf her son since his accident. Such a proud boy always, she had feared for him so, feared for his mental state. She had tried to help him but it had been no good – his pride was not such that a mother's love could easily bolster it – he had been ashamed in her presence, she could feel that.

Only Marcus had been allowed near him, and it was, slowly, Marcus, by his patience, his quietness and love for his brother, that had pulled Mac from the brink. But now that Marcus was married, what would it be like for Mac? If Marcus returned to Liverpool, as was his announced intention, to continue running the business, would Mac sink into loneliness and despair, seeing his brother happily married, while he, a cripple sat at home with his mother?

Looking at her two boys, so merry together at this moment now made her more afraid. Perhaps Mac could be persuaded to take up Marcus's offer and accompany he and Clarissa to Liverpool – he could lodge near to the business and take some part in it, or occupy a downstairs part of their house maybe. But even if he did agree, how might it affect Marcus and Clarissa? Even if Marcus were willing, Clarissa might resent the intrusion, with her husband inevitably spending a lot of time with his brother; unhappiness would surely follow. It was such a worry!

'Oh,' thought Constance, 'if only the business had been sold outright after their father died, or moved stayed here to Scotland, so we could all be together.' Instead Marcus had not only secured the move to Liverpool, but eventually bought Mathew Taylor's share when he retired. Marcus was now the sole owner of Taylor Stephenson, and Constance was very proud of her eldest son.

But her concern for Mac remained. It was like a pain that would not go away, a symptom of something potentially much more alarming. She would speak to Mac in a few days, when things had quietened down, discuss with him the idea of going to Liverpool with Marcus. But just as this thought calmed her, another, more acute realisation stabbed at her heart; if he did go, what would become of her - for the first time in her life, she would be alone!

"Mrs Stephenson?"

Constance looked around, and saw an elegant, grey-topped man holding out his arm in courtly fashion.

"Might I have the honour of this next dance madam?"

The distinguished figure was John Bamford, oldest brother of the bride, respected accountant and, at nearly forty, still a noted bachelor.

"Marcus tells me it's among your favourites," said Bamford, "Flower of Scotland."

"Why Mr. Bamford," said Constance, rising and taking his arm, "I'd be honoured."

"It's good to see the boys together again," said Bamford, nodding towards Marcus and Mac, still in jocular conversation."

"Yes, yes indeed it is Mr Bamford."

"Please, call me John – after all we're related now."

"Very well, John," said Constance as they took the floor, his hand sliding into place on her back.

She gave a little sigh. "And you," she said, "must call me Constance."

From the far corner of the marquee, Marcus observed his mother in full animation as the band played. As she turned, he saw that her partner was John Bamford. He gripped the stem of his wine glass. It was the first time since his father died that he had seen his mother, so ensconced, with another man.

CHAPTER THREE

A very suitable place

John Bamford had returned quietly to his guest accommodation. He had been given the turret room, situated high up in the Stephenson family's large country house. The room felt like an eagle's eyrie, with commanding views from its three windows across the vast estate as far as the Loch.

"A suitable place," he thought, "a very suitable place." He crossed to the mirror and removed his black bow tie. The face gazing back smiled a satisfied smile, the eyes glimmering with a sense of expectation. The next part of his plan had begun to work, and sooner and better than he had hoped.

Constance Stephenson had been a willing dance partner, her steps following his, her smiles responding to his warm compliments with gratitude and innocence. He had seen in her eyes she found him pleasing. If he had pressed her she would he knew, have taken that stroll in the gardens as he had suggested.

The only reason for her refusal was her watchful son, Mackenzie. Bamford frowned. Mac was going to be a problem, but not an insoluble one. He was a cripple for heavens sake.

He tugged off his shoes and stretched out on the bed, gazing at the intricate baroque patterned ceiling. He thought of Constance's other son, his friend Marcus, and how he had managed to wriggle out of the war and make a lot of money from it to boot. Good luck to him. As a lowly accountant Bamford made a decent living but his penchant for a good life cost him. The Stephenson family business had proved a ready source of discreet additional income.

Marcus had little idea about book keeping or even how much he was worth. He relied on Bamford for that. Bamford had creamed plenty off over the years to pay his gambling debts, but still he owed more, and wanted more - enough to spend whatever he chose and not have to worry about debt ever again. He had always craved money. He had needed love too of course, though not as much as he realised, not till he met Kitty.

After his call up in April 1916 he had been sent with his regiment to the east coast for training before leaving for France. There sat on a bench in a curious little beachside pub was beautiful, vivacious Kitty Mason, a fisherman's daughter, diamond eyed, with the smell of the salt water in her jet-black hair and all the romance of the sea in her joyful young soul. He had fallen utterly, hopelessly in love with her.

Within a month they were married, ensuring she would have her widow's pension if he should not return.

For reasons he was not himself entirely clear about he refrained from telling his family or any of his associates, especially the Stephenson family, that he now had a wife. That disclosure could come later if there was a need for it. The future for everyone was in God's hands that spring of 1916.

Kitty had written to Bamford in France and on his safe return was as besotted with her as ever. He found his debtors were just as eager to be reunited with their money, and the sums were far more than he could repay, or safely embezzle. Faced with bankruptcy, and prison if his accounts should then be scrutinised too closely, Bamford pleaded for time, and struck a deal.

While Kitty remained on the coast, he returned to work for Marcus in Liverpool, travelling back to see his wife when possible. Still he had told no one he was married. Meanwhile the creditors continued to pursue him; time would soon run out.

A plan began to take shape in his head. First he had to get even closer to the Stephenson family, and when Bamford had introduced his sister Clarissa to Marcus it was with just this thought in mind. And sure enough it had worked. Marcus had married Clarissa, making her a very wealthy woman. Now thought Bamford, it must be my turn. He needed a way out of his difficulties with money once and for all, a novel and radical solution, yes that was it he decided. Another idea then started to form - monstrous - but brilliant. Bamford had returned from the war a changed man, little wonder given what he had seen in Europe. But in the midst of the horror he had made a discovery – he had seen at close quarters just how terribly, pitifully expendable was a human life.

It was also so very easy to end another's life - it could be taken in an instant, by any number of simple means. Bamford knew, for he had done it, more than once in the mud and filth of the trenches, among the coppices and bloodstained barbed wire of the Somme. And now here he was, at an elegant society wedding, dancing with a multimillionaire widow, whom he now knew was attracted to him as more than a friend. Quite spontaneously he burst out laughing, his shoulders heaving with exhilaration.

CHAPTER FOUR

A Different Way of Life

"Marcus, don't you drop me, oh, do be careful!" Clarissa pleaded as he gathered her in his arms and lifted her over the threshold of their new home.

They had arrived at Crosslands railway station after two wonderful weeks spent in the Highlands of Scotland on their honeymoon. Marcus had insisted on the locomotive, yet was equally adamant they should travel first class.

The fact was he had never travelled any other way. Clarissa, especially after the lavishness of the wedding, still experienced difficulty with aspects of her husband's way of life, things which to him seemed normal struck her as immensely 'grand' – servants, possessions, opulence, getting waited on in restaurants and hotels, and generally being treated as 'a lady', despite her otherwise confident nature, made her feel a little shy and uncomfortable.

Whenever he witnessed this discomfort in his wife, Marcus wished he could 'tone things down' in some way for her. On the other hand, he could not resist the desire to give her everything, all the advantages of money that he had always enjoyed. If she felt at first, coming from her much more modest background, that these were excessive, she would soon, he hoped become accustomed to elegant living, embrace it, and be truly happy as his wife. He also reflected, and not without some amusement, how, if she thought him extravagant, she would have responded if, prior to his accident, she had found herself married to Mac instead.

Perhaps too, and this was a more sobering thought, taking a serene wife like Clarissa early on might have tamed Mac's dangerous excesses in the first place. Tame Mac though? Now that was a subject for mirth yet again!

64 Whindolls Road was a large, brand new detached house, built to Marcus's design and completed prior the wedding, as part of a small and exclusive estate on the outskirts of Crosslands. It had eight bedrooms, three bathrooms, a sitting room, drawing room, dining room, breakfast room and a very large kitchen, with a huge larder and cold store. The cellar he had planned especially for wine, most of which he already shipped in from around the world.

Waring and Gillow of Edinburgh had designed and installed the furniture, curtains, fittings and wallpaper. The directors themselves had called by appointment to see Marcus, of course; they knew the Stephenson family, and knew therefore that money was no object.

"I want the best for my wife," Marcus had told them. "Of course sir," Mr Waring had replied with due deference – "leave it all to us."

Marcus rented a large house in Liverpool, but he and Clarissa had decided they would live in Crosslands, for her sake, to be near her parents. He could also get away from the noise and bustle of the city. Mac now looked set to continue living at the old family home with his mother and Marcus was pleased about this. He had not got over his sense of shock at seeing his mother in such intimacy with John Bamford. John was a charming, handsome, educated man, but also some twenty or so years younger than Constance.

The idea of her and John, his old friend, trusted advisor and now his brother-in-law, associated with his own mother in any way that suggested anything more than familial friendship, well - it simply could not be. Marcus had not breathed a word of these dark concerns to anyone, not even Mac. But Mac's presence in the Stephenson house would of itself restrain the possibility of anything 'developing' between John and his mother, he felt sure of that. Privately, it was another reason for choosing Crosslands for his new home with Clarissa. In his absence, while the house was in preparation leading up to the wedding, Marcus had given Clarissa's parents, and his own family strict instructions not to allow her to even know its whereabouts. She was now looking at the finished article in all its glory.

"Well, my dear" said Marcus gently putting her down, "What do you think?"

Clarissa, wide eyed with amazement, was rendered speechless. Standing in the vast hallway, she gazed up at the staircase, which seemed to go on forever, leading to a long balustrade landing, and a seemingly unending series of doors.

Three-quarters of the way up, on the return landing, a stained-glass window stretched to the full height of the ceiling, a headspace the like of which Clarissa had only before seen in churches. This reminded her more of a small cathedral. Her eyes followed the line of the staircase back down, tracing the solid, gleaming white banister rail descending to form a magnificent, sweeping arc as it met the polished marble floor below.

On the ground floor, in the grand hallway, hung a huge gilt mirror, its frame adorned with winged cherubs and ornate, baroque scrollwork, and on the far side of the expanse of shining marble, a series of five, solid oak doors, hinted at further undiscovered splendour on the ground floor.

Clarissa's head spun, and for a moment she thought she might faint, either from the effort of looking up and the dazzling light from the stained glass window, or from the sheer overwhelming magnitude of this palace – she could find no lesser word to describe it – and the realisation that it was to be her home.

"Are you all right darling?" asked Marcus, who had by now crossed the marble floor and hung his coat on an enormous edifice of a hallstand, while Clarissa remained, appearing almost petrified by the front door.

"You don't think it echoes too much do you?" he asked. "We did discuss building a smaller lobby or ante room, but I think it's rather nice to come straight in and take in on all this, don't you?" He gestured with his arm, taking in the yawning ceiling, the dazzling stained glass and the perfect, glistening surface of the marble. "It is alright for you, I hope, you do like it?" Marcus was concerned. He had never seen her like this before. "Darling you are…"

"Marcus, yes, I'm all right." Clarissa's voice was faint, "I just can't believe this is ours, Can we really afford this?"

Marcus laughed heartily, greatly relieved. "You let me worry about that my dear;"

She turned to him and they kissed, a long, lingering, passionate embrace. He held her close to him, feeling the warmth and softness of her body; breathing the heady aroma of her perfume - oh how he loved her!

"So it meets with your approval Madam" Marcus said finally, bowing to her.

Clarissa laughed. "Well, it all seems, ah-hem - in order," she said clearing her throat and scanned the vast hallway again, this time as if conducting a works inspection. "Now if you would kindly escort me into the drawing room - I assume there is one, behind one of those doors?"

"Yes," said Marcus eagerly, "And a library, and two dining rooms, and a billiard room and a conservatory…"

Clarissa held out her hand. "One at a time please, one at a time –this is going to take some getting used to you know."

"I know that my precious. And I know its not what you're used to, but I so much want to give you everything – everything." Marcus kissed her again, pulling her close to him, pressing her warm bosom against him. She responded in kind, opening her lips eagerly to receive his questing mouth. Gasping for breath suddenly, they disengaged, and looking into each other's flushed faces.

"Clarissa my darling, have you ever slept in silk sheets?"

Her eyes sparkled. "My goodness young man," she panted gamely, "you're rather forward. Better not let the Master catch us."

Marcus placed his lips behind her earlobe, and in a voice tremulous with excitement whispered, "I don't intend to."

Then with a swift movement, her gathered his beautiful young wife bodily in his arms and bore her up the huge, white staircase.

CHAPTER FIVE

The Wedding Day

26th December 1921

Reflecting on the past year Mackenzie wondered if he should have taken Marcus's offer of sharing their home in Crosslands, it had been a very tempting offer. Mac adored James his first nephew, and wanted to spend as much time as possible with the tiny baby. But to do this he would need to spend a lot of time at his brother's home, much to the dislike of Clarissa so he decided to accept the city apartment Marcus had kindly offered to buy for him.

But all that had changed - the announcement of the imminent wedding of John Bamford and his mother had certainly put the cat among the pigeons. He had some concerns about his foolish mother and the frequent visits of John Bamford over the past year.
Bamford had turned Constance's head well and truly.

Flattering her with his charm he had wooed her and won the ultimate prize – Constance and all that went with her. He recalled the October day when the family, not knowing what was about to take place had been summoned to the house for the weekend. It was only when John Bamford had stood up after the evening dinner and announced the engagement and the date for the wedding had been set for boxing day 26th December that same year, that Mac realised what all the comings and goings by Bamford since Marcus's wedding had been about.

"Did you not suspect anything Mac?" Marcus whispered as Bamford carried on making the announcement.

"Not a thing," he replied, "Although I should have."

Later in the evening both he and Marcus had tried to persuade her to change her mind but she was adamant she was going ahead. They had escorted Constance away from Bamford to the privacy of the study with the hope of changing her mind, just the two of them trying to make her see sense but Clarissa had insisted she went with them and not wanting to upset his wife or arouse suspicion Marcus had allowed her to be present.

"You hardly know him Mother," Marcus had said in the privacy of the study "What's it been - a year?"

"One year and 6 months actually Marcus"

Marcus shook his head; Mother was beginning to sound like a lovesick girl not middle-aged woman.

"I don't know why you're so upset Marcus," Clarissa said, "Why, John loves her, any one can see that."

"Thank you dear," Constance said, "Glad to see someone is on my side."

Clarrissa kissed her mother in law's cheek. "Of course I am and I always will be. John is a good man and he will make you a fine husband."

"There my dears," Constance said "I will marry John in two months time – on the 26th of December. You are all I invited of course, but if you do not agree with my decision then I would prefer it if you stayed away. Now, shall we return to my fiancée, he will be wondering what all the fuss is about."

Mac and Marcus stared at each other – it was no use Constance was going to marry this man and nothing was going to change her mind.

"Well said Mama" Clarissa again kissed her cheek. "And I wish you all the happiness in the world, just like Marcus and I. We are very happy are we not darling."

Marcus beamed a huge besotted smile and nodded. Mackenzie looked from his brother to Clarissa holding his mother's hand in hers; she seemed, well - triumphant was the only word he could think of.

Suddenly he shivered, something didn't seem right, what was Clarissa and her brother up to. Well, he, Mackenzie Stephenson would do his best to find out.

He adored James, of course, the 4-month-old baby, his first nephew, and although he wanted to be near Marcus and his family, he would forego Marcus's offer and stay with his Mother, she needed him now, more than ever. He would do his level best to protect her from this rogue; Bamford was not taking all she had – not if Mackenzie had anything to do with it. And now the wedding day was here, he hastily tied his cravat, soon his mother would be married and if they couldn't change her mind he would do his level best to look after her.

CHAPTER SIX

The Dutiful Husband

December 27th 1921

Bamford rose from the immense four-poster bed, where Constance lay still deep in slumber. He put on his silk dressing gown, went to the window and parted the heavy drapes an inch or two. A grey dawn light was beginning to appear over the Loch. He yawned and smiled to himself. He thought he had acted his part particularly well in the last twenty-four hours.

During the ceremony and throughout the reception, aware that all eyes were upon them he had played the doting, deferential groom to his mature, dignified bride, mindful of her age and superior station in life. Then when they were finally alone, he had fulfilled the physical part of their compact with energetic conviction.

Constance had been a very willing and gracious conquest, and he had not found the duties of their wedding night quite the ordeal he had imagined. Indeed he had found himself surprisingly aroused by the older woman; horse riding was clearly good for the figure. He would not say as much to Kitty of course, quite the opposite. He could lie so easily, and sometimes wondered if all human beings found it so – Kitty for example. He felt a sudden stab of jealous panic; did she always go up to bed alone in that pub after closing time? No, Kitty wouldn't betray him for another surely, not Kitty Mason, his beautiful, loving and so very secret wife.

He had told Kitty some time ago that he was known to be a bachelor, and that it must remain that way; the next stage of his plan depended on it. It was then that he took Kitty fully into his confidence; he was to marry Constance with a view to inheriting her vast fortune. He and Kitty would see each other whenever they could.

After her initial horror Kitty's imagination was fired when she learned the extent of the Stephenson family's wealth. She was concerned however as to how she stood to benefit. Bamford stressed his love for Kitty, and that the plan was, in due course for them to be together, and extremely rich. Kitty agreed she would move and seek employment in the vicinity of the Stephenson home – preferably somewhere that Bamford could visit her often and discreetly.

The only possibility seemed to be barmaid in the village pub, a position for which Kitty was eminently suitable. Kitty's story was to be that of a war widow, of which there were innumerable up and down the country. Immediately on arrival the villagers had taken to her. Kitty was now one of them.

Mackenzie, a regular at the Highland Stag, had taken to her particularly; Bamford, realising this unexpected eventuality could assist them, suppressed his jealous annoyance, even over a cripple, and advised Kitty to be appropriately encouraging to Mac.

So far, so good, Bamford turned to the dressing table mirror and grinned now at his reflection. Today he would tell Constance she needed more help in the house, suggest she put an advert in the post office window, and he would make sure Kitty got the job. Once installed, they could have more of a proper, if discreet, loving relationship. The next move was to take over Constance's affairs. Marcus had engaged a replacement accountant as soon as the wedding had been announced; it was assumed Bamford would remain in Scotland in what was now his house. His house. Bamford turned back to the window and looked out across the landscaped terraces, the sweeping glens beyond.

In a few months he would advise Constance to change her will in his favour to minimise income tax; she would not question his professional judgement in such matters. Heaven help them all should an accident befall her. When it did, after a suitable period of mourning he and Kitty would sail for America. It seemed the place to be, a land of opportunity.

"Good morning John darling," said Constance, sitting up, "you look so happy today my dearest." Bamford returned to the bed and took his wife's hand. He kissed her tenderly. Smiling, he said: "I wonder why?" Constance sighed as he took her in his arms once more.

25

CHAPTER SEVEN

December 1922

Mackenzie Stephenson adored little Audrey. From the very first time he laid eyes on her, shortly after her birth on that warm September evening he knew he would do anything for the child, regarding her as if his own. There was something very special about the little girl. He was glad Marcus, Clarissa and young James had come to stay at the family home that past summer. Clarissa had been ill during the whole of the pregnancy and her doctor in Crosslands thought she would benefit from the Scottish air, while Marcus, ever the devoted husband and father, had employed a permanent nurse to assist mother and child.

Now, soon, they were coming again. It will give me some time with Marcus thought Mackenzie, some vital time. Ever since his mother's wedding, his sense of unease about John Bamford had slowly but steadily intensified.

After several urgent meetings called by her solicitor and her accountant Constance had dismissed them all, employing an unknown firm on the recommendation of her husband. Mackenzie was then further intrigued by the sudden appearance of Kitty Mason in the house, particularly after observing her and Bamford laughing together in the gardens. On later confronting him Bamford had of course denied any goings-on with the woman, suggesting Mackenzie was merely jealous and should try his luck with her. To Mac, this had seemed like a callous jibe at his supposedly hopeless physical state, his own interest in Kitty obviously having been noticed, and regarded as pathetic.

Lately Mac had seen Bamford making unexplained telephone calls, heard him in the early hours of the morning returning home. Other times he would be anxiously awaiting the arrival of the postman, grabbing the letters from him and tearing them apart, sometimes cursing as he read the contents. Constance seemed oblivious to all of this. When Mackenzie tried to talk to his mother on the rare occasions he could find her alone, she would hear not a word against her husband.

"John is a good man," was all she would say, "and, let me remind you Mackenzie, your stepfather." Stepfather – why there seemed barely a difference in age between himself and Bamford.

Mackenzie had telephoned his brother Marcus on several occasions to try to discuss his concerns, but either Clarissa had not passed on the message, or Marcus himself had chosen to ignore him. Now at last, with Marcus staying for Christmas and to celebrate his mother's first wedding anniversary, he would have a chance to talk to his brother face to face. Perhaps his suspicions about Bamford were all imagined. Since his accident his mind had begun to play odd tricks.

"I must keep things in perspective," thought Mac, "get a grip."
Bamford was an accountant, and accountants had always irritated him, chiefly in his father's day because they had always advised against extravagance, which had been Mac's middle name. Hopefully Marcus would set his mind at rest. And maybe he would try his luck with Kitty. She seemed to genuinely like him. That would show Bamford.

"No John, someone will hear us," whispered Kitty.
It was a few days before Christmas, and the big house was dormant. Bamford had taken his chance. He drew Kitty down on to the library couch. "How can anyone hear us? Constance is at her charity meeting and won't be back for another two hours. And the poke-nose cripple is out in the boat - fishing."

"How do you know," said Kitty, freeing her mouth from Bamford's eager kisses.

"Withers was pushing him to the boathouse, - I saw them from the turret room – through binoculars. It's a mighty long trek back from the Loch in a wheelchair."

"What about Clarissa and Marcus?"

"She's in bed in the west wing, got one of her 'heads' - and her dope of a husband won't leave her or the brat. Come, take off your dress."

"But John…"
Bamford silenced her with his own lips, his hand reaching for the buttons of her dress. Five minutes later they lay back together on the couch.

"When is it all going to happen?" asked Kitty quietly.

"When's what going to happen?"

"You know what I'm talking about John."

Bamford breathed out and curled a strand of her hair round his fingers. "What's the hurry?" he said.

"No hurry for you obviously; you and Lady Muck are sitting pretty while I'm still a skivvy; making do with the crumbs off the table."

"How colourfully you put things my love."

"Don't make fun of me John, this is serious."

"So is this." Bamford kissed her again, pressing his body against hers.

"Oh John...."

"John!"

Bamford leapt from the couch. Standing in the doorway of the library was his sister Clarissa.

"Clarrie – what are you doing here...wait a moment, listen..."

Before he could speak further, Clarissa was gone. Bamford ran headlong after her down the hallway. As she passed the door to the smoking room he caught up with her, grabbing hold of her arm.

"Clarissa, listen to me..."

"John...I'm sorry," said Clarissa breathlessly, "I was not here to spy on you, I've been worrying – I came down to see if Constance might know where I can find a new nursemaid for Audrey – you know ours has been called away, and I've been lying up there racking my brains...but I see that obviously Constance is not here! However – it is not my business to enquire..." Clarissa turned to leave. Bamford held her fast. "I'll make no excuses sister. What you've seen, you've seen."

"How long...?"

"Since Kitty and I were wed."

"What! What do you mean?" gasped Clarissa

"Kitty is my wife. We were married on my call up, before I left for France."

"Then you are...?"

"Yes – there is a word for what I am. I fell in love – with Kitty, but I wanted money too, I have always loved money Clarissa, you of all people know that feeling."

"I..."

"You cannot deny it. Would you have married Marcus without his money?"

"John how dare..." She broke off and looked away.

"Your silence is eloquence enough," said Bamford.

"John, I cannot condemn you for what you have done – what you are doing – it is just such a shock"

"I am sure."

"I have always known your weaknesses of course – as you…have known mine."

"Then you'll not betray me?"

Clarissa hung her head. "No. Now I must leave"

"Clarissa I have a proposition?"

What?"

"You need a new nursemaid for Audrey – I'm sure Constance would wish you to have someone who is known and liked in the village."

"You mean…"

"Kitty is very good with children."

"I imagine so…yes…"

"And of course, if the arrangement is acceptable I would be visiting you more frequently in future, both here in the west wing, and when you return to Liverpool – to ensure that things are working well, especially when Marcus is absent on business."

"I believe I understand what you are saying John." she said

John Bamford grinned, "I thought that you would."

CHAPTER EIGHT

January 1923

Kitty stared moodily into the fire and poured herself another glass of whiskey. Outside the wind was howling. It was two weeks after Christmas and, save for the butler she was alone in the house, the other staff, having been given leave till February.

Constance had gone to Liverpool to be with Clarissa, Marcus James and Audrey, and where Constance went, Bamford followed. Kitty was to take up her new post as Audrey's nanny at the end of January, Constance suggesting she too should have a proper period of holiday first, to which Clarissa had readily agreed. John had confided to Kitty that much as he would miss her, it would not look right if he stayed behind in Scotland. They had argued. Kitty wanted to go to America, she wanted money and she wanted Bamford; she demanded action.

Sipping at her whiskey, the firelight shooting patterns through the fine cut glass, Kitty pictured Constance and John, her John, laughing in each other's arms. She put her glass down with a bang, got up and strode purposefully to the hall. Lifting the telephone receiver from its hook, with the other hand she rummaged in the nearby drawer for Constance's" address book. Finding the Liverpool number she dialled, her heart now thumping.

"3502 – hello?" came an indistinct voice. The line was crackly, it sounded like John.

"Oh thank god its you - it's me Kitty, I've got to see you." She spoke in a breathless rush. "I'm sitting here thinking about you all the time, ever since I first saw you it's always been you…I know what everyone says about barmaids, but it's not always true. I want to be with you, make love with you properly, not worrying what people might say or do…I know its difficult for you, but I want you and I need you…hello, hello…?"

Kitty gave a start. A huge gust of wind had just burst the shutters of the hall window open, the long curtains now flapping madly. The phone had gone quite dead.

"What a night!" Sinclair the butler had appeared, and was now busily trying to secure the shutters. "Must have brought the telephone poles down – dear, dear, what a storm"

Kitty bit her lip hard. Attempting to reply to the butler she could only utter a strange, despairing croak as, dropping the receiver she ran sobbing back to the fireside and her glass of whiskey. She sat for a moment, deep in thought then crossing to the bureau, took out writing paper and a pen. Seating herself at the bureau she began to write.

Dearest John,

I telephoned you tonight because I had to speak my mind. I am sorry we got cut off and you did not have chance to reply, in any case I imagine she was in the room so you could not talk – the two of are so inseparable it seems!
Well, time will tell on that score John Bamford! And time for you is running out.
Tonight I told you again how much I loved and wanted you. It is now your turn to show me you care. It is now some years since you married me and told me you loved me.
Then you told me you planned to make us both rich by your scheme to get Constance's money. I wanted no part of this but you would not be dissuaded and I followed you to be near you, who are my legal husband.
You have repeatedly promised me you would leave Constance and return to me, but have not done so. I am asking for you now to do this.
Come back to me John. This is my last request. I should say my last warning. You married another woman, in the full knowledge you were already wed to me. This is called bigamy John, and as you well know is punishable by imprisonment.
There are also other things the law would like to know about, things you have already done, and things you have planned to do.
That is conspiracy, and also I believe a serious offence, as a solicitor would no doubt tell you John. America is a nice place I am told. I am also told prison is not a nice place, not a nice place at all in fact, far from it.

I love you John, but do not bank on this forever.

Kitty Bamford
Your lawful wedded wife.

Mackenzie's wheel chair bumped back into the sitting room.

"Who was that son?" asked Constance, not looking up from her needlework.

"Who mother?"

"I thought I heard the telephone ring."

Oh yes," said Mac, "it was a wrong number." He wheeled himself round to join his mother by the fireside.

An involuntary smile had appeared on his lips. The call from Kitty was quite unexpected. She sounded as though she had been drinking. Well, he thought, it often takes a drunk to speak a sober man's mind, and the same was true of women.

"I'm sitting here thinking of you all the time," she had said,

"I want to make love with you properly."

"Likewise my love" thought Mac, "oh likewise."

He would tell his mother nothing, nor Marcus, and certainly not Bamford. That added pleasure could come later. Perhaps in time they would be wed. All he could think of now was that she wanted him, body and soul. He must find a pretext for returning to Scotland. Kitty would be virtually alone up at the house for another fortnight at least. He closed his eyes and pictured Kitty's soft, perfect lips, her tiny waist, the round of her breasts. In the sweet wood smoke from the fire, he thought he could almost smell her.

Bamford crumpled Kitty's letter in his fist and thrust it in his pocket. The cheeky minx, he thought. Pretending to be so virtuous and loving and self-sacrificing when all the time the pound signs had been flashing in her eyes like fairground illuminations. So too for him, the difference was he made no pretence about it. And to dare to threaten him! Enough with her, thought Bamford. He had grown tired of her in any case lately – her cheapness, her thinly disguised artfulness; no Kitty's charms had already begun to pall, and now this letter put the lid on it. No one was indispensable, not a wealthy Scottish society widow, certainly not a common east end barmaid. He made his excuses and took a taxi into Liverpool. Finalizing accounts for a client he'd told Constance and she had believed him. He needed to think, clear his head.

The taxi pulled up along the dock road and Bamford went into the nearest pub and ordered himself a large brandy. The softening effects of the alcohol allowed him to think more calmly. Could he really do without Kitty? He took out the letter and read it again. The uneven scrawl betrayed tiredness, desperation – a desperate woman. And why would she not be, thought Bamford.

In a rare moment of empathy he put himself in Kitty's shoes; how would he feel if the situation were reversed? The idea of her living with, married to, another man, and he Bamford waiting on a promise, as she now was, would be unbearable to him.
Bamford's mood changed – her desperation showed she loved him surely, and all he had done was put her off. She was right, it was time to act, to be rid of Constance and follow through with the grand plan. He must see Kitty as soon as possible and reassure her.
Bamford fumbled in his pocket for some change, went to the telephone on the bar and dialled a number.

"Border Railways…can you tell me the times of this weekend's trains from Crosslands to Dunfallon in Scotland please?"

"How much do I owe you?" said Mac to the taxi driver as they drew up on the gravel drive beside the steps of the house.

"Ten shillings please Mr Stephenson. Wait there a moment I'll get your wheelchair out."

"There's a guinea – take it, for the time of year," smiled Mac as the driver took Mac's personally customised chair from the boot and unfolded it for him.

"Your stick sir, there - Christmas was over a weeks ago you know sir."

"I didn't see you at Christmas, your tip's overdue. Take it man."

"That's very generous of you Mr Stephenson sir. Sure I can't give you hand indoors?"

"I'm not helpless man!" chuckled Mac. "Be on with you - and a happy new year," called Mac as the taxi crunched its way back to the road.

Mac had caught the train up from Crosslands. He'd given no particular reason to his mother for deciding to return to Braeside early, and alone, other than a desire to do some fishing. Marcus and Clarissa were wrapped in the children and Bamford seemed to have disappeared off somewhere without saying a word to anyone, so there had been no real need for explanations.

33

He had not tried to communicate with Kitty either. Partly this was nerves, he was worried that in a more sober moment she might get cold feet about following up her heart's desires. Today was a Friday, and Friday had always been the butler's day off in the Stephenson home. Only Kitty would be in the house, Kitty and himself.

Mac pulled his chair up to the front door using the ramp and handrail that Marcus had put in for him. Entering quietly he waited for a moment in the hall and listened. Kitty must be in her quarter. He wheeled himself to the lift and entered.

Arriving on the second floor landing he exited the lift and turned right. The door to Kitty's room was closed. Should he call out or knock gently - he could not decide. A faint glow of light shone beneath the door. He felt so excited to think she was just behind it, a mere few feet away. Kitty was known to be an indolent soul; perhaps she was lying in bed reading or having an early evening nap – that beautiful girl, so vulnerable, so available and so wanting him. He felt his veins dilate with pleasurable anticipation. He was just about to call Kitty's name when he heard her voice:

"I'm so sorry – I don't know what I was thinking".
This was followed by a man's voice, one that Mac knew only too well. "That's all right, you were upset" Bamford said "I'd have done the same – I must say though it was a stinking good letter – you pulled out all the stops!"

"Now you make me feel worse!" Kitty answered,

"Don't be – you had every justification really. Now let's have a drink and think how we're going to go about things – I've bought a rather special bottle of Champagne…"

There was the pop of a cork, then the voices dropped to an incoherent murmur. Mac, who had sat rigid as he listened through the door, now gripped the wheels of his chair and forced them to turn. With beads of sweat coating his forehead, he groped his way unsteadily back towards the lift.

CHAPTER NINE

A Change of Plan

"What was that?"

"What was what?" said Kitty, taking a gulp of Champagne.

"A sort of, squeaking – do you know what it sounded like? – Mac's wheelchair."

"Don't be daft, he's still in Liverpool"

"How do you know?"

"He said – planning to stay there the whole of January."

"Suppose he changed his plan?"

"Why?"

"People do"

"Here, where you going John? Come back to bed - I thought you were going to warm me up in here…!"

Bamford had crossed quickly to the bedroom door, entering the landing just in time to hear the lift doors closing. He turned for the stairs and ran down taking the treads two at a time. "Damn you MacKenzie!"

As he reached the ground floor, Bamford saw the tail end of Mac's wheelchair disappearing into the library, the door then swiftly closing. Bamford raced to the door and pushed hard against it. Mac had locked himself in.

"Mac – Mac open up I must talk to you man – Kitty and I, its not what you think – Mac?"

There was no sound from within the library. Bamford hesitated a moment then hurried back up to Kitty's room. Kitty, nonchalantly pouring herself more Champagne looked at him in bemusement. "What on earth's the matter John – did you see a ghost?"

"No – Mac."

"What! Here?""

"I told you - he was outside this door. Now he's gone down and locked himself in the library."

"Has he gone crazy or what? Oh my god, do you think he heard us?" Kitty looked deadly serious now.

Bamford nodded, pacing the room, his brow furrowed with intense thought.

"But - I don't think we said anything incriminating – not about Constance, nothing specific."

35

"But he knows we were together, in my room…"

"We've got to stop him warning Constance before we…"

"Before we what?"

"You know what." John answered.

Kitty looked suddenly horrified, as if some vision of hell had opened up before her. Then, struggling to compose herself she said,

"Yes go down and talk to him John – he can't phone out from the library, you must talk to him."

"You come too. Kitty. We'll confront him together."

When they reached the ground floor, Mac was in the hall. He stared silently at them, his face expressionless. Bamford and Kitty stopped at the bottom of the stairs.

"Mac, listen…" began Bamford.

Mac interrupted him, pointing meaningfully at Kitty. "You – Jezebel!" he hissed.

"Mac, what on earth do you mean?" said Kitty.

"Mac, there's a perfectly innocent explanation for my being here with Kitty, in her room," said Bamford calmly.

Mac threw back his head and laughed bitterly. "You're priceless – the pair of you, a real double act. But you know, there is a funny side. What you don't realise Bamford is that while you're two-timing my mother with this harlot here, she's been doing the same to you."

"I'm doing nothing of the sort Mac," said Bamford as gently as he could. Then, his expression changing, he added, "what do you mean – Kitty doing what?"

"Ah now you're worried Mr Smarty-Pants!" crowed Mac. "When you're having the best of both worlds with the Stephenson largesse and a wee bit of skirt waiting, the skirt's telephoning me in the small hours and inviting me to her bed. You see I might be a cripple Bamford, but I've obviously got something you can't provide – I think its called charm. 'I want to make love to you properly,' that's what she told me – ask her to deny it I dare you!"

Bamford looked at Mac in disbelief then turned his gaze on Kitty.

"No, John, I swear, it's not true – I would never be unfaithful to you, never, there's been a mistake…"

"Too true sweetheart!" said Mac triumphantly.

"You little tart…" began Bamford.

Mac's loud, mocking laugh seemed to fill the house.

"You stupid, stupid little tart!" repeated Bamford.

Kitty's expression changed, confusion and fear giving way to a look of quickly rising anger. Her eyes blazing now she rounded on him.

"How dare you speak to me like that? I'll do as I please – if you want to know the truth I did want Mac once, and maybe I'll take him to my bed now."

"I wish you luck" Bamford scoffed, "an admirable sentiment grant you taking pity on a poor cripple - who knows he might even feel a little pleasure, while there's life there's hope eh Mac, though god knows not a lot in your case, I can't think why you didn't drown yourself in the Loch years ago instead of being such a burden to your mother. No sense of shame I suppose."

"You think you can wound me with words Bamford," snarled Mac, "the last resort of a scoundrel and a failure – yes a failure. If it wasn't for the Stephenson family you'd be polishing boots from dawn till dusk – or more likely drinking meths in the Gorbals!"

"Well said Mac!" cried Kitty. Jabbing her finger at Bamford she went on, "Mac's twice the man you'll ever be, wheelchair or no – you've given me nothing, nothing but empty promises – I want a real man, not a creeping, conniving excuse for one."

"Why you – I could…"

"What – kill me John? If I thought you were up to it I'd be worried – but I just don't reckon you've got the bottle for it."

Bamford's face contorted into a mask of rage. "I've killed before," he bellowed, "and by god I'll swing for you!"

Mac's eyes gleamed excitedly, swinging his wheelchair from one side to another, watching the opponents keenly as if a pair of fighting cocks he had an each way wager on.

Kitty, hands on hips now, jeered defiantly. "You know, while your mates were all getting shot, I think you spent the whole war hiding in that trench of yours. There's a word for you John Bamford - coward. And I'll tell you another thing…"

Before Kitty could finish Bamford had leapt forward and seized her by the throat. Freeing herself she ran down the hall and into the boot room. Bamford raced after her. Bursting through the door he came to an abrupt halt. Facing him was Kitty, in her hands a shotgun, aimed straight at him.

Behind him Bamford heard the squeak of a wheelchair, followed by Mac's voice, a soft, menacing growl, "Do it Kitty, do it and rid the world of this vermin. I'll protect you, you need have no fear."

There was a deathly silence as Bamford and Kitty stared one another in the eye. Kitty stood motionless, the barrels of the shotgun levelled steady as a rock at Bamford's head.

"Don't be a fool Kitty," he said. "You'll hang you know. We're all set for America, what do you think we've been waiting for all this time. Don't ruin everything now, everything we've worked and waited for, you and me Kitty, together now and forever."

"Don't listen to him," snapped Mac. "He'll sell you down the river believe me girl."

"Shut up!" barked Bamford. "Kitty – I love you - this is our moment."

"No John, this is my moment. I loved you once but I no longer believe you love me. I'm sorry…"

"The gun's not loaded," said Bamford.

"You're bluffing."

"The shotguns are all kept empty when they're in the house."

"Do it," growled Mac again.

For a split second Kitty's concentration wavered. Like a pouncing tiger Bamford leapt at her, knocking her to the ground. Their entwined bodies rolled over and over, the shotgun pressed between them, Bamford trying desperately to wrench the stock from Kitty's grasp. A moment later there was a loud report. Kitty's head lolled back, her body arching for a second then slackening. Bamford held her to him.

"Kitty, are you all right – Kitty?" Looking down her saw a red stain spreading across her dress. "Oh Kitty – oh god oh no – Kitty…"

"Arrgghh!" It was Mac's voice, bellowing like a banshee. Bamford leapt to his feet as Mac's wheelchair careered full tilt towards him. In Mac's raised hand was an iron golf club about to descend on Bamford's head. Intercepting the blow Bamford yanked at the handle of the club, but Mac's grip was vice-like.

The wheelchair danced violently back and forth as the two men preformed a desperate tug of war with the golf club. Unable to win, Bamford let go and retreated further into the boot room, stumbling over Kitty. Mac, his pursuit now blocked by the prone body, began to manoeuvre around it.

Meanwhile Bamford had removed the leather belt from his waist. He sprang forward, looped the belt around Mac's wrists and drew the two ends together. Mac's strong hands fought back as his assailant pulled hard. The added leverage of the belt proved decisive; Bamford now steadily and surely forced Mac's arms together behind him then tied the belt.

With Mac now powerless, Bamford fetched the shotgun and forced it into Mac's pinioned hands, pressing his palms and fingers around the trigger. Mac unleashed a hideous roar. Bamford hit him hard across the face with the back of his hand. Mac reeled, his eyes rolling as he slumped back unconscious.

The light was already beginning to fade as Bamford arrived at the boathouse Dragging Mac's wheelchair down the path and onto the jetty he positioned it at the very end, close to the edge. Here, below, the water was dark and deep. Mac was groaning, semi-conscious. Untying his arms, Bamford with a single, swift lunge jettisoned the wheelchair and its occupant over into the loch. The belt he had used to restrain Mac he flung after him.

Momentarily he stared into the blackness then headed back to the house. Casting a brief glance at Kitty's body, he kicked the shotgun to an appropriate position then went upstairs and retrieved his belongings, together with the bottle and champagne glasses, which he washed and replaced carefully in the kitchen cupboard. He had to get back to Crosslands before Kitty's body was discovered.
Under cover of darkness, John Bamford then set out on the long walk to the next railway station down the line.

CHAPTER TEN

The Inspector Calls

"John – is that you?" Constance called from the sitting room. Bamford appeared in the doorway, his hands behind his back and looked at her. Constance put down the sketch she had been working on and flew to his side.

"Oh I've missed you so much John," she exclaimed tenderly. "This house is so cold and empty when you're not here with me, and what with Mac having gone off somewhere without telling anyone…"

"Gone off?" said Bamford casually.

"Yes, disappeared without so much as a by your leave, we haven't seen him for two days."

"Perhaps he's courting. Don't look so surprised – surely he's entitled to a love life?"

"John what's wrong…?" she broke off, "why don't you put your arms around me as you usually do?"

"What – and drop these?"

Flashing a broad smile at her, Bamford produced the large bouquet of vivid red roses he had been concealing. Constance gasped with pleasure.

"Oh John they're beautiful," she said inhaling the flowers" fragrant scent, "where did you get them?"

"The local cemetery," said Bamford drolly.

Constance gave him a playful push. "You're a wicked man John Bamford," she smiled and gave him a playful poke in the ribs.

"You're enough to make any man wicked," breathed Bamford softly, as he curled his arms around her neck and began nuzzling her cheek with his lips.

Constance sighed. "Oh god how I've missed you."

Disengaging from him she stepped through the doorway and into the hall then turned and looked at him for a moment, her eyes smouldering with desire. Making her way upstairs, Bamford followed swiftly behind.

"Mother!" Marcus was calling from downstairs. "We're home." It was one hour later. Constance got up, put on her dressing gown and opened the bedroom door.

"Marcus – I was just having a lie down…"

"Oh – I'm sorry…"

"No matter." Tying the cord of her gown, Constance came to the top of the stairs.

"Any sign of Mac?" asked Marcus.

"No dear – I don't know whether we ought to be concerned, I mean it's not like him to go off without explanation, but then he has his own life I suppose," demurred Constance.

"Morning Marcus, look I don't know if this is any of my business," broke in Bamford, appearing behind Constance on the landing. "And it may mean nothing of course," Bamford went on, "but as I was leaving here to meet my client the other day, I heard Mac on the telephone."

"What about it John?" Marcus said. "I mean, who was he speaking to?"

"I don't know – but I got the impression it was a woman."

"You think Mac might have been involved in some sort of romantic entanglement?" said Marcus looking thoughtful.

"I wasn't implying anything morally questionable," said Bamford in a careful tone, "it was just that he sounded, well, emotional if you like."

A shadow of anxiety fell across Constance's features. "Mac was always an impetuous boy – and ever since the accident he's been…more unpredictable…oh Marcus you don't think he's done something foolish do you."

"I doubt it – Mac's got his head screwed on. Probably gone off to Liverpool to look at buying some newfangled adapted motorcar or other, wants to surprise us, you know the way his mind works."

"Yes I suppose you could be right," said Constance, "all the same it would be nice to have some idea – I mean one does wonder how he manages to get about so in that wheelchair, I'm sure he takes the most unnecessary risks …"

At that moment the front doorbell jangled loudly in the hall. Constance broke off.

"Oh I expect that'll be Mac now," she laughed. He was always so good at timing his entrances! I wonder what he's got to say for himself! Open the door Marcus."

Marcus looked puzzled. "I gave him a key…"

"Perhaps he's lost it," said Constance, "don't keep him out there in the cold there's a dear."

Marcus went to the door and opened it. A tall, middle-aged man in a raincoat and trilby was stood on the step. Lifting the trilby politely he enquired, "Is Mr Mackenzie Stephenson here?"

"Yes, yes he was staying here – but he's not here now, we…" began Marcus.

"I see sir, I thought perhaps that might be the case."

"Then why - what do you mean, who are you?" asked Marcus.

"My name's Inspector Reed, CID - I wonder if I might come in sir?"

With a hesitant, cautious look, Marcus ushered the stranger into the hall and closed the door. Constance had descended the stairs, her expression intensely curious yet composed. Bamford lingered on the landing.

"I'll come straight to the point sir, madam," said the Inspector, with a little bow towards Constance.

"Yesterday afternoon the body of a Miss Kitty Mason was discovered at your residence in Scotland – Braeside?"

"At Braeside, Kitty, a body…?" began Constance in alarm.

"Dead madam I'm afraid. Shot at close range by a person or persons as yet unknown."

"Good…gracious," stammered Constance, the blood draining from her cheeks, "how dreadful, whatever – but you mentioned my son – Mac."

"Yes madam, a wheelchair identified as belonging to Mr Mackenzie Stephenson was found near the property…"

"And where is Mac?" demanded Marcus

"The chair was found at the edge of the Loch Sir. A search of the vicinity is currently underway. I came here to ascertain whether any of you had seen or knew anything of the gentleman's whereabouts since yesterday. Or had noticed anything unusual about his recent state of mind."

42

Constance glanced briefly in the direction of Bamford, who was hanging back still on the landing.

"No, no – I mean we haven't seen Mac for three days," said Constance tremulously.

"As a matter of routine our men are already dredging the Loch," the Inspector went on, "but at the same time I thought it best to check what information you might have regarding Mr Stephenson."

Marcus bristled. "And did you not think of checking with us before rampaging all over our property Inspector whatever your name is!"

'Reed sir – and a woman has been found dead on that property – this is a murder investigation we're talking about here. I'm sorry."

"Murder?" gasped Constance. "But obviously…Kitty was not the most stable of girls…surely she must have…"

"Taken her own life? The evidence doesn't point that way madam I'm afraid. And the prime suspect at present has gone missing."

"You're surely not referring to my son!" Constance looked angry now, affronted.

Before the Inspector could reply, Marcus broke in. "Just a minute," he said haughtily, "what evidence?"

"The weapon that killed Miss Mason was not close enough to the body. There appears to be a shotgun missing from the gun cupboard at Braeside sir. We assume that's the one."

"Oh my god this is terrible, I can't believe it – Kitty dead, Mac gone missing," wailed Constance, breaking down now. "You don't really think Mac has…oh John, Marcus, what ever are we to do?"

"There there," said Marcus placing an arm around his mother's shoulder, " don't let's jump to conclusions," he said soothingly. "I'm sure there's a rational explanation for all this – its appalling news about Kitty of course, but I'm sure Mac had nothing to do with it. He probably went up to Braeside to do some fishing and took a bottle of whiskey with him in the boat. They'll probably find him asleep in the heather on the other side of the Loch. Inspector I'm sorry if I was rather abrupt, this has been something of a shock for us as you can imagine."

"Of course sir," said Reed sympathetically. "But there is something else I must tell you. The telephonist at the village post office up there says she placed a call from Braeside to your number here in Liverpool just a few days ago."

"How the devil did she know it was our number?" said Marcus, indignant again now.

"Local female telephonists' tend to notice a great deal that's outside the precise remit of their jobs sir."

"Bloody nosey you mean!" snarled Marcus, "I beg your pardon mother, I…"

"You said your son Mackenzie was still here at that time madam?"

"Yes," began Constance, "but I don't see how that implicates him in any way…" Then half turning towards Bamford" again, her hand flew to her mouth.

At that moment the bell clanged again. Marcus opened the front door to reveal a policeman in motorcycle gear.

"Afternoon sir, urgent message for Inspector Reed – understand he's with you?"

Reed stepped forward and took the envelope from the despatch rider's hand. After scanning the contents he turned back to Constance and Marcus.

"I'm afraid I have some very bad news for you. At 1.30pm today a body identified as that of Mr Mackenzie Stephenson was retrieved from the Loch at Braeside."

From her bedroom window at Braeside Constance gazed down towards the Loch. The surface looked calm as ever; rarely did even the strongest winds disturb the still waters of that deep, imperturbable place that had claimed the life of her husband, and now her youngest son. The room was warm with a blazing fire in the grate, but Constance shivered as she turned away from the window and looked back at her husband John, still sleeping in the grand ancestral four-poster. Her eyes moist with tears, she whispered: "You've been good to me John, thank god I've still got you."

Without disturbing him she dressed and went downstairs.

In the breakfast room she found Marcus and Clarissa.

"Good morning mother," said Marcus getting up

"Good morning both of you – no, no don't trouble, I'll help myself, oh good kedgeree, I'm glad cook decided to come back early, though I did urge her to take a fortnight."

"She's made of strong stuff," said Marcus as he poured them all coffee. "And Sinclair too – nerves of steel that man, he's been our butler since forever Clarissa, known Mac and I since we were kids - having to identify Mac's body, well, he must be as upset inside as we all are. And now the police are even suggesting Mac shot Kitty deliberately before drowning himself! I mean its obvious it was just a terrible accident, Mac showing off with the gun, then bang – he obviously couldn't live with himself – who could blame him – the guilt at not telling us he was seeing Kitty, then the appalling grief and shock when the gun went off …oh mother I'm so sorry please forgive me."

Constance had burst into tears. Marcus came quickly to her side and put his arms around her.

"No, no, don't mind me," sobbed Constance, "why shouldn't you talk of what has happened? Why shouldn't we all? These are facts we have to face – Mac is gone, Sinclair is upset yet stoical, and you are an honest brave boy – I must somehow try to follow your example…"

"Nonsense mother," said Marcus seriously, "I'm a damn fool with a loose tongue and a looser grasp of what's proper. I try to hide my grief with thoughtless chatter. Let's talk of other things. Clarissa has suggested a trip to Edinburgh, perhaps to a concert."

"Clarissa you are so considerate," said Constance, taking her daughter-in-law's hand. "And so kind to come up here, you must be missing the children so."

"They are happy enough; we managed to find an experienced governess, who is very good with them. We encourage their independence do we not Marcus?"

"Yes, we do dear," said Marcus absently, "though perhaps we can come here all of us in the holidays, if you would be agreeable to that mother?"

"Why I should love to hear children's voices ringing out at Braeside again, you know Marcus, your father always looked forward so to grandchildren, it was just such a terrible shame…I am sure his spirit will be aware and be overjoyed when he hears them tumbling down the corridors and…oh, yes Sinclair, what is it?
The butler had, in his customarily silent manner entered the room.
"There's a gentleman to see you Mrs Bamford," he announced. Marcus, as always, winced at the appellation.

Waiting in the library was Inspector Reed. "I'm sorry to intrude Mrs Bamford," he said. "But there's something I'd like you to take a look at. From his pocket the Inspector unwound a leather belt.
"It was found suspended from a branch overhanging the Loch, close to where your son's wheelchair came to rest."
Constance looked blank. "Should I recognise it Inspector? As far as I know it does not belong to either of my sons."
Inspector Reed held the belt closer. "How about anyone else? It's a man's belt Mrs Bamford." Constance shook her head. "No, "I'm sorry."
The Inspector picked up his hat. "No, you've been very helpful madam. We can now narrow down our enquiries."
As Constance led the way back into the hall, Clarissa and Marcus were coming out of the breakfast room.
"Oh Marcus," said Constance, "this didn't belong to Mac did it?" The Inspector proffered the belt again.
"No, don't think so," said Marcus. "He didn't wear belts anyway, not since his accident."
"Thank you sir," said Reed, "ladies, I'll bid you good day."
When he had left Marcus said, "Well, I don't want to speculate on what that was all about. The police are beyond me, forever barking up wrong trees. Are you all right my dear?"
He turned to Clarissa, who was stood still, staring after the Inspector, her eyes wide, her mouth twitching slightly.
"I'm sorry darling," she said, "I feel rather faint, would you excuse me?"

Constance touched her daughter-in-law's arm solicitously. "The shock is catching up with you my dear. You've been such a tower of strength to all of us, now its time for you to give in a little. Why don't you go and have a lie down? I'll ask Sinclair to bring you up a little brandy."

Clarissa lifted a hand to her forehead. "Thank you, yes, I think I'll do that."

Once on the first floor, after checking no one had followed her upstairs, Clarissa hurried along the corridor and tapped softly at Constance's bedroom door. Bamford appeared, his chin covered with shaving foam, a towel in his hand. "Clarrie, what…?

'Shush!" Clarissa slid past him into the room and closed the door partly behind them. "John," she said in an undertone, "where's that belt you brought back from the war?"

"Eh?" Bamford looked confused.

"The leather belt, with the snakes head buckle, the one you told me you took off a dead German."

Bamford looked startled for a second then composed himself.

"Oh I don't wear it around here," he said casually, "keep it in my army trunk, not the sort of thing a lady like Constance would care for – why do you want to know?"

"But perhaps a so-called lady like Kitty might be excited by your wearing it?"

"What do you mean…?"

"I've just seen it – in the hands of a police inspector."

"What!"

"The belt was found near where Mac drowned."

'Really?" Bamford's eyes were luminous now, his facial muscles animated. "Then Mac must have pinched it off me."

"You told me you always keep your trunk locked."

"Well it can't be mine then."

"You showed me the bullet marks on it, where you shot the German. Three rounds you said you put into him, you were proud of it, you showed me. I remember it distinctly. The first man you'd killed you said."

"Look this is nonsense Clarrie!"

"Quiet – you want Constance to hear?"

"Hear what for god's sake?"

47

"About what you did to Mac, to her son."

"What do you mean, are you out of your mind?"

"No, but I fear you are John – I fear you left your senses long ago. I should tell the police, you know that?"

"Clarrie the shock of events these past few days is taking effect. You're not yourself. Go back to bed, go for a walk, get some fresh air, do anything that helps you relax – and try to forget these foolish, upsetting thoughts."

"John I..." Clarissa fixed her brother with a gimlet stare. "John, I am your sister, we are one blood – tell me honestly now, did you kill Mac?"

Bamford returned the stare defiantly. "Of course," he said coldly, "and Kitty too, though that was an accident – not that it makes any difference - the impetuous, headstrong fool that she was, she'd have come to a sticky end sooner or later."

"John you are a murderer," said Clarissa, her voice equally cold.

"What of it, its just a word, no one can pin anything on me. Constance will vouch for me. And when she's dead I'll be a free man again."

"Dead!" Clarissa gasped, "You are the devil John."

Bamford grasped her two hands firmly in his. "And you sister," he breathed intensely, "can be my she-devil."

His voice now had a hypnotic quality, as if chanting an incantation.

"When this business is at an end, come with me to America. You don't love that stuffed shirt of a man you married, but bring your cubs along if you wish, there's little future for them here other than keeping the wheels of the Stephenson empire grinding relentlessly round. Do you really want your children to be as dull as Marcus? The United States is the land of opportunity Clarissa, especially when one has money, and I will soon have plenty. Why, one of them may end up as President. Anything is possible if you desire it enough. What do you say?"

"I say, if you stay here a day longer you will hang."

"Does that mean you are going to betray me?" There was a long pause as Clarissa studied her brother's face. Finally she said quietly, "No. But something might."

"I'll take my chance," said Bamford, "but think about what I said. I know you sister; you weren't born for a life of confinement any more that I was."

Just then Constance's voice chirruped from below. "Clarissa dear, I'm just sending Sinclair up with some brandy for you now, do ring if you want anything else, perhaps a hot water bottle…"

"I must go," hissed Clarissa, and without looking back she slipped out of the room.

Bamford shut the door after her and wiped his chin carefully with the towel. He then lay back on the bed, breathed out a long sigh and stared hard at the ceiling.

CHAPTER ELEVEN

Constance yawned and stretched an arm across the mattress.

"John," she murmured contentedly, her eyes still closed, her voice heavy with sleep. "Come back to bed John. The hills won't go away you know – I know how you love to stare out at them every morning, but they've been there forever, and they'll always be there – like you and me. Now come and put your arms around me – John...?"

Opening her eyes now Constance sat up and looked around. Something was out of place, and at first she could not tell what it was. Then, as her conscious mind connected with the familiar contents of her bedroom she knew; on top of the large oak wardrobe was an empty space, one that usually housed her husband's suitcase.

"Oh," she said aloud to herself – "oh he's gone to visit a client – he mentioned it, I'm sure, but..."

She rose, crossed quickly to her husband's wardrobe and looked inside. A look of alarm then came over her face and she ran to the bedroom door. Opening it she called loudly, "John? John!"

"Mother what on earth is the matter – it's not seven yet." Marcus had emerged from his room further down the landing.

"It's John," said Constance in a querulous voice, "he's gone, packed his things and gone. I knew it was all too much for him, I feared this might happen..."

"Feared what Mother? No one has seen John leave the house as far as I know - possibly he's in the garden, taking an early turn."

"No, no I fear the worst..."

"Hush now." Calmly Marcus ushered his mother back to her bedroom and sat her on the bed.

"There, look for yourself," she said. "His wardrobe, too many of his clothes are missing as well as the suitcase." Clarissa had come into the room now. "John has left me Clarissa. Constance wailed, "He's gone."

Marcus nodded. "It seems he has gone off somewhere at least." He pointed to the empty spaces in Bamford's wardrobe.

"It must have been all too much for him," Constance moaned, "I knew this would happen."

"Or something else." Marcus spoke this in an undertone.

Clarissa glared at him. "And what is that supposed to mean?" she demanded. "You think he had something to do with what happened to Mac and Kitty don't you? Well why on earth would he? It's nonsense - he's probably gone back to Liverpool, to see a client..."

"Yes, of course that's it...like he did over Christmas!" broke in Constance, a sickly self-assurance forcing her lips into a smile. "Yes, he'll have gone to see...oh what's his name?"

"But Mother," said Marcus, "you woke to find John gone. He gave you no warning of his departure, and so early in the morning – night time more like."

Constance's face registered concentrated thought for a moment.

"No," she said slowly at last, "John didn't tell me – or I forgot – yes that that will be the most likely explanation."

Marcus stared at his mother, shaking his head. Clarissa examined the wardrobe. "He's not taken much actually," she said mildly, "just a few shirts, some trousers and a jacket or two. He'll be back, Constance just you wait and see. Now I think you should get back to bed and wait for his telephone call. I imagine it was some urgent matter he remembered during the night, it had to be attended to and he didn't want to wake you. You know how sorry he will be to know he has caused you so much anxiety."

"You're probably right, I'm a silly woman Clarissa."

"John would never hurt you, he loves you too much."

"Funny he didn't even leave her a note then isn't it?" said Marcus under his breath.

Clarissa did not respond. Instead she took Constance's hand and helped her back into bed.

"I'll call Doctor Snook shall I?" she suggested, "He'll prescribe something to settle you."

Constance smiled. "Thank you my dear, I'm so..." She stopped short and listened as the front door bell rang repeatedly.

"Now what, I wonder," said Marcus sternly, heading out of the room. A moment later he returned.

"Its Inspector Reed, Mother, he wants to speak to John."

"So there you have it, the gentleman was seen and identified by a member of the public at Banfreeth railway station a few hours after the victims were thought to have perished. If so, he cannot have been several hundred miles away at the time, as claimed."

After this summing up Inspector Reed tapped his pencil softly against his notebook, and looked steadily in turn at Clarissa, Constance and Marcus who were sat opposite him in the drawing room. Constance was the first to reply. "I can't believe you suspect my husband Inspector," She said in a tremulous voice. "This so-called witness is clearly mistaken, John was with a client, he told me so, not at Banfreeth station. I appreciate you have to follow every line of enquiry, but this is a terrible mistake."

Reed nodded, but his expression did not alter. 'So where is he now exactly Madam? You said he was not in the house. If he's innocent he has nothing to fear."

"We don't know precisely," said Marcus. Looking quickly at Constance he added, "he visits a number of his clients, at…various times."

The Inspector nodded again and folded his notebook. "I see, well when he returns perhaps you'd be good enough to let me know. From what you say he'll no doubt be able to clear the matter up for us and we can eliminate him from our enquiries. And now I'll leave you good people in peace." He gave a brief, polite smile. "And thank you all very much for your co-operation."

"Not at all Inspector," said Marcus rising. "I'll show you out."

At the front door Reed turned. "I'll be releasing the bodies soon sir," he said quietly. 'So you can make your arrangements."

"Strictly between you and I Inspector," said Marcus, with a quick look behind him, "do you suspect Bamford of…of involvement in this, this…?"

The policeman looked at Marcus. "Oh I think you know the answer to that one. Good day sir."

When he had gone Marcus stood very still by the door for a moment, then with an effort returned much less steadily to the drawing room.

CHAPTER TWELVE

"I really think you should come back down to Crosslands with us mother."

They were in the dining room at Braeside, having just breakfasted, and were now sharing a pot of coffee. Clarissa had gone for a walk and left the two of them to talk. Marcus, who had now risen from the table, spoke slowly, as if choosing every word with infinite care, as if counseling a sick person. He was pacing the room, his eyes studying the pattern on the carpet intensely, as though hoping to find there the answer to some deep and troubling problem.

"I don't want to leave Braeside," said Constance distantly, staring from the window at the far hills. "Now Mac is buried here, I can't leave him."

"Father is here too in that sense," said Marcus, maintaining his careful, patient tone. "And you were able to respectfully leave him, to continue with your life elsewhere."

"Oh but that is quite different Marcus," said Constance firmly. "I loved your father, but after he died I took a new husband. Mac was my son, he can never be replaced."

"I too am your son," said Marcus, stopping his pacing for a moment and looking even more fixedly at the carpet.

"Of course dear," said Constance fulsomely, "and I love you as much, but you see I have a duty to Mac, to be here for him…oh I know it sounds mawkish, absurd even, but I feel him near me here near the Loch he loved so much. As his brother do you not feel that too?"

"Yes, yes of course mother," said Marcus, his teeth beginning to clench. "But will you not be lonely here?"

"Sinclair is here, and I have friends in the village. And when one has happy memories one can never be lonely!" admonished Constance. "And besides there is John to consider."

"Mother…"began Marcus, the knots of exasperation across his forehead tightening further.

"John loves Braeside as much as I do, and when he returns…"

"And when is that to be?" Marcus lifted his eyes from the carpet now and stared at his mother face to face. Constance broke his intense gaze and made a little fussing movement with her hand, smoothing down her dress.

"It could be next month, it could be tomorrow; the point is I must be here to welcome him, to reassure him, that whatever the gossips, the idiots and the rumour mongers have been saying, we know differently, we know the truth."

"And what of the police mother?"

"A bunch of fools and meddlers the lot of them! Kitty was a hopeless romantic probably intent on making a scene, only to shoot herself by accident. Whatever Mac's part in the affair he did the noble thing - he was in any case a proud boy who could no longer endure his physical plight, or the prospect of being an increasing burden on his friends and family. It was a brave act. There is no question of anything suspicious."

"So why are the police still saying John is somehow implicated?"

"I've told you – because they're fools!"

"You realise if John comes back they'll arrest him."

"No they won't." Constance disputed.

"Why are you so sure?"

"Because, I will prevent it; your father was an influential man Marcus. And that influence survives him, mark my words."

"I see." Marcus returned his gaze to the carpet. "Mother forgive me for asking this again," he said quietly, "but John has made no attempt to contact you since this terrible tragedy befell us. Have you ever had any shadow of doubt that he is innocent?"

"Never," said Constance. "Now I am going to take a walk down to the Loch. Mac always liked to go down there after breakfast. And John too of course."

"I've given her something to help her sleep. Insomnia can be a curse." Doctor Snook had just left Constance in the drawing room, and was now in the hall talking to Marcus.

"She doesn't seem to want to sleep, though I'm sure these night time vigils are doing her no good," said Marcus. "She just sits at her bedroom window with the curtains open, looking down the drive towards the road, waiting for her so-called husband to reappear. But nevertheless thank you doctor. I'm grateful for your spending time with her, and for advising her to come to Crosslands with us. Not that she'll take much notice I'm afraid. We've always loved Braeside of course, but I do fear leaving her alone. She still seems to imagine John is going to miraculously return if she stays here. And without us to contradict that delusion I'm worried her thoughts can only become more clouded."

"Your mother is a strong willed woman," said Snook sagely, "she'll not be swayed by any but her own mind. And forgive me if I speak out of turn, but sometimes laddie, one can do naught but respect people's right to, how shall I put it...?"

"Live a lie?" volunteered Marcus. The old doctor looked at him for a moment then nodding his head said, "A comforting lie. Good day to you."

Marcus returned to the drawing room and told his mother he and Clarissa would be leaving the next day on the early morning train for Liverpool. Constance refusing again his plea to come with them, took her chair and sketchbook onto the lawn to resume her finely detailed drawing of Braeside.

"John will be so pleased when he sees it," she said to herself as she shaded in the sloping roof of the turret room. She sat back and admired her work in progress. Though she thought so herself, it was really rather good.

The following day, after waving Marcus and Clarissa off, Constance went up to her bedroom and unlocked the drawer of her dressing table. Taking out the letter that had arrived for her the day before, she copied down the sender's address on to a sheet of her headed notepaper, and began to write:

"Dear John,

How wonderful to hear from you! I am so relieved to know you are safely in America, though of course I am missing you terribly! I have written to the Member of Parliament that was the trusted friend and confidante of my late husband Alexander, and asked him to intervene with Scotland Yard and advise them in the strongest possible terms of the gross error of their case against you.

As soon as the matter is cleared up I will write to you again and summon you home!

The warmest welcome awaits you John, as you can imagine, from me, and so too the family and community here at Braeside, once they realise the miscarriage of justice that has been perpetrated.

I am enclosing a cheque for the £5000 you requested, made out to the name you have stated.

Take all care my darling and here's looking forward to your safe return to my arms very, very soon!

Thinking of you every moment,

With all my Love, your Ever Faithful and Adoring Wife

Constance.

Constance then filled out and signed the cheque, folded it together with the letter inside the envelope and sealed it. She then went downstairs, put on her coat and boots, and set off for the village post office.

CHAPTER THIRTEEN

"Ah come in Marcus, come in!" said Mr Jenkins, "sit yourself down, this won't take a minute I'm sure."

He had been called up to Dunfallon village by the family's solicitors, 'Jenkins and Jenkins'. There was, young Jenkins had told him, a 'little matter to clarify.'

Marcus gazed around the serene, book-lined interior of Jenkins' office. He had known the place since boyhood, when his father had sometimes taken him and Mac in to visit old Mr Jenkins, the present incumbent's late father, whose dignified portrait now hung behind young Jenkins' desk, to discuss his legal affairs.

There was a solid, timeless quality within these walls that Marcus had always found reassuring. Through all that had happened in the last few years – his father's death, Mac's accident and sudden demise, his former friend Bamford's dramatic disappearance and his mother's intractable state of confusion – Jenkins stood firm, the impeccable, trusted guardian of the Stevenson family fortune.

As Marcus often mused, there was something undeniably consoling about knowing you had a great deal of money, and moreover, someone to look after it all reliably for you.

"So we just need to know who this person is..." With an effort Marcus focused his attention back on what Jenkins was saying. "Sorry, which person?"

"This Mr. Regent, Mr. Oliver Regent."

"Never heard of him, you must've muddled up our file with somebody else's Jenkins," smiled Marcus amiably.

"There's no mistake," replied Jenkins in an equally amicable tone. "I'm just slightly concerned about these cheques that's all. They're from your mother's trust account, which of course I oversee, and though I'm sure its in order, I don't know the payee, and thought it best to mention it. I know your mother is…delicate…at present, so I hoped you might be able to assist."

"If my mother has written a cheque to someone it's none of my business really," said Marcus.

"There have been a number of them," said Jenkins. He looked down at some papers on his desk. "Six in the last month to be precise."

"For how much?" Marcus asked.

"A total of, let me see…yes, just over fifteen thousand pounds."

"Phew!" Marcus looked thoughtful for a moment. "My mother has always been very generous with her charitable donations but this amount – perhaps this Mr – who did you say?"

"Regent – Oliver Regent."

"Perhaps this Mr. Regent is an official of one of her favoured good causes," suggested Marcus.

Jenkins spread his hands, placed them squarely onto the sheaf of papers and nodded. "Good, good," he said, "well so long as you are satisfied – I will of course leave it to your own discretion as to raising the matter with your mother, good, good."

Marcus then said, "Fifteen thousand pounds is a great deal of money

Jenkins nodded again. "And of course, looked at alongside the other arrangement…"

"What other arrangement?" Marcus asked.

"Turning the business and other assets over to Mr Bamford…"

"Bamford?" Marcus sat bolt upright.

"Yes, you see when your mother gave him legal authority…"

"What legal authority?"

"That which was arranged some months ago."

"No such arrangement was ever made."

"I'm sorry Marcus," began Jenkins, "is there some misunderstanding…?"

"There certainly appears to be," replied Marcus. "As you are aware, after my father's death, the title to the family property and all assets passed jointly to my mother, Mac and myself. My mother explicitly retained that title, in writing, on her marriage to John Bamford."

"Certainly, certainly," said Jenkins, "I drew up the papers in her presence. "Then, later, when she rescinded the title in favour of her husband…"

"When she did what?" Marcus exclaimed.

"When your mother decided to place her property in her husband, John Bamford's name, she asked me to draw up a legal document to that effect…"

"Just a moment," interrupted Marcus, his voice feverish with alarm now, "this must be a mistake Jenkins, because my father stipulated in his will, that any transfer of property outside our family could only be made with the agreement of Mac and myself."

"Oh yes," said Jenkins, "you're right on that score, quite right, of course."

Marcus sat back in the chair, looking relieved. Jenkins then continued, "Therefore, when Mr. Bamford brought the transfer document signed by your mother in to me, I made sure both your signature and Mac's were also on it."

Hearing this, Marcus's jaw visibly dropped. For a second he was speechless, then, almost stammering he said,

"But - Jenkins – no such document was - ever signed by me – nor I'll warrant by Mac!"

Jenkins stared blankly, then rummaged in the drawer of his desk and pulled out a box file. Leafing through he extracted some stapled sheets of paper. "I've known your signature – and Mac's - for over twenty years." He pushed the papers across the desk. Marcus picked them up.

"Yes Jenkins," he said quietly, "this looks like my signature all right, and Mac's. But I'm afraid, it was someone else who wrote them."

"So you see Inspector," said Marcus, "Bamford obviously forged both my signature and that of my late brother on these papers, in order to obtain control of my mother's finances."

Inspector Reed handed the document back. "That appears to the case I agree sir. When we apprehend Mr Bamford, this allegation, if proven, will certainly strengthen our case against him. May I ask if you have spoken to your mother about the matter sir?"

Marcus shook his head. "She won't hear a word against Bamford I'm afraid. She pretty fragile right now. Does she need to know?"

"No," said Reed, "we can keep her out of it for now. But when it comes to court, that could be another matter."

"I thought a wife or husband couldn't testify against their spouse in any case," said Marcus.

Reed pursed his lips. "That all depends sir."

"I see," said Marcus.

"And is your wife here at the moment sir?"

"No, she's in Liverpool with our children. It's rather awkward in any case, she's Bamford's sister you see."

"So I understand sir – I don't imagine, blood being thicker than water, that your wife's made any mention of Mr Bamford's likely whereabouts at all?"

"Like you say Inspector, blood's thicker than water – could that land her in trouble."

"We can't force anyone to disclose information sir," said Reed then added carefully, "though if anything were to come out later, there is such a thing as accessory after the fact."

"Hmm, yes of course, I'll bear that in mind," replied Marcus. "I was most concerned about the money if you must know, the family's money you understand, after finding out about this transfer of property…"

"Naturally sir, have you been able to safeguard things now?"

"I've managed to persuade the banks to freeze all the accounts temporarily, till we can substantiate that a forgery has been perpetrated and a theft attempted, but as it turns out our solicitor has just advised me that most of the cash and stocks had already been transferred into my mother's trust account – to which she still has sole access."

"Really sir?" said Reed thoughtfully. "I wonder why that was?"

" Presumably my mother realised she had made a mistake and somehow still managed to access the accounts even after she'd signed everything away to Bamford."

"How?" asked Reed.

"My mother has friends in high places Inspector."

"Ah."

They both looked up as Sinclair came in. "Mr. Jenkins is here sir," he said.

"Oh good, thank you Sinclair, show him in," said Marcus. "Our solicitor Inspector - I asked him drop by so the three of us could compare notes if need be. My dear Jenkins, do take a seat, thank you for coming over, this is Inspector Reed of the Yard."

"Pleased to meet you," said Jenkins sitting at the table."

"I'm glad - few people are pleased to meet a policeman – unless they've lost their cat," said the Inspector in a dry tone. Jenkins smiled politely.

"Jolly good news about the bank accounts Jenkins," said Marcus, "I'm awfully glad you found that out, it's a great weight off my mind I can tell you."

"Yes its an odd one that," said Jenkins, "all done after your mother signed the family fortune over to Bamford – and now that fortune's in her personal account!"

"This is the one only she can access you say?" said Reed.

"Yes that's right," said Jenkins. She obviously has the ear of one or two people upstairs, as it were."

"As I said Inspector," said Marcus, "friends in high places."

"Yes," said Reed, "well sir, let's hope your luck holds in that respect, and we catch this Bamford before he can do any more damage – financial or otherwise. Well I must be on my way. And I really think you'd better go and try to have a talk with your mother Mr Stevenson – make sure she doesn't change her mind and switch all the money back again!"

"Good work mother!" Marcus, finding Constance as usual behind her easel on the lawn, beamed at her.

It was the sort of bright, positive smile that people were prone to give to their elderly relatives, especially when something difficult had to be done or discussed. Marcus, aware of this, also wore a slightly shifty look.

"Oh thank you dear – it's almost finished, I think I shall hang it in the hall so John..."

"I didn't mean your sketch mother," said Marcus, making an effort to maintain his smile, and adding quickly, "which is superb of course - I like the way you've done the ivy round the turret room – no I was referring to the transfer of money, shrewd of you to put it all in your trust account after Bamford – after John - took control of the main finances."

A flicker of guilt crossed Constance's face for a second. Then composing herself she said, "Yes I'm sorry I didn't tell you and Mac about that at the time, but I felt you might not understand – and of course John is so clever with money, and when he comes back..."

"Yes mother of course, now you do realise its important to leave all the money in your trust account now? Jenkins can freeze that too if we have to, but in the meantime you might want to reconsider some of these big charitable donations you've been making."

"To whom dear?" Constance asked.

"Mr. Regis – or Regent is it?"

"Ah – oh yes, I um…"

"Jenkins flagged it up if you must know. I don't mean to interfere mother, but your generous nature is sometimes a little too much so."

"Yes, yes of course dear. I'll take heed."

Marcus leaned over and kissed his mother gently on the brow.

"Good. And the sketch is jolly good," he said, patting her shoulder.

"Thank you dear," replied Constance, "and you know, that ivy has a special meaning for me." Her pencil skimmed delicately across the paper as she went on, "you see when I was a young girl I used to come and play with the children who lived here at the time."

Marcus said, "You never told me that."

"No, but anyway, the family had a very strict governess, and if my friends and I were too noisy while their parents were out, she'd put us in the turret room and lock the door."

"How very mean of her," Marcus said.

"But we got our own back sometimes," smiled Constance, "because when it was time for tea we'd bolt the door from the inside."

"And the ivy?"

"Oh yes, well one time I completely flummoxed the governess by opening the turret room window, climbing down the ivy and creeping back upstairs to let the others out – the old battleaxe couldn't work it out – she never dreamed we'd be able to escape!"

Marcus put a hand on her shoulder again. "You really are a remarkable lady mother, very remarkable indeed!"

CHAPTER FOURTEEN

"So everything's tickity-boo now," said Clarissa. She and Marcus were dining in their favourite restaurant in the most fashionable district of Liverpool, a place where all the merchants, lawyers and bankers ate, along with well-known show people who dropped in when they were performing in the city or passing through.

"Hardly that," said Marcus. "My mother's supposed husband, yes I'm sorry, your brother my darling, on the run for the suspected murder of my brother and Kitty Mason, is also we now discover an attempted fraudster."

"I meant on the money side of things, said Clarissa, taking a sip of her champagne."

"Yes, thank god the family money is safe. Though my mother shows no sign of being able to grasp the reality of the situation as regards your brother."

"Maybe that's for the best."

"Burying her head blissfully in the sand you mean? That's what Dr. Snook said."

"Forgive me Marcus, but she's no longer young. Perhaps its her way of coping."

"Maybe you're right," said Marcus picking up his glass and staring into it thoughtfully.

"But as you say – thank god the money's all right. It is all right isn't it darling?"

"What? Oh yes, somehow I haven't felt able to question mother about the details, but after Marcus and Kitty were found she must have had some subconscious inkling about John, don't you think?"

"How else would the money have found its way into her personal trust account?"

"My reasoning exactly."

"And so the house, and the children's school fees are assured?" said Clarissa.

"Everything's assured!" said Marcus. "Their trust funds, the business, our home, Braeside, our stocks and shares – do you know they alone are now worth almost a two million pounds Clarissa?"

Clarissa's eyes shone behind her champagne glass. "Really?" she said.

"Father was a shrewd investor!"

"So it would appear. Well here's to him."

"To Alexander Stevenson – self-made millionaire!" Their glasses chinked together. As Marcus refilled them he said, "But how do you feel about all this my dear?" What your brother has done..."

"What has he done? I wasn't aware anything had been proven against him?"

Marcus looked uncomfortable. "Of course I...that's quite true as regards what took place at Braeside...and I myself recoil from the idea he may have...John was my friend...once..."

"He is almost certainly a fraudster, or as you say an attempted one it seems," said Clarissa coldly. "And on that count alone I must, as your wife, disown him. As to other possibilities...like you I find them too terrible to contemplate. Between ourselves I doubt we shall ever set eyes on him again."

"What makes you so sure?" asked Marcus, observing his wife closely over the candle flame.

"He is my brother, or perhaps I should say was," answered Clarissa, her voice devoid of expression. "Let us try to look to the future." She raised her glass again.

"To the future!" said Marcus boldly.

"Oh hello Marcus," said Jenkins over the telephone, "I'm sorry to bother you again."

"It's no trouble Jenkins," replied Marcus, "in fact I was going to call you, there's a few investments I was thinking of making..."

"Yes of course. But I wonder if you had spoken to your mother lately."

"Not for weeks I'm afraid. She's up in Braeside still and refuses to budge, or come to the telephone. Tells Sinclair to tell us it's "not convenient". What can one do?"

"Awkward yes," said Jenkins.

"Anyway, what can I do for you old fellow?"

"Well it's about your mother actually, another of these cheques I'm afraid."

"From her trust account?" asked Marcus.

"Yes – to the Regent charity."

"Oh well, I'll try and get up to Braeside at the end of the month, have another word with her."

"The thing is Marcus – this one's for rather a large amount."

64

"How much?"

"Fifty thousand pounds."

"Good lord I see why you rang!" exclaimed Marcus, "her bank would never let that go through though thank god."

"I'm afraid they have old boy," said Jenkins nervously.

"What! But that's impossible – I gave the manager strict instructions not to cash anything more than twenty a month from her account without reference to me."

"So you told me a few weeks ago. However it seems she rang the bank's head office in London and spoke to a former chum of your father's - insisted her instructions were followed without query, old school tie and all that. I'm so sorry old man."

There was silence for a moment before Marcus replied, "All right Jenkins, not your fault," he said decisively. "Do whatever you can to freeze that account – I'll call Inspector Reed and see what he can do. I'm leaving for Braeside by the first train tomorrow."

"This time I'm going to put my foot down," said Marcus to Clarissa as the taxi crunched up the drive towards Braeside. As the house came into view he sighed with relief to see Constance coming down the steps waving.

"Marcus, Clarissa, how marvellous," she called, "Sinclair told me you'd rung. He's gone now of course."

"A pity you couldn't have spoken to me in person then mother," replied Marcus as he stepped out and paid the driver. The taxi drove off and Marcus and Clarissa embraced Constance in turn.

"You're a rum one and no mistake," said Marcus, shaking his head as they went in.

"I've so much to tell you," chattered Constance, "first I have decided after all to leave Braeside."

"Well I'm glad to hear it," replied Marcus, "you can always come back to visit of course, but I've a lot to tell you first mother."

"Yes all in good time, don't fuss," smiled Constance.

"I'll come straight to the point mother," resumed Marcus when they had all three settled in the drawing room. "Jenkins has told me all about the cheque, and he has already written a letter to these Regent charity people insisting we have the money back or they'll be serious repercussions for them. All we need from you now is their address."

"Oh but that's quite impossible Marcus. You see the work they do in America is vital…"

"America…?"

"Yes they help the poor people get an education, and John is working with Mr Regent to build a school…"

"Hold on, did you say John – Bamford?" interrupted Marcus, shooting a glance at Clarissa.

"Who else?" Constance smiled.

"You mean you've been sending him money – you know where he is?" demanded Marcus. Both he and Clarissa stared intently as Constance went on, "But of course, and that's why I've decided to leave Braeside, leave Britain for good, to go to America and join John. We will work together there, helping the young people become educated, oh it will be so rewarding!"

Marcus made an inarticulate spluttering sound. When he had at last cleared his throat, he said slowly and firmly, "Now listen very carefully Mother, you are not gong to America. You are coming down to Crosslands tomorrow with us. Do you understand?"

"That too is quite impossible Marcus," said Constance brightly.

"Why pray?"

"Because all the arrangements have been made."

"What arrangements?"

"My passage is booked, I sail for New York in a few days."

"Nonsense mother – now you really must stop these fantasies…"

"But I have a ticket – look." Constance crossed to the bureau and handed her son an envelope. Marcus opened it and examined the contents. Mechanically he said, "This is a one way ticket."

"What have I just told you – Marcus dear please don't be an imbecile. Oh and here is John's latest letter." She passed him another envelope.

Marcus took out a cream coloured sheet of notepaper and unfolded it. In the same mechanical voice he read aloud:

"My Dear Constance,

Thank you for the cheque – now I know how much you really love me – that you share my vision for what can be achieved here. People forget how much poverty and ignorance exist in this great country of the United States – together we can change that – we will work wonders Constance! I am delighted you have agreed to sell Braeside..."

At this Clarissa gave a sharp intake of breath, while Marcus faltered for a second, before reading on in a cracked and tremulous voice,

"...Your family do not need that monstrosity and it will fetch a good price, more money to fulfill our dream here my darling. Be sure to remit the proceeds from the sale to my associate Mr Oliver Regent at the soonest opportunity.

Your ticket on the Queen Mary is enclosed herewith my dear, first class of course, no less would suffice for a lady of your unique standing, not to say beauty!

I will be on the quay at New York harbour waiting, yearning for you! Till then, sleep well and dream of me, as I will of you,

Your ever-loving husband

John"

Marcus folded the letter. For what seemed like an age, he stared silently at Constance. Clarissa looked from one to the other of them, attempting to speak, but finding no words.

At last, Marcus said quietly. "Well that's lovely, really lovely mother."

"Isn't it," replied Constance, making a girlish, pleased expression with her face and lifting her shoulders impishly.

"And now, as it's getting late," said Marcus gently, "perhaps you'd like to go up to bed and we can talk more about it all in the morning. I'll have Sinclair bring you up a jug of whiskey and some hot water."

"Have you forgotten Marcus?" said Constance, "Sinclair is gone."

"Gone?"

"I have paid him off, a most generous gratuity. He has a son and daughter-in-law in the village he can live with. He was upset of course, but at his age, and with the house going up for sale it made sense."

Marcus and Clarissa exchanged looks.

"I'll go to the village and speak to him tomorrow," he said in an undertone to Clarissa.

Turning back to Constance he announced, "Very well Mother, I will bring your whiskey up."

"Thank you dear, I do feel tired, I daresay its all the excitement."

"I daresay," said Marcus.

"But first, may I have my ticket please?"

"Ticket?" said Marcus.

"Yes dear, you have it in your hand…"

"You don't need it just yet surely?" said Marcus.

"I may leave here very soon – perhaps even tomorrow morning - take a hotel room in Southampton for a couple of days before the voyage. I'm so excited you see Marcus – you've no idea how much this means to me – it's going to be a whole new life…"

"No."

"What?"

"I must be frank with you mother. John Bamford is a swindler. He forged my signature and Mac's to obtain access to the family accounts. Mr Oliver Regent does not exist. The charity is an invention to extract money from you. If he receives the proceeds from the sale of this house I doubt very much you will ever see him again, not unless he sniffs even more money in the offing. It is plain he never loved you, and married you with this plan in mind from the start."

"Marcus I…" began Constance breathlessly, "I don't know what to say, I…"

"I realise this is painful for you, but for your own good you must realise and accept the truth. Your travelling to America would be at best a wild goose chase, and at worst a highly dangerous folly. This man has duped and deceived us all enough. It ends here and now."

"But Marcus it is you who are deceived," said Constance, as if she were reasoning with an awkward child. "John is a kind man, who has been much maligned. Since the prejudice against him here is insurmountable, I have no recourse but to go to him. I do so I might add willingly and of my own free will. Now since you are determined to traduce my husband it is better that I leave this house tomorrow morning. I will thank you to hand over my steamer ticket, and my husband's letter."

Mother and son stood facing each in the fading light of the drawing room, the lowering rays of the setting sun over the Loch casting a shaft of burning gold between them. Marcus's face was set firm, while his mother's eyes glinted like steel.

Several seconds ticked by in this standoff before Marcus, taking a deep breath said, "I must also tell you mother, it's highly probable that Bamford killed Mac - your son, my brother."

Clarissa emitted a slight whimpering sound, as if she might cry. Marcus looked to his mother expecting her to break down now, ready to take her in his arms. But instead Constance let out a terrifying howl of anger.

"How dare you speak to your mother like that Marcus Stephenson!" she shrieked. "You shall go to your room at once – and, I see you have been stealing," she said pointing to his hands. "Woe betide you when your father comes home!"

Petrified, Marcus dropped the letter and ticket and stared at his mother as if some alien being had suddenly taken her place. He began to stutter, "I'm sorry mother...I didn't mean to..."

Clarissa grabbed his arm. "Marcus," she hissed, "pull yourself together, she's having some sort of fit - we must do something - get her to bed, anything."

"Yes, yes, you're right...'said Marcus, his body now shaking.

Before he could speak again however, Constance had snatched up Bamford's letter and the ticket from the carpet and fled the room. "After her!" cried Marcus.

CHAPTER FIFTEEN

"She can't get far," said Clarissa as they emerged from the drawing room and looked left and right. "Not to Southampton at any rate!"

"I'm more worried about her heading for the Loch, especially in her current state of mind…"

"It's all right, look," said Clarissa, pointing to the lift, the lights above indicating it was in use. Marcus made a move for the stairs.

"Hang on." Clarissa pulled him back. "No point running up and down till we know where she's going."

"Her bedroom I imagine," said Marcus.

"No look, she's already on the fourth." Marcus looked above the lift doors where the number four was illuminated. Reaching for the call button he jabbed his finger at it.

"What's up there anyway?" asked Constance.

"The turret room – come on."

Stepping out of the lift Marcus approached the door of the turret room.

"Mother?" he called softly.

"Go away please I'm going to bed now," came Constance's voice.

"All right mother, but I'm just coming in to make sure you're all right." Marcus turned the handle but the door would not open.

"She's locked herself in," said Clarissa.

Then Constance called again. "I'll bid you goodbye now Marcus dear," she said. "I shall be phoning for a taxi at 6 am, to leave for America."

"She's mad," said Clarissa.

"All right mother, well sleep tight." Marcus called back. Hesitating outside the room he said to Clarissa.

"We can't just leave her in there – suppose she wanders off and does herself a mischief in the middle of the night?"

Clarissa looked at the key, which was on the outside of the door. Marcus had noticed it too. He stepped forward and turned the key in the lock, tested the door then stood staring at it. Clarissa took his arm.

"Come on," she said, "she's safe enough for tonight, she needs rest. Hopefully she'll come to her senses in the morning."

Back in the drawing room Marcus poured himself a large whiskey.

"Care for anything darling?" he said as Clarissa flopped down into an armchair with a sigh.

"Thanks, the same."

"What a business," breathed Marcus, handing his wife her drink and taking the opposite chair. "Need something to steady the nerves!"

"I'm still trying to take it all in," said Clarissa. "I'm genuinely sorry about what John has done, or may have done, if it makes any difference now. He's my brother and I wish him no harm, but I cannot condone his deceit, let alone whatever else he may be guilty of."

Marcus stared hard into his whiskey glass. "I wish him harm," he said darkly. Clarissa said nothing.

Then after a moment Marcus rose from his chair.

"I won't be a minute darling," he said then left the room and closed the door behind him.

A few seconds later, Clarissa heard the feint sound of a number being dialled on the hall telephone. Quietly she got up and pressed her ear to the door. She heard Marcus's voice:

"Hello, Inspector Reed, it's Marcus Stevenson...yes, look I'm terribly sorry to call you so late, but its about John Bamford...yes there's been some developments...I'm up here at Braeside...and it seems our man is in New York, and there could be a chance to catch him...it'll need liaison with the police over there I imagine, and we may have to use my mother to trap him, she's booked on the Queen Mary and expecting to meet Bamford in the States...look could you check the passenger lists? If you can come up here I can give you all the details...tomorrow...that'll be splendid, thank you so much, good night Inspector."

Clarissa hurried back to her armchair. Marcus returned to the drawing room, poured another large whiskey, sat down and closed his eyes.

Several hours later Marcus woke and looked around him. Clarissa was still asleep in the other armchair. Through the drawing room curtains he could see it was beginning to get light.

He got up quickly and ascended the stairs to the turret room. Turning the key he pushed the door but it would not yield.

"Mother?" he called, "mother how are you feeling? Open up now, its morning. Come down and have some breakfast. Mother?"

With a worried expression he shoved the door hard several times but it would not yield. He went down one flight of stairs, leaned over the banister and called loudly,

"Clarissa – I can't open the turret room. – I'm worried my mother may be unwell and I'm going to have to force the door – there's a crowbar in the garage, could you fetch it while I have another go?"

Hearing nothing, he hurried on down the stairs, crossed the terrace to the garage to the garage near the main gate and found the crowbar.

Returning to the house, Marcus looked up towards the turret room window and saw that it was open. Below the sill, he noticed some of the ivy had broken away from the wall and was hanging down.

"Mr. Marcus, sir!" Turning, Marcus saw a lone cyclist entering through the gate.

"Sinclair...?" he said recognising the old butler as the bicycle came closer.

"I apologise for calling out sir," said Sinclair, catching his breath as he leaned his conveyance against the low wall that surrounded the terrace. "But I know your mother has been...unwell, and before seeing her I wanted a word with ye in private as it were. I take it you've heard about the...ahem...dismissal?"

"Yes I'm so sorry about all that Sinclair," said Marcus taking his hand. "I'm sure we can sort things out and get you back, as you say my mother has not been at her best."

"Aye, aye, so Dr Snook said, I saw him in the village and he advised to bide my time till things are looking better, but listen there's now something much more important, about the house..."

"Braeside?" said Marcus.

"Aye, I've been trying to reach you on the phone in Liverpool, I didn't know you were here..."

"All right Sinclair take it slow, now what's this about Braeside?"

"It's been sold sir, sold!"

"Eh?" said Marcus, "no Sinclair, don't worry we've found out about that, only just in time mind you."

"But you're not in time sir – Braeside was sold last week on your mother's instructions, the new owners will be moving in at the weekend. Your mother arranged for the money from the sale to be remitted by telegraphic transfer to a charity in the United States of America."

"Sinclair - is this true?" cried Marcus in desperation, seizing the old butler by the wrists.

"I swear it sir, she did it all through the post office in the village, that's how I know, this is why I've been trying to got hold of ye, I'm so very sorry sir…good god man, what the…?"

Sinclair had broken off and was staring over the raised flowerbeds of the terrace, where, now visible below the strands of ivy dangling off the wall, a crumpled shape lay motionless upon the flagstones.

Marcus had seen the shape too now, and moved towards it slowly, then began running. As he drew closer a pitiful, strangulated cry, like that of some mortally wounded animal broke from his lips, the sound reverberating across the Loch and to the distant hills beyond.

"Mother…!"

CHAPTER SIXTEEN

1934

From the window seat of the drawing room Clarissa looked out across the garden. Taking in the flowerbeds, already bursting with summer colours, her gaze travelled over the three terraced lawns that fell gently towards the small stream, and the rolling hills beyond.

Crosslands was at its loveliest at this time of year she thought, but as she watched Audrey playing alone again her heart as always saddened. The six weeks of the school holiday that now stretched ahead would surely seem very long for the child without a playmate. And this year, for the first time James was not coming home. Maybe she thought she should suggest to Marcus they go away somewhere.

The past eleven years had not been kind to the family, especially Audrey, suffering the slurs and mockery of her peers.

"Would you like to invite your friends for tea dear?" Clarissa had asked her daughter on numerous occasions.

"I don't have any Mummy," had always been the heart searing reply, followed by, with downcast eyes, "The other children don't like me."

How should a mother respond to such a thing, how could she reassure, console her child, set the awful matter right? Clarissa had spent many a sleepless night agonising over these questions, these responsibilities, and still the matter laid there, perpetually as it seemed unresolved.

James had gone off to boarding school at the age of five, and hence been spared the ostracism; none had heard of her brother John Bamford where James boarded, or if they had, not made the association, and Clarissa prayed it would remain that way.

She had wanted Audrey to go away too but Marcus had insisted she stay with them, and thus she had attended Barnes-Stuart girls" school in Crosslands from the age of four. They had argued about this at the time and since, and always Marcus had got his way.

After his mother's death Marcus had rarely talked about her, and never about the fateful events surrounding her passing. The final straw for him had been the loss of his beloved Braeside, which he had tried heroically, desperately to prevent.

It was Marcus's coldness towards her that hurt Clarissa most. That, she could not get beyond. Of course, he blamed John for everything, and she herself could not help but blindly curse her brother sometimes.

"What did you do to us John?" she would whisper bitterly, clutching her brother's last communication, now some two years old.

Seated at the window of Crosslands, observing Audrey at her solitary game of hopscotch, she had that letter in her hands again. The closing words, and their meaning were clear and unambiguous.

"...So come and join me Clarrie, America's the place - and bring your children - there is a golden future for all of us."

How she wished now that she had gone with him that night. She recalled how she had planned his escape, putting the sleeping powder in Constance and Marcus's nightcaps then packed her brother's clothes, making sure the sharp-eyed servants saw nothing.

If only she had packed her own and the children's clothes too, boarded the train for Liverpool, and the great liner across the Atlantic. Audrey would not have had to endure the isolation, the inherited shame that was so grossly unjust. 'America does not judge, it respects only one thing: money.' John had written in one of his letters.

Somehow Clarissa felt this was true. None of us would be judged, she thought, and I would be free. I might even have fallen in love again. John had money now, and America was full of rich men. She saw Audrey had finished her hopscotch and was now talking to Watkins the gardener as he prodded around the vegetable patch. Was it really all too late now? Clarissa took one more look at the letter, then replaced it in her writing desk and locked the drawer.

Just then the door opened. Dorothy came hurriedly into the drawing room, smoothing down her pinafore with one hand, setting her cap straight with the other.

Seeing Clarissa at the windows looking out towards the garden she hesitated, then coughed softly.

"Beg pardon madam, all right to do this room first?"

"You're late Dorothy," said Clarissa coldly, her back still turned.

"Sorry madam, it was our Molly, she's been unwell again, one of her fainting do's."

In the stillness of the room, Dorothy heard her employer exhale.

"This really will not do Dorothy, you must make arrangements for your child."

Dorothy bit her lip. "As I say she was ill madam, wouldn't eat nothing, I didn't want to leave her alone, so the thing is this, I've had to..."

"You should take more care of her," interrupted Clarissa, turning to face her employee now.

"Yes madam, I know but it's expensive to get the doctor out and my Charlie, he don't earn that much."

"Then perhaps he should look for employment with better prospects. But we don't want to waste more time than is necessary on the matter now, do we. If you are expecting a full day's pay for today you will of course work the extra hour."

"Yes madam, I will, only there's something else I have to tell you."

"Yes, what is it?"

"It's Moll, I've had to bring her with me. There's no-one else to look after her at home you see."

Clarissa glared. "Your child is – here, in this house?"

"Waiting out the back madam."

"I see. Well this is very irregular you realise Dorothy? Make sure she does not meet my daughter, that would never do."

"Yes madam, and thank you - I didn't know what else to do with her."

"Well, be sure to keep her from any mischief and - out of sight." Clarissa adjusted her hair in the over-mantel mirror then walked briskly to the door. "You can begin in here. The laundry must be attended to before you clean the hall floor, then do the bedrooms. And tell Watkins to clear those leaves from the drive. I shall be upstairs."

When Clarissa had left, Dorothy went along to the kitchen and opened the back door. Molly, her thirteen-year-old daughter was sat on the step watching a trail of ants.

"Now you listen Moll," said Dorothy, taking the mop and bucket. "You be a good girl, sit at the table and read your books, or lie down on the mat if you feel poorly. I'll bring you some hot milk and biscuits in a while if you're up to it."

"But Mum, I want a wee." the child said.

"You must use the lavvy in the yard, over there, look. And don't go wandering. Just stay round the yard, or in the kitchen." Dorothy kissed her little girl and was gone.

Molly ran to the little wooden cubicle at the end of the yard then returned a minute later, hopped up the step and peered into the kitchen. It was a large, bright space, with a very high ceiling, and a big long table - not at all like her mother's kitchen at home, which consisted of a cramped lean-to at the side of their terraced house.

Molly walked round the table a few times, then sat on the chair and opened her books. After a few moments looking through them she got down again and went over to the door she had seen her mother go through. Gingerly, she opened it. On the other side was another room, even larger than the kitchen. Mollie gazed in awe; high above her head large joints of meat hung from hooks in the ceiling, and stacked along the shelves were row upon row of jams and pickles, the morning sun creating a rainbow of colours from the jars as it filtered in through the pantry window. Below the jars on a long table, under glass domes stood loaves of bread, succulent-looking cakes and various kinds of biscuits.

Molly, who first thing that morning had been unable to look at food was feeling better now, and had also regained her appetite. Tiptoeing over to the bench, she lifted the nearest dome took a large oat biscuit and munched it enthusiastically. Finishing it she reached for another, and was just about to take a bite when a voice said,

"What are you doing?" Molly turned quickly, hiding the biscuit in her apron pocket.

In the doorway opposite she saw a girl of about her own age, wearing a pretty summer dress and tennis shoes with white socks.

"I'm Audrey and I live here," she said, "now who are you?" Molly did not answer.

"Are you deaf?" asked Audrey.

Still Molly did not speak. Audrey approached her and poked her in the chest.

"If you don't tell me what you're doing I'll call Watty and have you thrown out," she threatened.

"Watty's in the garden," said Molly pointing.

Audrey looked surprised. "Watty's my friend!" she said crossly, poking her harder.

"Ow!" protested Molly, backing away. "Don't do that, it hurts. Anyway I don't have to speak to you!"

"Oh yes you do." Audrey replied. "And if I want to poke you I will. I can do anything I like, it's my house."

Molly looked down, then produced the biscuit from her pocket and held it out to Audrey.

"I'm sorry," she said, "I was very hungry. I wasn't well this morning, I missed my breakfast."

Audrey smiled. "I know who you are," she said.

"Who am I then?" challenged Molly.

"You're Molly!"

"How do you know?"

"Mama said."

"Do you go to school?"

"Yes I do but it's the holidays silly. I go to the council school. What school do you go to?"

"Barnes Stuart." Audrey replied

"The la –di –da one with all those other posh girls." Molly sniffed and screwed up her nose.

Audrey looked her up and down for a moment then took her hand,

"Come with me." she said

Molly shrank away. "Where are you taking me? I'm not going to the mistress. Mam will be cross with me." she began to cry.

Audrey put her arm around the frightened girl. "How old are you Molly Bratt?"

"Nearly fourteen, why" Molly wiped her eyes

"Oh! The way you were crying I thought you might only have been about eight. I was only going to give you some cakes and a glass of milk silly."

Audrey led her back into the kitchen and bade her sit at the table. She fetched a large glass of cold, creamy milk and set it down, together with a batch of cakes from one of the domes in the pantry.

"Tuck in," said Audrey.

Molly needed no further persuasion, and was soon devouring the cakes and guzzling down the milk.

"How old are you? Molly asked through a mouthful of cake crumbs.

"Twelve – soon be thirteen though. Have you got a brother?" Molly nodded head wiping her mouth clean.

"Two of them, Charlie and Billy and two sisters. I'm the youngest next to our Bill, he's only a baby."

78

"I have a brother called James. He used to pull my hair and make adventures for me but he's away at boarding school and hardly ever comes home. When he leaves he's going to help in Daddy's business. I might get married then, but I haven't decided yet. Mama says I have to choose a very special person and not just anybody.

Watty once said any chap would be the luckiest man on earth to marry me, but Daddy said that though he agreed I shouldn't be conceited. Are you conceited?"

"What does it mean?" asked Molly.

Audrey hesitated then said, "Being a show-off, I think. Listen, after this, what say we..."

"How dare you!"

The girls looked up with a start as into the pantry rushed Molly's mother, her face livid with anger and alarm.

"I'm so sorry Miss Audrey, she is a very cheeky, disrespectful child – I told her not to touch anything and to stay in the kitchen." Dorothy stepped towards Molly and lifted the raised the back of her hand. As she did so Audrey got up from the chair and stood between them.

"I gave the cakes to Molly," she said, facing Dorothy full on. "Don't you dare hit her."

Dorothy gave Audrey a surprised, slightly bewildered look and lowered her hand. "Well, I'm sorry I'm sure Miss - but I told her not to move and...."

"And she hasn't. I came into the kitchen for a glass of milk and found Molly sitting at the table reading. I offered her something to eat and drink and decided that she is now my new friend." She turned to Molly. "If that's alright with you."

Molly, wiping cream from her lips, and looking sheepishly at her mother, nodded.

"That's settled then. Molly when you have finished we will go out into the garden and I'll show you my new pram. Thank you Dorothy that will be all."

Dorothy, still looking uncertain shook her head. "You be a good girl Moll do you hear?"

"Of course she hears you Dot, she's not deaf!" Audrey said.

Then, laughing uproariously she grabbed Molly's hand and ran full speed towards the garden.

CHAPTER SEVENTEEN

Audrey and Molly had become firm friends, much to the dismay and annoyance of Clarissa.

"But darling what harm can it do?" Marcus pleaded with her one morning as they observed Dorothy, accompanied by Molly for the fourth day running, skirting the drive on her way round to the kitchen. "It's not as though we don't know the child."

"That is exactly the point Marcus," hissed Clarissa, ramming closed the drawing room door as the clunk of Dorothy's bucket was heard down the hall. "She is not the sort of child I want our daughter to associate with. I allowed her here for one day because the girl was ill. Now she's here every day, and bounding around our house treating it as her own."

"But Audrey begs to have her over. You said yourself she has no friends"

"We cannot allow our children to dictate to us Marcus, or for that matter our staff. The tail shall not wag the dog in this house."

"But I told Dorothy it was all right."

"Then it is you who must speak to her, and set matters right."

"But we've known Dorothy for years."

"We've known the postman for years – do you suggest we give his family the run of the place?

"It's hardly the same…"

"How so? Audrey and that girl are from completely different stations in life."

"So are you and I if it comes to that - a fact that used to embarrass you if I remember."

"Please don't try to undermine me Marcus. An association between our child and the daughter of our housekeeper can only lead to trouble and unhappiness. Not to put too fine a point on it, she and Audrey are, are - separate species - they will grow up to inhabit entirely different worlds."

"You never made this fuss with James."

"It has never been an issue with James. He has the correct instinct for such things."

"What things?"

"Protocol. It's a question of boundaries Marcus, surely you can see that?"

Marcus looked out of the window, to the lawn beyond the potting shed. Audrey and Molly were chasing gleefully round and round, throwing handfuls of grass cuttings at each other. Old Watkins was obligingly tipping out more ammunition from his mower box and chuckling at the girls' antics.

"Well?" said Clarissa.

"Hmm?" murmured Marcus, preoccupied by the sight of Molly and Audrey now engaging Watkins in the melee by hurling grass over his head.

"Well?" repeated Clarissa, "will you speak to Dorothy, or do I have to?"

"Yes darling," said Marcus, "I'll speak to her. But not today, let's let them enjoy the rest of the holidays at least."

"Come on Audrey, come with me to the beach," Molly said, tugging at her friend's hand.

It was a beautiful summers morning and the second week of the holidays and of their friendship.

Audrey pulled away "I can't Moll," she moaned "I promised Mummy that I would stay here, in the garden. If I go out she'll never let me play with you again." Molly looked downcast.

"Your dad says it's nice for us to play together," she said.

"Yes, but not leaving the house, and anyway we don't know the way to the beach."

"I do," said Molly."

"Bet you don't,"

"Bet I do. I'll prove it to you, come on."

"No, we're not allowed."

"I thought you were allowed to do anything," said Molly, a hint of daring in her eye.

"I can, most things. But no one's allowed to do everything stupid, not even grown-ups. Your ma would be mad at you."

"See if I care - you can stay here," said Molly in a defiant voice and headed for the garden gate.

"Moll wait, you can't go alone," called Audrey, "you've got to stay here with me - your ma will kill you – Moll! Wait for me…!"

"This is fun," Molly laughed, running towards the water. Audrey watched her friend.

———

After climbing the dunes they had tumbled breathlessly down the other side onto the glorious golden sands. The tide was way out and on either side the beach seemed to stretch forever. Ahead, the sea, a vast shimmering presence beckoned. Apart from a group of children picnicking on the dunes, the place was deserted.

"Don't go too far Moll," called Audrey as Molly's figure became smaller on the horizon. "Remember we mustn't be too long…Molly, Molly are you all right?" she stared at her friend then raced across the sand to catch her up. She saw that Molly had stopped laughing and was standing perfectly still.

"What is it? Come on Moll. Don't fool around." Audrey gently shook the girl. Still she didn't move. "Oh Moll! Molly had fallen to the ground and was shaking from head to toe. Audrey screamed, "Molly, Molly somebody help me!

The picnic group of girls and boys ran up. "It's Tumbledown and her posh friend," one lad laughed.

"Oh yeah," said a redheaded girl. "Fallen down again, Tumbledown?" she jeered.

"Please help us, please," Audrey pleaded, "my friend's not well; I don't know what to do."

The group began laughing and chanting, "Tumbledown Molly, Tumbledown Molly, fallen down again, fallen down again…"

"Please help us!" Audrey was screaming now, but this only made the children laugh more and continue their chant.

In desperation she shoved them, whereupon the boys grabbed hold of her and threw her to the ground. Then, hearing a voice behind them they stopped and turned around.

"Hey – you lot, get out of here!" A man was running towards the children, shouting and waving his arms.

"Run for it!" the taller boy shouted, "its Crackpot Jack!"

The group fled, leaving Molly and Audrey alone. Molly was laying still now, her eyes closed.

"Please wake up Molly, please." Audrey, tears streaming down her cheeks, shook her friend's arm, while casting agitated glances at the man that had shouted, and who was now approaching them. He wore ragged clothes and shoes tied up with string. From the stubble on his face Audrey guessed he might be a fisherman. But what had the other children called him – Crackpot Jack?

"You all right Missy?" said the man as he drew level and knelt down beside them.

———

Audrey gave a little shiver of fear as he reached out and stroked Molly's head. "Please - don't hurt her," she quavered.

"Old Jack's not going to hurt anyone," he rasped. He gave a crooked smile, displaying several gaps in his teeth, and a flash of gold.

"We'd better get her to my hut." He nodded at Audrey. "You come too little one, your friend's going to need you when she wakes up." He lifted Molly easily in his arms and made his way across the sand.

Hidden among the dunes stood a ramshackle old hut, its painted wooden boards bleached the palest of blue by the sun and salt air. Audrey trotted quickly behind them, her face full of fear and alarm. She had been told never, ever to go off with strangers, and while her first instinct was to run away as fast as she could and summon help, she also felt dread at the idea of leaving Molly alone, even for a few moments, with this terrifying looking man.

As they reached the hut Crackpot Jack turned and looked at her. "Well are you coming in," he said, "I'll not harm you, either of you. I know this young lady here, it's Molly Smith - we're old mates. We must get her out of the sun."
Audrey looked at the man, and saw now that behind the stubble and the wrinkled, dried out skin was a kind face. He pushed open a creaking door and they went in. The hut was rather like a makeshift summerhouse inside, with a couple of old wicker chairs and a low table lashed together from driftwood.
Audrey read the words Ceylon Tea on one of the boards. Along the back, with several springs protruding beneath was a couch.
Crackpot Jack spread a blanket over the couch and laid Molly gently down. "She'll be alright in a minute," he said. "Touch of the sun that's all." He went into a corner and lit a small oil-stove. "Drop of tea I think," he said, setting a little kettle on the stove. "Best thing, sweet tea."

When the tea was ready Audrey accepted some gratefully. Suddenly she felt very tired and thirsty. She had just taken a couple of sips when there was a little groan from the couch. Audrey ran to her friend's side. "Molly, Moll – oh thank goodness - are you alright?" She stroked Molly's head.
Molly opened her eyes. "Where am I?" she said.

"You're here, with your Uncle Jack," said Crackpot Jack smiling his crooked smile. Molly sat up and looked around. "How did I get here?"

"You had one of your turns love," Jack replied. "If it hadn't been for your friend here them blasted tearaways would have left you for the sharks."

"I don't think that's quite true Mr Crack…" stammered Audrey.

Crackpot Jack laughed. "Mr Jack Roberts is my name," he said. "But you can call me Jack."

"Uncle Jack can I have a cup of tea and something to eat, I'm starving hungry." Molly asked.

Jack went to the cupboard and took out a loaf and a block of cheese.

"Would you like some too Miss - there we go, I don't know you're name neither."

"Uncle Jack, this is my friend Audrey Stephenson, and this Audrey is my uncle Jack." Molly said.

Jack handed round the food and sat down on one of the wicker chairs, which creaked beneath him.

"Audrey Stephenson," he said, "you're from that posh house up in Whindolls Road are you?"

"How do you know that?" asked Audrey munching on her cheese.

"I knew your grandfather, in fact, he gave me this hut."

Audrey stared in amazement. Crackpot Jack smiled broadly at her.

"Yes ma'am, James Bamford, a kinder gentleman never lived, better than his son your uncle John of course. Generous to a fault your granddad was - not like his daughter with her airs and graces since she married money…"

Hearing a 'shushing" sound from the direction of the couch Crackpot Jack broke off in mid-sentence. Molly had a finger pressed to her lips and her eyes were indicating Audrey.

Coughing into his fist, he mumbled, 'sorry young lady, I didn't mean…me any my big mouth."

Audrey looked at him for a moment then threw back her head and laughed. "I quite agree with you Jack," she said boldly. "Mother is a frightful snob. Daddy thinks so too sometimes, it's true but I don't know much about my uncle John. I know something happened when I was very young. Daddy won't speak of it and Mummy says one day she'll tell me but from the jeering and remarks from outsiders, I think he killed someone."

Crackpot Jack offered a small, rueful smile. "You'll find out one day I'm sure young miss. Feeling better now Moll?" he asked. Molly nodded. "I'll bring some fresh fish and a round of strong cheese up to your ma, build you up my girl – and a case of brandy for her and your dad too."

"Where from?" enquired Audrey.

"Oh just a fisherman friend of mine," replied Crackpot Jack. "Now its time you two were getting off home. Your mothers will be worried wondering where you've got to." He rose and put on a crumpled brass buttoned jacket, then dusted off a peaked naval hat and placed it in a studied manner on his head.

"My goodness Jack," said Audrey, "you look like a real sea captain!"

Crackpot Jack smiled then gave a little salute and turned smartly on his heel. "I'll walk with you both, drop you off first Audrey and then take Molly."

The two girls yawned simultaneously and nodded. "Your charabanc awaits ladies - this way…"

"Charabanc?" said Audrey.

"You'll see," Molly replied.

Outside, from behind the shed Crackpot Jack wheeled out a curious contraption, a tricycle, attached to the back of which was another three wheeled trailer. Mounted on the trailer was what appeared to be a laundry basket.

"If you can both squeeze in," said Crackpot Jack, "and oh and Miss Audrey - I hope you don't mind the smell of eels…"

"What time is it Jack?" Audrey asked, as they drew up at the end of Whindolls Road.

Crackpot Jack pulled out a pocket watch. "Quarter past four." He peered round at the girls. "Will you be in terrible trouble?" he enquired.

Audrey swallowed hard. "No," she said forcing a smile. "It'll be all right."

"Well I wish I could come and put a word in for you, but I fear I'd not be helping matters."
Audrey pressed his hand as she climbed out of the basket. "Thank you Jack, and for helping Mollie."

"Now next time you tell someone where you're going. Whatever her faults your ma loves you, be sure of it, and it's not right to set her worrying."

"No, I suppose you're right Jack."

"And if you're ever passing my residence again do drop in, and there's no need for calling cards!"

"Good luck Audrey," said Mollie, kissing her friend on the cheek. "And thanks for looking after me."

"Good luck to you! I'll see you soon Moll, bye."

When the tricycle and sidecar had gone Audrey walked to her house, opened the gate and went in. From the drive she saw her mother, alerted by the sound of the gate, peering from the window. She stopped and turned for a moment, staring up the road.
One day, she vowed, Mollie and I will be together all the time, we will be friends always, always and forever.

"You are going to have to talk to her now Marcus," said Clarissa. "It cannot be put off any longer. She'll listen to you."
Marcus folded his newspaper, and sighed. He knew by now he wasn't going to be allowed to read until Clarissa had finished speaking.

"At least she's come home safe and sound"

"Heaven knows where she's been."

"Probably just to Molly's."

"Not all this time, Dorothy would have sent her back by now. That girl's led her off somewhere, mark my words."
At this point the drawing door opened slowly and Audrey's face peered round.

"Well come in if you're coming," said Clarissa briskly.
Audrey sloped into the room and perched on the arm of a chair.

"I expect you want to know where I've been," she said meekly.

"We certainly do," said Clarissa, "and we want to know why you left the house without telling us, despite everything you've been told. Well?"

"I went to the beach," said Audrey

"The beach!" cried Clarissa aghast, "that's miles away. Do you realise you could have got lost for evermore?"

"No it was alright really, Molly knew the way..."

"I might have known it! Are you hearing this Marcus?"

"And then she wasn't well and fainted, but these horrid children were jeering at her."

"Oh dear," said Marcus, "poor Molly..."

"Never mind the sympathy," interjected Clarissa in an aside to her husband.

"Well what happened then?" asked Marcus.

"An old man came and took us away..."

"What?" cried Clarissa almost choking.

"No, no, he was kind, he gave us tea and cheese..."

"And what else did he do?" snapped Clarissa.

"Nothing."

"Are you quite sure?"

"Well, one more thing - he brought us home."

"In his car?" enquired Marcus.

"No in a laundry basket – tied on to his bicycle."

Clarissa sat with her mouth open, her expression a mixture of horror and bewilderment. Marcus was smiling.

"It's all right Clarissa," he said.

"All right?" replied Clarissa looking at him in disgust.

"Audrey dear," said Marcus, "this old man, he wasn't called Jack by any chance?"

"Yes, how did you know?"

"Not...? Oh Marcus this is too much," said Clarissa.

"He's an old friend of ours - but..." began Marcus.

"He most certainly is not!" Clarissa interjected.

"But that doesn't mean you should talk to strangers of course."

"No Daddy – but I was worried about Molly, and I didn't know what else to do, and he did help us..."

"Never mind. Your father's right," snapped Clarissa. "You are too familiar with people all round, always bothering Watkins when he is supposed to be working..."

"But Watty's not a stranger Mama."

"Never mind. Your father and I will decide who you shall and shall not fraternise with. Is that not right Marcus?"

"Well…" began Marcus.

"And on that subject, he wishes to speak to regarding Dorothy's daughter."

"What about Moll?" asked Audrey, her eyes wide, looking in turn at each of her parents.

"Your father and I have come to a decision."

There was a long pause as Marcus fiddled with his newspaper, then finally he said, "Audrey dear, perhaps it's best if you and I have a word in my study.

CHAPTER EIGHTEEN

Three weeks remained of the summer holidays, and Audrey had no intention of spending a day of it without her new friend.

The fact that her mother had said she was not to play with Molly had only made her more resolute and loyal, and that morning she had taken care to ensure no one saw her leaving the house.

Molly had been waiting for her, as they had arranged, around the corner of the next street.

"What shall we do today Tumble?" Audrey asked, using her chosen nickname for her friend as they linked arms.

"Well," said Molly, looking unusually pensive, "I've got to look after our Billy. I've only come to tell you so as you wouldn't be waiting around for me."

"Couldn't you have put him in the pram and brought him with you," Audrey said with a conspiratorial twinkle in her eye.

"Audrey what are you turning into?" Molly laughed. "You know, he's only a baby."

"Then I could come to your house, Moll," Audrey suggested.

"But what about your mother - remember your dad said you should ask if you can go out."

"He's not home," said Audrey, "And if I ask Mummy, she will definitely say no." Audrey sighed. "But anyway," she added, the twinkle in her eye now a defiant gleam, "lets go!"

Half an hours walk later they arrived outside Molly's house. The terraced street was alive with noise and activity – boys playing football and calling out to one another, girls skipping and chanting in rhymes, while from house to house women in turban headscarves sat perched backwards out of their windows rubbing the panes with newspaper and soapy water till the glass glistened, or scrubbed their brightly painted front steps with stiff brushes, and ferocious energy. Young mothers with babies in prams stood in small groups chatting.

Suddenly above the general hubbub there came a loud rumble and thud followed by a cry of alarm. The two girls halted on the pavement and looked up.

A young woman, a ball of newspaper in one hand and a pail in the other sat pinioned on an upstairs sill by the window frame that had, without warning descended on her thighs.

Seeing Molly, she called down, "Moll, thank god – over here pet!"

"Not again Alice," sighed Molly.

"The sash has gone Moll, I told Charlie to fix it. I'll kill him when he gets home. Come on, give us a hand."

"What's she doing up there?" asked Audrey in bewilderment.

"Cleaning the windows of course." Molly replied, leading the way through the open front door of her home.

"Oh I see - we have a man come with a ladder to do the windows at Crosslands," said Audrey. Her tone was quite devoid of one-upmanship in this interested exchange of information between friends.

She followed Molly up the narrow staircase into the bedroom. Confronting Alice's dangling legs, and red face staring at them through the window, Audrey put a hand to her mouth to stifle an involuntary laugh.

"Get that book Aud" directed Molly pointing to a thick tome resting on the floor beneath the window. "I'll lift up the sash and you wedge it underneath." Molly took an even grip on the sash and heaved it up. Audrey quickly jammed the book on its end into the open space to one side of Alice's legs. Alice leaned in, shoved the window a little higher and squeezed the rest of her body back into the room.

"Thanks, Moll," she said, puffing slightly. "I could have been there all day for all that lot care." She thrust her head back outside to proffer a jubilant wave and some brief, raucously incoherent banter to all and sundry in the street, before closing the window down with a bang.

"Who's this?" she said, jerking a thumb at Audrey.

"Audrey Stephenson," said Molly. Audrey smiled politely.

"Ooh! Your posh friend from the big house!" she bellowed in mock grandiloquent tones, "we will have to mind our Ps and Qs won't we?" then adding kindly, "take no notice of me love, its very nice to meet you."

Alice smoothed down her apron. "Come on Moll lets get kettle on. Your mother's left Billy here safe and sound." She led the two girls into a small room, in the corner of which sat a large grey and cream pram. "Ah," she cooed, peering in, "all the excitement and he's still away with the fairies bless him! You leave him here with me Moll, if you two want to go out, he's no trouble."

"But mum said I was to look after him," replied Molly, "you're supposed to be going to work and she wont be back till this afternoon."

Alice smiled, "Not feeling too good today, been sick most of the morning, and that window didn't help - it's the baby love – mine," she explained, rubbing her stomach fondly. "They say your first is always the worst."

"Ok thanks Alice," said Molly, unable to conceal her pleasure. Come on Aud lets go and see what the others are doing." She took Audrey's arm and steered her back downstairs and out into the street. "Let's play football."

"That's only for boys isn't it?" said Audrey, puzzled.

"Nah, they don't mind – come on!" Molly charged into a nearby throng of boys and emerged triumphantly dribbling a ball, leading the boisterous pack up the street after her.

Audrey stood for a moment in amazement then laughing, followed on, whooping with the rest. She now realised that some of the footballers she had thought were all boys, were in fact girls.

With football, skipping, hopscotch, marbles and talking to Molly's friends, the pair were kept fully occupied, till all at once they realised it was the afternoon, and heading for teatime when Audrey would have to go home.

As they wandered back down towards Molly's house Audrey stared up and down the row of front doors and windows. They all looked identical except for their net curtains, and all small and tucked tightly together like Molly's.

"How many people live in your house Moll?" Audrey asked.

"Mum and Dad, Alice and Charlie and me – oh and Billy, I nearly forgot abut him."

"That makes six," said Audrey, "must be crowded."

"Yeah," Molly smiled. "And noisy when we all get together – Christmas is the best time, all our family come round - Gran, Aunty Brenda, Uncle Sid, Aunty Ethel, Uncle Arthur and all our cousins."

"How many of them are there?"

"Ten," replied Molly instantly. "That's easy to remember Mum says 'cos it's a round number. Dad says nought would be a better round number – nought, get it, a round number?"

"Oh, yeah," Molly smiled.

"We never stop laughing, mostly at Uncle Sid and Dad – I love it at Christmas.

"But how do you all fit in?" asked Audrey, gazing back at the little house.

Molly smiled. "With difficulty," as Mum says. "We make-do - there's the parlour and the lean to in the back yard next to the privy and the coalhouse. Dad's got his allotment across the alley – we always know where to find him when he wants a bit of peace, he grows some lovely vegetables. "I came here for a bit of peace" he'll say, and Mum will say "Never mind peace, I want some o' them peas!"

Audrey pictured the scene – the house full of relations, the funny Uncles and cousins, the jollity and laughter. How different Molly's life was to her own she thought. On a sudden impulse she said, "Could I come to your party at Christmas Moll?"

Molly smiled broadly and linked arms with her friend.

"Of course you can Aud, just need your mother's say so of course, which could be tricky...and then..." She stammered to a halt and looked away.

"What is it Moll?" asked Audrey, "have I said something I shouldn't?"

"No Audrey, course you 'aven't but the thing is see, I've got a job."

"A job?" said Audrey as if her friend had suddenly spoken some foreign language.

"Yeah it's in Liverpool, in one of the hospitals, in the laundry bit. I have to leave home and live somewhere else, near the work see. It's good money, so Mum says. I have to start soon see, so..." Molly, her voice tailing off again, lowered her head.

"It's alright Tumble," Audrey said in a conspicuously bright voice. "We'll still be friends."

"I'm fourteen next week," said Molly, looking up at her house with a distant expression in her eyes. "That's when I've got to go."

"We can write to each other," said Audrey quickly, the brightness in her voice giving way to a querulous wobble as if she might burst into tears at any second. "And...and I can come and visit you. Don't be sad, please Moll I couldn't bear it if we didn't stay friends...and...I'm going to jolly well make sure we do! I'll be leaving home and working soon too," she added spiritedly.

Molly looked pleased, then uneasy. "I thought you had to stay on at that school till you was a lady and then you was to marry a gentleman, I mean, you are a lady already, but, I meant…"
Audrey hesitated for a split second before replying.

"No," she said decisively, "I'll do what I want to do Moll. They can't make me stay, or marry if I don't want. So we'll both be grownup at the same time and can do what we jolly well like and my parents can jolly well lump it!"
Molly looked at Audrey with breathless admiration. She had never seen her friend quite so impassioned, especially on her behalf, and she swelled with gratitude and pride. The fire returning to her eyes she took Audrey's hand and gripped it hard. Audrey returned the grip, and the silent deep, look the two girls exchanged spoke all they needed to know; the bond of friendship between them was now forever sealed.
It was Molly who broke the silence. "I think you'd better get back now," she said, still gazing admiringly at her best friend. "Don't want you to get into any more trouble than you're already in."
Audrey smiled ruefully, her expression saying she knew what was in store for her back home.

"Suppose I had," she replied. "Will I see you before you leave for Liverpool?"

"I doubt it, but I'll write you a letter as soon as I've settled in. I can write you know Aud!" she added, seeing Audrey's look of surprise.

"Of course," said Audrey, "you can do lots of things Moll." She put her arms round Molly, and they hugged each other tightly.

"Who'd have thought it Aud, you and me best mates. Thanks for coming today, thanks for everything - and if ever you need anything you find me you hear, you just find me."
Audrey sniffed and wiped her eyes.

"Be sure to look after yourself in Liverpool, I won't be there remember."

"Oh yes you will, Audrey, in here, and in here." Molly pointed to her head, then her heart.

The two girls then began a slow walk back to Audrey's home. At the corner of her road they hugged once more before waving farewell.
Reaching her garden gate, Audrey turned and waved again, until her friend was out of sight.

CHAPTER NINETEEN

Clarissa picked up the morning post that had just clattered through the letterbox. Crossing to the breakfast room she sifted through the pile. There was a stack of business correspondence for Marcus, but nothing from America. She looked relieved, yet there was also a tinge of disappointment on her face.

Then she noticed something unusual among the pile. It was a letter bearing her daughter's name, written in an uneven scrawl. Opening it immediately, she quickly scanned the contents. With a sharp exhalation of breath she slammed the envelope down on the hall table and rang the servants' bell. A few seconds later, Dorothy appeared.

"What's the meaning of this?" demanded Clarissa, thrusting the letter into her hands.

Dorothy read silently then looked at her mistress apologetically. "Oh I am sorry ma'am, it's from our Molly…"

"I am aware of that," snapped Clarissa. "Which is why I want an explanation."

"I told her not to write…"

"What are you going to do about it - and where is my daughter?"

"I saw her in the garden with Watkins ma'am, but please don't be too hard on her - it's my Molly's fault all this."

"When I want a servant's opinion on how to discipline my children, I shall ask for it. Our agreement was that if I found your daughter employment you would keep her away from Audrey – completely away, in every sense. This eventuality," she said curtly, "is clearly a breach of that agreement and of the trust I have - misguidedly it seems - placed in you."

"I'm very sorry ma'am, but …"

Clarissa held up her hand. "No buts Dorothy, go and tell Audrey I wish to see her immediately."

Audrey was tending to the roses when Dorothy approached.

"Hello Dorothy how is Molly? She said she would write to me from Liverpool – the laundry must be hard work. I can't wait to see her again, will she come home to visit soon?"

Dorothy burst into tears. "Oh Miss, I'm so sorry, but the mistress – your mamma found our Molly's letter just now, and she read it, and I'm afraid you're in trouble, we're all in trouble… oh dear me…!" She wiped her eyes on her apron while chiding herself incoherently.

"Oh she did, did she?" bristled Audrey. "Mamma has no right to read my letters, a young lady's correspondence is private!"

"She wants to see you now," said Dorothy, struggling to compose herself, "oh, and she's in a terrible mood!"

"And I - want to see her!" stormed Audrey throwing down the pruning shears. "Watty I'll be back later to finish off." She walked briskly of towards the house, leaving Watkins and Dorothy exchanging diffident glances.

Audrey found her mother in the sitting room. "Can you please explain why you are now reading my letters?" she demanded immediately in a loud, adult voice.
Clarissa rose from her chair and stood facing her daughter.

"You will not speak to me in that manner Audrey," she replied firmly. "I have every right to know with whom my daughter corresponds."

"Mother please, what do you think I am, Molly is my friend. If she chooses to write to me, what of it?"
Clarissa offered her daughter a disarming smile, then after a brief pause said calmly,

"Darling I will overlook your impertinence on this occasion, since I see you are upset. Now one day, when you have children of your own you will realise parents want the best for them, and your father and I now want for you."
Audrey had sat down, her breathing subsided a little, though the truculent look remained on her face as Clarissa continued, "The lower, menial type of person is simply not an appropriate class from which to draw your friends."

"Who says so?" retorted Audrey insolently.

"Society – and your father and I."

"Daddy doesn't mind Moll, he said so…"
Clarissa put up her hand authoritatively. "Do not interrupt me Audrey. There are many eminently suitable girls at your school, whom I would not hesitate to have to have to tea. You only have to inform me who you wish to invite and it shall be arranged."

"But Molly is Dorothy's daughter," said Audrey.

"That," said Clarissa with a withering look, "is precisely the point child."

Audrey looked at the floor with a sullen expression then said in a quiet voice. "I'll not stop writing to Molly, Mother, or seeing her when she's home - she is my friend and that is that."

Clarissa gave a long outtake of breath. "Very well dear, then we must exert pressure upon you. You will either cease this nonsense now, or Dorothy will have to be dismissed. I will also find it my duty to inform respectable families that she is unable to control her children. She will find it hard to obtain employment in the area again."

Audrey looked aghast at her mother. "You wouldn't be so mean?"

"It is not meanness child. If it happens it will be a regrettable expedient brought on by your own selfishness. And while you are here there is something else I wish to tell you."

"Yes Mamma?" said Audrey, still gazing down at the carpet.

"Now you are thirteen years old I have decided to enhance your education."

"Oh."

"I have been speaking to the headmistress of Grenville House School in Surrey, and she thinks you have excellent potential and has agreed to offer you a place there."

"Yes Mamma," said Audrey in a disinterested voice.

"You may come home during the holidays of course…"

"What do you mean, come home?" Audrey looked up now.

"Grenville is a boarding school, you will reside there during term time."

"But Daddy wants me to stay at home, not go away…" Audrey protested, her face filled with alarm.

"Your father and I are in agreement on the matter…"

"That's not true you're lying! I hate you I hate you I hate you…!"

"Enough!" bellowed Clarissa, fixing her daughter with a steely eye. "You will leave here to begin your first term on Monday. Now I suggest you go to your room and start packing any belongings you wish to take with you."

CHAPTER TWENTY

September 1939

"Jack – Jack its me, Audrey."

The door of the hut creaked open and Jack Roberts's weather beaten face appeared.

"Why young Audrey, as I live and breathe! Is it really you?"

"It's really me!" cried Audrey, flinging her arms around the old man. "Though perhaps you don't recognise me now I'm taller. It has been five years since I saw you."

"Not only taller," said Jack, "why you're a beautiful young woman now!"

"Oh Jack you are kind," she said squeezing his hand, "but you haven't changed a bit – I mean you're as handsome as ever."

"Get away – I was born a grizzled seadog and that's the way I'll always be till Davy Jones comes for me. But come in, come in Audrey dear, and let me get you a brew and some bread and cheese." Jack led her into the hut and tugged aside the sacking curtain that hung at the window. Bright light reflected off the glittering sea streamed in, dancing round the dusty interior and illuminating the cornucopia of curios and salvage.

"I see you've still got the old lamp Jack," said Audrey fondly, touching a battered brass fog light hanging from the ceiling.

"Come from a pirate ship you know Audrey – or was it a French man 'o' war? I forget now...anyhow, tell me where you've been this long time young lady – I thought you'd run away to sea, or joined the circus!"

Audrey laughed. "I've been at that beastly school, in Surrey, a boarding school," she said then added in a bitter tone, "Mamma refused to let me come and visit you - I tried again and again to give them the slip in the holidays and come down to the beach, but she was always watching me like a hawk."

"Until today," observed Jack.

"Until today," repeated Audrey with a look of eager conspiracy. "I'm eighteen now, I've left that rotten school for good – and I'm home for good. I'm too old to let Mamma rule me, or any of them. I slipped out of my bedroom window early this morning."

Jack wrinkled his nose in concern. "You're lucky you didn't go breaking your neck lass!"

"No chance – Watty put the ladder up to the window for me." Jack erupted with laughter.

"You're a rum one girl and no mistake! Oh dear oh dear, old Watty's a case too. He told me how they'd sent you away of course, and I knew as how they were strict against you consorting with the likes of me. But I always knew you'd come and find old Jack when you got the chance – I knew my little Audrey 'ud not let me down! Ah I can't call you that now can I – you being taller 'an me girl!"
Jack chuckled as he placed a crust of bread and a hunk of cheese before her, followed by a steaming cup of black tea.

"Get that down you – don't reckon you had time for breakfast, what with your antics down that ladder – ah you'd a' made a fine smuggler Audrey!"

"Have you heard from Molly at all Jack," asked Audrey, munching hungrily on the bread and cheese. "I wrote to her, and you, but she never replied."

"No my fairest – I swear I never received no letter – and the postman knows where to find me as well as anyone," said Jack.

"I'll bet my mother had something to do with that," hinted Audrey darkly. "They'd do anything for her at that stinking school – all the while she was paying them the fees. Have you any idea where Molly is Jack? I'd like to tell her I'm home."

"I'll let her know for you Audrey, that's all I can do. Our Dorothy still needs to work."
Audrey nodded, "Yes Jack of course, I understand. There's something I don't understand though," she said thoughtfully.

"What's that my dear?" asked Jack, taking a swig of black tea.

"Well, the last time I was here you told me that Grandpa Bamford – and Uncle John – were once a friend of yours?"
Jack's face darkened. "That they were," he replied softly. "Once."

"Oh I see," said Audrey. "You also said I would find out about him. Daddy never mentions him, nor my mother. What is the big mystery, and why did he go away?"

"What's brought this on?" asked Jack carefully.

"Daddy and I were talking of the war, and he said you were there, you were a soldier - and that's how you came to live on the beach."

"I was in the war true, but why should he mention me?"

"I don't know Jack, but he did."

Jack sat back in his rocking chair and gave a long sigh.

"All right Audrey," he said at last, "now where shall I begin?"

"At the beginning?" suggested Audrey smiling kindly at him.

"Very well," said Jack, and began to rock his chair slowly and rhythmically as he spoke. "I told you your Grandfather gave me this hut."

"That's right," Audrey nodded, "I remember, but I never understood why."

Jack reached into the drawer of his sea chest and took out a dusty photograph frame. "This here's my wife and daughter," he said handing Audrey the picture.

Audrey studied the young woman and child smiling out at her through the foxed glass. "They're both beautiful Jack," she said, "what happened to them?"

"My wife was called Julia, our cheeky little girl was Charlotte - my lovely Lottie I used to call her." He put his head in his hands.

"Oh Jack I'm so sorry, I shouldn't have pried," said Audrey. She stretched out a hand and touched his arm.

"Please don't talk about it if you'd rather not."

"No no, I'm all right. I made an oath to myself never to mention their names again see – but that was foolish." He straightened up and blew his nose on a spotted handkerchief. "You have a right to know – to know everything, especially now you're of an age. But be prepared Audrey, what I'm going to tell will shock you my dear, and I have no wish to upset you."

"I am prepared Jack," said Audrey, her voice not entirely steady now.

"Very well," said Jack decisively. Many years ago I was a carpenter in Crosslands. I had my beautiful wife, an adorable little girl, my own honest trade, and my own house, a fine one - everything a man could want. In 1914 the war came - all be over by Christmas they said."

The old man gave a hollow laugh. "So like every good patriot I volunteered to do my bit for King and country. Though I didn't really have a choice; it was either go and fight or be drummed out of town. Julia and my brother in law would look after business, and for a while they did. I got letters at the front saying all was well and not to worry. When I came home on leave, sure enough everything seemed to be all right, and I returned to France, secure in the knowledge that when the war was over, if I made it through, I could carry on where I left off. But it was not to be." Jack paused, his eyes growing misty. "A few months later I got a letter telling me that little Lottie had drowned."

Audrey gasped. Jack made a movement with his hand, part placatory, partly a gesture towards the beach. "She was out there, dawdling on the sands, and wandered innocent as a babe into the sea. The tide was treacherous that day Audrey. Julia waded in to save her, and the current dragged both mother and child under. It took six weeks before their bodies washed up. The townsfolk carried them from the beach in a cart and buried them in the cemetery. By the time I heard the news they were already six foot under."

Audrey's face was solemn. "Oh Jack," she said softly, "I'm so sorry. It must have been such a dreadful shock for you."

"I took it hard I don't deny. But many others were suffering. And people were kind to me. One of them was your Grandfather, James Bamford,

"What did he do?" asked Audrey.

"After the war I had nothing," said Jack. "My business were gone, my house sold and the money all used up to pay my debts. I couldn't stop grieving. Your Uncle John and I had grown up together; we were friends. I knew the family well. And because of that your grandfather couldn't bear to see me brought low. He gave me money but I spent it on drink. I used to sleep on the beach here, so your Grandfather bought this hut for me off the old landowners, and the freehold to the sand that surrounds it. I was very grateful to him. I felt close to my wife and child see – that sounds foolish I know, if I'd been any sort of man I'd..."

"Oh no, no, Jack, it doesn't sound foolish at all," implored Audrey, "it must have helped I'm sure...to be close in spirit, and at one with nature too..."

"It was the sunsets, the sunsets and the sun rising - that was what gave me comfort," said Jack intensely, staring out now through the window of the hut to the azure sea. "Where the ocean meets the sky, day becomes night - and then eventually day again. This shoreline became for me, the place too where death could become life once more."

"The idea of rebirth," said Audrey, echoing the faraway note and following his gaze out across the shimmering sea.

"Yes – you can see anything you know...if you look long enough, long enough..." intoned the old man, his rheumy eyes fixed on the watery horizon, above which a few small, dreamy white summer clouds were now suspended.

They sat for a full minute before Audrey broke the silence.

"Thank you for telling me this Jack," she said quietly. "I feel very privileged. I won't speak of it to anyone, or again to you, unless you wish it. My Grandfather was obviously a very kind man. I don't remember him. But not so with Uncle John I think. He married my Grandmother Constance I believe. I could never understand why people round here made such hurtful remarks about him, or why he even went away so suddenly. My family simply do not talk about him."

Jack turned his face to hers. "Yes, James Bamford was a kind man. But the there is an awkward truth about the world Audrey – there are some men that have more than one side to them."

"What do you mean?" asked Audrey innocently then grinned impishly. "Was my Uncle John a bit of a cad on the quiet? Do tell!"

"A bit more than that child," said Jack, turning his face back towards the sea. "You see the truth is Audrey, your Uncle John ran away with all your Grandma's money."

"So – he became like an outlaw, a crook, a ne'er do- well?" said Audrey, her adolescent brow furrowing as she tried to frame this idea. "But," she said thoughtfully, "people say other things about him too – nasty, spiteful things, like he once killed someone, which is obviously not true – I mean, even if he was once a thief, there's no reason to go around saying he killed people as well – that's just horrid!"

"Maybe, maybe not," replied Jack pensively.

"Whatever do you mean Jack?"

"Well I pray you won't hate me for telling you this Audrey," said the old man in a leaden voice, "but it is almost certainly true that John Bamford is a murderer. Yes Audrey dear - he murdered twice, in cold blood; a young woman called Kitty Mason, and your dear, defenceless Uncle Mac."

CHAPTER TWENTY- ONE

1941

"You could have given me more notice Marcus." said Clarissa, looking faintly annoyed as she rang the servants" bell. "I'll telephone the butcher and see what's available; I hope they're not expecting prime cuts."

"Rupert's a military man Clarrie," replied Marcus, he knows all about iron rations, as well as rationing. Anyway" he laughed, "when did you ever say no to throwing a dinner party?"
Clarissa smiled ruefully. "I just hope his wife's equally understanding."

"Lady Challinor works among the poor," said Marcus.

"Whatever are you implying?" asked Clarissa.

"Nothing, just that…" Marcus was forestalled by the opening of the sitting room door.

"Ah! Dorothy," said Clarissa, tomorrow night you and your daughter in law will serve at table for me. There will be the two of us, together with Master James and Miss Audrey. Our guests will be Admiral and Lady Challinor. The Admiral is extremely high up in the Navy. Can you please be here at 6.30 to prepare?"
Dorothy nodded silently and curtsied her way out again.

"I really don't know how you manage my dear," said Lady Challinor. "A truly splendid meal; rationing clearly hasn't affected your household."
Clarissa smiled politely at her guest. "Thank you Lady Challinor," she said, "we make do I suppose."

"That's the watchword today, and an admirable example you set if I may say so." Lady Challinor returned the somewhat exaggerated smile. "And apart from "making do", what do you do for the war effort here at home?"

"I, well…"

"My wife helps me, don't you dear," said Marcus.

"Yes, yes, in a small way…" agreed Clarissa uncertainly, her face reddening slightly in the candlelight.

"Behind every successful man," proclaimed Lady Challinor imperiously, "lies the tower of strength that is womanhood. Where would the world be without us?"

"Here here," said Marcus.

"And if you do find any free time between your duties here and helping your husband in his business you would be most welcome at the WRVS. The work is essential, and spiritually rewarding."

"What is it you do with them exactly?" ventured Clarissa.

"Soup kitchens!" said Lady Challinor, as if it were a battle cry. "Whenever there's an air raid in Liverpool we turn up with our van and dish out hot soup and bread to all the poor souls who've lost their homes, and worse."

"A most worthy way to spend your time if I may say so," said Marcus. "As you say, those poor people, to know they are not forgotten, that someone cares…"

At this point, Admiral Challinor, who had sat silent for some time nursing his brandy, said in a deadpan voice, "If the bombs don't finish them off, the WRVS soup soon does the job!"
There was an awkward silence. The Admiral then snorted in amusement and delivered Dorothy, who was clearing plates from the table, a playful nudge in the ribs with his elbow.

"I must apologise for my husband," said Lady Challinor austerely, "Rupert fancies himself something of a dry wit."
The Admiral drained his brandy glass and gave a sideways wink at Dorothy and then Audrey, both of whom appeared to be trying to suppress a smile.

"Well, I am sure your visits are a godsend to those in need," said Clarissa. "I will look at my diary and see if I can find time to come along and join you if I may."

"Please do," said Lady Challinor graciously. "We need all the help we can get. How about you Audrey?"

"I'd love to do something for the war effort Lady Challinor," said Audrey enthusiastically.

"Audrey is employed in the business," said Marcus, "And plays a vital part in fact."

"Oh but I'd love to make soup Daddy," exclaimed Audrey. "That is, if you can spare me…"

"Well, perhaps, we'll see," said Marcus. He looked at the Admiral now. "And talking of the war effort Rupert, I wonder if we might talk ships for a moment. I know you were interested in requisitioning one of the Stephenson fleet."

The Admiral grunted. "If the ladies have no objection to us talking ships, then I would be glad to."

"Of course..." murmured Clarissa, with a glance towards Lady Challinor.

"Oh talk away," said the Admiral's wife, "that is after all why we are here is it not – as well to enjoy your hospitality of course my dear."

Clarissa nodded politely.

"Rupert, I will gladly release the Atticus Greensleeves for you. She can be at your disposal in a week."

"She's the finest vessel you have," said the Admiral, "I know how much it must mean to you to give her up."

"Well, the Navy will be paying me. I'm not doing it for nothing, not like your good lady here and her soup."

"My reward will be in heaven," smiled Lady Challinor. "But I don't blame a businessman for wanting his a little sooner."

"I can't believe the Navy will match what you can earn from chartering the Atticus on the open market, but be that as it may, 'said the Admiral, "we're most grateful. Don't bother about a refit though old boy; we'll strip her out to requirements."

"I'll at least make her seaworthy for her voyage to Portsmouth."

"That sounds worrying Marcus," demurred the Admiral, "you mean you're handing me a rust bucket?"

Marcus laughed. "She needs a lick of paint that's all. She's a good girl, she won't let you down."

"I know, I've been aboard her," said the Admiral. "You know, this is going to sound damn crashing obvious, but what a navy relies on are two things: good ships and good men. I've heard glowing reports about your seamanship, and your other attributes young man."

These last observations of the Admiral were directed at James, who had been listening quietly to the conversation.

"Oh really sir?" he replied modestly. "I wouldn't pay too much attention to my father if I were you, he tends to paint a rather rosy picture of his children as a rule."

"The reports come not only from your pater," went on the Admiral. "Your former headmaster is an old and trusted friend of mine. He's also a fine judge of character. It's character that's the backbone of a nation, especially in times of trial. What would you say to a career in the Royal Navy young man?"

Clarissa, who had been following the direction of the Admiral's speech with a look of concern, now drew in her breath sharply.

"James's abilities are fully engaged on the home-front Admiral," she said quickly, "and the smooth running of the Stephenson shipping line is as you know crucial to the war effort." She looked at her husband, waiting for him to confirm her statement. Marcus, pursing his lips, looked at James, then Clarissa.

"Well..." he said slowly, "perhaps we should let James answer for himself."

"Admiral," broke in Clarissa again, "it is most kind of you to take an interest, but James is too valuable – to the business, and..."

James now interrupted, "Like father says, mother, perhaps I should reply for myself."

There followed a pause, after which Clarissa said in a serious voice, "Very well dear, and what is your reply?"

This time the silence was more protracted and painful. It was the Admiral who finally spoke. "Good lord is that the time! I think we'd better be going," he said amiably, looking at this pocket watch. "Thank you for a most enjoyable evening, all of you - and I'm sorry if I put you on the spot just now young man. Last thing I wanted to do. Don't forget that in wartime, there are heroes in all walks of life. As the poet says: 'They also serve who only stand and wait' you know - Alexander Pope if I remember right."

CHAPTER TWENTY- TWO

Marcus looked tired as he stepped into the hall.

"Busy day sir?" asked Dorothy as she helped him off with his thick astrakhan coat and hung it up for him.

"Another two ships gone I'm afraid Dorothy," replied Marcus grimfaced.

"U-boats sir?"

"I'm afraid so," nodded Marcus solemnly. "The crew didn't stand a chance in mid-Atlantic. No survivors have been picked up yet, but we can't give up hope of course."

"Oh the poor devils," said Dorothy, her face ashen, "only young lads most of them I'll be bound." At that moment the sound of raised voices was heard coming from the library. Dorothy shot her master a nervous glance, and with a murmur of apology hurried off towards the kitchen.

Marcus approached the closed door of the library and hesitated. Clarissa's voice could be heard clearly.

"James I am adamant on this matter and so is your father," she was saying.

James replied, "Father says I have to decide for myself whether to take up the Admiral's offer – don't you want me to do my bit - to hunt down the Nazi swine who are drowning our men and sinking our ships day after day?"

Marcus gripped the door handle decisively and entered the library. His wife and son both turned towards him with imploring eyes.

"Marcus," began Clarissa. "Do tell him."

"Tell him what?" asked Marcus, crossing the drinks table and poring himself a large whiskey and soda.

"That he's just as brave and valuable to Britain and the war effort working for the Stephenson line on the home front."

"We've had this discussion a number of times now," said Marcus quietly, his back still turned away from them.

"You see," said Clarissa, "your father's tired, he's had quite enough of your disobedience..."

"I am not a child!" shouted James.

"I must ask you not to raise your voice to your mother James," said Marcus.

"I'm sorry," said James, "it's just that she refuses to..."

"Be quiet." Marcus's tone was now one of command. Facing them now he went on. "The fact is James, the question of your going on active service in this war is no longer in your hands. Or mine."

Clarissa, who had breathed a momentary sigh of relief, now looked uneasy. "What…do you mean?" she asked.

Marcus reached into the inner breast pocket of his suit, drew out a brown envelope and dropped it on the drinks table. Clarissa moved immediately to pick up the envelope.

Extracting the letter her face darkened as she read. She held the sheet of paper limply towards her husband.

"Marcus, James has been called up, it…it can't be." Her voice was cracked and dry.

"Yes," replied Marcus. He seemed bereft of any discernible emotion. "So as I say, there's little point in any of us arguing about the matter now is there."

"But what about your friends, your mother's influence – you said you'd put in a word, with someone at the Ministry so he didn't have to go."

"I'm afraid my word cuts little ice in this instance." Marcus took a hefty swig of whiskey.

Clarissa's expression changed suddenly to one of suspicion, "I don't believe you," she said accusingly, "I think you wanted him to go to war all along – to satisfy your own stupid manly pride…"

"Believe what you like," Marcus cut in. "It makes no odds now…"

"Makes no odds!" Clarissa had taken hold of his wrist now. "The odds are that our son is going to sail to his death, because you didn't have the guts or the ability to stop it…"

"You're being absurd, let go of me you stupid woman!" snarled Marcus, wrenching his arm away.

"I should have done that years ago, and taken the children with me," spat back Clarissa.

"Then it's a pity you…"

"Stop it – stop it both of you!" James, who until this point had stood looking at his parents with an appalled expression, now glowered at them. "Just look at the two of you – you're a disgrace. I am to have the honour of serving my country and all you can do is bicker like overgrown children. I will be proud to go into uniform, to be a fighting seaman in his majesty's Royal Navy. All I want is for you to love me, and, be proud of me too."

There were tears in the young boy's eyes as he spoke. Without a word Marcus and Clarissa came quickly towards their son, and with their heads hung low, wrapped their arms tightly around him.

"I'm sorry about what I said that day in the library." Marcus looked at his wife's reflection in the dressing table mirror, his gaze travelling down the sweep of her elegant neck and across the firm glistening shoulders revealed by her black evening dress.

Clarissa turned to him.

"Oh that. It all seems a long time ago now. We both love our son Marcus," she said, extending her hands towards him. "And I spoke in anger too."

"He was right wasn't he?" said Marcus, taking her outstretched hands in his and kissing them. "That we should be proud of him."

"Yes," said Clarissa, "he was right. It's just I couldn't believe it all happened so quickly – call up papers one day, then a week later he was gone."

"War doesn't hang about for anyone. But he came home, and we've had him to ourselves for two whole weeks."

"And now he's gong off again…"

"There'll be other leave - he'll come home again, for good. One day soon this god awful war will be over, thanks to young men like James."

"I know, but - oh Marcus I do so want tomorrow to be perfect for him."

"Yes, he's joining a new ship, but keeping very quiet about her – official secrets I dare say. We can all have lunch together in Liverpool, at the Adelphi, champagne on ice. It must be a be a real celebration Clarrie, a triumphant send off for our brave boy."

"Yes, yes you're right Marcus." She arched her back as he leaned forward and kissed her full on the mouth, his hands descending to the small of her back, pulling her body close to his. "I love you so much Clarrie," he said breathlessly, as, in a single, swift movement he lifted her on to the bed.

The great locomotive slowed, and with a hiss of steam and a long, shuddering squeal of its brakes came to a halt alongside platform number two of Lime Street Station. Marcus, Clarissa, Audrey and James jumped down and made their way through the bustling throng of soldiers, sailors, porters, travellers and businessmen towards the main exit. In the taxi, Audrey chattered animatedly to her brother.

"I feel you've only just arrived and now you're going off to sea again, and I've hardly spoken to you."

"I'll be back again before you know it sis," said James, digging her playfully in the ribs.

"Did you meet lots of girls in Portsmouth," asked Audrey grinning artfully.

"Don't embarrass the boy now Audrey," chimed in their father.

"Actually I thought it was a girl in every port wasn't it with sailors?" retorted Audrey.

"We do have a war to fight now and again you know," smiled James. "Anyway, there's girls and there's girls, if you know what I mean."

"No, what do you mean?" asked Audrey curiously.
Before she had time to pursue the question the taxi had pulled up outside the Adelphi Hotel.

Lunch was a sumptuous affair. James drew much attention in the restaurant, his fine figure in uniform gaining respectful nods from the civilian men, as well as garnering the admiring glances of several women. Though the boy would only consume one glass of champagne, Marcus made sure it was the finest vintage the house could offer. Quails eggs were followed by fillet steak in a pepper sauce and the freshest vegetables. Then came a tantalising fruit trifle laced liberally with rich amontillado sherry, liqueurs, and the best Havana cigars for the men.

Marcus was in expansive mood, dispensing his largesse proudly, every inch the prosperous businessman showing off his attractive wife and daughter, and handsome young officer son.

"If James eats any more," giggled Audrey over her trifle," his ship's not gong to make it out of port. And you've got cream on your uniform, look on the cuff."

"You're a fine one to talk," her brother grinned back at her, wiping his sleeve with a linen napkin, "isn't that your second helping of dessert?"

"Third!" snorted Audrey, "don't make me laugh or I'll choke on the cherries – oh I think I've just swallowed a stone!"
This set the whole table on a roar, as well the couple sitting next to them.

When lunch was over and James had been given his final toast, the family made their way to the naval dockyard.

"This is as far you're allowed I'm afraid," said James as they arrived at the naval sentry post.

"Oh but we were hoping to see your new ship Jamie," said Audrey.

"Yes," protested Clarissa, "is it really such a big secret?"

"More of a surprise," said James, with a smile. "In fact, here she comes now." He pointed to the headland, where the prow of a large vessel was just making its way into the docks.

"Good lord," cried Marcus straining his eyes seawards, "is that what I think it is?"

"The Atticus Greensleaves no less Dad, and I'm to be her second in command."

"Congratulations lad!" exclaimed Marcus, almost bursting with paternal pride and shaking his son's hand furiously. "And on the good old Atticus too, my you are a dark horse."
"But she looks different," said Clarissa, peering as the great ship veered slowly closer.

"Of course Mama," shouted James over the sudden loud noise of the Atticus's hooter. "She's a warship now – and that's her war paint."
Clarissa, raising one hand to shield her eyes from the lowering afternoon sun stared at the ship once so familiar. "Well..." she said at last, "the Atticus will look after you, I know it will."

Now the dockside seemed full of noise and activity – seamen shouting and running up and down with ropes, chains rumbling and clanging in a clamorous cacophony with the Atticus's growling engines as she came alongside. Clarissa looked back at James, who, now stood a few yards from her and Marcus, appeared to be locked in earnest conversation with his sister.

"What are those two discussing?" she said.

"He's probably telling Audrey to tell us not to worry. Or pouring his heart out about something he can't talk to us about. You know what young people are like."

"I do wish they wouldn't have secrets," said Clarissa.

"Don't we?"

"Don't we what?" said Clarissa.

"Have secrets."

Clarissa did not reply to this. Instead she said, "Come on Marcus, I think he's about to go aboard. Let's say our farewells."

"Molly…! The voice was just audible over the hum and thump of the presses, the swirl and gush of water, and the cries and chatter of a dozen girls as they filled or emptied machines and driers, while others wheeled around them heaving laden baskets of bed sheets, towels, collars, curtains, dresses and table linen over the hard stone floor of the laundry.

"Eh up, what you been doing now Moll?" chuckled a gap toothed woman folding pillowcases. "Look out here comes the governor."

A matronly woman in her mid-fifties approached Molly.

"Couldn't you hear me girl?" she said, "I've better things to do than come chasing after you with letters – and tell your fancy men not to send their billet-dos here in future, we're trying to run a business." She flung a brown envelope at Molly's feet. "And get them baskets of sheets moved out to the delivery bay, the van's due any time."

"Yes Mrs Mackay."

When she had gone Molly stopped and picked up the letter. She recognised the hand at once; it was from her friend Audrey.

Stuffing the letter in her apron and ignoring the curious stares of the other girls she braced her body behind a trolley loaded with baskets and steered it to the far end of the laundry. The delivery bay was still deserted. Tucking herself behind a wall she took out Audrey's letter and began to read:

"My Dearest Moll,

First of all forgive me for writing to you at your place of employment, but there is a reason, which I will explain. I have the most incredible news to report, something that completely surprised, and I have to say overjoyed me, and I hope and pray you will feel the same. You know how you met my brother James a few times when you and I had our occasional rendezvous? Well, recently, on the day he sailed on his new ship from Liverpool, he confided the most ardent secret to me, and implored me to impart the same to you, for you, yes you dear Moll are the subject, dare I say the object of his missive. In truth, Molly dearest, you are the object of my brother's deepest affections; yes – James is in love with you!

There, I have said it! He told me this much in the space of but a few moments snatched between brother and sister on the dockside as the navy were waiting to take him aboard. He now wants to take you in his arms, and his heart, at the soonest possible opportunity, and says he is sure even from your brief meetings that you feel the same. This is all as I say the most dramatic and exciting news for me, and I most fervently hope you, my best and dearest friend in the whole world, indeed reciprocate my dear brother's sentiments.

Needless to say not a word of this has been breathed to our parents; my mother at least is still dead set against my unshakeable bond with you Moll. That frankly shall remain Mama's sad loss, not yours, and certainly not mine, nor I hope James's. He urged me to write to you with this declaration, fearing any direct communication might be intercepted by his naval superiors, and passed back to our parents, with the danger that they – my mother at least – hatch some scheme to sabotage his, and your, blissful future union.

Such is the absolute importance he attaches to you; his sincere desire is that nothing shall mar your joint happiness.

As soon as you have the chance, send some discreet word to me via your mother that you have received this letter, and that you share the passion you have ignited in my brother James's breast. I will then find means to relay your reply to him, in code if need be.

Till then I shall be anxiously awaiting the joyous confirmation that my only bosom companion and my dear brother shall soon be man and wife. Such a state of affairs will be such as I could only have dreamed of till now!
With my most fond regards as always,

Your loving friend,

Audrey.

Pushing the letter deep into her apron pocket Molly, with pounding heart, hurried back to her work.

"Morning Dot," said the postman.

"Hello Alf," said Dorothy, opening the door wider. "Letter box got stuck?"

"No – just wanted to see your lovely face didn't I."

"Get away with you," laughed Dorothy.

"Well, that and I've got a telegram for madam. Has to be delivered in person so I'm told."

Dorothy took the envelope and examined it. "Oh its from the Admiralty," she observed. "Perhaps young James is coming home – that'll cheer her up."

"Yeah." The postman cast his eyes down at the mat. "Oh, and I nearly forgot," he said in a conspiratorial undertone, "our Rita, you know her as works over at the laundry, asked me to give you this note – its from your Molly - keep it to yourself, she says."

From his pocket Alf produced a folded slip of paper, which Dorothy secreted quickly in her sleeve.

"Well Dot, I'd better let you get on," said Alf, retreating down the path as Clarissa appeared in the doorway.

"What is it Dorothy?"

"A telegram ma'am – from the Admiralty, looks like Master James might be on his way... "

"Thank you," snapped Clarissa and snatched the envelope from Dorothy's hand. She took it into the library, shutting the door firmly behind her.

Dorothy hurried off toward to the scullery, took the slip of paper from her sleeve and read the note scrawled in her daughter's hand:

'Dear Mum, I hope you are all ok. Work here is not too bad. Please tell Audrey for me – its YES, YES, YES! She will know what it means. All you need to know for now Mum is that I am so HAPPY. PS, don't breathe a word of this to anyone else. Love Moll.'

Dorothy made her way to the drawing room where a fire was burning brightly and threw the slip of paper onto the flames. A second later she hear a scream of anguish from the library, followed by a loud and pitiful wailing. It was her mistress's voice crying out repeatedly the name of her son.

"James, no, it can't be, it can't be – James my beloved boy, oh James…!"

It was six weeks later before Clarrissa had in a roundabout way come to terms with James's tragic death.
Marcus's behaviour towards her was even more distant. They hardly spoke, avoided each other wherever possible, like strangers and now Clarissa had had enough.

As soon as Marcus had left the house that morning, Clarissa went to the escritoire in her dressing room and taking a small key from her neck pendant, unlocked the bottom drawer and took out a notebook, writing paper and an envelope. She began to write:

Dear John,

I write this letter to you in earnest hope it will reach you. The only address I have for you in America is from some fifteen years ago now, which is when I last heard from you. I cannot believe how the time has vanished, or how you seem to have disappeared so completely from my life.

Still less can I believe the event that prompts me to write to you now; for my news is sad beyond measure; James, my first born is perished, lost at sea in this dreadful war.

As you may imagine I have been, and am still wracked with the most unbearable grief. But bear it I must, somehow, for so many others are dying every day.

My sorrow is compounded by a dreadful bitterness though, and one that I cannot shrug off; it is borne of a deep regret: that I did not follow you with my children to America when you urged me so to do. Had I taken that course, James would be alive and well today.

The regret, the bitterness is fruitless, I know this with my rational mind, yet still it haunts and torments me. I feel that the only way to escape it is to do something decisive, drastic – perhaps come to America now.

My life with Marcus has long been stale. Where once there were shafts of happiness, with James gone, and my daughter Audrey I predict in rebellious flight from us soon, now sits only increasing misery and resentment.

Whether these feelings are mutual or not on Marcus's part does not concern me. People may say I am heartless, and they are right; what pride or pleasure I took in this provincial life has now completely abandoned me, and my heart has been ripped out by loss – the physical loss of my son, and long since, the spiritual loss of my daughter.

Perhaps, after all these years I am reverting to type once and for all. We are of the same blood John; perhaps I am, after all, the same kind of monster that people say you are. I feel I am going mad as I write these words – possibly I am, but the world is mad, so why should I be any different.

I have no way of knowing whether you receive this letter, save by a reply. I pray you will send me one. All I want you to know is that I would now willingly join you in America.

I also know your first love John, and that it is an insatiable one. Even as we both grow old, wealth can bring much comfort, much pleasure. Rest assured, there will be a great deal of money, Stephenson money, coming with me, if you will help me obtain it. I know you have the craft, and the means. I look forward to hearing how your fortunes have fared these last fifteen years.

Till then, your affectionate sister

Clarissa
.

Reading it through once again she carefully folded the paper, placed it in the envelope and sealed the flap. Writing the address on the front she slipped it into her handbag. Later that day she would post it and hope beyond all hope that John wherever he may be would receive it.

CHAPTER TWENTY- THREE

January 1943

"But I want to go into nursing Mummy, it's as simple as that."

Clarissa turned from the library window and looked at her daughter. Her face was pale her cheekbones noticeably sharp where the flesh had dropped away. "As simple as that?" she echoed. Her voice was empty, like that of a disembodied spirit. "I suppose it is. And suppose you catch an infection, suppose a bomb drops on the hospital?"

"Mother I…"

"Yes, you'll die, simple as that, and I'll have lost both my children. James dead, you dead, that's war isn't it, simple as that." Her tone, dry, lethargic, now had a trace of suppressed anger.

"Mother I understand you're bitter…"

"You're wrong Audrey, I've gone beyond bitterness. All I've got left is regret."

"I regret James dying too," said Audrey, "I grieve for my brother every day. But I can't sit here and do nothing, not when there's others suffering."

"Is that what you think I'm doing?" said her mother, suddenly imperious. "You think I'm an idle self-pitying woman Audrey, I've known that all along of course, children always judge their parents."

"No mother, I don't…"

"But if you knew even half the truth about this family, about me, you'd have a shock believe me."

"I may know more than you think." Audrey spoke slowly, looking directly at her mother. Clarissa returned her gaze, intensely curious now. "What do you mean, who have you been talking to?"

"Nothing, no one really," replied Audrey, awkward now. "But I know all the name calling at my old school wasn't for nothing – and, well, I heard things, about Uncle John. I'm sorry mother I shouldn't have brought the subject up, you're in enough pain…"

"I doubt if you heard the real truth, and you're not old or wise enough to understand it if you did. Life is more mysterious and complex than you could ever imagine child. As for my pain – wait till you lose a child Audrey, then you'll understand that."

"I hope it will never happen mother," said Audrey quietly, "as I am sure do you."

Looking back out towards the garden Clarissa said, "Go and be a nurse Audrey, go where you like, do what your heart tells you. It is what I should have done a long time ago. I cannot condemn you for following that impulse. In fact I applaud you for it, and I wish you well. I mean that. I do love you in my own way, and I know that I have been... difficult, and seemed unfeeling towards you since James was taken from us. But believe me I do love you, and want only the best for you. I pray God will keep you safe dearest."

Clarissa turned towards her daughter and stretched out a hand. Audrey ran to her, burying her face in her mother's tightly enfolding arms.

"You've given her your blessing?" Marcus peered at his wife over the morning paper.

Clarissa put down her teacup and said carefully, "I knew it was what you wanted her to do, if she had set her mind to it."

"I'm glad you qualified that statement," said Marcus. "I would prefer her here with us as much as you would."

"Yes, we've had this discussion." Clarissa looked weary, defeated. Then, the focus of her eyes suddenly sharpening with thought she said, "And there's something else."

"Oh, what?"

"She mentioned John."

"Your brother?"

"Who else? Marcus I think she's been talking to someone. Have you said anything?

"No, why would I?"

"To poison her mind."

"Don't be absurd! It probably that rumour that's going round."

"What rumour?" Clarissa sat up.

"There's a rumour, people are saying that your...that John Bamford has been seen in England," said Marcus. "Utter poppycock of course, the man's most likely dead by now, or he would be if he showed his face round here – sorry Clarrie but I..." he tailed off and looked down at his paper.

Clarissa's eyes were quietly ablaze, but she said nothing. Marcus then continued, "Anyway, as regards Audrey, I just don't want there to be any doubt in either of our minds Clarrie – that it is her decision to go off and work at this hospital – not yours or mine."

"Quite," said Clarissa, seeming wrapped in thought.
"It's better we let her go, and look forward to her return. Liverpool is as safe a place as any, probably as safe as here, more or less."

"Braeside would have been the safest of all, there's a cottage hospital there that would have been ideal..."

"Let's not mention Braeside," interrupted Marcus edgily. He cleared his throat and poured out some tea, then went on, "Audrey is a headstrong girl, always has been. If we tried to restrain her she'd only find a way to run off, or do something awful..."

"This is awful enough!" Clarissa was crying.
Marcus got up quickly and put his arms around her.

"Darling, there, I know...."

"I'm sorry," said Clarissa. "I miss James so much."

"We all do, darling, we all do."

"You know the thing that hurts me most Marcus?"

"What dearest?"

"That he never knew life really – he...he never had the chance to fall in love."

"Come in young missy." Jack smiled cheerfully as he opened the creaking door of his hut. "It's always a pleasure to welcome you in my humble home. Would you like some tea?"

Audrey nodded and sat down in one of the rickety chairs. Outside on the beach a flock of seagulls were calling to one another in plaintive cacophony, while through the little window came the glint of sun and sea.

"I've got something to tell you Jack," said Audrey.
Jack sat opposite her. "Why the sad face – I hope its not more bad news – after losing your poor brother I think you've had more than your share of misfortunes my dear."

"No Jack, its not bad news – well, for my parents I think it is. I'm going away to train as a nurse at Wetherton Hospital."
Jack uttered a low, respectful murmur of admiration.

"Why, that's a fine and noble thing to do Audrey, and your brother would be proud to know it. I suppose your mother and father don't take too kindly though."

"They like the idea I think, but don't want me to leave home – which is, well, difficult really."

Jack nodded knowingly and handed her a cracked mug of black tea.

"After young James, you're all they've got my love."

"Oh no - do you think it's really selfish of me Jack – you may be right…!"

Jack put up his hand to forestall her. "Now what I think is neither here nor there," he said. "But I'll tell you this, I've seen sorrow in my life and now its come to others I hold dear, like a cruel wolf descending on the fold. The way I see it is this, the world's gone mad all over again, and the only bit of sanity is for decent god-fearing folk to do something brave and good. And I can't see a better way than to reach out a kind and caring hand to the sick and dying in their hour of need."

The old man looked at his young friend steadily for a second then raised his battered tea mug in a salute. With deep gravity in his voice he said, "You're a good person Audrey Stephenson," he said, "one of the best. May God Almighty bless you."

CHAPTER TWENTY-FOUR

Uncertain Angels

Audrey stood looking nervously up at the large stone pillars either side of the main entrance of Wetherton Hospital. Taking a deep breath she mounted the steps and pushed through the heavy polished wooden doors.

"Are you starting today?" The voice was female, and unmistakeably scouse.

Turning, Audrey saw a friendly looking girl with a smile as broad as her accent.

"Yes I am," she said, "I hope I'm in the right place?"

"Well if you're not, I'm lost too!" chortled the scouser holding out her hand. "My name's Miriam Ikin but my friends call me Mimsy - what's yours?"

"Audrey, Audrey Stephenson."

"Bit lah di dah aren't we?" Mimsy laughed. "Where is 'madam' from then?"

"Where are you from?" Audrey retorted, slightly put out.

"Liverpool gal, slap bang in t' middle – and take no notice of me, I'm only having a laugh with you."

Audrey smiled uncertainly. "I'm from Crosslands, that's just outside Liverpool."

"Oh I know where it is gal – dead posh 'n' all,' declared Mimsy loud enough for the whole hospital to hear. Then seeing Audrey bite her lip and look down, she said more quietly, "A big mouth and a small brain's my trouble. You look like a real lost soul Audrey, helpless and hopeless as my old Granny used to say. Well I'm a sucker for lame ducks, being one me self, so allow me tuck you under me wing pet." She grabbed Audrey's arm and marched up to a desk presided over by a stern looking woman in nursing uniform. "Hey up Matron," she boomed, "Mimsy and Audrey, a pair of rookies reporting for duty!"

The Matron looked up. "Just wait over there with the other two new recruits if you please." She indicated two nervous looking young women seated in the corridor. They joined the pair, who introduced themselves as Ivy Curtis and Janet Sweet. Encouraged by Mimsy, the four of them were soon in giggling and animated conversation.

"Now girls," said Matron, her steely eye roving round the twenty junior nurses seated before her, "you have been studying here with us at Wetherton Hospital for two weeks now, and I am pleased to report your progress has been acceptable – so far. This, despite the flippant distractions of the fearsome four."

A muffled snort came from the back of the room.

"Why's she looking at us?" whispered Mimsy along the row of chairs in which Audrey, Ivy and Janet were likewise attempting to keep straight faces.

"Can't imagine," hissed Ivy.

"It will soon be time to inflict you, unsupervised, onto the poor defenceless souls known to us as patients," continued the Matron. "I hope that you will live up to the high standards of our profession, behaving at all times with dignity and responsibility, sobriety and compassion. In a few moments I will be taking the new government Minister for Health, together with the Chairman and Lady Secretary of the Hospitals Charitable Board on a guided tour of all departments. These important people are vital to the continuation of the good work we do here, so I expect you to create a good impression, as they are shown round. Now before you go, Janet and Ivy are assigned for the remainder of the day to the cleaning rota, Miriam and Audrey, there are some stores required for collection. Staff will give you the chitty."

As the others filed out, the staff nurse handed Mimsy a handwritten list of items.

"More bedpans!" she exclaimed "I told you that Matron's got it in for us. Hitler- in-knickers they should call her. Never mind Aud – we'll take a short cut to stores via the laundry."

"But this is the long way round," replied Audrey, following Mimsy down a narrow flight of stairs.

"I know – but there's a couple of new fellers just started in the laundry."

"How do you know?"

"Ask no questions and I'll tell you no lies, panted Mimsy as they reached the basement.

"Oh, what are they like gal?" laughed Audrey, mimicking her friend.

"Not bad – but your scouse is terrible!" They hurried on along a winding corridor, and arriving level with a set of double doors Mims pushed her friend playfully.

Audrey fell against the doors, which swung in and hit an obstruction on the other side. A girl, red faced and angry appeared.

"Mind my trolley you stupid cow!" she shouted at Audrey, who had fallen in a heap of linen that had tumbled from the trolley in the collision.

Mims leapt immediately into the fray. "Don't you speak to my friend like that you pipsqueak!" she yelled.

"Pipsqueak am I" retorted the girl, "I'll show you who's a pipsqueak."

The fulminating pair hurled themselves at one another, and stumbling against Audrey both toppled over, resulting in tangle of sheets and bodies rolling through the double doors. The laundry girl was the first to emerge, with raised fist ready to strike. "Take this you big..."

At that moment, from around the corner a small group of dignified looking people appeared. In front was the Matron, and behind her the new government Minister for Health, and the Chairman and Lady Secretary of the Hospitals Charitable Board, together with the local Reverend and a very grand looking woman if a fox fur wrap.

"...so you see ladies and gentlemen Minister," Matron was saying, "everyone here at the Wetherton works as a team. Our laundry staff in particular take their duties extremely seriously..."

The Matron broke off as an extraordinary scene met her gaze, and that of her party. In the doorway of the laundry two young women were engaged in what could only be described as a vulgar brawl, while a third writhed on the floor amid a pile of linen.

"What is going on here?" demanded the Matron, her face like thunder.

The brawling figures quickly parted and stared down in silence.

"You will all report to my office at three o'clock, and your future at this hospital will be decided upon. In the meantime you will clear up this mess immediately."

"Yes Matron," mumbled all three.

Turning to her VIP visitors the Matron went on, "Any indiscipline is of course dealt with most severely, we are not afraid to dismiss summarily which will almost certainly be the case in this instance I assure you." The VIPs nodded and cleared their throats appropriately.

"And now," said Matron, "perhaps you would care to inspect our stores first. We will return here when order is restored." She glowered sideways at the girls. "This way please..."

As soon as Matron and her dignitaries were out of sight the laundry girl flew into a rage again.

"You scouse trollop," she drew back her fist at Mimsy. "If you've gone and got me the sack I'll flaming well..."

"Molly!" cried Audrey suddenly, her face emerging from the jumble of sheets on the floor. The fist froze in mid swing. "Audrey?"

"Do you two know each other or something?" asked Mimsy mystified, still squared up to defend herself.

"Know each other? This is my best friend," cried Audrey.

Molly dived over and pulled Audrey to her feet and they fell into one another's arms.

"Oh Audrey I'm so glad to see you," sobbed Molly, "and I'm so sorry about James."

"I'm sorry too – for you I mean, that is, we were all so upset at home, and I knew you'd hear from your mother and I couldn't begin to imagine how hard it would be for you...he did love you, you know...I'm sorry, I wanted to come and find you but as time went on it seemed so difficult, and I was frightened, terrified, not knowing what to say to you...I thought you'd be angry with me..."

"How could I be angry Audrey, we both lost James..."

"Yes but..."

"I know; I know you don't have to say anything."

"Oh Molly..."

"Oh Audrey..."

"Oh heck!" said Mimsy, staring at the tearful reunion in amazement. "Is somebody going to introduce me or what, so we can all be friends - before the pipsqueak here decides to take another swipe at me?"

"Oh sorry – Mimsy, I mean Miriam, meet Molly, Molly meet Miriam."

"Mimsy will do," grinned Mimsy, "and sorry about calling you pipsqueak."

"Forget it," smiled Molly, "what's in a name eh. Pleased to meet you Mimsy."

The two girls shook hands.

"Here let me give you a hand with those sheets." Mimsy stooped and began gathering up the linen strewn across the floor.

"Thanks," said Molly, joining her. "And sorry about flying off the handle, I was going way too fast with the trolley. It's just that we've had a few run-ins with some of the snooty nurses from upstairs – no offence Aud – we're under strict orders not to talk to them unless they talk to us. I don't know what they've got to be so high and mighty about."

"Yeah, bloody stupid," agreed Mimsy, "I mean we'll all go down in the same bleedin' boat if it sinks won't we..." Then, catching Audrey's eye she added quickly, 'sorry Audrey – I forgot about your brother – she told me all about James, he must have been a real hero – did you know him Molly?"

"I'll tell you later Mimsy," said Audrey hastily. "But listen Moll, I've got to get back to work, while I've still got a job that is - when can we get together and have a proper talk? You haven't even told me what you're doing here at the Wetherton."

"Nor you!" chuckled Molly. "Look, my address is 112 Jericho Road – better still meet me tonight by the Feathers Arms, you know the one, at the end of Jericho Road?"
Audrey nodded. "I'll see you later then, about seven o'clock? I'll meet you outside."

"Ok." said Audrey.
Molly squeezed her friend's hand, and giving Mimsy a cheery wink, disappeared with her laden trolley back into the noise and steam of the laundry room.

It was seven-thirty by the time Audrey reached the pub. She looked up and down the street but Molly was nowhere in sight.

"Hello darlin, lookin' for a good time?"
Spinning round in alarm, Audrey saw a large, rough looking dirty faced man lurching in her direction.

"Aye you, Monty!" broke in a sharp high-pitched voice. Molly was crossing the road with a warlike stride. "That there's my friend and definitely not the sort of girl you're looking for!"
The huge man gave a beer sodden belch. "Sorry Moll," he slurred. "I thought for a minute my luck was in, she's a cracker that one." Laughing loudly he staggered towards the door of the pub and disappeared inside.

"Oh Moll, I thought I'd missed you, I didn't know what to do and when that man came up to me I...."

Molly laughed. "Calm down, that's Monty. He works down the docks. He's harmless enough. I heard Hitler-in Knickers made you and Mimsy work an extra two hours. I got a right ticking off from my guvnor too."

"Yes, but at least we kept our jobs."

"Are you joking – they can't get rid of the likes of us Aud – who else is going to slave like we do for a bob a week?"

"Plenty I imagine, the way things are."

"Don't you believe it – we're workers us girls, and the bosses up at the Wetherton know it."

"That man just now Moll," said Audrey, still looking perturbed, "who was he, what did he want?"

Molly shook her head with a wry smile. "My word Audrey Stevenson, you really have led a sheltered life. Come on," she said taking her friend by the hand and leading her into the pub, "let's continue you education."

The two girls sat at a table in the corner of the pub. Molly had set two glasses of sherry in front of them. Audrey looked distinctly uncomfortable.

"I can't drink this Moll," she whispered, "and I don't think you should, with your illness."

"I'm all right now," Molly lifted her glass to her lips. "I grew out of what ever it was."

Audrey continued, "Anyway what are you doing in a place like this – women don't go in pubs on their own."

"Hey hey, this is my local," Molly protested looking around at the cosmopolitan array of people enjoying them selves. "The salt of the earth, these folk, and all of them my friends too." She waved to Monty as he rolled past their table. He raised an unsteady hand in response and blew a kiss at Audrey who buried her face in her hands in horror.

"Take no notice of Monty," she said, "just tell him where to get off when need be. Audrey I live here, with these people, they are all good souls."

"I thought you lived with your parents. Have you all moved here?"

Molly shook her head; "No I live here on my own for now. I've got a boyfriend Aud, Bill's his name; he's abroad somewhere fighting the Jerries. Got this house so when he comes back we're to be married, whenever that will be."

"I didn't know you were even courting Moll."

"It's not been long but I just knew he was for me." She took several more slugs of her drink then began explaining how she had lost her job at the old laundry and got taken on at the Wetherton, then launched into a detailed, description of the onerous regime in the hospital's laundry room.

"The most important rule is we're not supposed to fraternise with the "ladies with the lamps" upstairs. Just like old times eh Aud," she laughed, "They're still trying to keep us apart – fat chance eh!" She raised her glass in salute.

"Hear hear," rejoined Audrey, taking a tentative sip of the sherry. Then she asked, "But why did you get the sack from the other laundry Moll?"

"Like I said Aud," sad Molly leaning towards her friend and narrowing her eyes, "they're still trying to keep us apart."
"Who?"

"I'm not one to speak ill of anyone's family Aud."

"You don't mean - not my mother?"

Molly tapped the side of her nose. "She has friends in high places. The Freemasons own a lot of businesses in Liverpool Aud. Your mother must have known we were still in touch, somebody would have reported you'd been writing to me at the laundry, and getting me the sack from the laundry could have been a warning – stay away from my daughter. Then there's that brother of hers, ran off to America, done some dark deed a long time ago, so rumour had it.

"My Uncle John," said Audrey, "yes old Jack told me a few amazing things about him."

"I've heard folk say he still pulls strings in Liverpool," continued Molly, "puts money into charitable causes and such like."

"Oh then there must be some good in him – just as there is in my mother if she weren't so unhappy – I really wish I could meet him. Oh I'm so sorry if she had you thrown out of your job Moll," lamented Audrey.

Molly put down her glass and looked equally apologetic. "Listen to me, and my big mouth; I've no proof of anything, I shouldn't take no notice of gossip. All I know is the overseer came over one day and said they had no need of me anymore. It could have been they just didn't have enough work."

"No, I don't believe that," said Audrey pursing her lips. "I wouldn't put anything past my mother, she was always against us, we know that."

"Now I've gone and turned you against your own mother," said Molly ruefully. "A sniff of this stuff and I'm a blathering idiot."

"Not at all Moll; do you know, I bet she's got spies everywhere…"

"No, no, forget what I said, please," implored Molly. "Don't blame your mother there's enough hating in the world. Whatever or whoever got me the elbow has done us a right favour don't you see - it's brought us back together again, courtesy of that distinguished seat of medical learning the Wetherton Hospital." She raised her glass again.

"Together with a bang!" exclaimed Audrey snorting into her sherry.

"The look on Hitler-in Knickers face when she saw us rolling about on the floor like all in wrestlers…." Molly screamed, doubling up with mirth.

"I thought that vicar was going to pass out!"

"Or pass on! Ha, ha, ha, ha…!"

As the girls" raucous laughter echoed round the room, Monty, looking on with a broad, drunken grin, gave a huge bellow of approval and promptly fell off his stool.

An hour later, Audrey climbed unsteadily aboard the bus back towards the hospital. Alighting opposite the nurses' home she slipped through the gap in the railings that Mimsy had told her about, cursed under her breath as her shoe caught a stone, which rattled noisily onto the quadrangle, then made her way into the building on tiptoe. At an upstairs window, a shadowy figure observing this nocturnal activity withdrew behind the curtain.

CHAPTER TWENTY-FIVE

The Nightingale Sings

"There's a dance tonight you know girls, over at the air base." Mimsy, carrying a bedpan in each hand towards the sluice, performed a little two-step and warbled a snatch of The Boogie-woogie Bugle Boy from Company B.

"Careful with that lot," laughed Ivy, "or you'll be sitting the next one out. Anyway, count me in. What time's it start?"

"Seven o'clock," replied Ivy. "How about you Aud - and your friend Molly?"

Audrey, on her knees, looked up from the bed she was making.

"No thanks," she said, "better not, and Moll's working tonight."

"What will you be you doing instead then? Janet asked. "Don't be so boring, come with us. There'll be lots of lonely Americans just waiting for some pretty English girls like us."

"We not good enough for you is that it?" said Mimsy light-heartedly.

"Oh Mims I don't know," Audrey sighed and got to her feet. "Mother never approved of me going to dances…oh but why am I saying that – I don't know." She shrugged, and sighed again.

Mimsy looked at her open mouthed.

"You mean to say you've never been to a dance? Never danced with a feller?"

"A what?" said Audrey.

"A chap, a beau, you know – a *feller* - " said Mimsy in mock aristocratic scouse tones.

"Oh a boy. Well I went to an all girls" school you see, though we did have Scottish country dancing lessons with a nearby boys" school a few times."

"This'll be a bit different Aud," said Ivy archly, and winking at Mimsy, "waltzes and foxtrots, and maybe a jitterbug or two if we're lucky with the Yanks. Everything's a lot closer if you know what I mean." She winked again.

"Don't our dance halls frown on that – the jitterbugging I mean?" said Audrey.

"See - you know more than you let on!" grinned Mimsy.

"Well one does hear things." Audrey lowered her head bashfully.

"Listen," said Mimsy, sidling up to Audrey and putting a sisterly arm round her shoulder. "Your mother's in Crosslands and you're here in Wetherton – how's she going to know what you're doing? So if 'one' would like to accompany 'one's' friends to this ere dance this evening, they will make sure 'one' has the well-deserved time of 'one's' life, and finds out why Yanks are so-called. What does 'one' say?"

"Not sure I understand that last bit," said Audrey awkwardly, "but all right – I'll come!"

"Whoopee – you won't regret it Aud, will she girls?"

"Never!" chorused the others, as Mimsy, grabbing a floor mop as a dance partner, mimed a spirited foxtrot down the ward.

Hearing a sudden fusillade of coughing from Ivy and Janet she spun around to see Matron stood in the doorway watching her. Hastily righting the mop she proceeded to polish the floor with her full, and energetic attention.

"Oh Ivy I feel so nervous," bemoaned Audrey, taking hold of Ivy's arm as the four friends alighted from the bus at the perimeter of the U.S. base. "Do I look all right in this dress?"

"Right as nine pence," declared Ivy.

"Only nine pence?"

"All right then a million dollars," chipped in Mimsy. "Honest Aud, you look a treat."

"Not as nice as you three," demurred Audrey, as they showed their nurses ID cards to the tough looking military policeman on the gate. He waved them through with a smile and a whistle, seemingly intended for Audrey.

"See what I mean!" said Ivy."

Following the Map's directions they made their way past a series of Nissan huts and jeeps and arrived at a large hangar with some bunting strung across the large double doors. Swing music could be heard beating out a seductive rhythm.

"In for a penny in for a pound," whispered Mimsy. "Come on girls."

The four friends entered the hall in a tight group. The room was hazy with smoke, the music very loud. Through the crowds, on a rostrum at the far end Audrey spied the gleam of a swaying saxophone, while a tall elegant looking crooner in tuxedo and bow tie inclined his slick head towards the microphone.

A throng of young women stood around near the doors, while groups of young servicemen in uniform chatted, casting their eyes towards the opposite sex. A number of couples were already dancing energetically.

"Ooh I love this song," exclaimed Janet, launching into the chorus of Chattanooga Choo-choo as the crescendo approached.
Forming an impromptu conga line, with Audrey tagging on at the end the girls threaded their way towards a trestle table where a steward was serving drinks.

"Just a lemonade please," said Audrey as Mimsy tried to press a glass of potent smelling liquor on her.

"Sensible lass," remarked Mimsy. "But don't be too sensible – you'll miss all the fun."
With that she took off decisively for a huddle of GIs sporting identical close-cropped centre partings and glistening hair oil. There were smiles all round as Mimsy disappeared into their midst.
Seeing a vacant chair Audrey sat herself down by the drinks table, and observed the scene. The others had all been swept off their feet now and were dancing enthusiastically to an up beat jazz melody. A series of young men had courteously asked Audrey to take the floor with them, to which she had politely declined.

"Excuse me ma'am?" The enquiry was made in a low, languid, southern drawl.

"I'm sorry my feet are…" Audrey began the excuse she had already used four times.

"I just wanted to ask if anyone was using this here chair ma'am. My feet are kinda sore, if you'll pardon me saying so. Yours too?"

"Yes…no…" stammered Audrey.
"Actually mine aren't either," confessed the American.
"Oh but why…"
"No it's my ears."
"Your ears?"

"Yes ma'am, my ears are red raw as a crocodile's back when he's been out of water in the sun all day. You see the lady I've just been dancing with has talked my ears fair off my head and no mistake ma'am. I thought Southern women talked a lot, but this little lady, she must be the world goddam champion o' non-stop talking without ever stopping for breath. There she is, over there."

The young man nodded his head discreetly to the corner of the room, where Mimsy was now holding forth to a rather dismayed looking GI.

"She's gotten hold of my buddy Ed now. Poor old Ed!" He threw back his head in laughter, smacking his thigh with gusto.

Audrey likewise began to giggle uncontrollably. "Oh dear, poor Mimsy – I am sorry, she's always like that I'm afraid, but she has a heart of gold."

Her companion looked instantly mortified. "She's your friend? Oh gee I'm sorry ma'am, I would never have said those things If I'd have known, you must think I'm the most unfeeling person ever walked the earth…"

"No it's quite all right," said Audrey, "please don't apologise."

"Well, in that case, if I've not offended you too much, I wonder if I might have the pleasure of the next dance with you – oh and you can talk all you like, honestly."

Audrey looked at the handsome, eager young face, the broad shoulders rippling under the smart US Air Force uniform and open flying jacket. "Thank you," she said, I would be honoured."

Then, seeing a young woman being launched acrobatically into the air by her partner she said in sudden alarm, "Oh – but I don't know how – that dance…"

"Hell I can't jitterbug either, I like a slow dance."

"I think I could manage that," said Audrey, but its all jazz tonight isn't it…"

At that moment the tempo changed sharply down. The band had segued smoothly into A Nightingale Sang in Berkley Square.

"They must have read your thoughts sweetheart"

Taking her hand he led her onto the floor. She felt his hand slip gently around her waist. They began to move naturally to the music. The saxophone's low wistful notes sent a shiver down Audrey's spine. Suddenly she began to cry.

"Why what's wrong?" asked her partner in a concerned voice. "Is my dancing that bad?"

"No," sniffed Audrey, her face lowered. "You dance beautifully."

"Then what?"

"It's just that…no one's…no one's ever called me sweetheart before…."

The next second, their lips had met in a passionate kiss.

CHAPTER TWENTY-SIX

The Americans Come to Tea

The chunky US military jeep, like some powerful metallic brown beast let loose in the sedate neighbourhood, growled its way noisily along Whindolls Road, slowed then with a mashing of gears nosed up onto the pavement outside the imposing red brick façade of number 64. The four occupants, Mimsy and Italian Joe, Audrey and Martin, alighted. Audrey skipped up the three stone steps to the big oak front door and rang the bell.

"Why hello Miss Audrey," smiled Dorothy as she opened the door. "Come in, we've all been expecting you."

She stepped back as Audrey entered the hallway.

Mimsy and Joey and Martin were still stood at the bottom of the steps not daring to venture further until instructed.

"Come on you three," called Audrey, 'stop dallying about." She went back, took Martin's hand and steered him up into the house. The other two followed tentatively.

Uncharacteristically, Mimsy still hadn't spoken. She stood in the large hallway, mouth open in apparent awe of her surroundings.

"Mims, dear," said Audrey, "do you want to take off your coat."

"Sorry," whispered Mimsy, wriggling awkwardly out of her jacket and handing it to Dorothy. "Do you really live here?"

"I'm afraid so," Audrey smiled, "at least I used to. And why are you whispering? We're not in the library."

"And this must be your young man," said Dorothy looking at Martin. "May I take your hat and coat?"

"Pardon me," said Martin, snatching off his US Air Force beret. "Martin Corbett ma'am, how do you do?" Martin held out his hand, which Dorothy, after a second or two of surprise took, recoiling from Martin's energetic shaking. "I want you to know ma'am how honoured I am to be invited to your lovely home. Your daughter is a fine young lady, and I'm very pleased for the privilege of meeting you, and I can sure see, if you'll allow me to say so ma'am, where Audrey gets her beautiful looks…"

"Martin…" Audrey stopped him in mid flow. "This isn't my mother."

Behind them in the hall Mimsy snorted loudly, trying to suppress a huge burst of laughter. Martin looked at Audrey, then back at Dorothy.

"Martin this is Dorothy," said Audrey, smiling, 'she's Molly's mother."

There was a second's embarrassed pause then Martin beamed again.

"Then I can sure see where Molly gets her good looks," he said unabashed. "Molly, she's your other friend right? Well I'm mighty glad to meet you Dorothy."

Dorothy, as if to avoid another handshake, backed away slightly. Smiling politely she said, "Won't you come this way ladies, gentlemen?" and led them along the corridor. "Your mother's in the conservatory Miss Audrey."

Clarissa, looking cool and reposed in an elegant pink chiffon dress rose as Audrey and her guests came in. A profusion of flowers and plants filled the room around her. Audrey exchanged a perfunctory kiss with her mother then said, "Mother these are my friends Mimsy and Joe, and this is Martin."

Clarissa shook hands with Miriam and Joe. Martin then stepped forward boldly.

"Martin Corbett ma'am," said Martin giving Clarissa's beautifully manicured hand the same bone-crushing treatment he had inflicted on Dorothy.

"Yes I've heard about you. I've heard about all of you. The Matron at the Wetherton Hospital happens to be an old friend of mine. There's little that happens in and around Wetherton she doesn't know about."

There was silence for a moment as the four friends exchanged nervous, uncertain glances. Audrey began, "Mimsy has a nickname for..." then thinking better of it stopped short. Instead she said, "Martin flies the B17 bombers, he joined up after Pearl Harbour."

"It was the duty of every American," said Martin, "to do what he had to do, to do whatever he could, just as your fine young men..."

"Yes, quite," cut in Clarissa, her voice cracking slightly.

Audrey said quickly, "Joe's his co-pilot. Don't you think he looks like Chico Marx, Mummy? Everyone says so."

"I never go to the cinema," said Clarissa blankly. "Besides you are embarrassing the young man."

"Oh he never gets embarrassed ma'am," said Martin. "He's too stupid. I can say that "cause I'm his friend."

He gave Joe's ear a playful swipe.

"Actually he's more like Harpo, 'cause he hardly speaks, for an Italian at least. And he's a terrific boxer, Air Corps champion you'd better believe it. One day he's gonna knock my head clean off my shoulders for being smart."

"You talk enough for the both of us," grinned Joey, his slick New York wise-guy accent a contrast to Martin's lazy southern drawl. "And behave yourself in a lady's house."

"I'm sorry ma'am, I am saying too much, pardon me," said Martin humbly. "And I'm sorry too if I caused you pain by referring to your young British men in the service back then. Audrey told me about her brother, your son who nobly gave his life at sea, and I should have remembered and held my tongue."

"Well, don't mention it young man, we can't be forever walking on eggshells can we," said Clarissa briskly. Martin looked mystified. "Eggshells ma'am?"

Clarissa turned to Mimsy. Looking her up and down she asked, "What is your real name?"

Mimsy replied, "Miriam, ma'am... Mrs Stephenson, from the Bible, with Moses in the bull rushes..."

Audrey noticed her usually brazen friend was blushing slightly, and assuming a deferential manner, as well as making an unsuccessful attempt to suppress her broad scouse accent. To forestall the awkwardness Audrey laughed self-consciously and said, "Mummy, may we go into the garden? I'd like to show my friends Daddy's favourite plant."

"Of course, Audrey dear, I'll have Dorothy serve tea on the veranda. I presume the boys will take tea, we don't like, or want coffee in this household."

"You know I'm getting to like your English tea!" said Martin in a very enthusiastic manner.

"Oh you are a terrible liar Martin Corbett," whispered Audrey, squeezing his hand as they filed out of the room. He put a strong arm around her.

"Come on honey," he whispered back, 'show us this special plant now, I love anything that grows, like love for instance."

"Oh, then you're sure to like this," replied Audrey, her voice querulous with emotion now.

137

When they were out on the veranda she said, "I'm sorry everyone if my mother seems a little...austere...touchy. It is true she's gone through a rough time of it. She can't get over James's death you see, it hit her hardest of all of us I think. Sometimes I think she blames my father, and even me for encouraging him to join up in the place. Nowadays you never know how she's going to react, one minute all sweetness and light, the next ready to murder someone..."

"Murder? You mean homicide right? That's a strong word. Is there a history of murder in your family?"

Audrey froze suddenly. "How did you know...?" she began, then seeing the twinkle in Martin's eye said with relief, "Oh, no, I'm just using a figure of speech of course..."

Of course; your mother is a sweet lady, which is the name of my aircraft as it happens – yeah 'Sweet Lady'. She's no more capable of killing than I am."

Audrey's expression darkened. "Who - your plane or my mother?"

"Well a bomber is a killing machine, sure, but if we're talking human beings I guess that given the motive, many otherwise placid people are capable of cold blooded homicide."

"Surely not you, what would be your motive?"

"Money."

"Money?"

"Yeah, like when Joey here keeps winning money off me at poker – I think to myself, I could kill him!" The only reason I don't say it is cause he's the Corps champion, eh Joey!"

Martin delivered another slap to his friends ear and the two comrades squared up to one another, sparring playfully, and shadow boxing their way boisterously around the conservatory.

"And it's anyone's fight here at Madison Square Gardens tonight folks!" shouted Martin.

In high spirits now, they both began laughing loudly, while Mimsy, forgetting the diffidence that had stifled her since arriving in the salubrious surroundings of Whindolls road, clapped her hands and cheered the contenders on. Suddenly however her tone changed.

"Oh mind that big pot thing!" she screamed in alarm as Martin's shoulder collided with a large jardinière set upon a tall stand. The jardinière and stand tilted as one, and seeing the whole edifice about to crash to the floor, quick as lightning Joey dived forward, catching the jardinière and its contents deftly in mid air, while Martin's foot intercepted the heavy wooden stand as it fell to within inches of an exquisitely decorated, and delicate looking Chinese vase.

"My Love Lies Bleeding!" cried out Audrey. Her sudden resonant utterance, like the arresting voice of the chorus proclaiming the climax in some high flown, classical drama, caused everyone in the room to stare at her.

"That's it," she said, "the plant I wanted to show you, my father and I are both so very fond…"

"Amaranths Caudatus to be precise."

Now, all eyes turned towards the garden. Marcus, dressed in a smart blue tailored suit, his gaze fixed on the mass of foliage cradled in Joey's arms, stood at the open door between the conservatory and the garden.

"Daddy…!" cried Audrey running up to him. As father and daughter embraced, Joey and Martin quickly righted the wooden stand and replaced the jardinière upon it.

"Not many people use the Latin name of course," continued Marcus, kissing his daughter on the forehead. "Where's Dorothy? I rang the front door bell but no one came."

"Making tea," smiled Audrey, clinging to her father's hand. "Martin loves our English tea."

"Who's Martin?"

"Martin Corbett, my father, and Daddy this is Miriam and Joey."

"Sorry about the…incident there…sir…" mumbled Martin awkwardly.

"Mm, well, never mind, accidents will happen, no harm done I'm sure," nodded Marcus. "Marcus Stevenson - pleased to meet you - Miriam, Joe."

As the introductions were being made, Dorothy arrived with the tea.

"Sorry I didn't hear the front door sir, I was down in the kitchen," she apologised, adding with a sideways look at the two young men as she adjusted the position of the jardinière stand, "and there was rather a lot of noise, elsewhere if you know what I mean." Martin, still looking apologetic cleared his throat.

"My co-pilot and - we were just giving a demonstration Mr Stevenson sir, of er…"

"Yes I observed your match through the window," said Marcus. "Used to box a little myself at college. Well it's an honour to meet our American allies, and may I say friends. He raised his teacup.

"An honour to be here sir," rejoined Martin. "Your daughter said this plant is special to you sir." He indicated the jardinière now returned by Dorothy to its correct place.

Marcus nodded. "I don't why, but it's always had a rare significance for me – the name as much as anything, so sad of course, but at the same time quite beguiling don't you think?"

"Like Greek tragedy sir – terrible and beautiful all at once?"

"Something like that – rather like life itself in many ways, especially now - forgive me," Marcus blinked away a hint moisture in his eye. "I didn't intend to sound morbid…"

"Daddy, daddy," Audrey was tugging her father's hand. Mimsy's had a wonderful idea. She's brought her box brownie and would like to take a photograph of us all – sort of hands across the sea with us and Martin and Joey, would it be all right?"

"Oh yes, you go ahead."

"But you must be in it too, mustn't he Martin."

"You bet, if you'd care to that is sir," enthused Martin.

"Mims are you ready?" asked Audrey excitedly.

Martin looked thoughtful. "But if Mimsy takes the shot, she won't be in the photograph. Here let me take it Mims…"

"Then you won't be in it Martin," objected Audrey. "I must have you in the picture, I simply must."

"Perhaps - Dorothy would you oblige?" suggested Marcus, seeing the housekeeper returning with a fresh supply of hot water for the tea.

"Oh I'm no good with those gadgets I'm afraid," laughed Dorothy, "you'd all come out upside down!"

"I will take the photograph." All eyes turned to see Clarissa, who had just entered the room.

"Mummy oh thank you," said Audrey.

Clarissa took the camera from Mimsy and positioned herself by the door, while the others assembled themselves in the centre of the room around the jardinière stand; to one side stood Joey and Miriam, on the other Martin and Audrey.

The four young people linked arms, exchanged fond smiles at one another then looked out at the camera. Marcus took up position at the back, behind Audrey, his face brushing the delicate, vibrant red blooms of the Love Lies Bleeding.

"Just a minute," said Audrey. "Now you won't be in the picture Mummy."

Clarissa, her face a mask of stillness said, "Oh but it was never my intention to be my dear, never." Her voice seemed tired, yet at the same deadly serious, brimming with some larger meaning. The others fell silent, watching her, as if waiting for a revelation, and there was an air of something immense, portentous in the room. Then looking down into the camera she said in a hollow tone, "Now smile everyone."

CHAPTER TWENTY-SEVEN

Passionate Rendezvous

"I bought the place as a weekend retreat," said Marcus.
He and Audrey were sat alone in the breakfast room at Whindolls Road. Through the window, Clarissa could be observed in the garden. She was wearing a large floral patterned hat and tending to some roses.

"So we could get away from the bustle of Liverpool now and again," continued Marcus. "After Braeside went, god knows we needed somewhere…tranquil, remote. Your mother fell in love with it. But lately, with one thing and another…of course it's only a cottage, nothing like Braeside…"

"A cottage sounds perfect," beamed Audrey. "Tell me more about it Daddy, how would I get there?"

"Well its in the middle of nowhere really, the nearest station is a mile or more. I believe there are omnibuses but how frequently I've no idea. We always took the car. It's a long walk otherwise, you have to find Pothole Lane."

"Pothole Lane!" Audrey clapped her hands. "Daddy – I love it already."

"Well it's yours – if that's how you want to spend your time off from the hospital. How long are they sparing you for?"

"Just the weekend – well three days." Audrey's eyes lit up. "Thank you Daddy." She kissed her father's cheek. "I promise we'll leave it clean and tidy."

At that moment Clarissa came in from the garden, pruning shears in hand, and an inquisitive look on her face.

"Leave what clean and tidy?" she asked.

"Rain Tub Cottage," said Marcus. "Audrey wants to spend the weekend there."

"Whatever for?" Clarissa asked.

"To get away from the bustle of the city," smiled Audrey. "That's what Daddy said he bought it for. And I've never seen it, it sounds heavenly and Daddy says you fell in love with the place."

"There's been a lot of water under the bridge since then," said Clarissa.

Marcus raised his eyebrows discreetly at his daughter. "Well I suppose you might find it charming enough," continued Clarissa, "but its very remote."

"I've told her that," smiled Marcus.

"And it's hardly the place for a young woman to stay alone, and I would not allow you to do that. The nurse's home is one thing, an isolated house in the countryside quite another."

"Oh I won't be alone Mummy…"

Clarissa's expression stiffened. "If you are thinking of offering hospitality to your young man there in our absence," she said, "think again young lady."

"There are four bedrooms at Rain Tub Cottage," volunteered Marcus. "And Martin is a gentleman do you not think?"

"Yes, I know all about gentlemen," muttered Clarissa darkly.

"Whatever do you mean my dear?"

"Suffice it to say Marcus, that our daughter will not be entertaining a man who is not her husband, overnight and un-chaperoned, at Rain Tub Cottage."

There was an awkward silence for a moment, then Audrey said in a slightly aggrieved tone, "Well mother, you needn't worry on either of those points, because Mimsy, Janet and Ivy will be coming with me."

"The four musketeers?" chortled Marcus, "Rain Tub Cottage will never be the same!"

Clarissa studied her daughter's face closely for a moment then said, "All four of you allowed a long weekend off at the same time? The matron would hardly allow that."

"But its true Mummy," protested Audrey, "they're reorganising the wards, and it's being done this week – we were only told the other day that we all have to take our leave together now, and they'll be no more for the rest of the year, its because they need more space for all the soldiers coming in…"

"I know all about the reorganisation at the Wetherton," said Clarissa raising her hand. "What does surprise me Audrey is that you would wish to use this free time to go off with your friends rather than invite Martin to spend time here with you, with us. The two of you have seemed inseparable these last few months. He will be free to leave the base as usual this weekend I imagine? Well?"

Audrey looked down at the tablecloth. Tracing the pattern of the stitching with her finger, she said quietly, "Well, as a matter of fact Mummy, Martin has to go away this weekend."

"He is being deployed?" said Clarissa.

"No…not exactly…"

"Then what exactly?"

"Training," said Audrey, 'special training, highly classified actually, and I shouldn't really be telling you, he wasn't supposed to tell me even…some kind of mission they're preparing for…"

"I think you'd better stop right there," said Marcus. "Before we all breach the official secrets act – walls have ears, as they say, walls have ears."

"Exactly Daddy." Audrey gave a sly glance at her mother. "Otherwise of course I would be seeing Martin this weekend. As it is I want to take my mind off things, and I thought the cottage with Mims and Ivy and Janet, who really need a break themselves, would be just…"

Clarissa lifted her palm imperiously again. "Very well, very well, just make sure you don't all frighten the poor neighbours with your raucous behaviour."

"There are no neighbours," said Marcus. "Only old Mrs Caldwell, and she's deaf."

"Speaking of Mrs Caldwell, I'd better see if I can get word to her to air the place out if four of you are going down," said Clarissa."

"Oh don't go to any trouble Mummy, I'm sure we'll manage…"

"Nonsense. She'll need to get sheets organised, and provisions for three days."

"Well, well," said Marcus thoughtfully, 'so the Yanks have got something cooking eh? You see darling," he said with a smile, "there are some things that even you don't get to know about."

Clarissa did not return the smile. "As you say Marcus," she said, "the less said about that now the better. You'll miss your young man Audrey, I understand, but you'll see him again soon."

Getting up to leave the room she paused at the door and turned back to her daughter. "I did not intend to sound critical of Martin dearest. I want you to know that I like him. But there is such a thing as proper behaviour Audrey. I hope I am not too bold in my presumption, that one day you and he might stay at Rain Tub Cottage together – but as man and wife."

"Forgive me God," said Audrey under her breath as, with a quick glance up and down the street she entered the call box at the end of Whindolls Road and fumbled in her bag for some coins. Finding them she opened her address book and dialled a number written down in the back.

"Hello – US Air Force Base West Wetherton Park England, Personnel Recreation Officer speaking," announced a broad Brooklyn accented voice.

"Hello, could you give a message to Airman Martin Corbett for me please?" said Audrey softly.

"Could you speak up please?"

"A message, for Martin Corbett."

"Yes ma'am, Airman Corbett, what is the message?"

"Tell him, it's on."

"What's on?"

"Oh…he'll know," replied Audrey, glancing nervously up the street again.

"Ok, it's on," said the Personnel Recreational Officer. "Who shall I say is giving this message?"

"Audrey."

"I'll get this to Airman Corbett ma'am, Audrey says it's on, and he'll know what's on, right?"

"Yes, I mean right – and I'm most grateful, thank you."

The Personnel Recreational Officer laughed, "You bet sweetheart. He'll be grateful too."

Audrey looked at her watch as the train slowed. It was 3 p.m. A light, early October rain had begun, falling with a gentle hiss on the engine as it pulled into the little station. She lifted her suitcase from the rack and opened the carriage door. The air seemed warm, sweet with the smell of hedgerows and ripe apples.

"Excuse me, is there a bus to Pothole Lane?" she asked the stationmaster as she handed over her ticket.

145

"Yes madam, next one's due ten o" clock tomorrow morning."

"Oh well," she smiled, "its not raining terribly hard."

An hour later she arrived outside Rain Tub Cottage. Her father's directions had been easy to follow. She surveyed with a sense of enchantment the picture before her.

Indeed the cottage was pretty as a picture she thought – the thatched roof, whitewashed walls and aged, criss-crossing timbers, the crooked little latticed windows. There were even roses round the door. And all perfectly enlaced in a white picket fence. All it needed was a fairy godmother!

Audrey opened the gate and took the key from her handbag. The door was a little stiff, but with a slight push it swung open. She took off her hat and coat, gave both a shake and hung them on a hook behind the door.

The interior was charmingly quaint and cosy, with comfortable winged armchairs and button back couches, deep pile rugs and softly gleaming brass.

In the large Inglenook a log fire was burning merrily. Vases of fresh cut flowers filled the air with their sweet perfume, and when Audrey investigated the delicious aroma coming from the kitchen she discovered a pot of hearty beef stew simmering gently on the range. This Mrs Caldwell whoever she is, has certainly been busy thought Audrey. Upstairs, the beds in all four rooms were newly made up, with crisp linen sheets and neatly laid eiderdowns.

Suddenly there was a loud engine noise outside. Audrey's heart skipped a beat. She ran quickly back downstairs and opened the door. Martin, magnificent in a long military greatcoat and Air Force beret stood smiling in the doorway.

"Sorry about that," he began apologetically. "I think she needs a de-coke." He indicated his jeep, slewed at an angle under some trees. Audrey threw her arms around him. They kissed passionately for a full minute.

"Come in," she said breathlessly at last.

"Ouch!" Martin had hit his head on the hard oak lintel above the door to the sitting room.

"Oh sorry my darling," said Audrey, rubbing his scalp tenderly. "I forgot you were so tall!"

"Hey but this is great," he exclaimed, plunging down into one of the armchairs, his long legs stretching as far as the fireplace. "Its like Hansel and Gretel!"

"It is a bit," agreed Audrey sitting herself down on the rug and wrapping her arms affectionately round his knees. "It's certainly like a fairy tale having you here. You found the place all right then?"

"Clearly," smiled Martin, stroking her damp tousled hair. "Once I got used to your winding English lanes. Nothing is in a straight line in this country, but you know I really like that. Though I wish you had let him me bring you down in the jeep. Did you walk all that way from the station in the rain?"

"Too risky to travel together, someone would be bound to see us. And I don't suppose I'll rust."

"Ok. And you know what honey?"

"What? Audrey turned to look at him as Martin lowered his head towards hers and inhaled. "Mm!" he said softly, "the rain does wonderful things to your hair."
Their lips brushed, then melded in a long, slow, kiss.

"That was...nice," breathed Audrey at last, her cheeks flushed from the warmth of the hearth, and the fire now blazing within her.

"Nice? That was - ecstasy," purred Martin.

"Hmm," murmured Audrey dreamily, gazing into the glowing logs and pressing her face against his side. "By the way," she said, "what did you tell Joe?"

"Like you said, that as far as the hospital and your folks are concerned, the girls are all down here with you this weekend, and no-one knows where |I am."

"Mummy and Daddy think you're on a top-secret training mission. I hate having to lie."

"Is it worth it?"

"Every bit." She smiled up at him. "What did Joe say?"

"He'll square Mims and the others - said he'll take "em all out of town somewhere nice while we're down here. Give "em a good time. Joey's an ace."

"Bless him," sighed Audrey. "Yes I'd hate to think how I'd explain it to my mother if any of the girls were seen in Liverpool over the weekend – or if Hitler-in-Knickers rumbled us – it would just mean more lies - oh what a tangled web and all that."

147

Martin put his nose in the air and sniffed like a well-trained bloodhound.

"Hmm, not only your hair that smells good around here," he said.

"Mrs Caldwell's beef stew," said Audrey. "She's the old lady that looks after the cottage for my parents, she lives in a little house at the top of the lane apparently." Audrey put her hand to her face in alarm. "Gosh I hope she doesn't spot your jeep in the lane."

"What if she does," said Martin. "There's other military in the area she'll think nothing of it. Don't fret honey."

"I hope you're right," said Audrey. "According to Daddy she keeps herself to herself whenever the cottage is occupied. They let her know in advance if anyone's coming down by telephoning the village post office, and the postman passes on the message."

"Hence the delicious stew waiting for us,"

"Exactly."

"And the cosy beds all made up. Though we'll not need all four of them of course. How many are we likely to need sweetheart?"

Audrey said nothing for a moment, then, giving his hand a little squeeze, got to her feet. "I'd better take a look at that stew," she said. She went to the kitchen and lifted the lid off the pot. "Another ten minutes should do it," she called to Martin.

Noticing another door at the end of the kitchen, she opened it and gazed in upon a spacious, cool pantry room, it's shelves filled with crusty loaves of bread, cakes, biscuits, pots of jam and preserves. On the far wall stood a laden wine rack, while a separate cold safe revealed a generous leg of ham, a quart jug of milk, cream, a large round of cheddar cheese, two dozen eggs, several pats of butter and a dozen rashers of bacon.

"Martin," she called in amazement, "come and look at this."

"What is it honey, a spider?" said Martin hurrying to her side, "I'm good with spiders…wow!"

"I know," said Audrey, as together they surveyed the Aladdin's cave of provender. "There's enough here to feed an army."

"I'll tell Joey, he can bring the boys down," laughed Martin.

"I wonder how Mrs Caldwell got her hands on this lot," pondered Audrey. "Certainly not with her ration book." She broke off a hunk of crusty bread and handed some to Martin. "I suppose living near a farm helps. Hmm, delicious."

"Do they make this on the farm too?" asked Martin. He had taken a bottle from the wine rack. Audrey examined it.

"That's surely not… champagne?" she gasped.

"That's what it says right here on the label," said Martin. "But they say don't judge a book by its cover. I guess there's only one way to find out right? Do you know a good vintage Madame?"

"I've only had champagne once – no twice," said Audrey. "The first time was when Daddy opened a new factory - the bubbles went up my nose and I just got hiccups."

"And the second time?"

"The last time I saw James."

"I'm sorry." Martin looked down. As he was about to replace the bottle, Audrey touched his arm.

"No, don't be," she said quietly. "I mean, I'll always be sad about James of course, but I don't want to not do things because of that."

"You mean like, drinking champagne?"

Audrey looked at him then nodded.

"Sure?" said Martin.

"Sure."

He opened the bottle with a resounding pop.

"Ooh wait," Audrey scrambled for glasses as the creamy foaming liquid rose up.

"To us honey," said Martin.

"To us."

"Maybe Mrs Goldspell too," grinned Martin.

"Caldwell," corrected Audrey. "Though where she got this - Daddy must have sent it down, but I don't know how he'd have done it in time."

"Well, to Mr. Stevenson too then." Martin raised his glass again, "for providing not only the most beautiful daughter in the world, but the finest champagne. Your pa seems to be a kind of miracle worker Audrey – in fact, from what I hear your whole family's something special – unusual if you don't mind my saying so."

"You don't know the half of it."

"Perhaps you could tell me some day."

A ruminative, faraway look came into Audrey's eyes. "Come to that," she murmured, "I don't think I know either. And I'll tell you another strange thing."

"What's that honey?" said Martin.

"This champagne is the same as we had for James's send-off, his...last one. Same origin, same vintage."

"That's quite a coincidence."

"No," said Audrey, "I don't think it is...oh, quick...!"

A hissing noise had alerted her to the stew, which had risen and boiled over, sending a splash of rich sauce sizzling on the range.

"Stand back!" Grabbing a tea towel Martin lifted the heavy iron pan and set it down carefully on a breadboard on the table. "I guess dinner's ready," he announced.

"I guess," smiled Audrey. "Shall we open a bottle of this red to go with it?"

"Should we?"

"That's what it's here for," smiled Audrey. "We can finish the champagne..."

"At bedtime?" said Martin.

After the beef stew, washed down with a fine full-bodied burgundy, they ate treacle tart with cream, followed by crisp apples with cheddar. They were now sat at the table, dreamy and replete, each with a glass of thick warm vintage port.

Martin had lit the oil lamps and found some candles. He gazed intensely at Audrey, her face glowing in the flickering light.

"Martin, what are you looking at?"

"You my darling." He rose and took her hands, leading her out of the kitchen and into the living room. Then, gathering her up in his strong arms he mounted the stairs effortlessly.

On the landing were four doors, each ajar." Martin I..." began Audrey.

"Spoiled her choice honey." He took her into the nearest room, laid her gently on the bed and sat down beside her.

"Martin, not yet..." she whispered.

"I understand honey," he said softly. "I shall be next door. Well, goodnight and thank you for a wonderful evening. I love you."

Suddenly Audrey's arms were around his neck, her lips on his, their bodies forging together, galvanised by the powerhouse of their mutual passion. Martin began to undress her, gracefully, tenderly, marvelling in her beauty, while Audrey, quivering with desire, let her hands rove, thrilling to his touch, and her own as she explored the taut, perfect contours of the young airman's muscular physique.

They made love slowly, savouring each moment in their journey of discovery; each on a pilgrimage to the heart, the very centre of the other's being. Their bodies and souls quickened by wine and food and firelight, the joy of romance and the intensity of their feelings for one another, they gave and received pleasure equally.

When the final, earth-shattering moment of their union came, Audrey cried out her lover's name, gripping his shoulders with her fingertips, as his mouth once again found hers.

Outside, a new moon had just appeared from behind the shadowy clouds. A gust of autumn wind blew briefly through the surrounding trees, gently ruffling the thatch, and then the air was calm again.

In the warmth of the cottage, the lovers, their glowing bodies entwined, sank immediately into a deep slumber.

CHAPTER TWENTY-EIGHT

Red Sails In The Sunset

"My, aren't we blooming!" Molly, mindful of the proximity of the ward sister, offered this compliment discreetly to Audrey as they neared each other in the corridor.

"Had a good weekend I take it?"
There was a twinkle in her eye as she stopped and pretended to adjust the wheel of her laundry trolley.

Audrey, a stack of bandages in her arms paused and smiled broadly. "You could say that."

"I must say," hissed Molly, "you do look like a cat that got more than the cream."
Audrey blushed. "Moll," she whispered, "it was wonderful, or should I say he was wonderful. I would so like you to meet him.
Molly's face lit up. "Right, bring him round to the house tonight, and I'll give him the once over."

"Whatever do you...?" said Audrey slightly alarmed.

"Have a look at him that's all," reassured Molly. "I won't touch, I promise, well not unless he..." she tailed off with an arch grin.

"Get away with you!" Audrey laughed and pulled at Molly's cap.

"Oh oh, look out," warned Molly, seeing the sister approaching, "Hitler-in-Knickers second in command."

"Nurse Stephenson!" boomed the sister. "Come along with those bandages, on the double now!"

"Yes sister," called Audrey.

"Tonight at eight, my house" hissed Molly as they parted.
"You and lover boy, can you both make it?"

"I'm not sure if Martin can, I'll send him a message, it all depends on his C.O..."

"Nurse, how many more times!"

"Sorry, coming sister..."

At ten minutes past seven Audrey ran from the hospital to the nurses' home, changed out of her uniform and into civvies, then hurried outside to the steps. She looked at her watch. It was now twenty past seven and almost dark.

Suddenly she felt something snake around her waist and grip her tight. As she let out a scream a hand came over her mouth.

"Hey, don't wake the neighbourhood now."

"Martin, oh my goodness you scared me!" Audrey panted, turning round to face him.

Bringing his hands up to her cheeks he kissed her softly on the mouth. "I'm sorry honey, that was a foolish thing to have done. I should have known you'd be frightened. I was just being playful – and goddam stupid as usual." He shook his head, clicking his tongue in disapproval at himself.

"Oh no it's all right," said Audrey, still a little breathless. She squeezed his hands affectionately. "It's just that one hears stories, about things happening to girls in the blackout..."

"Of course, I'm sorry."

"I didn't hear you coming, how did you manage to sneak up on me so silently?"

"We're taught all the arts of warfare, even us simple airmen. And I've been stalking jackrabbits since I was knee high to a racoon," he mused in his lazy Southern drawl. "Or was that the other way round now, I quite forget."

They both laughed. "Do I look like a jackrabbit?" asked Audrey.

"I never saw one this pretty, that's for sure."

She squeezed his hands again. "I'm glad you got my message, come on, let's find a bus, Moll's simply dying to meet you."

They began walking. Martin said, "On the way, could we get some fish and chips?"

"Don't they feed you on that base?"

"Joey said he and the girls went to the coast last weekend and they had English fish and chips, and they were just the best thing ever, food from the gods he said. Mimsy said the King of England eats fish and chips in Buckingham Palace all the time."

Audrey laughed. "Did she?"

"Off a silver plate, so she said. Would that be true honey?"

"Oh, absolutely – oh look there's our bus, come on Martin, run..."

"What kept you?" beamed Molly opening the door.

"Hello Moll," said Audrey, "we brought you some supper. Martin insisted – Martin this is Molly, Molly, Martin."

Martin removed his beret and leaned forward to give Molly a peck on the cheek.

"I've heard a lot about you Molly," he smiled. "Here, with our compliments," he thrust a bulging paper parcel into her hands. "Please."

"Ooh, still hot," said Molly, "thanks ever so, love. Come in the pair of you."

She ushered them into the little living room. "Sit yourselves down. Well its nice to meet you Martin, I've heard a lot about you too. We've never had a real live American in our house."

"Really?" said Martin, plunging into the armchair and stretching out his long legs towards the open fire. "What kind have you had?"

"Oh get away," grinned Audrey. "Eh, I tell you someone we have got – Bing Crosby, only on a gramophone record of course, Red Sails in the Sunset."

"I love Bing!" exclaimed Martin. "And I love your home, it's so…homely."

They all laughed.

"Come and help us find some plates Aud?" Molly nodded towards the kitchen and Audrey followed her out.

"Well?" asked Audrey in a hushed, excited tone.

"Well what?" replied Molly clattering in the kitchen cupboard.

"What do you think of him?"

"Don't be daft Aud, he's gorgeous." She set three plates on the table.

"Do you think so, really?"

"Really - tall and dark and handsome as Prince Charming, and a real Southern gent too."

Audrey sighed. "I'm lucky aren't I? I can't believe he's all mine – at least I hope he is."

Molly took her friend's arm. "He's sold on you, love, you've only got to look at the two of you together to see that. Come on, let's feed our faces, I'm starved."

As the three of them tucked into their supper Audrey asked, "Are they as good as Joey told you Martin?"

"Hmm, better," Martin, mumbled though a mouthful of fish and chips. "Only he said that Mims said, the proper way for ordinary English people to eat them was out of the newspaper. Why don't you do that Molly?"

"Cos'she's dead posh," smirked Audrey, imitating Molly's accent.

Molly aimed a chip at her friend. "No actually we take the newspaper off so we can read the news. It tends to be a few months old, but you catch up."

"Oh right, yeah," said Martin still munching. "After we got the fish and chips tonight, I saw something on the wrapper about Mr Churchill, and what he said about fighting the enemy on the beaches."

"And in the hills," rejoined Audrey.

"And on the landing strips," added Molly.

"I couldn't see the landing strips," said Martin.

"Why not?" asked Audrey

"There was this grease stain on the newspaper."

Audrey and Molly laughed.

"And another thing," continued Martin, his brow wrinkling with earnest curiosity, "Molly, people have been telling me that the King of England's favourite dish is fish and chips, and that he and his family always eat it off silver plates. Now is this true, or is everyone having a joke with me?"

With a deadpan expression Molly replied, "Of course. That's why the Royal Family never have the foggiest idea what's going on in the world."

"Really?" Martin gawped at her.

"No newspapers."

"Ah." Martin pursed his lips, then seeing the amusement on the girls" faces broke into a sheepish smile. "I guess I'm going to take a little while to get used to your English sense of humour now aren't I."

"Sorry love," said Molly. "I don't mean to tease. I'm always doing it to Audrey, but she's getting wise now. Let me find you a beer to make up?"

"That'd be more than adequate Miss Molly."

"Brown ale all right?"

"More than."

"Actually," said Molly, turning back at the kitchen door, "the Royals only use silver plates for their fish and chips on state occasions. My mother says we ought to have silverware too, cause our house is more than occasionally in a state."

Martin picked his teeth thoughtfully for a moment; then said, "Would that mean in a state like, the State of Tennessee for instance?"

Molly and Audrey stifled a fit of giggles.

Molly found Martin a glass of brown ale and a gin and it for her and Audrey then went over to the gramophone. The mellow voice of Bing Crosby floated into the room.

"Aren't I the lucky one," she said, raising her glass, "two Americans in my house – in one night."

"And I've got," smiled Audrey wrapping her arms affectionately around Martin's neck and pressing her nose to his, "the real live one."

Martin rose from the chair and took her in his arms. As the music swelled, filling the tiny living room, slowly, tenderly, cheek-to-cheek, they began to dance.

Molly remained seated and watched them in silence. Very soon she had tears in her eyes.

Red sails in the sunset, so far away,
Carry my loved one, home safely today,
She sailed at the dawning, all day I've been blue,
Red sails in the sunset, I'm counting on you.

"Thank you Mrs Stephenson for a wonderful tea once again," sad Martin, shaking Clarissa's hand. He turned to Marcus. "And thank you sir for showing me your garden, it's beautiful."

"A pleasure young man," replied Marcus. "We don't have the wide, open spaces of your homeland I'm afraid. Our cities grow ever more crowded, and thus our gardens more valued as a haven of nature."

"My brother is in America," said Clarissa suddenly in a strained, faraway voice, "though of course no one is quite sure where he is. Isn't that strange? That's English families for you I suppose, and the English character, or lack of it in some – who judge others in absentia on the back of hearsay and gossip. One day they'll all know the truth, oh yes, mark my words."

"The truth Mrs Stevenson?" enquired Martin politely.

Marcus coughed loudly and took Martin's arm.

"Listen," he said briskly, "has Audrey taken you to see the sunset yet?"

"No Daddy, I haven't," said Audrey. "Should I do you think?"

"I suggest you both go now," said Marcus heartily, bundling the two of them into the hall. "You'll be just in time."

"What was that all about?" asked Martin as they walked arm in arm down the path that led to the beach.

"Oh, about my Uncle John," replied Audrey. "The skeleton in the family closet, some say. Not mother of course, she's very touchy on the subject. One never knows what will set her off."

"Is it true he is in America?"

"He's thought to be, but no one really knows where he is."

"And what exactly is he supposed to have done that's so awful?"

"Something quite dreadful actually."

"Like what - Fraud, theft, adultery?"

Audrey stopped on the path and turned towards him, her face serious yet composed.

"Murder! - Martin I must tell you this now because you'll probably hear it from someone else round here. You said you'd already heard rumours."

"I'm listening honey."

"Before the war, several years ago in fact, my Uncle John, my mother's brother married my paternal grandmother Constance."

"Your dad's mum."

"Right, she was a widow, he was much younger - it caused a bit of a scandal apparently."

"Sure."

"Then one day, up at Braeside, the house our family once owned in Scotland, two bodies were found. One was a woman, a local barmaid whom my Uncle John was thought to have been having an affair with, she had been shot."

"And the other?" asked Martin.

"A man drowned in the Loch. He was my other Uncle, my father's brother Mackenzie. He'd been paralysed some years earlier, and was in a wheelchair."

Martin gave a long low whistle.

"Wow, your poor dad, to lose his brother like that, and your grandma her son." He shook his head and stared at the ground. "And the finger was obviously pointed at Uncle Johnny right?"

"Right," said Audrey. "But as I say, I don't believe anything was ever proved."

"So that's why he skipped the country?"

"The police were on his trail, everyone pointed the finger as you say, and I suppose he was frightened. They say my poor grandmother always believed in his innocence, and in the end it drove her insane."

"She's dead right?"

"She fell from the turret room at Braeside, landed fifty feet below on the flagstone terrace. Some say she threw herself out because...because..." Audrey's voice had become querulous, her face puckered with distress.

"Because what?" asked Martin, taking her hand.

"Because my parents had locked her in there."

"Oh my Lord," breathed Martin. "But that can't be true right? Or if it was they'd have done it to protect her maybe?"

"I don't know Martin." She blinked away a tear and cleared her throat. "I don't even know which bits of the story are true. But as I've grown up it's been like a dark shadow in the background, always hanging over us. Then when we lost dear James. For a while Mummy and Daddy seemed to pull together more, there was real love. But then Mummy after a while started blaming my father for what happened, not openly, but hints, comments, you know the sort of thing.

And the stuff about Uncle John surfaced again – my mother staring into the distance and talking about wishing she'd gone off with us and left my father behind, while he poor soul tries to ignore her and laugh it all off to keep everyone happy.

Except that the cloud, the shadow won't go away by laughing at it. The past is haunting our family Martin, and as I get older, the strange thing is it seems to be moving closer."

"The sins of the fathers," intoned Martin.

"What?"

"The sins of the fathers shall be visited on the children."

"It's exactly like that!" exclaimed Audrey, "except that we don't know for sure if there were any sins, or if there were, who actually committed them. If only I could somehow find out the truth. I'd give anything to know for sure what happened all those years ago. It might then lay these ghosts once and for all and perhaps give my mother peace, and Daddy too."

"Or the reverse," said Martin quietly.

"How do you mean?"

"Have you heard of Pandora's box?"

"You think I have a fatal curiosity," asked Audrey, "that my world might turn to darkness if I open the lid on the past?"

Martin shrugged. "I can't say, I just think be careful honey, that's all."

"There's darkness already, which I'd like to banish." Audrey threw her arms in a dramatic gesture towards the sky, "to let in the light, let it stream in and put an end to the dark shadows for evermore!"

She turned to him and kissed his cheek fondly. "But you make everything beautiful and bright for me darling, you've transformed my world, and I should thank God I have you. I do have you don't I?"

She looked up into his blue eyes, light and clear as a summer sky.

"I'm here honey," he murmured, pulling her to him and kissing her again. "And that's where I'm staying, every minute I'm allowed."

Audrey smiled and held him tight, gazing out towards the white-flecked sea just visible over the horizon.

"You're right I know, and perhaps it's best not to meddle, but oh – I'd give anything to meet Uncle John, just to see what sort of a man he really is. I don't remember him, I was a baby at the time, and had no idea any of this was happening. I've only learned bits and pieces over the years – comments from my parents, people at school and overhearing neighbours talk – and then Jack."

"Jack?" said Martin.

Audrey smiled excitedly. "Of course you've not met Jack have you? Well come on darling let's go find him now." She pulled his arm eagerly, leading him off at a trot along the path. By now they could hear the sound of the waves crashing on the beach, mingling with the cry of the gulls overhead.

"The sunset is near," she shouted into the wind, "and I think that tonight it is going to be the most beautiful we have seen, because we'll be seeing it together Martin, you and me, come my darling, come!"

As they raced together over the sand dunes, Audrey waved to Jack, who was already sat on a rock near the water's edge, watching the sun dip slowly towards the sea.

From high up in the cliffs, perched on a grassy knoll, a lone seagull fixed its curious gaze on the distant figures, observing as the old man rose, embraced the girl and took the young man's hand.
The gull spread its wings and took to the air, soaring high above the sea, it's gimlet eye trained all the while on the trio of humans. As the wind changed, the bird wheeled, turned and like a bolt of lightning plummeted down towards the sparkling ocean.

Martin, transfixed by the magnificence of the red and gold fires of the setting sun, gave a brief shudder as, for a split second, a dark shadow cast itself across the three of them and then was gone.

"Are you all right son?" Jack enquired solicitously. He had observed the look on the young boy's face, just at the moment the sun had gone down.

As the three of them made their way up the beach to the dunes, Martin now looked pale and thoughtful.

"No, no I'm fine," he replied. He turned to look back at the horizon. Wisps of inky black cloud were gathering in the sky.

"It felt so strange there for a moment," he said, 'so beautiful, yet strange. What do they call it – like someone walking on your grave?"

Audrey took his arm. "You shouldn't say things like that."
"Sorry, it was just…"

"It was the sunset lad," said Jack. "I should have warned you. The sunset here is like nowhere else. It lifts your heart like the singing of a heavenly choir - it's like...like the creation of the world itself, in all its divine and infinite beauty. Creation and..." he paused for a moment then said more quietly. "The sunset you see can bring shadows too." He stopped and looked down.

"Jack - " Audrey gazed at him, her face pensive, concerned.
The old man drew himself up again and stared out towards the darkening sea. "Once you have looked upon that there sunset," he declaimed, "you're never the same again. It burns itself into your memory, into your soul, and then it has you. From now on a part of you will always remain here, on these sands, for all eternity."
Listening to him, Martin shivered again.

"Forgive me son," said Jack shaking his head, "forgive the ramblings of a foolish old seaman."

"I don't think you're foolish sir," said Martin. "I felt that exactly, what you said. I feel it now."

"Come on," pleaded Audrey, "let's go, it is getting cold now."

"Yes, yes, come up to the hut both of you," said Jack jovially, slapping his strong, leathery hand on Martin's shoulder.
"We'll light the lantern, put on the old oil stove and pour a drop of rum that'll warm your heart like toast lad. And I've a round of cheese that needs eating, and a tin of old ships biscuits, a mite hard, but like Ambrosia when you soak them in a little milk. And then you'll hear some stories lad. Audrey, did I ever tell you about the time in the South China seas, when we ran across the ghost ship? Well, one dark night there was a storm blowing up, and the Captain says to me, Jack, he says...."

As the old man, already lost in his tale led them back, Martin stopped and turned towards Audrey. Putting his arm around her he said. "You told me Jack was a soldier in the first war?"
Audrey nodded, "He was, he likes to tell these tales, maybe he wished he had been a sailor."
Martin smiled and held her even closer.

"Actually, between ourselves," he whispered, "I have no idea what Jack meant about the shadows."

"Really?" she replied.

Martin shook his head. "I'm from Carolina, remember. It's the English climate makes me shiver." He blew loudly through his lips, making her laugh. "And what is Ambrosia?"

"I have no idea!" confessed Audrey, and they both laughed.
Martin then looked at her earnestly.

"For me," he said kissing her forehead tenderly, "the sunset can only be beautiful, as beautiful as the sunrise. Want to know why?"
She looked at him.

"Because," he said softly, "I have you my darling, and that makes everything perfect, even a thunderstorm is perfect because I have you."

"A thunderstorm, truly?" asked Audrey.

"Truly."
Placing his lips on hers, he kissed her passionately.

At that moment there was a low rumble in the sky. The rumble came again, more loudly, followed seconds later by a sharp crack as the beach was illuminated in a flash of lightning, the heavens opened, and rain began lashing down on them in great torrents. Martin quickly put his coat over her.

"Did Jack say something about rum?" he shouted above the thunder.

"Yes!" Audrey shouted back.

"Then what are we waiting for?"
Hand in hand, the lovers ran, stumbling, laughing, dancing with excitement, across the storm swept dunes, towards the friendly, glowing light of the old hut.

CHAPTER TWENTY-NINE

Appointment at the Northwestern Hotel

The first thing Audrey noticed as she mounted the steps and entered the foyer of the Northwestern Hotel, in Lime Street Liverpool, was the Christmas tree.

Stopping on the plush, carpeted floor, oblivious to the porters and guests bustling around her, she stood transfixed in wonder at the tall tree, its profusion of lush, green branches, the perfectly arranged confection of gleaming silver and gold baubles and tinsel and lights.

"Can I help you madam?" said a dour voice.

Audrey started. A smartly attired man with a managerial air was looking at her enquiringly.

Slightly flustered she replied, "Oh...I was just um, admiring your wonderful tree."

The manager gave a little bow. "It has attracted much favourable comment madam." He looked at her closely over his half moon glasses. "May I ask, have we had the pleasure of your company at the Northwestern previously madam?"

Audrey hesitated. "No," she said turning her head away.

When the manager showed no sign of departing, she continued awkwardly, "The Christmas tree...um...is it an English fir?"

"We were fortunate to have the tree donated madam, from the United States."

"Oh."

"A kind gesture from a philanthropic foundation, that supports many worthy causes all over the British Isles, Liverpool being one of them. Our guests are invited to contribute to the work of the foundation." He pointed to a tin, marked 'Donations' placed near the Christmas tree.

"Oh yes, yes of course," said Audrey, fumbling in her handbag for a coin. "What's the name of the foundation?" she asked. The manager pointed to a poster.

"The Regent Trust, madam,"

Audrey looked thoughtful. "Where have I heard that name before?"

"The foundation began in America in the 1920's to help the homeless and expanded to London. A very worthwhile cause it is and proved its worth in the bombings. I daresay you'll be hearing a lot more of it though; the founder wants to bring the Trust to Liverpool. He has great plans for the city."

"When is all this taking place?"

"The sooner the better; the Luftwaffe didn't spare us either." Audrey sighed

"Have you a reservation madam?"

"Reservation? Well I um actually no…I was going to take tea in the lounge."

The manager breathed in. "Then forgive me madam, but our facilities have no provision for, how shall we say, unaccompanied ladies."

"I'm waiting for someone," said Audrey quickly.

The manager narrowed his eyes. "May I ask whom madam?"

"Yes, I'm waiting for…um…"

"Her husband of course!"

Audrey spun round to see Martin, a greatcoat over his arm and dressed in an elegant blue suit.

"And he's late as usual," continued Martin, giving Audrey a peck on the cheek. "Hi honey, sorry about the hold-up. How're you doing buddy?" He shook the manager's hand vigorously. "Love your tree by the way, isn't the tree a picture honey?"

"Yes…" said Audrey shakily, staring at Martin. "We were just talking about…"

"Say feller can we get in our room, my wife's tired, aren't you honey? We both need a hot bath pronto. The name's Corbett – Mr and Mrs Corbett, we're all booked in you'll find." Smiling at the manager, he squeezed Audrey's arm tightly.

For a second the manager's eyes narrowed again. With a blank faced expression he gestured towards the desk. "Very good sir," he said, "If you'd just like to come over sign the register both of you."

Martin signed his name with a flourish and handed the pen to Audrey, giving her arm another squeeze.

Audrey leaned forward, made a squiggle on the page and turned away. The manager peered closely at the entry.

"My darling wife's still getting used to the Corbett part" Martin patted Audrey's hand and gave the manager another broad smile. "We've not been married long. Could you send our case up? We only have the one, we share everything, don't we honey? Thank you so much."

The manager signalled to a porter, and a few moments later Martin and Audrey were being ushered into a double room on the third floor. Martin tipped the porter, ensured the door was closed then turned and took her in his arms.

Audrey, who had remained tight-lipped and nervous in the presence of the porter now exclaimed, "Martin, whatever is going on?"

"I would have thought it was obvious darling." He spread his arm out, gesturing at the spacious room.

"I thought we were meeting for tea in the lounge."

"Darling it's Christmas, and I wanted to make it special. They only had this one double room left when I booked. You do like it don't you?"

Audrey sat on the bed and took off her hat.

"Oh darling of course, it's marvellous." She breathed out a long sigh and shook out her hair, the tension in her shoulders dropping away. She smiled at him fondly and held out her hands. "It was just a bit of a surprise that's all."

He took her hands and sat beside her. "That was rather the idea."

She leaned her head against him then sat up suddenly.

"Oh but I haven't got any clothes, any night... things...I mean..."

Martin patted his suitcase. "All taken care of. I had a word with Joe, who had a word with Mims, who was on shift at the hospital last night and took a look in your quarters. She picked out your favourite dress, apparently, and um...other things. I hope you don't mind? "

Audrey's mouth had fallen open slightly.

"Oh Martin you're, you're – incorrigible, and so is Mims – wait till I see her!

"Not angry?"

She paused, looking into his blue eyes for a moment then said, "Angry? This is the best Christmas present I could have wished for, thank you."

Martin kissed her tenderly.

"Oh but I feel in such a whirl, downstairs waiting for you, and the manager looking at me as if I were some…"

"Scarlet woman?" said Martin

"Exactly! I do hope he didn't remember my face."

"Why would he?"

"I've had lunch here with my family before the war and I'm pretty sure the manager knows Daddy, certainly by reputation. Oh Martin, suppose he tells someone?"

"Tells what? That you stayed in the hotel?"
Audrey looked suddenly anxious again. "Martin, you know what I mean, that I stayed here with you – as Mrs Martin Corbett."
Martin got up from the bed. "Well I'm sorry about that honey."

"Goodness don't be sorry," said Audrey, "I didn't mean that – if it means we can be together tonight…"
Martin rubbed a hand over his neck and walked to the window. With his back to her, he said, "Thing is I've got something to tell you, two things actually."

"What?" asked Audrey, still seated on the bed.

"I'm going away."
Audrey put a hand to her face. "Away?" she said tremulously. "When, where?"

"Tomorrow night," replied Martin quietly, still facing the window. "Of course, I can't say where to."

"Oh Martin…"

"Which is why I wanted to make this special, our last night…"

"No…!" Audrey gasped, and looked about to cry.

"Whoa, whoa honey, I meant our last night before Christmas, before I go on operation." He turned to her now, and stood in the centre of the room, clasped his hands in front of him.

"You look like you're going to make a speech," spluttered Audrey, her voice now teetering on the edge of tears.

"I am, kind of," he replied.

"So what was the other thing you had to tell me?" said Audrey very quietly, her eyes now moistening.

"That you won't have to worry about that name signing thing again, as Mrs Corbett. "Cause next time you do it; it'll be all legal and proper. At least I hope so, if you like what I'm about to say."

Audrey stared at him, her eyes widening now. "Martin," she said, struggling for breath now, "are you…"

"Yes Audrey, I'm asking if you'll do me the very great honour of becoming my wife. I love you more than words can say, and I want to make you happy for the rest of our lives together."

Audrey stared up at him. Her eyes wide, her mouth hung open.

"Oh Martin…" she cried, "Martin what can I say?"

"How about, yes?"

Now she flew to him, into his outstretched arms, which immediately enfolded her. Her tears of joy wetted his shoulder. "Yes, yes, a thousand times yes!"

"The once will be fine," he murmured, kissing her forehead, "but it's good to be reassured."

Audrey's lips met his and they kissed, tenderly at first, then as their passion mounted, more eagerly. As one they moved to the bed and lay down. The undressing was also eager, their bodies seeking one another with an urgency of desire that could not wait.

After they had made love, they lay together in silence under the sheets. Audrey's head rested on Martin's shoulder. Her eyes were open, yet restful, calm, her face expressing nothing but perfect repose. It was Martin who spoke first. "I've got an apology to make Darling."

Audrey moved her head a fraction. "What?"

"Well two apologies in fact," he said quietly. "One, a matter of protocol – I didn't ask your father first, for your hand in marriage I mean. I wouldn't want him to be offended."

This made Audrey smile. "That's so thoughtful of you," she said kissing his shoulder. "You can always do that later. We won't tell him about tonight of course."

Martin frowned. "Supposing he says no?"

Audrey smiled even wider. "He thinks you're pretty wonderful – you needn't worry. What was the other thing – that you wanted to apologise for?"

"I have no engagement ring to give you – I feel bad about that."

"Oh don't be silly Martin."

"It would be a token, a kind of proof about my intentions."

"You think I need proof? Oh Martin you're so sweet and…and old fashioned, in the most beautiful way. I have all the proof here in my arms. Baubles and bangles can wait. How can you afford to pay for this room and a fancy ring on an airman's pay?"

"Who's talking about fancy? In the fairy tales they always use a brass curtain ring don't they? You wouldn't mind a curtain ring right?"

Audrey smiled and gave him a playful poke with her elbow.

"Not everything's true in fairy tales."

"That's true."

They both laughed.

Suddenly Audrey sat up. "Oh Martin!"

"Is it an air raid? I didn't hear the siren."

"Don't you have to be back at the base by eleven? You'll be in the most frightful trouble…"

"Relax, Honey, I have a night pass."

Her caressed her shoulder.

"Oh then you can stay…"

"All night, that's right."

She turned to face him, "And then you'll be going – going away?" Her voice was sonorous, grave.

"We fly out tomorrow. I can't say what time. I can't say where."

Audrey was silent, still, staring out at the darkening sky through the open curtains.

Feeling her shiver, he rubbed her shoulder again. "But hell, I'll be coming back."

Audrey said quickly, "Where will we live Martin, when we get married? Here? America?"

"Wherever you like, Honey; my folks aren't rich and I'll probably leave the service after the war. Ah might become a lawyer – they say there's money in that line of work – and you get to help folks out of their problems, so yeah, I figure an attorney would make a good career, especially if we're going to raise a few kids. You'd like children wouldn't you?"

"I'd love them – oh Martin, we're going to be so happy!" She put her arms round him and held him tight."

"We are happy now Darling. But we can't live on the fruits of love alone sweetheart - would you like to go down and eat before the dining room closes?"

"Oh I hadn't thought of food – oh but can you afford it, I believe it's frightfully expensive here?"

"All paid for already. Come on – I want a romantic dinner with my fiancé – and to dance too."

Audrey nodded eagerly, and the couple dressed and made their way down to the hotel foyer.

As they passed the Christmas tree, Audrey paused to look at it. "It's so magical don't you think Darling? Like something from a storybook, those stories about long ago Christmases, where all the characters are kind and the bad ones end up repenting, and forgiving and being forgiven."

Martin smiled and stroked her arm. "Mr. Regent would like that I guess."

"Mr. Regent?"

Martin pointed to the poster. "The Regent Trust – whoever this here Mr. Regent is…"

"Mr. Oliver Regent sir – good evening Mr. and Mrs Corbett."

Audrey gave a little start.

The manager had materialised out of nowhere and was standing at their side. He gazed closely at each of them, as if trying to decipher something. "Yes sir," he continued, "I was telling your good lady wife last evening about the work of the Regent Trust. Among other enterprises there is a fund raising dinner planned for next year, to be held here at the Northwestern Hotel. We are hoping to have the very great pleasure of welcoming Mr. Oliver Regent here on that occasion. Perhaps you would be interested in applying for tickets sir? They are strictly limited of course, but those attending would have the opportunity of meeting Mr. Regent in person – a very great honour indeed if I may say so sir."

"Ahem, good evening feller," said Martin. "Yes well Mr. Regent sounds a very great and honourable guy from what you say. We'll think about that won't we Honey?"

Audrey nodded quickly then hid her face behind Martin's shoulder.

"But first we're taking dinner here this evening," said Martin.

"I think you'll find we're all booked in."

The manager bowed obsequiously. "This way sir."

The dining room was almost full as they went in. The waiter showed them to their table, which adjoined the dance floor, just a few feet from the band, which was just taking a break. Martin ordered Champagne and oysters.

"Martin this must be costing an absolute fortune," whispered Audrey, "you must let me help with the bill."

Martin raised his hand. "The US Air Force don't treat us too bad, in fact your British boys think we get paid too much. Over paid, over…"

"Yes I've heard that expression," said Audrey hastily.

After they had eaten the band struck up. An elegant chanteuse took to the rostrum.

"Oh Darling, they're playing Red Sails!" exclaimed Audrey. "We danced to it at Molly's remember?"

"I do recall, with fish and chips, the food of royalty I'm told."

"But the fact they're playing it again now, here – it must mean something."

"Must it?"

"It must be our song, don't you see?" said Audrey insistently. "And it means you're going to be safe, that the sails will carry you back to me – oh, but except it's about the sea." She looked disconsolate. "You fly a plane, you don't sail…"

"There's a reason for that," said Martin in a hushed, conspiratorial voice. He bent his head towards hers. "It's highly classified of course."

"What?" Audrey sounded intrigued.

"I get seasick. Don't ever tell."

Audrey giggled, then hiccupped. "Sorry, the Champagne."

"Mrs Corbett," would you give me the honour of this next dance."

"You shouldn't call me that, not between ourselves – not till we're married!" said Audrey, a little louder than she intended. At the next table a middle-aged lady raised her pince-nez and looked over at them. Audrey lowered her face behind the menu.

Martin leaned towards her. He whispered "Well Honey, just remember we've done a lot of things we shouldn't before we're married. Marriage is a feeling between two people, not a piece of paper, or a ring or a preacher's say-so.

170

Some might say we should have waited, that what we've done is immoral, and there's folk back home get horsewhipped and worse for such things. But I love you Audrey, and as far as I'm concerned we're already man and wife. Pardon my speaking so open on the matter, and maybe this is blasphemy, but this fine Champagne has loosened my tongue. When I come back I want to walk down the aisle with you. But right now, I want to hold you close."

He stood up. Audrey, her eyes misty with tears rose and took his arm. They took to the floor, the music swelled and slowly, tenderly, under the glittering lights they danced. - *Red Sails in the Sunset*....

It was early morning. Audrey was still slumbering. Martin, already in his uniform leaned down and kissed her gently on the cheek. "Honey, I have to go. Don't get up. I love you."

"Oh Martin, no…" Audrey lifted her head drowsily then put her arms round his neck.

"Don't go!" she slurred loudly.

"I'll be back." He pressed his cheek to hers and whispered softly in her ear. "Sooner than you think Mrs Corbett – to be."

"Hmm…how much Champagne did I drink last night?"

"They're still counting the bottles – it's going to be a long job."

Audrey gave a sleepy smile. "I feel so…tired."

"You sleep Honey, the room's ours till noon."

"Ours…hmm."

She dropped back down onto the pillow. Martin drew the sheet up to cover her.

"Martin?"

"Yes Darling?"

"You do want to marry me don't you?"

"More than words can say." He kissed her once more. "Next Christmas we'll spend together, I promise." He held her hand and she smiled up at him.

When she had closed her eyes again he picked up his kitbag and walked to the door. Turning, he gazed back fondly at her for a few seconds, then without a sound was gone.

A few moments later Audrey stirred. A familiar sound coming from the street below had stirred her to consciousness. It was an engine, loud, brash, the sound of Martin's jeep. She hauled herself from the bed and ran, almost falling over herself unsteadily to the window. She pulled back one half of the curtains, then blinked in the sudden, unusually bright light.

The scene outside was like a Christmas card, the streets and buildings covered with snow. Only a few early morning footprints pocked the soft white blanket, and on the road were two broad tracks leading away from the hotel, the tyre marks from where Martin's jeep had been parked.

Audrey gazed down, tears welling in her eyes. The snow began to fall more quickly, huge flakes filling the air, piling steadily deeper on the pavement and road. After a few minutes the tracks of the jeep had completely disappeared.

"Did he give you a ring?" asked Ivy.
They were in the nurses' staff room, having a mid morning cup of tea.

"Not yet," replied Audrey, "but he will of course. He only proposed three days ago."

"How longs it take to get a ring then? Isn't it normal to give a girl a ring when she gets engaged?" Ivy persisted, stirring her tea noisily. "Sounds a bit fishy to me."

"Don't be so cynical Ivy," interjected Mimsy. "Martin's a man of his word, you've only got to look at him."
"Oh aye, and there'll be a lot more girls doing that – looking at him, and more. Amy Bradshaw had a Yank propose to her one night, she accepted, and the next night she saw him in the pub with two WAAFS, one on each arm."

"They were just having a knees-up," said Mimsy to Audrey, who was looking downcast now.

"Is that what they call it nowadays?" said Ivy archly.

"Ivy, please!" chided Mimsy.

"Sorry Audrey love," said Ivy, "don't mind me I'm just jealous my Albert hasn't proposed yet. "I'm sure your Martin meant every word he said."
Audrey was still looking despondent when the door of the staff room opened and the Matron looked in.

"Nurse Stephenson?"

Audrey started guiltily, almost spilling her tea. "Yes Matron?""

"There's someone on the telephone for you."

The Matron's manner was curt as she led Audrey to her office. "Hurry along and please be brief, we don't encourage personal calls to the hospital as you know."

Audrey took the receiver. "Sorry Matron, I've no idea who..."

"My sweet English Rose."

"Martin!"

The matron gave her a disapproving glance then turned her attention to the filing cabinet.

"Martin where are you?" her voice was trembling. "Sorry, I know you can't say..."

"I can say I love you."

Audrey glanced quickly towards the Matron, whose face was obscured by the open drawers of the filing cabinet.

"I love you too," she breathed, cupping her hands round the mouthpiece.

"Did you get the parcel?"

"What parcel?"

"Miss A. Stephenson?"

Audrey spun round. Clive the hospital porter had just knocked and entered the office. He was holding out a small brown paper package bearing her name.

"Thank you Clive – Clive's just given me a parcel as a matter of fact, the address is in your handwriting ..."

"Who's Clive?"

"The porter."

"Hey now that's what I call efficiency, they told me the deliveries are sent round about this time," said Martin.

"But what is it Martin, is it a surprise – should I open it now."

"If you like."

Audrey laid the receiver down on the desk and with her two hands tore open the package. Inside was a small box. Opening the lid she gasped, then picked up the receiver again. "Oh Martin..."

"I'm sorry - it was the best curtain ring I could find."

"It's beautiful..."

"Not as beautiful as you; that's the engagement taken care of, now I have to find another curtain for the wedding ring."

"Oh Martin! When are you coming back? I'm missing you so much."

"Likewise Honey, and I'll be with you just as soon as our job is done out here. But I think it'll be over soon enough. How do you feel about a spring wedding little lady?"

"Oh Martin, I can't wait...."

"Neither can your duties on the ward Nurse Stephenson!"
Audrey jumped. The Matron was glaring at her from behind the filing cabinet.

"No Matron, sorry...Martin, I have to go."

"I love you."

"Goodbye..."
Replacing the telephone, Audrey put the ring carefully back into its box and pushed it deep into the pocket of her uniform then hurried out of the office and back to the surgical ward.

"Slow down girl, where's the fire?" Mimsy said as Audrey came dashing in.

"Oh Mims, Mims that was him, Martin," Audrey panted. "He's sent me a ring – I'll show you later."

"I can't wait!"

"Neither can I Mimms – neither can I, in fact I'll show you now!" She took out the ring and held it up.

"Wow" said Mimsy, "those look like diamonds to me. Congratulations Aud." She called out to Ivy who was helping a patient into bed. "And Ivy takes back all she said, don't you Ivy?"
Audrey skipped over to Ivy and held the ring up, its stones flashing in the morning sunshine streaming through the window. The patient, an elderly man winked at both girls.

"Ooh, I'll say," exclaimed Ivy. "Never doubted Martin for a minute." They all laughed. "Wait till I tell my Albert – hopefully he'll buck his ideas up a bit now!"
This sparked a renewed burst of laughter. Then quite suddenly Audrey doubled over.

"Hey it wasn't that funny Aud," said Ivy. Then seeing her friend's complexion she enquired, "Are you all right love?"

"Ooh, just feel a bit queasy all of a sudden. Probably the excitement – look will you cover for me for a few minutes, I think I'm going to be..." She rushed from the ward, while Ivy and Mimsy exchanged glances.

Through the half-open door of her office, the Matron looked up to observe Audrey, her hand clutched to her stomach, running hastily into the washroom. The Matron closed her door and looked thoughtful. She carefully removed the silver chain from around her neck and opened a small locket. She gazed down at the photograph secreted within, the portrait of a young man in the British Army uniform of the First World War.

"Oh Ernest," she said softly and ran a hand across her face, touched her greying hair. "I miss you so much." Holding the portrait to her lips she kissed it tenderly. There were tears in her eyes.

After a moment or two she snapped the locket shut and fastened the chain back around her neck. Searching beneath her desk she retrieved the remains of the package that Audrey had discarded in the waste bin.

She un-crumpled the paper and examined the handwriting. On the reverse she saw there was a sender's name. The Matron reached for her telephone and lifted the receiver. "Operator? Would you get me Crosslands 53 please?" A moment later a woman's voice came on the line. "Hello, this is Clarissa Stephenson speaking - who's calling? Hello, who's calling?" repeated Clarissa's voice again over the telephone.

Without replying the Matron replaced the receiver. She rose from her desk and gazed out of the window of her office at the thin line of trees on the other side of the road.

As she looked there, in her mind's eye there appeared among the trees the feint outline of soldiers, bayonets fixed, crawling from a trench. They began running, across the mud and barbed wired of no-man's land. A crackle of machine gun fire broke out, explosions, clouds of smoke rose. Amid the chaos and confusion, some of the soldiers continued to run, others stumbled, fell. There were shouts, cries of pain.

The Matron drew the blind across the window, shutting out the scene. She closed her eyes. Clutching again at her locket, she held it tight.

CHAPTER THIRTY

A Counsel of War

December 1944

Mimsy entered the nurse's washroom. She found Audrey, bent over a sink.

"Aud…!" She hurried to her.

"Ooh – I'm all right – just the excitement like I say." She turned to her friend, her cheeks pale, attempting a smile.

"You been sick?"

Audrey nodded. "Only a bit."

"How long has it been like this?"

"Like what?" Audrey was washing her face noisily.

"The morning sickness."

"I don't know what you're talking about," said Audrey loudly over the running water. "It's nearly ten."

Mimsy reached out and turned off the tap.

"I come from a big family Aud. I've seen a lot. I think we need to have a talk."

"Thank you," said the doctor, removing his stethoscope. "You may come back over and take a seat now please."

He crossed to his desk and studied some notes on a file. Audrey, who had been lying on the consulting room couch, got up, tidied her clothing and sat opposite him. The doctor looked up from his notes and peered at her closely over his half-moon glasses. "I see you live in the nurse's quarters at the Wetherton." Audrey nodded. "And you came all the way over to Jericho Road to see a doctor?"

"Oh, you know how people talk – I didn't want anyone at the hospital to think I might be unwell, I want to keep my job, I'm sure you understand. I've a friend lives nearby here," said Audrey hastily. "I was seeing her today too, so it was convenient."

"What I'm about to tell you might not be quite so convenient. I see you're not married?" He looked at her hands.

"I'm engaged," said Audrey proudly. "I've got an engagement ring, it needs adjusting."

"It's not all that'll need adjusting."

"You were going to tell me something doctor – am I ill?"

176

"Not at all, you're in perfect health." He answered

"I knew it, what a relief! I told Mims it was just excitement. You see I'm getting married when my fiancé comes back, he's in the US Air Force...I'm sorry - you said something would be inconvenient? Oh goodness, you're not going to say I can't have children are you? I know some women are unfortunate that way..."

"No, there's certainly no problem on that score."

"Thank goodness."

"In fact, assuming nothing goes wrong I would say you're going to have your first child in approximately six months time."

"She can't just do nothing," said Molly.

Molly, Audrey, Ivy and Mimsy were gathered in the living room at Jericho Road. Janet was on a late shift. Molly was looking at Audrey with a mixture of sternness and concern.

"Exactly, you have to make some decisions Audrey love," said Ivy.

"So what are the choices?" Molly asked

Ivy leaned towards them conspiratorially. "My cousin said gin worked wonders when she was in Queer Street." Then whispering she added, "and my Auntie Rose knows a feller who can sort women out – a sort of a doctor – he charges a few quid, but I'm sure Aud can tap her old man, tell him its to help a poor widow or summat..."

"I'll pretend I didn't hear any of that Ivy," Mimsy interrupted her.

"I was just saying," protested Ivy, "we can't rule anything out..."

"The one thing you all seem to be ruling out, is me!" said Audrey suddenly, having till now been sitting, silently looking down at the carpet. There followed a deathly hush as all eyes turned to her.

"Aud," began Ivy, "I'm sorry pet..."

"It's all right," said Audrey in a quieter voice. "I'm sure you all mean well, but I must admit I'm rather confused by your attitude. This has just been such a… surprise, I don't know whether I'm coming or going, and my head's spinning so fast I think it might fall off if I don't try to think calmly and not panic – which I wasn't till you all started making me feel like something disastrous had happened. When I told you my news, what the doctor had said, and you asked me to come here tonight I thought you wanted to congratulate me, not talk about me as if were, I don't know…an unexploded bomb that had got to be defused!"

Ivy quickly stifled a snort of amusement and joined in a general murmur of apology and nodding.

"We're here for you Aud," said Molly gently, "whatever you decide to do." They all nodded again in agreement.

"I don't see there's anything to decide," replied Audrey. "You see, you've all been thinking of this – my situation – the baby - as a problem."

"Well it is…" began Ivy. Molly shot her a silencing look.

Audrey continued calmly. "Why should that be so? The way I see it, this is a most wonderful thing that has happened. This baby is mine, and Martin's, my husband-to- be. I simply cannot wait to tell him, I intend to write to him tomorrow. He'll be overjoyed I know it."

The others exchanged glances.

"When is he due back then Aud?" asked Mimsy.

"He can't say for sure, but he promised we'd have a spring wedding – and think, we'll have a son or a daughter too!" She was beaming now.

"From what I know of Martin, I think you're right Aud," said Molly encouragingly. "Its not him, its….."

"What Moll's trying to say is, we don't want to throw a spanner in the works," said Ivy, "but there's the little matter of your parents, and then how are you going to manage till then? If Martin isn't back till after the baby's born, I mean, where are you going to stay and what-not?"

"We'll find a little house together afterwards. And till then I'll stay at home in Crosslands of course," said Audrey airily. "My parents will be only too pleased."

"So…when did you plan on telling them about the baby Aud?"

"Straight away naturally," said Audrey folding her arms.

"You - think they'll be alright about it, knowing it's out of wedlock and all?" asked Mimsy tentatively. "Your Dad's a sweetheart, and I know your mother's been through a lot, they both have, but think for a minute Aud - do you really believe she'll take this in her stride?"

Audrey looked thoughtful for a moment then said, "Daddy's often talked about how nice it would be to have grandchildren. They might be a little disappointed I suppose, not to have things the other way around – I mean the wedding first – but they'll understand I'm sure."

"They'll understand, oh that's good." Ivy said, raising her eyebrows discreetly at the other girls.

"Yes, they'll understand," repeated Audrey, her eyes shining fervently.

"What?" Marcus shut the drawing room door quickly then sat down again. Audrey was on the couch. They were alone.

"I'm going to have a baby," Audrey repeated.

"But why, how...?"

"Martin..."

"Yes I realise that, but – oh Audrey how could you be so foolish! And we assumed Martin was a gentleman." He got up again and began pacing, running one hand distractedly through his hair

"I realise it's a shock Daddy..."

"A shock! That's an understatement!"

"But Martin and I are going to be married, he proposed. His engagement ring is a little too small, I think my hands have swollen, the work at the Wetherton, the carbolic Mims says..."

"Audrey will you shut up! Oh I'm sorry my darling!" He came over to her, wrapped his arms around her. "I'm sorry Audrey, we've always loved you - you know that, but I...I just don't know what to say to you. I mean, what do you want me to say to you?"

"That you're pleased?" said Audrey quietly. She gave a little snuffle and took out her handkerchief.

"Pleased! oh." Marcus gasped the word, as if he were about to suffocate. He sat with his head bowed for a moment in silence. Then turning to his daughter he took her hands in his.

"Audrey, do you know what? I am pleased...I would be pleased, at the idea of a grandchild..."

179

"You often said how much you wanted one," said Audrey meekly.

"Yes, but not a…!" Marcus's face contorted, complex emotions almost visibly wrestling with one another while he sought to control them, to find some way of dealing with the situation with which his daughter had confronted him.

"We must tell your mother," he said at last. "I must tell your mother."

"Yes Daddy of course."

"Then we'll have to figure out what to do."

"What do you mean Daddy – what to do?"

Marcus attempted to speak, but could not. Instead he got up and left the room. Audrey sat in silence. Approximately two minutes later he returned. Clarissa was with him. She did not sit down but stood by the door. She fixed her daughter with a heavy stare.

In a low modulated voice, she said, "Audrey your father has just informed me of what you have told him. May I first ask why you saw fit to disclose this first to him, alone, and not the two of us, together?"

Marcus shot a look at Audrey then his wife. Again he seemed about to speak but did not.

"It is an irrelevance I suppose," continued Clarissa. "The crime that you two irresponsible young people have committed remains the same, as sordid and regrettable no matter who hears it first."

"What do you mean by that?" exclaimed Audrey, her mouth dropping open in dismay. "If you must know Mother, Martin…"
Clarissa held up her hand. "I have little desire to hear the details, or any attempt at an explanation, excuse or heaven forbid, justification. Knowing of your 'modern' views I would expect the latter to be already well formed in your immature, and ill-formed mind."

Marcus sat down, then stood again, turning this way and that and looking at his wife and daughter in turn. He appeared to be in a state of some agitation. Audrey meanwhile still looked incredulously at her mother.

Clarissa went on, "There is little point in dwelling on the circumstances that created this problem. The task now is to solve it. Marcus, I suggest that at an appropriate time, Audrey is removed to a private sanatorium in the countryside, some place at a suitable distance from our home. Nature will take its course, and an agency for the adoption of unwanted infants will be charged to take care of the matter from thereon. Audrey can then return here if she wishes, or resume her position at the Wetherton Hospital. The choice will be hers, and afterwards we will not speak of this matter, or the young man in question again." She looked at Audrey, then at Marcus. "Well?"

Marcus cleared his throat and looked nervously at his daughter.

"Well, Audrey?" he asked.

Audrey stared at him, then at her mother.

"I can't believe what you've just said!" she exclaimed, this is my baby, mine and Martin's, your grandchild Mother...."

"There is no point becoming emotional about this Audrey," interrupted Clarissa. "There has clearly already been too much emotion altogether and a complete absence of forethought, and morality."

"How dare you lecture me..." began Audrey again.

"How dare you!" rejoined her mother in a voice like thunder. "How dare you betray the trust and care we have invested in you, by seeking to abuse us in this unspeakable, this unforgivable way Audrey! It is heinous enough that you burden us with your shame. If you have any shred of decency in you, you will not now seek to question our judgment, and the assistance we are generously prepared to offer to extricate you from the quagmire of sin in which you have so willfully steeped yourself."

Audrey got to her feet. Facing her mother, her voice trembling with emotion she said, "I came to Daddy first because I feared in my heart that you would judge me. I see I was right. But I do not accept your judgement Mother. I hoped for understanding from you, for tolerance, for love, yes love. Instead I have received condemnation. You speak of morality and standards, yet there are far more questionable acts in the history of our family than the things I stand accused of by you – which is merely to love a man and now to want to bring his child into the world."

"Be careful what you say Audrey," said Clarissa sharply.

"I will speak as I wish - of my Uncle John, your brother. I have overhead you seeking to defile his name, for unsubstantiated crimes. Or if he indeed committed those crimes, perhaps you were in collusion with him. I have heard talk of letters, that you have communicated with him, that you do still. Is he truly a monster then Mother, or are you both monsters? If so, then in his case at least he is no hypocrite, unlike yourself."

"Audrey I will not allow you to speak to me in this way, you will go to your room immediately."

"I have no room here Mother, and you will hear me out."

Clarissa looked to her husband. "Marcus, speak to her please."

"Audrey, please, desist now, you have said too much already," pleaded Marcus.

"I have only just begun," said Audrey warmly. "You dare to judge Martin, a man who is fighting for his country, for the whole free world against tyranny, risking his life, for us, yes you and I, just as James did. And you, you preen yourself in this horrid house, pruning the roses and ordering the servants about while pontificating about morality. And now you seek to steal my baby from me – you are wicked Mother, you are evil, do you hear me, evil…"

Clarissa was breathing hard. "You are naïve and foolish, do not compound your stupidity by insulting me in this ridiculous manner. As for Martin," she said through clenched teeth, "he has proven himself to be a thoroughly common, ignorant ne'er-do-well who deserves to be thrashed at the very least. By god I'd arrange it if I could, and far worse."

Audrey, holding her head high said, "Martin, is an officer and a gentleman." Then, in a colder voice she continued, "It is you who are truly common Mother, you are not fit to wipe his shoes."

Clarissa moved two steps forward, then like a demon she flew at her daughter, her fingernails tearing at Audrey's face. Marcus flung himself between the two writhing bodies, taking hold of his wife's shoulders, attempting to pull her away.

"Clarissa, Clarissa, this is not the way, she's overwrought - Audrey you will apologise to your mother!"

"Never!" yelled Audrey, retreating towards the door.

"It's too late for apologies," snarled Clarissa, as Marcus struggled to hold her back. "You will leave this house immediately you, you, she-devil – take whatever you need, because from this day on you will never darken our door again do you hear – your allowance will be severed forthwith, your trust fund rescinded, you'll have nothing, nothing and no-one, then see how you like it – you're on your own!"

There was deathly stillness in the room. Only the sound of Clarissa's laboured breathing broke the silence. Audrey looked at her father.

"I...think it's best if you do go," he said mutely, not looking at her.

"Very well," said Audrey. "I shall go. I realise it will be impossible to remain now." She opened the drawing room door, and pausing for a moment, looked back at her parents. "You know I feel sorry for you, for both of you. But you needn't worry about me. I won't be alone. I shall have Martin."

CHAPTER THIRTY-ONE

Outcast

The snow had turned to sleet when Audrey finally reached Jericho Road. She had just caught the last train from Crosslands then walked the rest of the way. As the sleet spotted her face she intoned her lover's name repeatedly, "Oh Martin, Martin, if only you were with me, if only you were here…"

On the corner she saw a couple eating fish and chips out of a newspaper, which made her smile briefly in spite of her misery. Arriving outside Molly's house she dropped her suitcase, knocked on the door and then sank down exhausted on the step.

"Now then, girl, it can't be as bad as all that." She looked up to see Monty, the burly dockworker on his way home from the Feathers.

"Why it's you Miss Audrey." He gazed down at her in bemusement, and at her suitcase. "What you doing here – and in such a right old state?

Audrey immediately broke into a fit of crying.

"Oh heck," he grimaced and banged on the door. "Maybe it can be as bad as all that!"

"Stop that noise!" came an irate shout as Molly flung the door open. "And what do you mean by…"

About to chastise the figure on the step she then realised with a shock it was Audrey, obviously in a state of distress. She bent down and took her arm.

"Aud," she exclaimed, "whatever's the matter? Never mind, tell me indoors. We'll get the kettle on, c'mon."

She beckoned to Monty, who picked up the suitcase, and followed the two women through the narrow hallway, his large frame brushing against the hanging coats and scarves as they made their way towards the small kitchen at the back of the house.

"Come on Aud, its nice and warm in here. She steered her friend to the armchair by the fire then pulling up one of the rickety wooden upright chairs sat next to her.

"I've left home," Audrey wailed, "left Crosslands - I mean for good."

Molly looked aghast. "How, why?"

"I had to – I told Daddy about the baby – it was a big shock, I thought it might be all right, then of course he told Mummy, and she was perfectly beastly and said I should go away and have it in secret, and then get it adopted…"

"We were all worried for you love, we thought there might be problems there," said Molly shaking her head sympathetically. "Eh, I hope you didn't agree with the old…with your mother."

"Of course not, I was horrified, but then she was even more beastly, and then I said some horrid things about her, and about our family."

Molly bit her lip and glanced across at Monty. "And then she flew into the most frightful rage – a sort of fit, Daddy had to hold her off, She ordered me to leave the house and never, ever go back, so here I…here I am…oh Moll what am I going to do…" She collapsed into her friend's arms, sobbing convulsively.

I'll tell you exactly what you're going to do," said Molly rubbing her back tenderly, "and that's stay here with me."

"Oh Moll you're so sweet but I can't, I can't…"

"Why on earth not, pray?" Molly replied. "Be company for me. Rattling round in this place all on me own – Bill's not going to move in for the foreseeable, he's too busy shooting at the Jerries."

"Wish I was with him," said Monty, "only me flat feet let me down – that's years of humping crates round the docks done that you know." He handed Audrey a cup of strong looking tea. "Get that down you girl. And give us that wet coat, before you catch your death."

"It might be a good thing if I did," Audrey lamented. "Catch my death I mean."

"Now we'll have none of that talk under this roof Audrey Stephenson." Molly leaned forward. "What would Martin say? Oh Aud – does he even know yet, about the baby I mean?"

"No, it's terrible I know but I just haven't been able to sit down and write a letter yet – I must, because it'll take a while to reach him I imagine, wherever he is. Oh and don't call me Stephenson again Moll – that family's disowned me, so I'm jolly well not going to use their name if I can help it. Besides I'll be Mrs Corbett in a few months time."

She rummaged deep in her pocket and took out Martin's engagement ring, wrapped in a handkerchief.

"I really must get this altered without delay now."

"There'll be time enough for that later on Aud. What you need right now is rest. I'll make up the spare bed and sort out your clothes in the morning."

She placed her hand affectionately on her friend's arm, then gathered up some freshly laundered sheets from the clothes maid and disappeared upstairs.

"She's a grand lass," said Monty, swilling down a mouthful of tea. "The best, most loyal friend you could wish for."

"I know Monty." She gave him a forlorn smile then began to cry. Monty looked perturbed. He stretched his huge hand towards her shoulder and patted it awkwardly, then hurried out to the hall.

"Molly, Moll...!" he called up the stairs. "Come "ere pet – this needs a woman's touch."

Molly came back down. "There, there Aud – don't fret now, I've done your bed, you can go up now if you like."

"I'll get off home now," said Monty. "Leave you ladies to it. And you keep your chin up young Audrey."

"Thanks Monty," sniffed Audrey.

When they were alone Molly turned to her friend with an earnest, eager look in her eyes. "Oh, do you know what, I think I'm as keen as you for Martin to come home Aud. I know it's going to be difficult till then, but it'll all be worth it you'll see, it'll all come right." She grasped Audrey's hand and squeezed it "And do you know what else?"

"What?" Audrey summoned a meek, inquiring smile.

"Your ma and pa are going to come round, I feel sure of it."

"What, come round here, to your house..."

"No, dopey, I mean they're going to accept you, accept the situation, the baby, Martin, everything. Once they've calmed down, thought about it all, stopped worrying about what their fancy friends will think – they'll be begging for an invite to the wedding."

Audrey looked doubtful.

"I'm not so sure Moll. I don't know that I'd want them there – not after what was said tonight – you should've seen my mother, heard her, oh, it was awful, awful." She shuddered as she recalled the scene that had taken place at Crosslands only a few hours previously.

"You're in shock Aud," said Molly, "they're in shock. When the dust settles they'll realise its not the end of the world that their unmarried daughter's got a bun – is...look the main thing to remember is, time is a great healer so the saying goes. And after all, since losing James you're all they've got. If Clarissa turns her back on you she'll be making a big mistake – cutting herself off from her daughter, a wonderful son-in-law and a beautiful grandchild. She'll end up a bitter old woman. Mark my words Aud, it'll all turn out champion – your family will come round, Martin will return in a blaze of glory, you can set the date, book the church, choose your dress, order the flowers..."

She broke off as Audrey yawned loudly and her head flopped forward. "But right now, you need to sleep. Go on, up you go."

As Audrey ascended the stairs Molly tidied the kitchen. She heard the floorboards creak as Audrey got into bed in the room above. Molly sighed. Not for one minute did she believe what she had told her friend. She knew full well Audrey's mother would never forgive or accept the situation.

And then there was Martin; she liked him, but would he really come back, or was he just another Yank, full of promises that would never be kept? Only God knew the answer to that one. Molly resolved to pray that night and, hoping with all her heart that God was listening.

CHAPTER THIRTY-TWO

"So that's the whole story Matron – more or less," said Audrey. They were in the Matron's office. "I was terrified of telling you but I thought about it, and I decided it was best to be honest, I didn't want you finding out from someone else – you know how girls talk, and I knew you'd be sure to overhear something soon. And the thing is I want to keep my job here as long as possible. I love it, and to be honest I need it desperately – I'm obviously going to have to support myself till Martin – that's my fiancé – comes home from the war, and probably afterwards too. You may have been aware I had some other income of my own, but because…of what's happened, my parents have decided to…withdraw it. I don't wish to paint them in a bad light, but there it is, I'm sure they have their reasons, and perhaps later when…when things come to pass they'll change their minds and look on my circumstances more favorably. But obviously I can't rely on that, and one can't live on fresh air. I am very fortunate in that my friend Molly has offered to accommodate me in her home, but she has very little money and I must contribute."

Matron, who had stayed silent during this speech, now took off her spectacles and looked long and hard at the girl sat nervously before her. She had turned out to be a good nurse much to her surprise and she didn't want to loose her, good nurses were hard to come by. At last, with an air of great deliberation, the Matron spoke.

"Nurse Stephenson – Audrey, sit down child," Matron said, "There are a number of things I wish to say to you, as well as certain things that I…" she paused, "that I have to say. I will begin with this. When you began your training with us here at the hospital I was apprehensive, both for you and us. Nursing is a difficult and demanding profession, which can tax the stamina of even the strongest young women. The discipline, industry and uncongenial nature of our work are aspects that do not readily appeal to girls brought up in – shall we say – comfortable surroundings. Many of our nurses here, as you will have found, come from homes that are a far cry from your own background, from families of a different class altogether.

You have however, managed to fit in admirably, and I have observed how you have made many friends here. These things are important; a good team spirit is as crucial to an efficient, caring hospital as practical skills – and the latter I am delighted to say you have mastered admirably. Other senior colleagues have also made these observations. In short Audrey, I am pleased with you, we are all pleased with you. You are credit to your chosen profession."

Carefully, meticulously, the Matron's fingers reached out to realign a thin sheaf of papers on her desk. The wall clock ticked on monotonously.

Audrey cleared her throat. "Thank you Matron," she said quietly. "I'm glad you think I've coped all right, and I did so want to do my best…" She tailed off.

The Matron made a slight, gracious nod of assent. Then shifting forward slightly in her chair, and without looking at Audrey, she began speaking again. "Now I must come to what I am obliged to say, what it is my difficult duty, to tell you."

Audrey's chair creaked as she sat up.

The hospital adheres to certain standards, both public and private. These standards are reflected throughout this institution – from its senior staff and management, to the women who work day to day on the wards. The basis of these standards lies in the Christian tenets of decency and morality. Whilst I am not unsympathetic to your predicament, it is for this reason that I am now obliged to say that your position at the hospital is – no longer sustainable."

Audrey flinched, and put her head on one side, looking at the floor.

"If the decision were mine alone, - it might be a different matter."

There was a long pause. Audrey's reply was slow, painstaking.

"Thank you Matron," she said, "for explaining everything so - thoroughly. I understand of course…except - "

"What is it my dear?" asked the Matron.

"I am to be married, Matron, when Martin returns."

"But you are at the moment an unmarried mother working on the wards. The hospital will not permit this; it will be seen as immoral and would go against what we stand for."

"But I am going to be married!" protested Audrey.

"Please do not split hairs. I have told you all you need to know." She held up her hand decisively. There was silence for a moment.

189

"Well, if there is no more you wish to say, it remains for me to wish you well – and I do wish you well Audrey, I hope you can believe me."

Her eyes appeared to glisten and dilate. Then briskly she said,

"Finally, as for the practicalities - may I ask that you move your belongings from the nurses home by the end of the week. That would be most helpful."

"I'll go today if that's alright Matron. Molly is expecting me." Audrey replied

"Jericho Road? Are you sure that's going to be…"

"Good enough for me Matron…It's perfectly acceptable. Molly's my friend – we'll be fine."

Matron smiled "Very well then Audrey, there's no more to be said and if you should ever need a reference or…anything."

Audrey nodded "Thank you Matron for all your help and understanding."

Matron took Audrey's hand in hers. "I only hope my dear, that all goes well for you" she said, genuinely meaning every word.

"It will have to Matron," Audrey replied "I don't really have a choice.

The Matron took out a handkerchief and blew her nose.

Audrey rose from her chair. "Thank you again Matron, she said, "for explaining things."

"Thank you Audrey, for all you have done for us at the hospital." She began busying herself with some papers on her desk.

At the door Audrey stopped and turned back. The Matron did not look up. "Matron can I ask you, did my mother have anything to do with this?"

For a moment matron's usual composure seemed to crack."Of course not Audrey" she replied without raising her head, "Rules are rules

Audrey gave a wry smile. "Of course Matron I understand fully." And without speaking she opened the door and slipped quietly out.

When she had gone the Matron picked up the telephone.

"Crosslands 584, please…hello Clarissa? Yes, she's gone. I hope its what you want." Replacing the receiver she turned to the window and gazed silently out at the line of distant trees. Above them the afternoon sky was already growing dark.

CHAPTER THIRTY-THREE

A Christmas To Remember

Two hours later Audrey was knocking on the door of 112 Jericho Road. Molly took a few minutes to open it. She looked surprised to see her friend.

"Audrey? What you doing here? I thought you were on a shift today?" Then her hand flew to her mouth. "Oh no, don't tell me, not the old tin tack."

Audrey looked bemused.

"The sack – down the road – the boot – not a week before Christmas?"

"Oh, yes, they've thrown me out of the Wetherton. Matron called me in as soon as I arrived on the ward today."

"Hitler-in-knickers – the old...! Oh, of all the bare faced, ungrateful...after what you've given to that hospital..." she tailed off, wringing her hands in exasperation. "How you feeling Aud?"

Audrey sniffed. "Pretty miserable actually."

"Then come on in – this is your home now after all, c'mon give us that bag. There's a pot of tea brewing."

Audrey almost collapsed into the hall. "Oh Moll," she said, half weeping, half laughing, "I do love you - there's always, always a pot of tea brewing in your house."

"It's the eleventh commandment of Jericho Road – thou shalt always have kettle on th' hob! Anyway as I say, its your house now too – and you can always stay after Bill moves in too if you like, be like a family."

"That's so sweet – I expect Martin will want to get our own place jolly soon, especially once we have our little one."

Molly looked pensive for a second then said quickly, "Of course love, yes – anyway now look, come on through." Molly led her into the kitchen and began busying herself with the cups.

Audrey flopped into a chair by the table.

"Oh when do you think this blessed war will be over Moll?"

"If I had that kind of crystal ball," said Molly wryly, "I wouldn't be slaving in that laundry – I'd be sitting in a tent at the fairground – a string of sovereigns round me head and a bucketful of pound notes under the table."

"Madame Molly," said Audrey with a smile.

Molly's eyes lit up. "Yeah – we'd be millionaires!"

"My father is a millionaire," replied Audrey, "it's not made him especially happy, not lately anyway – and certainly not my mother. No, Moll, I shouldn't want to be a millionaire. I would've been of course, if…this hadn't all happened. Now I wouldn't take their money if they begged me."

"They could try begging me instead," smirked Molly. "Don't take this the wrong way Aud, but for those that's never had nowt, even a few quid seems like the pot of gold at the end of the rainbow."

Audrey reached out and touched her friend's arm. "I know Moll, I didn't mean…"

"I know you didn't." She put two cups of tea on the table and sat down. "Now tell me, what pathetic excuse did Hitler-in-knickers come up with for giving a wonderful hard working nurse like you the sack?"

"Well, she didn't really – make excuses I mean. She was quite honest about it; said the governors" moral standards would be offended if an unmarried mother-to-be was working on the ward."

"She wants locking up – it's all the fiddlers and profiteers that want sacking, not young girls like you doing an honest job."

"She more or less said that if it was down to her, she'd keep me on. I don't blame her - I think she felt bad about it. I expected it to happen really, sooner or later."

Molly stared thoughtfully at her teacup. "Hmm, I wonder who put her up to it though?" she said.

Audrey shrugged. "I'm not going to worry about it, I've decided."

"Good for you girl!" Molly beamed and refilled the teacups. "And remember, my house is your house."

Audrey smiled gratefully. "But I'll help all I can Moll, you won't have to keep me."

"Never thought I would, but there's no need to worry about that - I've a good wage, and my savings. If nothing else this rationing's taught me how to manage – make a little go a long way." She laughed. "But listen, you mustn't even think about work, not the way things are."

"Oh but I've already got another job Moll," said Audrey brightly. I called in at the recruiting office on the way here."

"What job?" Molly looked surprised.

"In the tank factory, you know making the fuel tanks for the Wellington bombers."

Molly was aghast. "You can't do that in your condition!"

"I didn't tell them – I'm not showing yet and the money's good."

"But - when do you start?"

"A weeks time, the day after Boxing Day."

Molly looked concerned. "You just be careful Aud. There's not only you to think about now."

Audrey sighed. "I don't need reminding of that Moll," she said patiently. "It won't be for long in any case; Martin should be home soon, two months - then we'll have the spring wedding he promised me."

Molly flashed a smile. "I'll drink to that love." She drained her teacup. "Now," she announced, getting to her feet, we must get ready for Christmas."

She opened the pantry door wide. "I've been buying a little extra each week," she said a satisfied smile as she surveyed the contents of the pantry.

"Did I tell you you're invited to my mum's for Christmas Day?"

"Me?" said Audrey.

"Mum insisted on it when she heard what had happened – she'll insist even more now you're out of a job. Oh, we'll have such a good time Aud!"

"Christmas…oh." Audrey looked wistful. "Oh how I wish I could turn the clock back, to when I was seven years old. I loved every Christmas but that year was such a very special one. I remember Mummy and Daddy bought me a bicycle, and for James, a fort and soldiers. And all the presents so beautifully wrapped by the ladies in Lewis's department store. We had a large Christmas tree in the hall and one in the drawing room, and every room in the house was decorated with the most delightful garlands and ribbon and streamers and holly wreaths…"

Audrey stared mistily into the distance with a look of deep nostalgia, her eyes luminous with the memory of happy times gone by.

"That Christmas seems so long, ago, Moll," she said dreamily, and yet at the same time I can picture it all, every sight and sound and smell as if it were yesterday."

"It does sound magic," sighed Molly.

"That's exactly what it was," breathed Audrey, her eyes shining. "Magic."

"I'm afraid there won't be anything too fancy with my lot," Molly laughed. "It's brown paper and coloured string for the presents - and Dad goes off into the woods to lop the top off of a fir tree and bring it home, and the little 'uns make paper chains at school. They've barely two bob to rub together round here, but they make the best of it, we have our own kind of magic, you'll see."

Audrey smiled. "I'm sorry Moll. I shouldn't reminisce out loud like that."

"It's all right. You probably need to."

"I can't go back to that life now can I, not ever? For one thing James is no longer there –and if he was.." She broke off and the two girls exchanged a brief, intense, empathetic look.

"It has to be best foot forward now," said Audrey boldly.

The spirited moment did not last long. It was soon followed by a muffled wailing sound, as with her head in her hands Audrey began weeping, crying bitter-sweet tears of remembrance for her lost brother, for the family that had abandoned her in her hour of need, and for the life of innocence and love she had left behind.

The Holly and the Ivy,
When they are both full-grown,
Of all the trees in the wood,
The Holly wears the crown

"Oh heck who's that – not more carol singers?" Molly opened her front door to see Monty's large frame on the step. Over his back was slung a bulging sack.

"Happy Christmas Eve!" he declared, doffing his cap in her direction.

"And to you – and don't call me Eve - aren't you going to sing us another song?"

Taking his cue, Monty held his cap to his chest, and in a rumbling baritone began to chant to the tune of *'In The Bleak Midwinter'"*

"There once was a lady from Ealing, who had a peculiar feeling…"

"Stop!" shouted Molly, you'll get us all arrested, now come on in."

"Who is it Moll?" called Audrey from the kitchen.

"Father blooming Christmas," replied Molly, "needs his mouth scrubbing with a bar of carbolic."

"Sorry I don't know the proper words."

"Oh, it's a right proper education working down them docks isn't it," said Molly clicking her tongue.

"Hello Monty! Happy Christmas," Audrey greeted him as he lurched into the kitchen.

"Same to you young Audrey."

"Whatever do you have in that sack?"

"I told you, he's Father Christmas," explained Molly.

"He's a day early," laughed Audrey.

"So is this lot," replied Monty as he swung the sack off his shoulder and emptied the entire contents onto the kitchen table.

Audrey stared in bewilderment, while Molly's eyes lit up with excitement as she examined the pile of items -there was a tin of red salmon, a tin of ham, a jar of pickles, a bag of sugar, a large wooden box of tea, a bag of potatoes, a bag of oranges, two large tins of peaches and three large bottles of sherry."

"Oh, I've not seen one of these for ages!" exclaimed Molly, picking up an orange and holding it to her nose, inhaling as if it were some fragrant and vastly expensive perfume. "Oh, and even my dad will take a while to get through all this tea – all the tea in China."

"Where is all this food from?" Audrey asked.

"It's all bomb damaged love," Monty replied gravely. "There was nothing could be done to save it." He made the sign of the cross over his chest.

"It all looks all right," observed Audrey in an equally serious tone.

Molly and Monty burst out laughing together and began to sing

Good King Wenceslas Looked Out,
On the feast of Stephen
Where the snow lay round about,
Deep and crisp and even…

"Come on in Audrey – might I call you that now, and not Miss Audrey?"

Dorothy looked fondly at the young woman whom she had known since she and her own daughter were little girls playing together. Molly and Audrey were stood in the doorway of Dorothy's house.

"Of course," said Audrey awkwardly, "I'm a guest, a very grateful one, in your house. And I'm quite happy to help with peeling potatoes or setting the table…"
Dorothy held up her hand. "All taken care of love."

"Well are we going in or what?" laughed Molly, chivvying her friend over the threshold. "I think its going to start snowing in a minute, we'll be like two frozen snow women in the street – the kids will be chucking snowballs at us."

"Actually you did used to call me Audrey," said Audrey as Dorothy took their coats, "when we were children at Crosslands, which I really liked – of course I realise it had to be different when Mummy was around, that is…isn't it terrible, I almost forgot you still worked there oh dear…"

Audrey looked more than awkward now, appearing positively uncomfortable. Dorothy put a hand on her shoulder. "You don't have to say another word pet. And if anyone at Crosslands asks after you I'll say you're as well as can be expected. I shan't say more, or less."

She would tell her soon that Clarissa had asked her to leave because she would not discuss Audrey, but Marcus had defied his wife and for the moment Dorothy had still got her job. It had caused such animosity between Marcus and Clarissa and Dorothy was glad he had stood up to her. She was going to tell Audrey but today was not going to be that day.
Audrey visibly relaxed. "Bless you Dorothy."

"Come on through, I think you've met my husband Charlie, Molly's dad."

"Yes, hello Charlie, Happy Christmas"
Charlie, seated among a crowd of other people filling the living room to overflowing, raised a glass of stout and bellowed some friendly if unintelligible greeting in her direction.

"Don't worry, Dad's done a huge chicken," said Molly, "and a big side of pork – they'll be plenty to go round."

"Done it?" enquired Audrey.

"In every sense – Dad's a slaughter man," said Molly cheerfully. "Now let me do the introductions – everyone, this is my dear friend Audrey."

She then gestured towards the various occupants of the cramped room, who gazed at Audrey with friendly curiosity.

"That's Uncle Tom, then we've got Auntie Maggie, Uncle Jack, Grandma Bratt, and almost out of the window over there, is Auntie Mabel." Molly added in a whisper, "the maiden aunt."

"But who are the others?" asked Audrey, "You didn't mention everyone's name did you?"

"The others here are my nine cousins – though some couldn't fit in here, so they'll be upstairs or in the kitchen – and you'll get to know all their names as you go."

"Yes I'm sure I will," said Audrey smiling timorously at the assembled company, who all nodded and smiled back at her. "Learn the cousins names as I go," she murmured, "yes I'll try to…" This provoked a huge roar of good-natured laughter.

"Mum," said Molly, opening the laden knapsack she had arrived with, "I've got a few bits from Monty in here."

"Oh sherry, I don't mind if I do," beamed Dorothy in approval as she inspected the bottles. "Good old Monty."

"Good old Monty," cheered the family in unison as the tins, and bottles and other bounty were held aloft

"And we've Charlie's homemade beer or ginger wine if you prefer Audrey," said Dorothy.

"Ginger wine sounds lovely, thank you Dorothy."

After a few drinks and much animated conversation it was time for the Christmas dinner to be served. As Molly's father expertly carved the chicken, making sure all had fair shares, Uncle Tom called out "Are you sure its dead Charlie?"

The quip brought the house down, while maiden Auntie Mabel had to subdue a fit of hysterics with an additional glass of sherry. There was a momentary silence as the homemade Christmas pudding served up for each and every one with the rum sauce poured lavishly over each bowl was consumed with great relish.

"Compliments to the chef," cried Uncle Jack raising his glass when the meal was finished.

"That's no chef, that's my wife," chortled Charlie, prompting fresh gales of laughter, accompanied by glances towards Auntie Mabel and a few comments of 'steady on now Mabel dear."

Afterwards there were charades and parlour games, which Audrey joined enthusiastically in, and the children excitedly opened their presents – a delightful model sweet shop, a two-penny doll in elegant home-knitted clothes, a charming post office set, and tangerines and halfpennies in each of the stockings that hung from the mantelpiece.

When the early evening came, Dorothy and the aunts brought in the Christmas tea – cold chicken and pork sandwiches and pickled onions and home made Christmas cake with brandy, washed down with Monty's China tea.

"Who's for a song," cried Charlie.
In a jiffy, Auntie Maggie was at the piano, and the strains of "Bye, Bye Blackbird" were filling the house. Halfway through the third chorus a shout went up, 'shush, listen everybody – it's the Sally Army."

Auntie Maggie's fingers froze in mid octave, the voices fell silent, and in their place was heard the sombre murmur of a trombone, the slow, rhythmic beat of a drum.

As the sound grew louder Dorothy led the way to the door, the others following. Outside they found a scene of transformation. Against the soft lamplight, snow was falling silently, a white blanket already thick on the cobbles, the street bathed in an amber glow.

Through the falling snow the uniformed musicians, in regular step, one by one appeared. By now the whole family were outside the house – Dorothy and Charlie, the aunts and uncles, the cousins, Molly and Audrey, every mouth moving in time to the verse of *'Once in Royal David's City'* - gazing enraptured at the marching figures in their caps and bonnets, their brass instruments and buckles gleaming as they passed under the lamplight and each one carrying a lighted candle lantern.

Other families had emerged from their homes now, the whole street it seemed turned out to honour and pay tribute to the Salvation Army and their gratitude for it's presence among them on this most special night of the year.

Moved by the music, the words, the magical spectacle, every heart was stirred, every soul uplifted.

As the band drew level with the house, the assembled mouths of the Bratt family began to sing, joining the other families, rising up in one joyful voice:

"Where a mother laid her baby, in a stable for a bed…"

Audrey looked around her, how happy everyone was. Friends, families, neighbours, sharing the happiness of the season, differences and troubles put aside and forgotten for the moment. Even the two policemen, on duty at the bottom of the street were not left out, Dorothy made sure of that taking two glasses of beer and some sandwiches to them and receiving a Christmas kiss as payment much to the dislike of Charlie.

They had all made the best of Christmas and now were together – the whole street together.

"This is truly magic," she whispered as the ambience enveloped her.

In the midst of this scene, as the chorus swelled, Molly suddenly noticed that Audrey was crying.

"Hey love, what's wrong?" she said, putting an arm around her friend.

Audrey sobbed.

"Come on love," Molly said, "it'll all be all right, you'll see."

Audrey nodded through her tears, "Oh Moll," she spluttered "I'm sorry, it's just…"

"Just what?"

"Just that…I've never seen so much love and kindness and friendship, as I have here today with your family." She placed a hand on her midriff and looked down.

"This Christmas," she said solemnly, "is the Christmas we shall have little one, when your daddy comes home.

CHAPTER THIRTY-FOUR

March 1945

"Nurse Ikin!" The Matron's voice rang out down the ward like the stentorian bellow of a sergeant major.

Mimsy, on her hands and knees making a bed, popped up like a startled rabbit appearing suddenly from its hole. All heads, patients and staff, turned to look at her as she made her way to the nursing station by the double doors, where Matron stood with hands on hips, her face a mask of simmering anger.

"Yes ma'am?" enquired Mimsy, with as much calm and equanimity as she could muster before her superior's glowering expression. "What is it?"

"Nurse Ikin, how many times have I told you girls about not encouraging your gentleman friends to the hospital?"

"Sorry, Matron, I don't understand – I've only got one um, gentleman friend, honest - and he's in North Africa with the 8th army, last time I heard at any rate."

The Matron narrowed her eyes and breathed in. "The perhaps you can explain why a young man in American Air Force uniform is presently in the corridor, demanding to see you – he is in a state of some agitation. When Sister O'Rourke asked him his business, he made an extremely rude remark."

Hearing a muffled snort of amusement, Matron fixed her gimlet eye on Ivy, who immediately resumed scrubbing the floor with great alacrity.

"I would have the porters remove him from the premises, but like us they have patients to attend to. Unless you can persuade this young man to leave immediately I shall be forced to take such action."

Mimsy muttered a garbled, "Probably some misunderstanding..."

"He knows your name, girl," rasped the Matron.

Oh – right, Matron, very well, I'd better go and see what its all about then."

"Indeed."

Mimsy disappeared hastily through the double doors.

The rest of you can get on with your duties if you please," boomed Matron at Mimsy's gawping colleagues.

A few yards along the corridor, she saw the figure of a uniformed man with his hands in his pockets and his back to her.

"Hello," she called, "were you looking for me...? Joey!"

Italian Joe turned and saw her. He said nothing.

"Joe, what a nice surprise, I thought you were in Italy – when did you get back? Gosh it's good to see you lad...Joey - what's wrong? You look so serious – you've not been injured have you? Was that why they sent you back?" The young airman's face looked gaunt. He seemed older, his dark Latin eyes rheum-filled, his olive skin parched and drawn.

"Hello Mims." His voice was like gravel. "I'm not hurt."

"That's a relief," sighed Mimsy. "You look like you've been through it though."

He nodded. "I'm one of the lucky ones. Where's Audrey? That sister that was needling me – she told me Audrey's not here no more."

"She left, just before Christmas, got another job for now, just until – oh but did Martin not tell you about...?" Mimsy hesitated. "Oh - Audrey was going to write to him, but she kept putting it off – I suppose he doesn't even know."

Joe looked at her blankly. "We don't always get mail."

Mimsy said in a whisper, "Audrey's pregnant Joe, nearly six months gone now."

"Pregnant?" echoed Joe. He stared at her.

Mimsy nodded and began talking excitedly now. "She's going to be so thrilled Martin's back, she can have her wedding at last, oh its going to be such a grand affair Joe, and all the boys at the base are invited of course, we're going to lay it on real special for Audrey, all pitch in. We can set the date, get her dress and all."

Joe rang his fingers through his black hair. "He didn't know, about Audrey, the baby," he muttered half to himself, "God, he didn't know..."

"Well he's got a wonderful surprise waiting hasn't he, oh I can't wait to see his face, or Audrey's when I tell her you're all back...!"

"We're not all back Mims," Joe interrupted her in a plangent tone. Mimsy looked at him in sudden horror.

"Martin's plane was hit over Italy. The crew were all killed."

There was silence in the corridor, like the stillness after a violent explosion.

The colour had drained from Mimsy's face. "No Joey," she said, "it can't be…you said all killed – but you were his co-pilot."

"A few days before, I got my own crew, my own plane. I didn't want to fly without Martin, we were buddies from way back, you know. But he wanted me to do it, to have the promotion, for me you know. That was the kind of person he was – generous, always looking out for the other guy, for his friends. I'm sorry to have to come here and tell you this news today Mims. But Martin always said if anything happened to him, I was to tell Audrey - that was his wish. I know what a good friend you've been to her." He shuffled awkwardly, wringing his cap with his hands. "Well, if she's not here,- I have to get back to the base now. You look after yourself Mims."

Mimsy stood rooted to the floor, blinking, dazed. As he turned to leave she said quietly, "Listen, Joe - you can tell her, if you, I mean, if you want to do it, that way."

"It was Martin's wish," he repeated.

"Meet me at the hospital gate tonight – six o'clock?" Mimsy said "I'll take you to her."

Joe and Mimsy were stood outside 112 Jericho Road. Audrey opened the door. On seeing Joe, her face lit up.

"Joe!" she exclaimed, "Oh Mims, my goodness, oh heavens – come in, come in." She almost pulled them into the living room, then leapt forward and hugged Joe. She was laughing, babbling with excitement, her eyes filling with tears of joy, relief and exhilaration.

"This is such a wonderful surprise, Mims did you know about this? Well of course you must have done, and, oh my goodness, Martin! – I never wrote the letter to him, it sounds so stupid but somehow I was worried it would fall into the wrong hands and I got all sort of superstitious about it – but does he know now – have you told him Mims? I mean, where is he?"

"Audrey…" began Mimsy, trying to forestall her friend's excitable outpouring.

"This is so wonderful," Audrey continued, "Do you know, I've been moping all day, and they've been teasing me as usual, and then to cap it all one of the girls on the conveyor belt had a letter from her chap and I felt so envious as she read it out to everyone - but now I'm the luckiest girl alive - they'll all be envying me tomorrow, or even more spiteful probably, but what do I care..." She began to sing: "Oh when the lights go on again, all over the world - " She broke off. "Why, whatever's the matter Mims?" Finally she had taken notice of their faces: Mimsy's ashen hue, Joe's rigid, tight-jawed expression.

"Best sit down Aud," said Mimsy. "Joe's got something to tell you."

"Oh-oh, this sound ominous, don't tell me, one of your japes," laughed Audrey, perching herself on the edge of the armchair "Come on then what's the lark? You always were a joker Joe. If you're going to spring Martin from round the corner better make it quick, it looks like it's going to rain any minute."
She peered at Joe quizzically, then at Mimsy. "He did fly back with you I assume Joe? Oh don't tell me he's still out there – I was reading in the paper about the mopping up operations, but they officially surrendered ages ago for goodness sake – can't the Italians sort themselves out by now – oh gosh, no disrespect Joe."

"None taken," said Joe quietly. "Audrey, what I have to tell you is going to be painful for you to hear, very painful - "
Audrey's face suddenly changed. She opened her mouth to speak but no words came. She shot a look at Mimsy, then back at Joe.

"What?" she said. "Not...?"

"Martin's plane went down over Italy," said Joe. "There were no survivors. I'm so very sorry."

"Martin had asked Joe, that if this ever happened, to tell you in person," said Mimsy.
Audrey's mouth was twitching. Her eyes had grown wide. "And now - it has happened," she uttered inanely. Her voice had a strange, disconnected quality.
Joe swallowed and cleared his throat. "He also wanted me to tell you, to tell you that – that he loved you very much."
Audrey's whole body had begun to quiver, and she was making a low whimpering sound.

"Thank you, Joe," she said. Then, letting out a shriek of pain as if suddenly she had been stabbed, she tipped forward off the armchair and collapsed in a heap on the floor.

"She's sleeping now," said the doctor. He had just come downstairs. Mimsy and Molly were sat in the kitchen at Jericho Road. "I'm sorry I can't do more for her. Medical science can cure many things, but broken hearts.." He shook his head. "It's going to be hard for her."

"Will the baby be all right Doctor?" asked Mimsy.

"As far as I can tell; the effects of shock can be unpredictable. See that she has as much rest as possible, and gets enough good food to eat." The girls nodded.

"Can anything be done to persuade her to return to her home in Crosslands? I know Marcus Stephenson and the family by reputation of course." He looked round the tiny kitchen, at the chipped plates on the drainer. "She might find it more, ahem, comfortable there."

Molly gave him a look of cold contempt. "I wonder what kind of reputation you might be thinking of as regards the Stephenson family," she said caustically, "one that sees fit to turn their own out on the streets? We're Audrey's family now Doctor, and Jericho Road's where she'll stay, and be well cared for - I'll thank you to close the door on your way out."

"Of all the cheek," remarked Mimsy indignantly when the doctor had gone. "And under your roof too - who does he think he is – God all-bleedin-mighty? I'm glad you told him what for Moll."

Molly smiled. "Well, you can't let folk walk all over you can you. Listen Mims tomorrow's Sunday and we're both off work, so if you don't mind the couch and an army blanket, why not stay here tonight – I've half a bottle of brandy somewhere, and a bit of bread and cheese for supper."

"Thanks Moll, that'll be lovely."

"Right, That's settled then. I'll just go and check on our Audrey."

She went quietly up the stairs and opened the door of the spare room. Audrey was lying peacefully on her back breathing softly, her eyes closed. Molly tiptoed in and pulled the blanket up slightly.

"Don't you worry about a thing pet," she whispered. "You're safe here. And we'll manage – somehow or other, we'll manage." She crept away, pulling the door to behind her.

In the darkened room Audrey opened her eyes. They were sore and swollen with crying. Raising herself up she gave a little shudder. Martin was not coming back. The words, the thoughts, had echoed in her head till they were almost meaningless. How could they mean anything – it seemed impossible; her world had suddenly changed, collapsed about her ears, and nothing made sense any more.

It was so awful she could barely comprehend it, let alone contemplate the future, for until that afternoon the future had consisted entirely of Martin, her fiancé and her love, her whole universe...the father of her child; she put a hand on her stomach. There was a future, right here inside her, but how could she face it now, how could she possibly explain to her child about this terrible thing, this loss, the magnitude of which she had no notion of how to bear? How could such love be given only to be so cruelly snatched away? When my family rejected me, she thought, I could bear it because I had Martin, and his perfect, unquestioning love. Now I am lost, lost just as he is, strewn through the air into a thousand pieces, drifting helpless on the wind.

She pictured his plane, droning peacefully over the fields and olive terraces, then an explosion, a shattering of metal and propellers and oil, flesh and blood, scattering out in a thousand pieces across the crystal blue Italian sky, blown for miles and miles until disappearing at last to nothing – dust to dust, earth to earth, ashes to ashes. But where was Martin now, where was his soul? It was simply not possible for him not to exist, somewhere.

At that moment a gentle breeze rattled the ill-fitting sash windows, parting the curtains and letting in a shaft of light. Through the narrow slit Audrey caught a glimpse of the moon, its soft glow illuminating the scudding clouds.

"Martin..." she cried out imploringly and stretched her hand towards the window. "I'm here, yes...I'm here my darling."

Then just as quickly the moon was gone and the sky was dark once more, the breeze dropped and the gap in the curtains closed. I must hold on, thought Audrey, hold on and never let go – for his sake, and mine.

Reaching to the bedside chair she took hold of her clothes. Rummaging in a deep inside pocket she took out the box containing Martin's engagement ring. She tried it on her finger. Still it would not fit. She closed her palm over the gold band.

"No matter," she said quietly to herself. "You'll be with me always Martin, always."

"Ooh summat smells good." Mimsy had just wandered bleary-eyed into the kitchen.

Molly was bent over a sizzling frying pan. "Just a few rashers of bacon Monty dropped off the other day."

"That man's a miracle worker."

"That's one word for him. Sit yourself down Mims, there's an egg each too and some more of Ma's homemade bread. I'll take Audrey's up in a bit - let her lie in."

She served up the bacon and eggs, sliced some bread and poured out two cups of tea. "Only powdered milk today though I'm afraid, makes the tea taste like dishwater, but beggars can't be choosers."

As they ate Molly took an envelope from her apron pocket. "Strictly between you me and the gatepost, I had a letter from my Bill this morning."

"Bill?" said Mimsy, looking intrigued.

"My fiancée." She put a finger to her lips.

"Oh, Moll!" Mimsy now looked both surprised and excited. "You never said you were engaged."

Molly gave an awkward, sheepish smile. "I was going to tell you, all of you, but I felt a bit superstitious about it to be honest, him being away – and now, after what's happened to Audrey, Martin and all - well."

Mimsy looked down at her plate. "Of course."

"I daren't say a word about it to Audrey, about me and Bill, it's break her heart even more than it is already."

"Maybe it would help her - she'd be pleased for you, I'm sure, don't you think?"

"I can't risk it – she's in a delicate state, especially with the baby on the way now too."

Mimsy nodded. "Perhaps you're right, I'll keep mum. But tell me about Bill, what's he like?

"Gorgeous!" beamed Molly, unable to contain herself as she reopened the letter. "He's in the Royal Engineers, and last I heard he was headed for North Africa, Egypt I think – of course he doesn't say here, they're not supposed to, but daft bugger, he's put some sand in - look." She tipped up the envelope and a few tiny, silvery grains trickled out onto the kitchen table.

'Dearest Moll,' she read, 'since my last letter me and the boys have gone somewhere very hot – the enclosed should give you a clue – and since I have not got you an engagement ring yet, I hope you will accept the said enclosed as a temporary token of my affection – it came out of the ground, just like diamonds do!"

"Sure his mob's not camping out on Blackpool beach?" grinned Mimsy.

"That's a thought – maybe it'll be a donkey next." She read on: "When I come home love, I promise we'll be married"

"Eh, he told me that the night before he went off you know," she said with a confidential wink. "I said: you can promise all you like Bill Marshall, but you're getting nothing on account!"
Mimsy put her hand over her mouth in scandalised amusement.

"No? What did he say to that?"
He said in a very serious voice, "Molly Bratt, if you think that's all I'm after, you're very much mistaken. I can wait my girl - I just hope you can!"
Mimsy roared with laughter. "Oh blimey Moll – well I can see I'll have to keep an eye on you girl, and give Bill a full report when he gets back to Blighty!"

"So long as that's all you give him!"
Both girls erupted into further hilarity. Calming down Molly said, "Oh dear, I've just got to find the right time to tell our Audrey now. Apart from anything else I want you both as my bridesmaids…"

"Morning Moll, morning Mims," called a voice.
The pair turned to see Audrey, rubbing her eyes sleepily coming along the hallways towards the open kitchen door. Molly hurriedly stuffed Bill's letter back in her apron.

"I heard a lot of laughing," yawned Audrey.

"Sorry about that pet," frowned Molly.

"Don't be, I could do with hearing something cheerful – I've been doing enough crying."

"I was going to bring you some breakfast in bed, why don't you go back up, sleep in?"

"That's kind Moll." Audrey pulled out a chair and joined them at the table. "But I'm not an invalid, and I'll just be miserable lying up there all on my own staring out of the window. I was thinking of going to church as it's Sunday, but I think it might upset me even more, and I'd hate a lot of strangers staring and leaning across the pews and asking me in kindly voices what the matter was – if I told them they'd probably disapprove and think it served me right or something."

"Churchgoers can be a bit like that," nodded Mimsy sagely. "They think because they put on a posh hat and shake hands with the vicar once a week they've got a seat all booked upstairs, if you know what I mean." She gestured towards the kitchen ceiling.

"What?" Audrey, still dozy stared at her. "Oh – a seat in heaven you mean? Yes, I see, perhaps you're right. I don't know what Martin's religion was – isn't that awful. He was from the South of course, where I believe they're awfully God-fearing. Oh goodness, you don't think he's going to hell do you – because of..." She touched her midriff, her eyes suddenly filled with fear.

"You mustn't fret about that Aud." Molly put an arm around her friend. "Martin was a good man, good in his heart, where it counts – and God knows that."

Audrey squeezed her friend's hand and nodded. "I know." She looked pensive. "Moll, what were you talking about when I came in?"

With only a flickering glance at Mimsy, Molly replied, "Oh – only about how horrible this powdered milk is. If I could afford it I'd buy a cow."

"Perhaps Monty could get us one," suggested Mimsy.

"I wouldn't put it past him."

"Mind you he'd need to supply a meadow to go with it – there's nowt for a cow to chew on in your back yard Moll."

"I'd gladly buy you a cow and a meadow," sighed Audrey, "except I haven't a bean. And I'm afraid there'll be no work for me at the factory soon - I can't hide this much longer." She stroked her bump. "Another three months and I'll be having the baby. Then what do we do? The rent won't pay itself Moll – I'm sure you can't manage to keep both of us – and a little one."

Molly felt in her apron pocket and closed her fingers around Bill's letter. "We're going to be alright Audrey," she smiled. "Just trust me."

CHAPTER THIRTY-FIVE

July 1945

The warm weather of June had continued into July. Audrey, nearing the full term of her pregnancy, found the heat exhausting. Then, after the euphoria of V.E. Day, with the demand for aircraft fuel tanks grinding to a halt, the factory at which she had been working announced its sudden closure, and she had found herself out of a job even sooner than she had anticipated.

Though glad of the respite, the practical implications were worrying. They became even more so when Molly broke the news that her own employer, which sewed overcoats for the army, was also reducing its workforce. Molly having been only recently taken on was among the first to be let go.

Fortunately she had managed to return to her old job at the Wetherton Hospital laundry on the late shift. This paid better wages, though the hours were long and unsocial, and the work more physically demanding. Molly however seemed to take the change in her stride, and assured Audrey not to fret on her account, to think of 112 Jericho Road as her home, and gather her strength for the happy event that was soon to take place.

Busy at the factory, her eyes and mind dulled by the rolling, rhythmic movement of the conveyor belt, there had been days when Audrey hardly thought of Martin. Instead she re-imagined the good times she'd had as a child with Molly, sneaking off from Crosslands and roaming the lanes and meadows together. Would there be times like that for them again – picnics and days out on the beach with her little boy, or girl – how dear Jack would love to see them!

Then, retuning home tired to Jericho Road, she would exchange a few words with Molly - if their hours happened to coincide - snatch some supper and yawn her way up to the little spare bedroom and fall between the sheets.

This was when Martin would visit her – in the small hours, when the pubs had closed and Monty had gone by, his singing faded away, and the street outside lay quiet. Only then, in her dreams would Audrey relive their days and nights together – curled up with Martin by the fire at the cottage, dancing cheek to cheek at the Grand, laughing at the funny, inquisitive manager, gazing in wonder at that magical Christmas tree, then ascending the great staircase to their room and closing the door, shutting out the world and tumbling into each other's arms.

She felt Martin's face close to hers, his warm smile and his soft blue Southern eyes, their bodies entwined, his lips on her lips, his warmth so comforting and snug against her breast, his beating heart against hers, Martin, Martin, Martin…!

Then she would wake, with a silent, strangulated cry, clutching her throat in horror as again she heard the ominous breeze, the thief in the night rattling through the windows and snatching her love away, taking him, taking him, taking him from her – for ever, and for ever, and for ever.

So desperately did Audrey long to return to these dreams again and again, yearning, hoping each night for the spell to be cast, to step back, through the looking glass of time, back to that wonderful world, of innocence and beauty, in which she and Martin still lived and breathed and laughed and loved one another.

It was a particularly warm evening when, after retiring at around 9.30, Audrey slept fitfully for an hour before waking with a sharp twinge in her stomach. The pain struck again.

"Ouch!" Her breathing quickened, her body damp with sweat. With an effort she sat up, pushing away the sheet, sucking in the air from the open window. Then the twinge returned, a stabbing, crippling pain now.

"Molly," she yelled, "I think it's coming…the baby…oh…!"

Molly, still pulling on her dressing gown came rushing in.

"Aud – oh crikey – but you're not due for another fortnight."

"I know, but…ah, oh…ouch…!"

Molly ran her hand through her hair, her mind racing.

"Heck – listen, don't move, I'll fetch Old Mother Sarah."

"Why her?" Audrey gasped.

"She delivers babies," gabbled Molly frantically tying her dressing gown. "Lays out the dead, cures things, and bakes the best sponge cake you'll ever taste. Some folks say as how she's a witch."

"I don't fancy any cake right now," panted Audrey, "and I hope I won't need laying out, not just yet…"

Molly, dressing gown tied, turned towards the stairs. "Stay right there pet."

Audrey gave a sickly smile. "I'm certainly not going anywhere."

Two minutes later Molly was on Mother Sarah's doorstep.

"Oh Sarah, thank goodness - it's Audrey, the baby's coming." The old lady nodded, and without a word threw a shawl over her shoulders and followed Molly's hurrying footsteps.

Audrey's cries were audible as soon as they entered the house. Mother Sarah took charge immediately.

"Fetch some hot water, she ordered, "and we'll need some towels. I'm going up to the lass."

Molly did as bidden, and swiftly heated a saucepan of water and brought it into Audrey's room, together with a pile of clean towels. Audrey was laid back on the pillows now, her face contorted with pain.

Mother Sarah spoke to her in a calm, soothing voice. "There love, don't worry, it's agony for you I know, but it'll all be over soon, you've just to be brave a little bit longer. She held a handkerchief towards Audrey. "Bite down on this, you'll find it helps. And you come round this side of the bed Molly, help her out won't you - That's it love, you're doing well now gal, steady as she goes eh. You'll come through gal, you'll see."

With Molly gripping her hands, and the old lady patiently and expertly directing the proceedings, talking her through, reassuring all the while, it was a long and tortuous night for Audrey.

Finally though, just as Mother Sarah had foretold, she did indeed 'come through', and at precisely 6 am on the 9th of July 1945, the cries of a beautiful newborn baby girl rang out through 112 Jericho Road.

"Well done love," beamed Mother Sarah placing the pink, bawling infant carefully in Audrey's arms. "She's a beauty and no mistake."

Audrey kissed the top of the baby's tiny head, her exhausted tear stained face now radiant with joy.

"Yes," she whispered tremulously, 'she is, a real beauty."

"What are you going to call her Aud.?" asked Molly, gazing in awe at the scrunched up little face.

"Margaret I think – it's my middle name."

"Like the young Princess." smiled Mother Sarah.

"Yes – except this one's my little Princess - aren't you darling, yes that's right." She gently tickled the pink nose.

Her eyes then met Molly's, the two of them communicating in a single glance a whole host of feelings – pride, relief, sadness, hope, and the kind of deep, loving understanding, quite beyond words, which only true friends can share.

Their faces said: this is a very special moment, and whatever happens now, we will be there for each other, and the care, the absolute trust we have had for and in each other since our childhoods will go on, and that same care and trust will be there too now for this child, for little Margaret.

"I want to ask a favour Moll," said Audrey. They were sitting in the small back yard of 112 Jericho Road, shaded from the hot midday sun by the kitchen wall. Cradled in Audrey's arms was baby Margaret, fast asleep. "Its about me going back to work."

Molly gave her friend a censorious look.

"You're not ready yet pet, it's only been two weeks, and Margaret's still feeding."

"Not for much longer," Audrey replied. "I'm drying up in that department, and we need the money. I know you've been dipping in your savings to keep us going, don't tell me you haven't."

"What if I have?" replied Molly, "That's what savings are for."

"What about your bottom drawer?"

Her friend flinched. "Bottom drawer – how do you mean?"

"You and Bill's."

There was an awkward pause before Molly said, "Who's been talking to you?"

"Nobody – I just heard more than I let on that Sunday morning on the stairs – you'd just got Bill's letter, remember?"

Molly cast her eyes down in embarrassment. "I'm sorry I never said anything Aud. I mean, I was going to, but then when we heard about Martin, it didn't seem right to go crowing about me and Bill, and talking wedding bells."

"I appreciate that Moll." Audrey reached out and squeezed her arm. "But I'm thrilled for you, honestly. I can't wait to meet him."

Molly smiled. "Thanks. I know you'll like him; he's a real down to earth sort, decent as they come. He'll take a shine to you I don't doubt, not to mention little "un here." She proffered an indulgent smile at baby Margaret, still slumbering contentedly. "But back to what you were saying Aud, you've got to be sensible, how can you manage a job and a baby?"

"I've thought about that – I'm going to get a job on alternate shifts to yours, then, you could look after Margaret while I'm out at work – if you were willing to of course. That's the favour.

"Well I…"

"And there's something else."

"What else?"

"I'd like you to be Margaret's Godmother."

Molly stared at her. "Oh Aud, "That's a…very special thing…"

"Of course, it's rather a lot to ask, I understand if you prefer not to."

Molly's face lit up. "A lot to ask – why it's a lot for you to give, I mean, oh Aud, I'd be thrilled, honoured, a privilege, do you really mean it?"

Audrey nodded in great earnest, "But of course I mean it, it would be my greatest pleasure – you are my oldest, closest, dearest friend, dear sweet Molly."

"And you, mine!" She rose and wrapped her arms around mother and child, kissing them both profusely.

At that moment there was a loud knocking from the front door.

"Who the hell's that on a Sunday morning," exclaimed Molly. "I'll get it, you sit there."

It was Monty. "Hello Moll love."

"Hello Mont…eh, that's never yours is it?"

Molly stared at the burly docker's large fists, which were gripping the handles of a shiny, and very new looking Silver Cross perambulator, in navy blue and white.

" brought it for Audrey's little un," said Monty proudly. "Do you think she'll like it?"

"Like it – she'll love it. Hey, did you wheel that thing all the way here, through the streets and all?" Molly chuckled.

"And why not?" Monty replied imperiously. "The hand that rocks the cradle rules the world you know."

"Aye, but there has to be a babe in it first."

"Well see about putting one in then."

"Right, I will – Audrey!" Molly shouted through to the back yard, and a few seconds later Audrey with Margaret tucked in her arms joined them at the door."

"Monty's got a little present." Molly indicated the pram.

"It's for you, Miss Audrey." Monty, now suddenly sheepish pushed the pram forward slightly.

"Oh Monty," gasped Audrey, That's so awfully kind – my goodness." She looked about to burst into tears. "But Monty I couldn't possibly accept it – it must have cost you a small fortune..." She broke off. Molly was nudging her with her elbow. Molly then coughed and looked meaningfully at Monty, who, taking the hint said quickly,

"Oh it didn't cost me owt, no my dear– it were a friend's, they didn't need it any more, see."

"But it looks brand new," said Audrey in wonder, running her hand appreciatively over the pram. "Oh and look inside Moll, an embroidered lace pillow to match the cover, and such a beautiful shade of pink."

"Yes, yes my friend's right handy with a needle and thread," said Monty.

Really?" said Molly, winking at him archly.

"Oh, Monty, thank you, thank you so very much. I was so worried about how I was going to afford a proper pram, and this one is magnificent. Now I can go out walking and take Margaret with me."

She bent over the pram and lay her sleeping baby carefully down inside. Without opening her eyes Margaret gave a little sigh of contentment as her head settled on the pink lace pillow.

"Bless her cotton socks the little darling," said Molly, her own eyes now looking distinctly moist.

Monty cleared his throat. "Well she seems comfortable enough there," he said. "So I'll bid you ladies good day – all three of you. I've an appointment with some people vital to the brewing industry."

"He means the Feathers is open," translated Molly. Monty made a brief, courteous bow.

Audrey, on tiptoe, kissed him on the cheek.

He turned and gave a bashful wave. "Oh dear me, I can go in the Feathers a happy man now," he grinned. "I'd have been worried leaving a pram outside the four ale bar to be honest."

"I'd be more worried if you'd took it in with you Mont!" joshed Molly.

Linking her arm through Audrey's she beamed down at Margaret. "Come on Madam, let's wheel you round the estate, or as we like to call it, the back yard - That's the way to travel now isn't it, eh bless your cotton socks!"

Next morning Audrey rose early and made breakfast for herself and Molly. At around 11.30, when Molly had left to begin her shift at the hospital laundry, she tucked Margaret into the pram, and, singing a little song to her, set off along Jericho Road in the direction of the town centre.

Half an hour later, with some difficulty, Audrey nudged her pram through the doors of the Labour Exchange.
She found herself in a kind of hall, sparsely furnished and filled with people queuing in a long line that snaked back on itself. Though the place was poorly lit, the peeling paintwork and generally dilapidated state of the building was evident. There was also a stale, rancid smell, suggesting inadequate ventilation.

As the heavy doors closed loudly behind her, one or two heads moved languidly in her direction then turned away again. The queue comprised young fellows in their de-mob suits, many looking weary and dejected, older men in overalls and flat caps, while women of all ages, shapes and sizes stood amongst them.

Throughout the room could be heard the low, indistinct murmur of muted conversation and shuffling feet, and from behind the desks at the far end, the head of the queue, the occasional scraping of a chair, the scratch of a fountain pen or the reverberating thump-bang of a rubber stamp.

As unobtrusively as she could, Audrey steered her pram forward and approached a middle-aged woman in the queue.
"Excuse me," she said timidly, "I'm looking for a job."
The woman turned a hatchet face towards her. Looking her up and down she muttered in a low, sardonic voice,

"Oh really, who'd have thought it love?"

It's my first time here," said Audrey apologetically. "Please, where do I have to go?"

"Back of the queue, same as the rest of us."

"Yes of course, thank you so much."

As Audrey turned to look for the back of the queue, she felt a hand grip her wrist. The hatchet-faced woman was glaring at her. "A bit of friendly advice."

"Yes?"

"You won't get a job with that in tow." She jerked her head towards the pram.

"Oh – you mean…"

"Best get rid of it."

Just as she spoke there came a sudden outburst of noise, echoing loudly round the room, drowning out the rubber stamps and the shuffling feet and the scraping chairs; Margaret had burst out crying, bawling her tiny head off for all she was worth.

Behind their desks the Labour Exchange officials stopped scratching their fountain pens and looked up in baffled indignation from their form filling, while along the queue the murmured conversations abruptly ceased.

All eyes were fixed on Audrey, standing, all alone with her crying baby, and the gleaming Silver Cross pram.

CHAPTER THIRTY-SIX

August 1945

"Hello Moll, where's Margaret?" asked Audrey eagerly as she came into the kitchen. Under her arm was a large brown carrier bag.

"I put her out in the yard as it's such a nice day again," replied Molly, who was making a pot of tea.

"She's been no trouble, she's a little angel really."

Audrey put down her parcel and went into the yard. She peeped into the Silver Cross pram. Margaret was sleeping blissfully. She bent down and delicately kissed the little nose.

After adjusting the hood of the pram slightly, ensuring the shadiest position, she stood and gazed fondly at her daughter for a moment. Rejoining Molly in the kitchen she said wistfully,

"I'm so lucky to have her. And lucky to have you to look after her, Moll."

"You do more than your bit. And how were your comrades at the biscuit factory today – still swearing enough to make troopers blush?"

"The air can be a bit blue round the conveyor belt sometimes, but they're a good bunch you know Moll." Audrey peeled off her regulation hairnet and overall and sat down at the kitchen table.

"It's taken me a month, but I think they're finally accepting me there. One or two of the older ones still look down their noses knowing I have a child, but most treat me just like one of the girls – which is all I want to be. Of course some of the younger ones are in the same boat as me. And they've let me in on the perks now too."

She emptied the contents of the carrier bag out on to the table.

Molly raised her eyebrows at the cascading mountain of bread, cakes and biscuits.

"Hmm, this lot will come in handy," she said approvingly.

"Some of the bread's a bit stale I'm afraid," said Audrey.

Molly picked up a loaf and tapped it against the table. "No matter, it's perfect for bread pudding. The cakes look fresh as daisy's mind – "ere I hope you didn't half inch them." She gave Audrey a studious look.

"Half inch?" said Audrey bemused.

"Pinch – steal."

"How dare you suggest I would be dishonest Molly Bratt!" said Audrey indignantly.

It's just I know what those factory girls are like."

"Like Monty perhaps?"

"Don't get "cute Aud," reproved Molly. "Monty's got his head screwed on; he's long enough in the tooth to get away with it down the docks. Besides, you're a lady – ladies don't go about nicking stuff. And getting light fingered is the quickest way to lose your job."

"Oh Molly, do stop all that lady nonsense, we've been friends too long – and I've told you, its perks, some of the cakes and loaves come out the wrong shape and get labelled rejects - we're allowed to take them home, all the girls say so – so long as we wrap them up well as we leave the factory gate."

Molly burst out laughing.

"Oh Aud, you're priceless. Come on then, let's tuck into some of these "ere "perks" eh."

She took out a knife and cut two thick slices from a huge, rich looking fruitcake.

"Hmm, delicious - tell the girls to keep sticking the reject labels on this lot. Oh heck, look at the time – a quick cuppa and I must be off. Hitler-in Knickers will have my guts for garters if there's no clean sheets. Thank the lord I'm off tomorrow and Thursday."

"That reminds me Moll," said Audrey stirring her tea. "As well as working at the biscuit factory, I was thinking I might take a part-time job as well; we could use the extra money to have a little break, all three of us, a holiday somewhere, or just some days at the seaside, go and see Jack too, while the weather's so lovely."

"Hmm, I don't want you overdoing it now girl," demurred Molly.

But a break would do us so much good, I wouldn't be overdoing it at all. Moll, you know it's you that needs a rest – I hate seeing you scrimp and scrape and look so worn out all the time, and having nothing to show for it – you deserve more.

"But I'm not worn out," Molly objected.

"I don't believe you Moll – you put on a brave face all the time, but I know you're helping out your relatives with money, as well as trying to save for when Bill comes back, and your wedding - and you're putting in extra hours at the laundry to do it."

Molly looked pensive for a moment then said, "All right, maybe I do spread the shillings around a bit, but That's what families are for where I come from, and what life's like for ordinary folk Aud. We toil, we sweat, and we're glad of the chance to earn our living, and at the end of the day we put our feet up for ten minutes if we're lucky, and now and again we have half a stout down the Feathers, and folk like Monty, who work like mules, help us out with a bit extra. We don't expect much, and we're never disappointed - we count our blessings." She looked at Audrey expectantly, as if waiting for a response.

"I admire you Molly," said Audrey, "you know that. I always have. I grew up with money, and through foolishness or pride or stubbornness, or a matter of principle, or simply loving Martin, I don't know - it looks like I've lost it all, for good. If I did have the inheritance that was once coming to me, I could help you. I could buy this house for you, and your mother's house, and then for a start Dorothy wouldn't have to go on working like a slave for my family.

At her age she should be retiring, taking it easy, and you could see more of each other. I make out I like working at the factory and in some ways I do, and you say you like going out to work in the laundry for a pittance, but we're both deluding ourselves – there's a better life for all of us, for you and Bill when he comes home, for your mother, for me and Margaret – there has to be..."

"Audrey," snapped Molly, "it's you that's deluding yourself. I for one can't afford to live in cloud cuckoo land. For me, and my kind, life is life - its hard, grinding, difficult, but you get by, you snatch what contentment you can, and only the rich can have it otherwise."

"That's just defeatist talk," said Audrey insistently.

"Aud," said Molly quietly, "I gave you a roof over your head here because you're my friend, and you were in need. Are you telling me now, that here's not good enough for you?"

"Oh Moll," cried Audrey. Her expression now was one of hurt, of being grossly misunderstood. "It's quite the opposite. Don't you see, it's because you're my friend, because you're so good and kind and pure and generous, that I want to give you something back, make things better for you, and your mother, and your brothers and sisters and cousins and friends – for people like old Mother Sarah, bless her heart."

"You think we're not happy in Jericho Road, is that it?"

"No Moll, I think your capacity for happiness is extraordinary, you and all your family and friends I'm utterly in awe of you all. And because I'm so grateful – for your kindness, your friendship, the way you've accepted me and helped me, I desperately want to do something for you, don't you understand – I feel so inadequate, and I want to change that. Wouldn't you like your mother to be able to put her feet up a little more often, for you to be able to take her away to the seaside now and again? Even if don't want anything more out of life for yourself, don't you want it for the people you love? The war is over, we've been through so much – don't we deserve a better life if we can get it?"

There was a pause as the two friends looked at each other long and hard. Molly took a deep breath.

"I'm lost Aud I really am," she sighed. "I admire your sentiments, and I know you mean well, and yes, things are tough, and I'd dearly love to set my mum up and not see her work her fingers to the bone, but how's it to be done? As you say, you've lost your inheritance, but if you're thinking a couple of nights a week scrubbing floors is going to earn it back -" She threw her hands in the air.

"I know what you're saying Moll, but listen to this." Audrey leaned forward, her eyes bright and animated. "What I've got in mind would be a really easy job, a girl at the factory told me about it – she said some of them do a couple of nights a week at this place, and that the pay there is very good…."

"Oh, where?" asked Molly.

"At the cinema – the Magnet…"

"What!" Molly looked suddenly alarmed.

"There's no need to sound so horrified." Audrey smiled. "For heaven's sake I already work in a biscuit factory, so don't say its no job for a "lady". I always rather fancied being an usherette. It must be rather fun, you get to meet people, and show them to their seats with a torch, and in the interval you just sell sweets and cigarettes and things."

"I know what an usherette is." Molly said flatly.

Audrey continued, her voice rising enthusiastically, "There are perks too - you get to watch all the latest films for free. I haven't been to the cinema for ages – perhaps you and I could both work there, that would be such fun, I can leave Margaret with Mother Sarah. But the must important part is that once I start working there I can learn the business, maybe become a manager, or even open my own cinema one day, they say the industry is going to really start growing, I could make lots of money, my own money, not inherited, and give people good jobs, a better life…"

Seeing Molly's stony-faced expression Audrey stopped in mid flow.

"Why whatever is the matter Moll?"

"Aud, I'm your friend, your best friend I hope…"

"You certainly are, the best I've had and always will be."

Molly nodded. "Good. So I'll say only this to you now, and take heed – go and work at the Magnet by all means – but please Aud, for your own sake, be careful."

Audrey began giggling.

"Oh Moll you are funny sometimes; what, do you think I'm going to do - trip over in the aisles and spill all my choc ices?"

The following Thursday Audrey fed and settled her daughter then wheeled her in the Silver Cross pram along Jericho Road to Mother Sarah's house.

"Thanks ever so much for doing this Ma," she said, as Sarah helped her over the doorstep with the pram. "I won't be long."

"Going for an usherette job down the Magnet you say?"

"That's right – they're showing "The Corn is Green" this week – Nigel Bruce and Bette Davis – I can't wait. I'm going to learn all about the cinema business too – see behind the scenes."

The old lady gave her a searching look but said nothing.

It was a warm August evening, and rather than wait for the bus, Audrey, with time in hand, began the half- mile walk into town. The Magnet, a large and imposing structure built in the 1920's as a theatre and with the advent of talking pictures had been adapted for use as a cinema.

On arrival there was already a queue formed for the early evening showing. She stopped for a moment and gazed at the poster outside: "The Corn is Green" there was a still depicting Bette Davis bravely gazing into towards the new day. From what she had heard the story of a middle aged lady (Bette Davis) who set up a school in a Welsh Coal mining village against all the odds.

Audrey smoothed down her dress, straightened her hair and mounted wide marble steps. Bypassing the queue she went through the chrome and glass double doors and entered the grand, deep-carpeted foyer. She looked about her, and felt a little tingle.

There was something thrilling, magical about the softly lit interior, the secret entrance to a place of enchantment – beyond lay the silver screen, a world of untold romance and excitement.
To either side, a staircase, with ornately scrolled balustrades led to the circle. In the centre of the foyer were two more large doors with a round glass panel at the top of each, which led through to the stalls.

one side was the ticket booth, where, seated behind the glass a young woman was taking money and handing out the tickets. On the opposite side was the sweet and cigarette kiosk, where a young woman in an orange and cream outfit stood serving.

Guarding the doors the commissionaire, a young man in an immaculate green and orange uniform with gold epaulettes on the shoulders and a peaked cap, was directing the patrons through to the ticket booth

"Can I help you Miss?" he asked Audrey.

"Oh yes, thank you - I've come for a job."

"Really?" he gave a rather impertinent grin and looked her up and down. "You're a bit different to the other girls – I dare say you'll be popular though."

"Oh, yes…" said Audrey uncomfortably. "Is the manager about? I was advised to see him – about the job."

"In there." He nodded to an unmarked door to the side of the ticket office. Audrey went over and tapped lightly.

"Come in," came a soft voice from within. She entered and found herself in a small, windowless room. Sat behind an oak desk was a diminutive, bald headed man dressed in a brown tweed suit.

"Yes, what can I do for you?" he asked courteously.

"I've come about the job, the girls from the biscuit factory, Aggie and Elsie, said to come and see you - they work here a couple of nights a week."

The manager's eyes, like tiny pinpricks, stared at her. "Ah, I see. So you…" he hesitated, "you know what they do here?"

"Oh yes. And I'm quite happy to turn my hand to anything – all that might be required, to keep the customers satisfied – I'm sure I'd make a good usherette."

"An usherette…?" The manager looked at her blankly for a moment. "Ah yes I see, of course – well yes there is a vacancy at the moment, two nights a week - its yours if you want it."

"Oh." Audrey looked surprised. "Don't you want references?"

He coughed. "You seem a bright enough girl. Come in tomorrow night about 6.30. Gladys will show you what to do. Here take this - it should fit by the look of you dear." He handed her a brown paper parcel. "The girl that's just left was about the same size as you."

"Thank you Mr.…?"

"Pendleton, Maurice Pendleton - Gladys will be on tomorrow night, keep an eye on what she does, it'll give you an idea of what's expected of you."

"Well what do you think?" Audrey, stood on a chair in the living room of 112 Jericho Road, twirled round in her usherette's uniform.

"Well you certainly look the part," said Molly. She narrowed her eyes for a moment. "And you're sure it's just an usherette job you'll be doing at the Magnet?"

Audrey stopped twirling and looked at her.

"Why does everyone keep asking me that? Of course, what else would I be doing in a cinema? I've got to start at the bottom Moll, get experience."

"There's experience and there's experience," said Molly darkly.

"What do you mean?"

Before Molly could reply, baby Margaret began crying. Audrey jumped down from the chair and went over to the Silver Cross pram. She rocked the handle gently to and fro. "Mummy's her darling," she cooed. "Only Mummy in a silly old costume." She unbuttoned the jacket of her uniform. "There, that's better isn't it?"

"Hello Elsie, hello Aggie." Seeing the two girls seated together in the biscuit factory canteen, Audrey waved cheerily and went over to their table.

"Just to let you know," she whispered conspiratorially, "I got the job at the Magnet – I start tonight. Bit nervous though."
Aggie and Elsie exchanged a look.

"Oh aye?" said Elsie guardedly. "We're working tonight n'" all. Should be busy, Fridays usually are. We'll see you down there then, if you're not too pushed, being a new girl."
Audrey looked quizzical for a second then smiled,

Oh, yes – well that'll be nice, you can give me a few tips."
Aggie gave a hollow laugh, "Yeah, we can do that all right."

"Well, thanks Elsie, That's very good of you."
Audrey walked towards the door that led back to the factory floor. The two girls watched her silently then exchanged another meaningful look.

Audrey, her freshly laundered uniform under her arm, arrived at the Magnet at 6 p.m. Finding the doors locked she looked up and down the street and a moment later saw Elsie appear on the corner. She waved. "Elsie – hello."

"You're early," said Elsie as she approached. "It doesn't open till seven."

"Oh Mr. Pendleton told me to be her for half past six, so Gladys could show me around, I think."

"Better come with me." Elsie led her down an alleyway at the side of the building. By a small door, two young men were loitering.

"Evening else," said one of them. "Who's this then?"

"A new girl – usherette." Elsie replied without looking at him. She knocked on the door.

"Not working with you then?" the young man asked. Audrey sensed him staring at her.

"No," replied Elsie clearly. "She's up front."

"I bet she is," remarked the young man's companion. They both laughed cockily. Audrey, feeling a hand on her arm as they went through the door, gasped.

"Eh, lay off Freddy." said Elsie. "She's too good for the likes of you."

"Get off." Audrey snatched her arm free of his grip

"Ooh, hoity-toity are we?" sneered Freddy.

The other man laughed. "Elsie's right mate – she's way out of your league."

On the other side of the door Audrey found herself in semi darkness. Then suddenly she stepped back, as out of the gloom appeared a startling vision, a woman of somewhat indeterminate middle age, with bright ginger wavy hair, her face heavily powdered, and wearing thick mascara and a lurid shade of red lipstick.

Her floral patterned dress was gathered in sharply at the waist, from which rose a tightly laced bodice that emphasised a pair of extremely ample breasts, the plunging neckline above revealing an immodest depth of very defined cleavage.

Audrey noticed that the woman's hands, as they held the door to the alley, were leathery and aged, the fingernails painted with varnish of an even gaudier red than her lipstick.

"Who's this?" she said, jerking a thumb towards Audrey.

"The new girl," replied Elsie.

Audrey then flinched as the older woman shone a torch directly into her face. The beam then roved slowly over her body.

"Not bad Else," said the woman." "Not bad at all"

"She's front of house," said Elsie.

"We'll see" the older woman grinned, "we'll see"

At this the two young men from the alley laughed again

"Hop it you two," she rasped, "We're not open yet." She shoved the protesting pair back out into the alley and shut the door firmly. She then turned back to Audrey. "Sorry about that dearie, you got to tell these fellers what for, you'll learn that soon enough. I'm Mrs Skillycorn, I run the accounts office."

"How do you do," replied Audrey timidly, and held out her hand.

Mrs Skillycorn ignored it and walked off along the darkened corridor. Elsie nudged Audrey and they followed the flickering light of the torch, Audrey tripping and stumbling several times.

A few seconds later, seeing the shadowy rows of seats and the heavy velvet cinema curtains stretching up behind her, she realised they were now at the front of the auditorium. The vast blank enormous emptiness, with its dark corners and blacked out spaces, the dizzying height of the ceiling, felt eerie.

"Bring the new girl into my office Else," said Mrs Skillycorn.

225

At that moment Audrey started as another figure appeared suddenly behind her. Then she saw that it was Mr Pendleton.

"Oh, Maurice, it's you," said Mrs Skillycorn. "I was just taking the new girl under my wing."

"So I gathered," said Mr. Pendleton. "But there'll be no need thank you Mrs Skillycorn. Audrey's our new usherette. Follow me please young lady."

Before Audrey could look round, both Mrs Skillycorn and Elsie had disappeared into the shadows. Mr Pendleton took her arm and guided her up the sloping auditorium and out into the foyer. Audrey blinked in the bright light.

She followed Mr Pendleton towards his office. "In future Audrey," he said, there's no need to use the side door when you come in."

"Oh sorry, I just followed Elsie in that way, I thought…"

"Yes well she works for Mrs Skillycorn in the accounts office. Now if you'd like to get changed, Gladys will be here to show you the ropes shortly." He indicated a door marked 'Ladies.'

Audrey donned her uniform and returned to the office. A young woman was now stood by Mr. Pendleton's desk.

"Audrey, meet Gladys," said Mr. Pendleton. The two women smiled at each other. "Well, I'll leave you ladies to it. He nodded politely and left the office.

Audrey liked Gladys. She'd seen her the previous evening working in the kiosk and carrying her tray down the aisle, and had been impressed by her competence and easy manner with the cinemagoers – counting out change efficiently, and always having a cheery reply couldn't be easy; she hoped she would do as well. Gladys was tall and slim, and looked awfully smart in her uniform.

"May I say I like the way you wear your hat Gladys," Audrey complimented her, "it really sets off your blonde hair beautifully – and that hairstyle is so wonderfully fashionable."

Gladys beamed. "Thanks pet – well, let's get going, that queue will be starting soon, and Fridays is always busy – I'm right pleased to have you here I can tell you, we could do with two usherettes every night really, the way things are going, what with the kiosk, and showing them in."

"Business is good then? Audrey said, as Gladys led her over to the kiosk.

"Booming pet; they say there's no money about, but this place makes a mint; mark my words. Not that we see much of it. Here try this for size." She handed Audrey a cigarette tray.

"I'd like to learn the cinema business actually," said Audrey, adjusting the strap of the tray around her shoulders.

Gladys smiled. "I can see you've got your head screwed on." Then, lowering her voice, she said, "Though this place is a bit different to some cinemas."

"In what way?" asked Audrey, counting out the change in her float.

"Let's just say not everyone comes in to watch the film."

"Oh – courting couples you mean?" Audrey gave a bashful smile. "Well I suppose that's all good for business too."

Gladys was about to make a reply, then appeared to change her mind. Instead she said, "Come on then, battle stations." She called over to the commissionaire, who was in position on the doors. "Let them in Ernie!"

Audrey followed her colleague into the auditorium, where the house lights were now up, and took up position as directed, in front of the screen facing the left aisle, while Gladys took the right.

Within a few moments people began drifting in and sitting down. Some made a beeline straight for either Audrey or Gladys, and asked for cigarettes, ices or chocolate, or all three.

Most were friendly, and some of the chaps quite chatty. Once Audrey had located the little light on her tray and switched it on, she found she could handle the change quite well, and several people in any case were helpful enough to provide the exact coins.

`Suddenly music began playing from loudspeakers high up on the walls. The house lights dimmed, and with a squeak and a rattle, the great red and gold velvet curtains drew open. There was a buzz of anticipation along the rows of seats, and some 'shushing'. Audrey looked over at Gladys, uncertain whether to remain in place. Gladys made a 'stay put' gesture with her hand, then came a few steps towards her.

"This is Pathe News," she whispered. "We stay on the aisles till the big flick starts, then move to the side, and stand about halfway up – there's always a few customers that'll come and find you, so you've got to keep on selling, but you should be able to watch the film as well if you want – I've seen it four times already, so I won't tell you what happens. In the interval, you walk back into the middle, and face the enemy again! I'll be doing the same in the circle then, so you'll be on your own down here, but if you need me, just shout. Good luck pet. Oh and by the way, did Pendleton mention that door over there?" She pointed towards a barely visible door on the side aisle. Audrey shook her head. "Isn't that the accounts office or something – where that woman with all make-up works."

"That's right," said Gladys emphatically. "So don't go near it whatever you do. Mr. Pendleton doesn't allow it. Even if you're asked to, don't go in there, understand?"

Audrey looked puzzled. "Why, what's so mysterious - won't I have to go in there to collect my wages…?"

"No!" snapped Gladys. "It's…its not safe."

"Not safe?"

"There's lots of old wiring and machinery lying about. Mrs Skillycorn makes up our money and gives the wages to Mr Pendleton, he'll pay you at the end of the week."

"But…"

"Oh and there's rats behind there too."

Audrey shivered. "Ach – I hate rats. Oh but poor Elsie – having to work in there! Why doesn't she complain?"

Gladys looked flustered for a moment. "Some folk don't mind I suppose. Time we were in position pet. See you in the interval, good luck."

CHAPTER THIRTY-SEVEN

September 1945

Audrey had been working at the cinema for six weeks and enjoying every minute of it. Despite an intense curiosity, she had obeyed Gladys's warning never to go near the mysterious darkened doors of the accounts office.

The thought of rats was quite enough to deter her from any attempt to peep through and find out what Mrs Skillycorn and Elsie were up to in there. Perhaps the place was a health hazard, and Mr Pendleton was worried the Town Hall would close down the cinema if anyone found out. It was probably nothing more than that Audrey decided.

Since the first night however she had not seen Elsie at the Magnet, and only glimpsed her fleetingly at the bakery, not long enough to speak to. She had formed the distinct impression Elsie and Aggie, were both avoiding her of late.

"I don't know what I've done to upset them Moll," she complained to her friend one Saturday afternoon over tea and the latest 'reject' cakes from the bakery. "I saw them both in the canteen yesterday morning and they put their heads down and shuffled out ever so quickly. They're deliberately avoiding."

"Perhaps they think you think you're better than them, the way you talk," mused Molly. "You know what some folk are like, judge a book by its cover."

Audrey pursed her lips. "Some of the girls do, you're right Moll. But Elsie and Aggie have never been like that, not till a few months ago."

"Not till you started at the Magnet you mean?"

"Exactly!" Audrey eyes lit up. "There's something going on their Moll."

Molly looked at her friend anxiously. "What do you mean?"

"I don't know. But, I intend to find out."

"Aud – look don't waste your time on them," Molly said quickly, "I told you that lot are wrong-uns'."

"I tell you one thing," said Audrey decisively, "If I see Elsie tonight I'm going to have it out with her. I don't like being shunned for no good reason. We were friends before, and something's wrong."

"It's Saturday night Aud," protested Molly. "You're not going to work again surely - this is the fourth night this week. Stay home for once, there's no sense stirring up trouble…"

"Moll, if those girls are in some sort of trouble, they need help." Audrey gathered her uniform together and put on her coat. She then kissed Margaret, and gave Molly's arm a little squeeze. "Don't worry – I can look after myself.

Hearing the front door close Molly bit her lip and gazed down into her teacup, her expression was one of intense concern.

Reaching the bus stop just in time Audrey boarded the 5.15 into town and paid the penny fare. Settling down in the seat she reflected on Molly's remarks. She loved her friend dearly, but did she always have to be so overprotective.

As the bus swayed and bumped along, she began to feel slightly annoyed. Who did Molly Bratt think she was – her gaoler?

As she alighted opposite the cinema the church clock struck six. It was early so she decided to wait on the steps. She had just sat down when Elsie turned the corner of the road.

Thinking: here's my chance she waved. Elsie immediately began running for the alley at the side of the cinema.

"Oh no you don't Elsie Dodd," Audrey sprang up and intercepted her, catching her by the arm.

"Here, what's the game…?"

"I want to know what I've done to upset you and Aggie," said Audrey politely but firmly.

Elsie averted her face. "Nothing Aud, honest, don't know what you talking about?"

"Then look at me, Elsie, tell me, what's wrong?"

Elsie slowly turned to face her. Audrey gasped. Elsie's left pupil was barely visible – the flesh around her eye swollen by a huge angry-looking bruise.

"Whatever happened to you?" asked Audrey

"I fell over," said Elsie, quickly covering her face with her hand.

"I don't believe you," challenged Audrey.

Elsie nodded somberly. "I did so - and that's an end to it – what of it?"

Audrey hesitated. Then as Elsie was about to walk away up the alley she stood in her way.

"That doesn't explain why you and Aggie have been avoiding me. Is it to do with me working here?"

Elsie stared at her. "No love," she said quietly. "It's got nothing to do with that."

Audrey changed tack. She smiled, "Were you drunk when you fell over?"

"Might have been," replied Elsie, returning the smile sullenly.

"And you thought I would disapprove? What a silly goose you are." Audrey put an arm around her.

"Elsie Dodd - get in here!" The raucous voice reverberated down the alley like an air raid klaxon. Audrey saw Mrs Skillycorn's hatchet face at the side door. She felt Elsie stiffen.

"Sorry Audrey, I've got to go."

Audrey looked into her eyes, wincing at the sight of the lurid injury.

"We are friends again then Elsie?"

"Always Aud," she muttered, and shuffled off hurriedly towards the side door. Mrs Skillycorn had already disappeared. The door closed with a bang and the alley was deathly silent.

Audrey walked back to the cinema steps and waited. The church clock struck the half hour. She looked anxiously along the street for Mr Pendleton. If he didn't arrive soon she would have a rush to get the trays and the kiosk stocked up it time. Audrey hated rushing.

Suddenly, behind her the main cinema doors opened.

"Mrs Skillycorn…" she exclaimed, surprised to see her here after the earlier apparition in the alley.

"Maurice won't be in tonight," said Mrs Skillycorn abruptly.

"Oh…why…?" said Audrey nervously.

"He's been taken queer. I'll be in charge."

Audrey sat rooted to the steps. She felt the woman's eyes boring into her.

"Well, don't hang about," rasped Mrs Skillycorn. "Get in - you're on your own tonight, Glad's away too."

Audrey hurried inside and into the ladies toilet, changed into her uniform and headed for the kiosk.

"Just a minute you." Mrs Skillycorn was behind her again. "Now listen, I'll be paying the wages at the office out back tonight. After the show, you're to come in and get your money – down behind the screen, you know the doors?"

Audrey gulped. "Mr Pendleton told me not to go through there…the rats…"

Mrs Skillycorn gave a mocking laugh. "If you want your money, you'll come." She pushed open the auditorium door and disappeared into the stalls.

The evening flew by. Audrey had prepared her tray quickly and efficiently and filled the kiosk counter. She had sold a lot of stock over the two hours, moving busily between the kiosk, stalls and circle, and people had been ever so friendly. One couple kept coming back for ices and giggling loudly.

Her shift over Audrey had changed out of her uniform and was now feeling worried. Mrs Skillycorn had quite given her the creeps earlier, and now, if she wanted her wages she was going to have to go through those hideous doors. There was surely no reason why they couldn't bring her pay packet out to the foyer; she felt sure the woman was just trying to spite her.

She walked slowly backing into the empty auditorium and waited till Marjorie the ticket office lady and Bruce, the doorman had gone through the doors and seen them come out again. Bruce gave her one of his sly, smirking looks as he passed her.

Now it was her turn. She turned the handle and pushed open the left hand door, as she had seen the others do. Finding herself in a small dimly lit hallway she recoiled at a strong smell of stale alcohol. In front she could just make out another set of identical doors; this must the way through to the alley, where she had been led blindly on the first day. She heard the sound of muffled laughter from the other side of the doors.

"Hello?" she called, taking the handle and going in.

"Well if its not Miss posh knickers!" It was Mrs Skillycorn, her derisive greeting rang out over a cacophony of chatter and the sound of gramophone playing a loud, scratchy, slightly out of tune, wailing melody. Mrs Skillycorn's face was framed eerily in a pool of light from somewhere within a small hatch. Audrey saw the words 'Pay Office' etched on a pane of glass above.

232

"Welcome dearie - come and join the fun," she cackled."
Audrey felt her knees trembling. "I...just want my pay please," she stammered.

"Oh everyone gets paid here dear – and sooner or later everyone has to pay an" all – one way or another – ah ha-ha-ha...!'"
Audrey moved a little further into the light, and stopped, rooted to the spot, staring in horror at the scene before her. To the right were a series of small doors, on her left a small, open-sided anteroom, within which an assortment of men – some in uniform, soldiers, sailors and airmen, others civilians, were sat, drinks in hand, leering at a small group of semi-naked women stood in their midst

As she watched, one of the soldiers grasped one of the women roughly by the arm and pulled her through one of the small doors.
Suddenly Audrey caught her breath; emerging from one of the doors, a flimsy negligee barely concealing her, was Elsie. With unseeing eyes she walked over to Mrs Skillycorn and handed her something. With another spasm of shock Audrey realised it was money.

"That all?" demanded Skillycorn.

"Course it is," muttered Elsie.

"Cos' if I find you holding out on me..."

"That's what he gave me, I swear."

"It better be."

"I've gotta go now Mrs Skillycorn..."

"You go when I say! I've customers waiting."
Elsie turned away, and it was then she saw Audrey. Her face a mask of mortification and shame, Elsie turned again, this time to run. Audrey took her arm and steered her to a corner.

"Audrey! Dear God I told you never to set foot in here..."

"I invited her!" shouted Mrs Skillycorn. "Now get back to work Elsie Dodd...why hello Major, haven't seen you for a while." She turned her attention to a great-coated man who had just arrived, giving him a sickly smile.
Audrey gripped Elsie's arm. "Elsie," she whispered intensely, "why are you doing this?"
Elsie snatched her arm away. "I've got kids to feed," she hissed. "Harry's still away, what am I supposed to do."

"But your job at the bakery – isn't that enough?"

Elsie gave a hollow laugh, "I make more in a night here than a week at that place. I've three nippers – they don't live on fresh air – and I want some money of me own. It's all right for the likes of you."

Mrs Skillycorn, overhearing their conversation smirked,

"These lads pay good money. You should try it Audrey they'd enjoy a bit of posh meat like yours love."

"I am not your love!" snapped Audrey. She turned back to Elsie. "So this is how you got the bruises?"

Its all part of the job." Mrs Skillycorn grinned savagely her teeth gleaming like knives in the half-light.

"Elsie, you must…" began Audrey, but stopped short as something grabbed her from behind. "Ach! Leave me alone you…!"

Turning her head a fraction she saw a sallow face, its features contorted, two piggy eyes gleaming with lustful intent. She began to struggle but the man's vice like hands held her shoulders tight.

"How much for this one Mrs S?" he slurred. His breath, rancid with alcohol made Audrey's stomach churn.

"Ten bob Stan." Mrs Skillycorn held out her hand. "In advance."

"Let her go!" Elsie had sprung forward and grabbed the man's hand.

With a shove he threw her off effortlessly and she fell to the floor. Mrs Skillycorn came forward, and dragging her to her feet again pushed her face into Elsie's.

"You'll get back in there, and do your job," she said, then added menacingly: "if you know what's good for you."

Audrey was still held captive by the foul breathed man with piggy eyes.

"Bit frisky this one Skilly," he muttered.

"Take her leave her," said Skillycorn. "She's new."

"Yeah, I can see that…" he gave Audrey a hideous leer. "I'll take her." He fumbled in his pocket and threw a ten-shilling note into the hatch.

"Fifteen minutes," barked Mrs Skillycorn pocketing the note.

Audrey screamed the man slapped a hand over her mouth. Dragging her through one of the small doors he slammed it shut behind him and threw her onto a low, grubby looking bed.

"I like 'em when they fight," he grinned.

Audrey smelt his breath again, she screamed again, and again, louder and louder. The sound seemed to vanish into the walls. He laughed. "No one can hear you, it's a cinema see – soundproof ha-ha-ha..." He came towards her, his fist raised.

Suddenly the door burst open. "Get off her now!" Elsie stood there, nervous, but defiant. The piggy eyes turned and stared drunkenly at her. "You don't want her -she's no good, here have me Stan, I'm much better." She came towards him, lowering one strap of her negligee. She began to rub her body against his. "Besides, I've always liked you Stan - you're a real man if you know what I mean, not like the others."

"No," grunted Stan. "I want her." He turned back towards the bed where Audrey lay terrified.

Elsie pulled him closer to her. "Stan, you know what I'd like to do to you?"

"What?"

She leaned over and whispered in his ear. The piggy eyes lit up. He grunted again, this time with pleasure. Elsie jerked her head towards Audrey, indicating the door. Silently her lips mouthed the words "Run, run, run..."

Audrey leapt up and hurtled through the door. A she ran headlong past the Pay Desk, and out into the empty auditorium she heard Mrs Skillycorn's mocking voice calling out behind her.

"You'll be back Posh Knickers, you'll see, one day you'll be back, everyone pays in the end, one way or another, ha-ha-ha-ha! "

CHAPTER THIRTY- EIGHT

"I tried to warn you about that place Aud."

They were in the kitchen at Jericho Road. Molly was consoling Audrey after hearing about her ordeal.

"We all knew something was going on there, I just wish I'd told you straight out what it was."

"If I had known," Audrey sobbed, "I'd never have set foot there."

Molly put her arms around her friend. "I know, but consider it a lesson - you were dead lucky tonight."

Audrey shuddered. "Don't say it like that!"

"Sorry."

"Because if Elsie hadn't been there…" Audrey gave a sudden wail. "She saved me Moll, saved me from…oh that man had such a terrible look in his eye."

"It's all over now, you need never go near the place again."

"What about the money they owe me?"

"That's the least of your worries! I think we'll manage." Molly stroked her hair. "The main thing is you're all right."

Audrey nodded and dried her eyes. "I'd better go to bed, work tomorrow."

"You're not going into the bakery are you? Elsie will be there."

"Exactly. For a start we need the money, but mainly I want to thank Elsie for helping me tonight – and tell her off at the same time, try to persuade her not to do what she does."

Molly sighed and shook her head. "You'll be wasting your time, and your sympathy. She's tasted the money and she'll not give it up. And she's got kids - women will do anything for their family."

"I wouldn't do that – I couldn't, I'd find some other way."

Molly smiled kindly. "I know you would love but not all folk are as clever, or strong-minded. Take my advice Aud, keep away from Elsie."

Audrey looked puzzled. "But why should I do that, just because I disapprove of what she's doing?" she said earnestly. "She's obviously frightened sick, caught in a terrible trap. Apart from anything else I owe her a great deal after what happened tonight. I must help her don't you see?"

A look of deep concern clouded Molly's face. "Audrey I admire your good intentions pet, but you know what they say about the road to hell." Taking Audrey's hand she leaned towards her. In a low voice she said, "you don't know what you're dealing with. The Magnet's run by dangerous people, I'm begging you Aud, don't mess with them."

Arriving at the bakery ten minutes before the morning shift began Audrey took up position just inside the works entrance. As soon as Elsie came in she approached her. Elsie, with a look of alarm, immediately sheered off into the ladies' lavatory. Audrey followed.

"Oh no you don't," she called out, hearing a cubicle being bolted. "I want to talk to you."

"Well I don't want to talk to you," came the muffled reply.

Audrey banged loudly on the wooden door.

"Elsie - come out now. I want to thank you for last night, and I want to help you get away from that dreadful place."

There was silence for a moment then the bolt rattled back and the door opened. Elsie wore a slightly truculent look.

"What's dreadful about it?" she said. "And who says I want to get away? All right it's not for the likes of you, That's why I had to get you out of there, simple as that, someone had to do it. But I don't want any la-de-da thank you – or your interfering advice."

She pushed past Audrey and began scrubbing her hands and face furiously at the sink. As she did so Audrey noticed that her left eye was now also bruised, her cheek swollen, and there were several deep scratches across her throat.

"Oh Elsie," she gasped. "Why do you let those men do this to you?"

Elsie gave a quick snort of contempt. "It's not the punters you stupid arse. It's that old witch Skillycorn. Keeps us in line, she says." Then suddenly the hard face crumpled and she began to cry. "I'll never be free of her."

Audrey put her arms round her. "Oh Elsie of course you can be free, just don't go there anymore, try to make do with the wages from here, I'll give you some extra when I've got it."

Elsie dragged her sleeve across her wet eyes and turned away. "I don't want charity. Oh you'll never get it, not the likes of you, you just don't understand…"

"Then make me understand," pleaded Audrey.

Elsie looked furtively around as if someone might be listening,

"I can't get away," she whispered. "I've tried before. Skillycorn will tell my husband, and get my kids took off me. I only started there to get a bit of cash for Christmas - that was a year ago. The old cow's got me over a barrel. I daren't say no to her."

Audrey struggled to think. "She might be bluffing,"

Elsie sighed heavily. "Her sort don't muck about. Besides, she knows people, people who…do things…to other people."

"Then go to the police Elsie, they can stop all this…"

At that moment the door opened; it was Aggie. "You know you can't." she grinned. For a moment she stood and glared at Audrey. Then she continued, "Leave her be, there's no way out of it, not for any of us."

Elsie now put her head down, pushed past Aggie and rushed out. Aggie, shaking her head fixed her gaze on Audrey again.

"Leave her be," she said, an unsavoury menacing tone in her voice. "Leave us be. There's no way out of for us."

"There's always a way out!" Audrey exclaimed spiritedly. "Go to the police, just tell them everything."

Aggie threw back her head and laughed bitterly, the noise reverberating round the cubicles. "That's a good one. The coppers are Skillycorn's best customers!"

"Then I'll go to the police myself," fumed Audrey, "There must be something we can do."

Aggie grabbed Audrey's arms roughly. "Listen you silly bitch, leave us alone!" she spat. "You don't know who you're dealing with. Skillycorn's vicious, but so long as she gets her money she'll look after us. If she don't –its just another prossie dead on the dock road - along with anyone else that gets in the way." She stared meaningfully into Audrey's eyes.

Audrey snatched her arms free. Desperately she said, "There must a way out, surely?"

"There is - if Skillycorn was dead. And by God I go to bed every night praying for it. But no one can kill a devil like Skillycorn Audrey, no one, because you see she's inside of us, inside all of us I tell you!"

She began laughing again - a cruel, rattling, deep throated, monstrous noise. Audrey remembered with a shiver of pure terror that it was almost exactly the same sound she had heard only the night before: it was Mrs Skillycorn's laugh.

Aggie and Elsie kept their distance for the rest of the day, only nodding to her briefly as they left the factory together. Audrey noticed how sad and afraid Elsie seemed, the painful looking bruises on her arms and face still very apparent. Walking home she couldn't get Elsie out of her mind.

"What's wrong?" Molly asked. Audrey sat down glumly in the kitchen at Jericho Road and related her encounter with the two girls that morning.

"I told you not to get involved," Molly said, almost angrily. "They got themselves in that mess, leave them to it, and be thankful you got away when you did."

"But that woman is evil," said Audrey emphatically. "And I'm really afraid for Elsie."

Molly wagged her finger. "Nothing to do with you! Keep out of it."

Audrey nodded, stirred her tea and said no more. But her mind was working hard. She knew Elsie would be at the cinema that night. She resolved to go along and wait for her outside, try again to stop her from going through the side door into the hellhole that lay behind it. Or, what if, Audrey then thought, what if she went in herself and spoke to Mrs Skillycorn? She swallowed: Did she really have the courage for such a daring course of action? She would find it; she had to find it if she were to help her friend.

It was 11 pm before Audrey felt it safe enough to leave the house. Margaret was in her cot in Molly's room under the pretence she had wanted to stay with Aunty Molly, so if she awoke Molly could tend to her. She would face Molly's wrath later if that should happen. Hopefully it would not come to that, thought Audrey, and she would be back before her absence had been noticed, and with any luck, her mission accomplished. Luck, yes, she was going to need a lot of it.

Slowly creeping down the stairs Audrey took her coat from the hall and quietly opened the front door and set off for the Magnet cinema.

It was a mild evening, the streets taking on a different, unfamiliar persona in the darkness. She negotiated the pavements cautiously, avoiding the drunks weaving their way home after being ejected from the various pubs on route.

Arriving at the cinema she saw the lights were still on, and a few stragglers coming down the steps after the last showing.

The side alley was in complete darkness save for a faint insipid amber glow at the upper windows. Giving a quick glance up and down the street, she began walking slowly up the alley, her feet feeling their way along the uneven ground.

Suddenly the side door sprang open casting a shaft of dim light into the darkness. With a start Audrey lurched towards the bushes that lined the wall on the right and pushed her way in. Her heart beating fast she peered through the branches and saw Mrs Skillycorn pushing a group of cheerful sounding drunks out into the alley. Laughing along with them, she cackled, "Come again boys, we're open every night – always a warm welcome at the Magnet."

Audrey could see the fearsome woman's buxom silhouette in the light, waving to the group. As they came past her hiding place Audrey froze, then held her breath as one man staggered and fell against her.

Uttering a foulmouthed curse, he righted himself and walked unsteadily on. When they had turned the corner Mrs Skillycorn disappeared slamming the door shut. Audrey paused momentarily then moved forward from the bushes, but stepped quickly back again as the door reopened.

In the shaft of light another figure appeared. Audrey stiffened: it was Elsie. Looking about her the girl took from her coat pocket a brightly coloured flowery headscarf, put it on her head and tied it firmly under her chin then walked along the alley towards the main road. Once she had gone by, Audrey waited again; other women were emerging from the side door. She heard again Mrs Skillycorn's voice. "See you tomorrow girls – and make sure you're on time, we're going to be busy." Her harsh mocking laugh echoed down the alley rattling the crates of empty beer bottles.

Without speaking the girls hurried towards the road. The door closed again. Audrey waited till their footsteps had faded away and all was silent once more. Elsie would be long gone, she thought, and Mrs Skillycorn was alone. This was her one and only chance, but her nerves were jangling.

She took a long, deep breath and began to leave her hiding place - then came more footsteps. She stopped abruptly.

From out of the shadows a figure was emerging. Audrey hid again behind the bushes and watched the solitary figure walk quickly by.

"Elsie?!" she whispered softly to herself. Why had she come back?

Reaching the side door Elsie removed the headscarf, shook her hair free and went back inside the cinema. Audrey stood listening, thinking: she must have forgotten something. Mrs Skillycorn would still be inside; she could only come out this way, as the front doors would all be locked by now.

The minutes ticked by. Audrey began to feel cramped and uncomfortable. She did not want to move a muscle yet lest Elsie should spot her when she came out again. She wanted Mrs Skillycorn alone. Then a terrible thought came to her: What if Elsie had been told to come back after the others had gone?

Suppose Skillycorn had arranged for those horrible men, those people all too willing to "do things", to be there - and what about those injuries on Elsie's face? Perhaps this was how she had got them; was Elsie even a willing participant in all this? And most terrifying of all, thought Audrey, what if any moment they discovered her hiding in the alley?

Panic swept over her: what on earth was she doing here? How stupid she had been; thinking she could face down this crazy, tyrannical violent woman? Molly was right: leave Elsie to it, if only she had listened to Molly. Now she had to get away. Go; run, before they found her...

Just at that moment the side door burst open with a loud bang and Elsie ran out full tilt down the alley. Revealed for a split second in the half-light, her damaged face had a look of utter horror. Audrey's mind was whirling again. She craned forward, waiting to see if Mrs Skillycorn would follow. There was no sound, only the side door quietly squeaking now as it swung gently back and forth in the night breeze, the shaft of light widening and narrowing in time with the movement.

Several minutes went by, while Audrey's heart pounded. Finally she moved cautiously from the bushes and with careful steps approached the side door. She blinked in the sudden light, which now seemed brighter and shining straight in her eyes.

Reaching for the wall she felt her way slowly along pausing occasionally to listen. All was quiet, the silence oppressive. After a few feet she stumbled against something soft and heavy on the floor and looking down saw what appeared to be a tangled stage curtain. Then she saw something that made her gasp and stagger: a face was looking up at her. It was Mrs Skillycorn. The eyes were open and still, the lips twisted into a macabre grimacing smile. From within the mouth came a glint of gold teeth. At the back of the head was a pool of something red, viscous and glistening. Blood.

Audrey froze, summoning every sinew of her body not to scream, faint or fall onto the limp, lifeless form at her feet. At any moment she knew, with an absolute terror, that she was surely going to do one of these things. She felt dizzy now, her head lolled...then something caught her eye; on the floor near Mrs Skillycorn's crumpled body, a piece of brightly coloured fabric showed itself in the half-light. Audrey bent down; it was Elsie's scarf.

"Phyllis!" The voice coming from the direction of the auditorium brought Audrey quickly to her senses. It was Maurice Pendleton. "Phyllis – are you down there?" He was getting closer. "I want my money, and I'm not leaving without it tonight I'm telling you straight! Twenty pounds tonight or there's going to be trouble - we agreed – Phyllis...?"

Audrey didn't wait any longer. Snatching up the scarf, she stumbled to the doorway and ran as fast as she could towards the road. The last thing she heard was a chilling scream, echoing along the alleyway. Maurice Pendleton had found the body.

She didn't know how far she'd run before her breath expired and the sickness overcame her. Stopping on a corner she gulped in great lungs full of the night air. Hot, yet still shaking with terror at what she had witnessed, she felt in her pocket; Elsie's scarf, the incriminating evidence she had taken from the scene of the crime was still there. Looking about her she saw familiar shops; she was close to Jericho Road; home was just around the corner.

Closing the front door carefully Audrey then paused. The house was silent. With some relief she removed her coat and hung it on the peg, took the scarf from the pocket and crept upstairs, only stopping briefly to peer through the half open door of Molly's bedroom. Both Molly and Margaret were sound asleep. She felt a desperate urge to take her little girl in her arms and hold her, but held back; she could not face Molly right now, nor answer any of the searching questions that were bound to ensue.

Audrey closed her bedroom door and sat on the bed. Looking at the headscarf she turned over in her mind the awful truth: Elsie had killed Skillycorn; the proof was in her hands. The police must be informed, justice had to be done.

Tears pricked her eyes as the significance of this hit her: Elsie – the girl who had saved her, and whom she had tried so desperately to rescue from the clutches of those vicious, corrupt people, from the spiral of poverty and exploitation and fear that had engulfed her, would hang. And Skillycorn, that evil woman, even in death would have won. Was that justice? Even Aggie had wished her dead.

In anguish, Audrey wound Elsie's scarf around her fingers, "Oh, what am I to do?" she whispered to herself. Aware of something sticky on her fingers she saw with a shock that the scarf was stained with blood, Skillycorn's blood.
Audrey's stomach churned. Retching, she rubbed her fingers frantically on the clean part of the scarf and threw it down. There was no doubt in her mind now what she must do.

By heck!" exclaimed Molly. Her eyes were glued to the front page of the local paper. "Have you seen this Aud?"
Audrey looked across the breakfast table. "No, what is it?" she replied with careful nonchalance.

"There's a woman been found murdered, night before last – at the Magnet!"
Audrey bit into a slice of bread to steady her nerves. "Oh - why?" she mumbled.

"In the wake of what is thought to have been an attempted robbery," read Molly with gusto, "a woman believed to be in her late fifties was found dead from head injuries at the Magnet Cinema – now wait for this," she paused for effect, "The manager, a Mr Maurice Pendleton, has been arrested and charged with her murder. I always thought there was something funny about that manager feller, but wouldn't put him down as a killer, no, there's more to this than meets the eye mark my words...eh and listen to this: Pendleton is further alleged to have collaborated with the victim in using the cinema to live off immoral earnings – that means running a brothel I suppose – and a large sum of cash had been recovered from a concealed area at the rear of the premises. Police believe the pair may have fallen out over these illegal earnings, which culminated in the woman's violent death. A police spokesman said: We are appealing for anyone who may have any information about the events at the Magnet Cinema to come and speak to us: all information will be treated in the strictest confidence."

Molly gave a low whistle and passed the paper across the table. "You knew this woman didn't you – she was the one you told me was there that night you got jumped on"
Audrey felt goose bumps creeping up her body. She nodded. "I wouldn't say I knew her." She shivered.

"Sorry love," said Molly. "I'm sure you don't want to be reminded of that."

"No I don't Moll. Audrey got up from the table as the clock on the mantelpiece chimed seven. "If it hadn't been for Elsie...."
Molly tut-tutted. "That's neither here nor there - she should never have got you involved in that place..."

"She didn't," said Audrey firmly. "And whatever you think of Elsie, she saved me that night, and for that I am grateful to her."

"Fair enough Aud, but how do you know it wasn't her did this?" she jabbed her finger at the newspaper.
Audrey froze. "What?" she said quietly.

"Elsie – how do you now she didn't stove the old woman's head in? You reckoned Elsie was desperate – well folk are capable of anything when they're desperate."

"Molly..."

"All right the old cow might have had it coming to her, but murder's murder Aud."

Audrey breathed hard. "Molly Bratt," she said tight-lipped, "I'm going to work." She went upstairs to her sleeping daughter, kissed her, then picked up the headscarf and put it in her handbag.

As Audrey and the rest of the staff arrived at the bakery that morning they found a surprise in store. Waiting to interview them in the canteen was a team of police officers. She looked discreetly around for Elsie but could not see her.

Slipping away from the others she went back to the perimeter gate. A few minutes later Elsie appeared. Audrey ran quickly towards her. "I have to talk to you," she said urgently, casting an anxious glance towards the bakery.

Grabbing her arm she drew her away from the stragglers still mooching in to work and into the shadows of a disused outbuilding by the gate.

"Get off me," hissed Elsie angrily.

Audrey maintained her grip. "The police are in there, they're asking questions."

"Police - what's that got to do with me?" replied Elsie her voice suddenly unsteady.

"I saw you last night - at the cinema." She heard Elsie give a sharp intake of breath. "I know what you did - I don't blame you, you found a way out."

"What do you mean - what did I do? I didn't do nothing - what you saying?" She snatched her arm away. "Get away from me, you're nothing but trouble." Pushing past Audrey she began walking quickly through the gate.

"Elsie," Audrey called after her, "I know what you have done."

Elsie stopped, turned and walked back to her. "Now you listen to me," she said menacingly. "I've done nothing, you hear, nothing, so keep your posh little nose out of my business and leave me alone, or else - you might live to regret it."

The canteen was full. The police were questioning everyone. Most of the tables and chairs had been pushed against the wall. A few had been set up in a row at one end, and sat behind each were two police officers.

The men and women had lined up separately forming two orderly queues that snaked around the large room. Audrey was immediately in front of Elsie and Aggie, she could hear their low unsavoury murmurings directed at her.

As she sat down at one of the tables in front of the police officers she glanced quickly behind her. Aggie glared, but Elsie looked troubled and edgy. Aggie was gripping her arm.

"Now young lady, can I see your identity card?" asked one of the police officers.

Audrey opened her handbag, sorted through it and withdrew the card, but as she did so her fingers caught in Elsie's brightly coloured headscarf. The scarf slithered from Audrey's grasp, fluttered down, and came to rest under the table by the policeman's feet. Audrey bent down quickly, but the officer was quicker. He retrieved the scarf and held it up. Audrey heard Elsie gasp.
The policeman looked at Audrey. She stared back at him.

"Must be alive," he said. Smiling, he handed her the scarf. "Here you are Miss."

"Thank you," she smiled back. "But it's not mine." She sensed Elsie stiffen behind her.

"Well it came out of your bag Miss."
Audrey paused and made a half-turn to Elsie. "I know," she said. "But as I said, it's not mine." She stood up and pointed to Elsie. "It belongs to her."

Elsie was visibly shaking and beads of perspiration were forming on her forehead. Audrey took her arm and stared deep into her eyes. Elsie bent her head. "I found it last night, Elsie, after you left my house." Elsie looked up. Audrey smiled at her. "It was on the chair, under the cushion."

"Oh, yeah, thanks," muttered Elsie weakly. She returned Audrey's stare, and a look passed between them, a look of understanding and absolute trust. Nothing more needed to be said.

CHAPTER THIRTY-NINE

Wedding Bells and Warfare

Autumn 1945

The post had come early. Molly rushed downstairs as soon as she heard the familiar rattle of the letterbox. Sifting through the envelopes she found the one she had been waiting for; Bill's masculine handwriting was unmistakable. She tore it open eagerly and sat on the bottom stair to read.

Audrey, rubbing a sleep crumpled face appeared at the top of the stairs. "Anything for me Moll?" she yawned.

"It's from Bill," replied Molly excitedly, not lifting her eyes from the page "he wants me to arrange the wedding."

"Oh that's wonderful Moll, I'll help you if you like." Audrey said cheerfully. Molly looked up at her friend. Her lips were pursed now. "What's the matter Moll?"

Molly cast her eyes down at the letter again. Tentatively she said, "I told you Bill was coming home soon." Audrey nodded. "Well it's sooner than expected - next week, and he wants me to arrange a special licence for the week after...."

"Marvellous," beamed Audrey. "I can do that for you – I know where to go, I can sort out the forms for you and everything....Molly, why are you looking like that?"

Molly sighed. "Bless you Aud, but..."

"But what?"

"There's something else we have to sort out first, you and me. Now, I don't want you to take this the wrong way Aud, but I mentioned to Bill that you and me were sharing this house and..."

"You want me to move out."

Molly frowned. "Why would I want you to do that?"

"Because you two will be starting a new life together and you won't want me tagging along," said Audrey matter-of-factly."

"As a matter of fact, the boot's on the other foot."

"What do you mean?" Audrey, looking confused, came and sat on the stair above Molly. Her brow furrowed. She had been bracing herself to be asked to leave Jericho Road once Bill came home and he and Molly got married, but as Molly said, that moment had come a bit sooner than expected. But now, what was this new twist of fate?

"Boots, feet, whose boots?" she yawned. "I don't think I'm quite awake yet."

"It's quite simple," said Molly, waving the letter. "Bill actually says here, that he hopes you won't mind if he comes to live here with us. You see I told him all about you Audrey, and little Margaret."

"Gosh, wasn't he shocked – I mean me not being married?"

"No, he says he's quite looking forward to taking his turn looking after Margaret. He comes from a big family you see, loads of kids around - misses the company I shouldn't wonder. The question is Aud – will you stay?"

Audrey stared in amazement. Moll, I…I think I'm the one that's shocked, to be asked to stay." She laughed. "Yes, yes, yes! Of course I would love to stay, if you think there's room. I promise I won't get in the way, and I'll be awfully discreet, you won't know I'm here. I'm eternally grateful - to you both, I can never repay your kindness to me."

"That's what friends are for." Molly smiled. "And come to think of it there is one thing you can do for me."

"Anything, just name it."

"Make the breakfast today!"

Audrey laughed heartily. "It would be my pleasure." She felt Molly really was her guardian angel, in every sense.

It was November 6th 1945, when William Marshall made an honest woman of Molly Bratt at the small Wesleyan chapel two streets away from Jericho Road. They had both wanted a quiet wedding with only a few family and friends in attendance. Dorothy, Molly's mother cried all through the service, only staunching her tears while the photographs were taken.

"Oh she's so happy Miss Audrey," she said, sniffing and looking on fondly as the bride and groom posed together by the chapel gate.

"Yes," Audrey agreed, "they make such a lovely couple, and from the bottom of my heart, I wish them all the happiness in the world."

Dorothy turned to her. "You've been such a good friend to my Moll," she said warmly, 'stuck by her through thick and thin. And it'll be your turn to walk down the aisle one day Miss Audrey, you'll see..." Seeing Audrey's face she tailed off.

Audrey's smile had vanished. "Dorothy how could you be so insensitive. I know you mean well, but please don't say anything like that again. I will never marry. Martin was my one and only love. Frankly I find your remarks impertinent."

Dorothy, flustered, endeavoured to control herself. She felt a powerful urge to slap Audrey's face.

"No need to fly off...I only meant - look I'm sorry Miss Audrey. Moll told me how special he was, how you felt about him...it was just...oh dear, I didn't meant to upset you."

Audrey, breathing rapidly, seemed also to be battling with strong emotions.

"Yes well, in future perhaps you could refrain...oh no, no I'm sorry, I shouldn't be so - I don't know...sensitive. Perhaps I shouldn't dwell in the past, maybe life won't let me, perhaps it's a sin to do so, oh I don't know what's the matter with me..."

Tears were filling her eyes. Dorothy delved in her handbag and proffered a large pink lace item from her store of hankies.

"Oh dear oh dear," she said apologetically, "now I've gone and spoiled it all for you. We were having such a nice time."

Audrey wiped her eyes and forced a smile back onto her face.

"Not at all," she sniffed. "I'm just being silly as usual. Now Dorothy, dear Dorothy," she linked the older woman's arm in hers. "Let's join your daughter and son–in–law on this unique day. When all's said and done, I think we all have a lot to celebrate."

The two, walked arm in arm, the difficult exchange diplomatically put aside, Dorothy reflecting on Audrey's sudden tirade. When the girl was angry, she thought, how like her mother she could be!

Bill and Molly, now Mr and Mrs Marshall, returned from their two-week honeymoon in Scarborough bearing gifts of all shapes and sizes, postcards and rock for everyone.

The couple were now sat looking proud, healthy and radiantly happy in the living room at Jericho Road. Audrey, beaming, brought in a tray of tea. Baby Margaret was gurgling in her pram by the window.

"Here Audrey, this is for you." Molly handed her friend an elegant black leather purse.

"Thanks Moll, oh it's lovely, oh look there's even two little pockets with windows to put photographs in – I shall put in one of you two at your wedding, and one of Margaret."

"Hey we could have mashed the tea Audrey," Bill protested, "You shouldn't be waiting on us hand and foot."

"No – let her earn her keep!" Molly joked. "And this is for my beautiful goddaughter." She bent down and kissed baby Margaret and placed a fluffy black and white teddy bear beside her in the pram. The child gurgled happily and stroked the bear. "Uncle Bill chose him, didn't you love. Looks a bit like him doesn't it – especially when he hasn't shaved."

"Who hasn't shaved, the bear?" quipped Bill.

"Go on you, get them cases upstairs, then you can have your tea." Molly laughed

"You'd have done well in the army my dear," said Bill, then sang, "Come on: Kiss Me Goodnight Sergeant Major…." He nuzzled her neck on the way out to the hall.

"Eh, there's a time and a place Bill Marshall."

"Aye-aye Sergeant Major!" Saluting, he went into the hall and picked up the suitcases.

Audrey whispered, "Are you sure it's ok for me to stay here Moll?"

"Course," replied Molly as she poured the tea.

"What about Bill?"

"Bill love!" called Molly, could you come back down here as soon as you've done them cases?

Bill reappeared a moment later. "What is it, love of my life?"

"Audrey's got something to ask you."

Bill looked at Audrey enquiringly. Audrey was blushing.

"No I haven't."

"Audrey, ask away, any friend of Molly's is a friend of mine." Bill's honest, open face beamed a big generous smile. Bill was one of those people for whom no secrets were hid, and he had not a bad bone in his body.

"It's just that I'm worried," began Audrey awkwardly, "if it's still alright my being here – now you two are married…and…"
Bill came over and put a big muscular arm around her.

"Of course it's all right love. It's lovely to have friends around, especially good ones like you Audrey. I'm just glad you let me come here to live." In a quieter voice he added, "Moll's told me what you've been through."
Like razor blades at her heart Audrey felt a sudden searing grief for Martin, as fresh and piercing and painful as if his death had been only the day before.

With an effort, she replied quickly. "That's all in the past now." She ran a hand through her hair. "Hmm, yes well, thank you, both of you, for being, well for being you, my good and true friends." She kissed each of them on the cheek then went to the pram and scooped up Margaret and held her close. "Perhaps later Moll," she said, "we can ask Mother Sarah to baby sit Margaret and we can go down to The Feathers. You can show off your new husband. And I'm buying the drinks."

"Oh I like you more than ever now," said Bill.

"Don't encourage him Aud."
Bill looked adoringly at Molly. "We'll drown our sorrows."

"We've got none to drown," said Molly.

"Come here then girl." He kissed his wife tenderly on the lips.

Audrey, her eyes brimming with tears turned away towards the window, tightening her arms around her daughter.

CHAPTER FORTY

December 1945

Bill was lucky. He had found a job when they were hard to come by. When he had been offered a start at the docks he had jumped at it. He had been there four weeks now.

"Here's your baggin," Molly said, handing him the khaki satchel. "And I've put a piece of apple pie in for afters."

Bill kissed her cheek. "You are one wonderful wife. I'll see you later Moll. Wish me luck." He always shouted this on his way out.

Molly gave her customary reply: "Go on with you," she laughed. "You're lucky enough."

She stood on the doorstep waving till he was out of sight then returned to the kitchen. She had given up her job at the hospital laundry soon after they married. Now she looked after her husband, Audrey, the house, and last but by no means least, baby Margaret.

She looked at the clock: it was 6 am. Audrey had already left for work at the bakery, and she and Margaret had the house to themselves.

"Plenty of time," she said to herself. "I'll have a brew first then see to the little one." She began humming a little tune as she pottered about the kitchen.

This now was her time - her and Margaret's, and she savoured every moment of it. Indeed she had grown to love the child as if she were her own, and often felt a pang of envy when Audrey came home and took all her attention.

"I must remember," she sighed to herself for the umpteenth time, "I'm Margaret's godmother, and I must be grateful for that."

She wondered, also for the umpteenth time, when she would start a family of her own. Bill had raised no objections, understood her broodiness and seemed in fact to look forward to parenthood as much as she did. He was also a passionate man, their bedtimes were satisfying and there was no apparent problem in that department. It was only a matter of time, thought Molly with a smile, before Margaret had a little playmate in the house.

That evening, as they all sat round in the living room talking, with the wireless playing soft classical music in the background, Audrey brought up the subject of the war.

Turning to Molly's husband she asked, 'so what was it like in the army Bill?"

Bill hesitated, and after taking a long, slow sip of his brown ale he said, "Well love, Egypt was very hot - and lots of flies, and the fellers all wore funny hats."

"Fezzes," piped up Molly, who was knitting a cardigan for Margaret.

"That's right – fezzes they call them, red they were, with little tassels, right comic."

But how did you feel out there," asked Audrey. "Were you ever afraid, afraid you might never come home?"

Bill shifted uneasily in his chair. He darted a sort of pained, pleading looked at Molly. He liked Audrey, but couldn't the girl take a hint, he thought; fancy asking him things like that.

War was dreadful and that was a fact, yes of course he had been afraid, and he had lost some good friends. He hadn't wanted to join up, but who did? He had done his bit and was proud of it. But he didn't want to talk about it.

Least of all to a posh girl whom he realised now he hardly knew, and who seemed to be coming over all Lady Bountiful towards him all of a sudden. She had lost her fiancé, surely he could expect a bit of tact from her. He did the pleading look to Molly again. She took the cue.

"Where's all this leading Aud?" she asked. "Why do you want to know what Bill felt about the war?"

Audrey blushed slightly but didn't answer.

"Is it to do with Martin?" asked Molly.

Audrey suddenly looked furious. "How dare you think that?" she exclaimed. "Can't I have a conversation now? I'm sorry Bill if I seemed intrusive, but Molly, if I am to live here I have the right to speak to your husband."

"Speak?" Molly put down her knitting. "It sounded more like you were interrogating him."

"Nonsense, I simply asked him a perfectly civil question."

"Well it was out of order. He's been through enough, and if he'd rather joke about fellers in funny hats rather than titillate a nosey parker like you by telling you how scared he was and what happened to the poor lads who never made it, then he's every right. I'm sorry about your Martin, everyone is, but Bill's a brave man too, but just because he was bloody well sharp enough, with his head screwed on, and lucky enough to have come home in one piece, that's no reason to knock him."

"Molly, are you suggesting Martin was somehow irresponsible, or…or incompetent?

"Don't be daft."

"And I was not 'knocking' Bill, as you so quaintly put it…"

"And don't you start criticizing the way I speak young lady – all I'm saying is folk have a right to a bit of privacy where we come from."

"Now we're getting to the truth aren't we – you don't think I belong here with you do you? For years you've pretended so, but you see me as different, not one of your jolly working class, salt of the earth merry band – not a 'real" person at all in fact. What you forget though Molly Bratt, is that my family have disowned and disinherited me, and I have nothing, I'm a nobody just like you."

"A nobody am I! I'm a darn sight more than you, you little madam!" Molly had risen to her feet and was shouting now. "And I've got more – I've got self-respect."

"You wouldn't know the meaning of the word!"

"Wouldn't I, then I'll show you what I do know."

"You'll not get the chance!"

Suddenly Audrey flung herself across the room, grabbed Molly's hair and began twisting it for all she was worth.
Molly fought back, yelling, "Ah, you cow! Get off me or I'll give you what for!"

Locked in combat back and forth across the room the lurched - pulling pushing, shouting insults and tearing into each other. As they collided as one solid mass with the sideboard, Molly's elbow nudged against the volume control sending the crescendo of Beethoven's Fifth Concerto up several decibels.

"Girls, girls," pleaded Bill in desperation above the noise, snatching up his glass of brown ale just before the pair went crashing into the table sending it rocking. Meanwhile, in the upstairs room, unheard by anyone, baby Margaret was crying her head off.

CHAPTER FORTY-ONE

A Peacetime Christmas

It was Bill, once he had turned the wireless down and the girls had paused momentarily for breath that first heard Margaret's plaintive crying.

"Now look what you've gone and done the pair of you – you've woken the little one."

Audrey and Molly exchanged mortified looks for a brief moment before Audrey released her grip on Molly's blouse and ran quickly from the room. As Molly started to follow, Bill restrained her.

"Leave her be," he said. "She'll be all right in the morning. It must be hard for her, seeing us together. I should have talked to her when she asked me about the war – it doesn't do to bottle things up. It's difficult to express though – women are better at that sort of thing – she lost her feller, that kind of hurt doesn't go away in a hurry - and here's us two lovebirds playing happy families and canoodling without a care in the world, and she's got a babby up there who's never going to see her father..." Bill hung his head as tears fell from his eyes. "I should have talked, when she asked, not dodged out...and now there's upset between you two..." He sat and put his head in his hands.

Molly came and wrapped her arms around her husband. "What a good kind soul you are Bill Marshall. It weren't your fault. Audrey had no right to pester you about bad memories, and the truth is she knows it and feels bad about it herself. And don't worry about our little tiff. Me and Aud go back a long way, we grew up together, against all her parents" wishes – the more they tried to keep us apart, the closer we stuck – it runs deep, and nothing's going to change that, however many times we might fly off the handle at one another – in all but name we're sisters. And you're a hero for putting up with the both of us."

Upstairs Audrey had closed the bedroom door and picked her baby up. The crying had stopped almost immediately. Margaret was now making a low, peaceful gurgling sound. Audrey sat on the bed, rocking her very gently to and fro in her arms. She felt full of remorse. Whatever was she thinking of asking poor Bill all those questions.

"I'll go down in a minute and apologise to him," she said to herself. Then quite spontaneously memories of Martin came flooding back.

"How he would have loved you, my sweet one," she smiled, stroking her little daughter's blonde curls as she laid her back down in her cot. From the bedside drawer, from beneath her silk hankies she took out a photograph. It was the portrait of her and Martin, the one her father had taken in the garden at Crosslands that happy day.

She kissed Martin's face tenderly. "My darling," she said softly, "I will love you for all eternity, and our darling daughter, lying here by my side will know of you and love you as much as I. Goodbye my sweet, sweet man, my lover, my life." She kissed the portrait again and replaced it in the drawer.

She gazed down at her sleeping child. "We would have made a lovely family the three of us, together." She pictured the scene: Martin, irrepressibly cheerful and funny and full of energy and ideas as always, playing blissfully with Margaret, watching rapt as she took her first steps, spoke her first words...Daddy...!

As this image, so magical, so painfully intoxicating became unbearable, Audrey forced her mind further back, to her own parents, her old home in Crosslands with its beautiful garden, her safe haven; Watty, tending the beds so carefully and dear Dorothy.

Both had always been her friends and advocates. But what did Dorothy really think of her now she wondered?

"You don't miss the water till the well runs dry." Dorothy had oft chanted these words.

Only now did Audrey appreciate their meaning. She was missing so much. She had existed, basked, safe and content in that world of Crosslands, which had been made heaven on earth by the arrival of Martin in her life all those months ago.

Now it seemed an age away, another lifetime another universe, a kind of perfect wonderful dream that had been destroyed by cruel gods.

What, thought Audrey as she lay down on the bed and closed her heavy eyelids, has happened to me? And whatever will now become of me?

"I can't wait for Christmas Aud" Molly said. That cake's going to be the main attraction. I'm not sure if I can wait three weeks for a slice."

"You'll have to."

Christmas was indeed coming - Molly and Bill's first together, and Molly was eager that this year the festivities would be more hospitable and enjoyable than ever, and what was more, had arranged, after some tricky negotiating with her mother to host the affair herself at 112 Jericho Road. She was aware of the challenge this posed; rationing was still in force, and even with sufficient coupons certain comestibles were not always available.

Fortunately everyone had rallied round, and with Bill and Monty now both working at the docks, there had been a steady supply of dented tins containing all manner of foodstuffs – peas, beans, carrots, artichokes, spam, corned beef, soup, ham, mussels, oxtails, ravioli, sardines and mackerel - brought home to Jericho Road to supplement the Christmas turkey or more likely chicken, as and when one could be found. Molly had carefully stowed the tins in a special cupboard in the kitchen marked "Christmas" in red chalk.

Audrey meanwhile, remembering early lessons from Dorothy in the large kitchen at Crosslands, had made a large Christmas cake, rich with plump fruit and laced liberally with rum from a broken packing case Monty had come across unloading a freighter in from Trinidad.

Molly had been more than happy to hand over responsibility for the cake to her friend. "You're doing a grand job Aud, much better than I would have done," she said, wiping her finger round the mixing bowl and licking it.

"You'll be sick as a dog," chided Audrey, "there's raw egg in there."

It would also be baby Margaret's first Christmas. Everyone, relatives, neighbours, friends and acquaintances, and even people Molly and Audrey had never heard of, but who had somehow heard about Margaret, were looking forward to spoiling the "little angel." Mother Sarah and Monty had of course been invited along, with Dorothy and Charlie and all of Molly's family.

Mother Sarah had already delivered a tin of red salmon, a tin of old oak ham and a jar of pickles for the Christmas tea, and Monty had just called in and left two large bags of tea and sugar. Molly's Christmas cupboard, not to mention her heart, was already near full to overflowing.

On Christmas Eve, Bill and Molly and several of Molly's kith and kin and Monty all went down to The Feathers. Audrey, politely declining Mother Sarah's offer to baby sit, stayed in with Margaret and hung a stocking on the chimneybreast to await Father Christmas.
She then sat by the fire with a mug of cocoa, reflecting on her life, and the events of another year now drawing to a close and what on earth was the new one going to bring.
On Christmas day morning Bill cleaned the pickle jar and polished the cutlery till it gleamed. More of Molly's cousins arrived, and Father Christmas did not disappoint Margaret, mysteriously filling her stocking with a pink wooden rattle, an adorable small white fluffy teddy bear, several tiny oranges and an assortment of minute chocolates wrapped in bright shiny paper of gold and silver, red and purple.
Margaret gurgled and giggled obligingly with innocent delight as Molly's younger cousins vied with one another to produce the most mirthful reaction by rustling the sweet papers, clacking the rattle loudly or playing peek-a-boo with the teddy bear.
With Boxing Day came Dorothy's turn as hostess. After tucking in with much merriment to the leftovers and Mother Sarah's pickles, salmon and ham, and making very short work of Audrey's cake, washed down with copious tea, in the late afternoon, hearing the distant beat of a drum the whole party decamped outside the house.
Through the fading light, a flutter of stray white flecks heralding the heavy snows even now pendulous in the darkening sky, the good old, ever comforting Salvation Army Band had just turned the corner.

As the sober, upright uniformed musicians processed in perfect step past 112 Jericho Road to the bitter sweet strains of In the Bleak Midwinter, as on every year for as long as anyone could remember the assembled onlookers, stirred by drink and bonhomie, by religion, deference and respect, wistful sentiment and some immense powerhouse of pious emotion infinitely deeper than thought, had not a dry eye among them.

Audrey remembered last Christmas and the sadness she felt. Her life had changed spectacularly, in the short space of 12 months. She had grown, found herself. The life she had at Crosslands seemed at the very least dreamlike. And as the music played Audrey, her heart querulous with joy, grief, hope and gratitude, crewed with the rest.

CHAPTER FORTY-TWO

January 1946

The New Year brought some good news for Bill and with it a worry for Molly. It was Sunday morning, and she and Bill had just finished a leisurely breakfast of eggs and bacon supplied by Molly's father's allotment.

"I don't know how we're going to tell Audrey Bill, I really don't."

"I didn't think she liked bacon." Bill looked up from his copy of the Daily Herald and shrugged at the empty plates on the table. "Plenty of eggs left."

"I don't mean the bacon," Molly said exasperatedly. "I mean your new job."

"Why should it bother her?" Bill shrugged again. "It's obvious Audrey and Margaret will come with us – once we've made the arrangements. There'll be more money in my wage packet – we can afford a bigger place I daresay. I thought you'd told her all about it."

Molly's frown deepened. "I wasn't sure how she'd take it – being uprooted again. Bristol's a long way."

"She'll get used to it – what's she got round here?"

"Her family for one thing."

"Thought they didn't want to know her?"

"They don't – at least - "

"What?"

Molly sighed. "Oh, I don't know. Audrey's in a bad way still Bill, she smiles and laughs and jokes all day long, but at night when I'm walking past her room I hear her crying, crying her heart out."

Bill looked thoughtful then nodded. "I know," he said quietly. "I've heard her too."

"She's got memories here Bill, not just her family and Jericho Road. Ivy said she was on the bus one day and saw her outside the American air base."

"What?"

"Saw Audrey standing by the wire, just staring in."

Bill shook his head. "All the more reason to get her away; she can't go on living in the past."

"I think she knows that, but it's hard for her Bill."

"She can make a fresh start – maybe meet a feller down in Bristol, once Margaret's off to school. She's a good-looking woman. Let's face it she can't stay here – what's she going to pay the rent with - fresh air?"

He took a large bite of toast and returned to the Daily Herald. Just then the hall door banged.

"She's on her way down," whispered Molly.

"Morning, you two," Audrey voice was cheerful as she entered the kitchen. "My you both look awfully serious."

Molly pursed her lips. "Bill's got something to tell you."

"Eh? Oh yes, sorry, I finished all the bacon." Bill doffed an imaginary cap and bowed his head.

"I don't eat bacon," replied Audrey.

"I told him that."

"I'd love a fried egg though."

"I'll put you a couple on love, you sit down." Bill got up and began busying himself at the stove.

Audrey looked on in bemusement. "I didn't know you could cook Bill," she smiled. "What's brought this on?"

"Aud," said Molly, leaning her elbows on the table. "Listen, we're moving away. That was what Bill wanted to tell you."

"Away, oh…" Audrey looked from one to the other of them.

Bill, his back to her, bent intently over the frying pan said "I've been offered a job see, only it's down in Bristol, warehouse foreman on the docks there - got a letter from the firm last week."

"We didn't tell you because we've been thinking it over, haven't we Bill."

"Have we?" Molly shot him a glance. "Oh, yeah, that's right, we're been thinking it over." He shook the pan vigorously making it hiss.

Molly, seeing Audrey's ashen face said quickly, "Of course we'd like you to come with us, wouldn't we Bill?"

"Oh definitely," Bill replied over the sizzling eggs, "and Margaret of course – can't leave her behind – ha- ha!"

Audrey felt her heart thudding in her chest. It's like a death knell she thought. Just when I thought I had found a place I could be, if not happy then settled, safe, a home, it is all going to be swept away. "But I…like it here…" she began unsteadily.

"We like it too Aud," said Molly, "but times are hard and they're laying men off on the docks here. Bill's very lucky to be offered a good job with more money."

Bill tilted the frying pan and flicked at the fat with a knife. "You'll get to like it in Bristol soon enough Audrey. It'll be a new start for all of us."

Audrey was shaking her head abstractedly and looking down at the floor. "Sorry, no, I can't come with you I'd only be in the way..."

"You're not in the way here, so what's the difference?" pointed out Bill. "Besides I've already organised it, the rent's paid here till the end of the month so you can stay on till then, and join us when we've found a proper place down there."

Audrey looked up aghast, then indignant. "You should have consulted me first," she exclaimed haughtily. "What makes you so sure I want to carry on living like a spare part with you two anyway? You both treat me like a...like a sick child, or someone mentally deficient." Her eyes were smarting as she tried not to burst into tears. Molly bridled. "Well if that's your attitude young lady we don't want you to come with us. We thought we were doing you a favour, but carry on Miss know all, stay here on your own."

Hearing this Audrey's face began to smoulder with rage. Before she could reply Bill came quickly to the table and set a plate of fried eggs and bread and butter down in front of her.

"Sunny side up!" he beamed, "just the way you like them."

"I don't..." began Audrey.

Cup of tea everyone?" interjected Bill again. With a noisy clatter of crockery he poured out three cups of tea, while intermittently whistling the tune of a popular song.

Audrey and Molly shot peevish looks at one another across the table. Bill opened his paper again.

"Eat up Audrey, before it gets cold," he said kindly. "Margaret awake yet?"

Audrey shook her head glumly, then picked up a knife and fork and began slowly to eat. Molly sipped her tea and said nothing, the three of them sat in silence.

When Audrey had finished her breakfast Bill said, "Want a look at the Herald Audrey?" She took the paper without speaking and began to turn the pages slowly. Bill winked surreptitiously at Molly. Molly did a little flick of her eyebrows.

Suddenly Audrey gave a kind of horrified shriek, followed by a long low wail of despair. Thrusting the newspaper violently away, she rose from her chair and ran sobbing from the room.

"What now?" Bill spread his hands in disbelief. Molly retrieved the Daily Herald and scanned the page Audrey had been reading.

She groaned. "Oh no." She pointed to a large picture of an ocean going liner. A paragraph underneath read: "First of the happy G.I. Brides to leave for America on the Queen Mary."

CHAPTER FORTY-THREE

Eternal Sunset

The atmosphere in 112 Jericho Road had been, to say the very least, frosty since the night Bill and Molly announced their move. Audrey had apologised several times to Bill, who, in his easy going, philosophical way was quite all right about it.

Molly however was a different matter, and relations between the two girls were still distinctly strained; Molly seemed moody and resentful, unable or unwilling to bury the hatchet, and every now and then firing little darts of criticism in Audrey's direction.

"Lady Know-All thinks we're offering her charity I shouldn't wonder," she remarked loudly to Bill one afternoon as Audrey came into the kitchen.

Audrey opened her mouth to offer a retort but stopped herself. Instead she said, "I was just going to take Margaret out for a walk in her pram. Would you like to come with us Moll?"

Molly shook her head and said nothing.

"How long is this going to go on?" Audrey sighed.

"Don't know what you mean,'" murmured Molly, "nothing's going on that I know of."

Bill looked at his wife with a pained expression.

"All right, please yourself," Audrey shrugged, and pouring herself a glass of milk took it up to her bedroom. It was where she seemed to be spending more and more of her spare time she reflected.

"But today is different." She beamed cheerily at Margaret and hummed a tune as she began to wash her, "because we are going on an adventure."

She gave her little girl a playful tickle. She then got her dressed and carried her downstairs, put her in her pram and left the house, setting off in the direction of the railway station.

Audrey had a new job now, at a nearby sewing factory, and as today's shift had finished early and the weather was pleasant she had decided to take Margaret out and enjoy the fresh air.

"Who cares if Molly wants to carry on being cross and won't make up?" she thought as she pushed the Silver Cross pram briskly along Jericho Road.

"The sun is shining and it's good to be alive. Isn't it Margaret? That's right little lady! And I tell you what," she added as an idea came into her head, "we'll go and see someone who I think *will* be pleased to see us." She flashed her daughter a bright smile as the pram bounced along.

An hour later, Audrey arrived outside the faded green wooden panelling of Jack's beach hut. The sky was azure blue, the sea racing as a brisk breeze blew across the sands. She tapped lightly at the rickety door.

"Jack it's me, Audrey," she called softly into the breeze.
Slowly the door creaked open and Jack Roberts her old friend appeared. Seeing her, his rheumy eyes lit up with happiness, his cheeks crinkling into the warmest kindest and gentlest of smiles – the dear familiar trusted face she had known all her life.

"Hello Audrey my dear, what a lovely surprise!" He leaned forward and pressed his cheek to hers. "And this must be little Margaret."
He reached a leathery finger towards Margaret's tiny pudgy hand. She gripped it, gurgling with delight. "She likes you Jack!"

"Oh our Dorothy's told me all about her you know, now come in, come in, there's a brew on the stove and bread and honey. And milk for the baby." He ushered Audrey and the pram through the narrow doorway. "I did wonder if I would ever see you again Audrey, after Martin I mean."

Audrey's face puckered. She threw her arms around the old man and sobbed. "Oh Jack I'm so sorry I didn't come to see you before now, you must think I'm awful, but so much has happened, and I didn't know how I could face you, its sounds stupid I know…it's just that…I know I should get over it and I've tried, believe me I've tried…but I…I still miss him so very much." Her shoulders heaved with great sobs.

He patted her back gently. "There, there girl, I don't doubt it my love, he was a fine young man, and you've every right to miss him and be sad. Time might be the great healer people claim it to be but we never forget those we've loved and lost, never. But you're a credit to him, you and your little one. She's got his eyes you know."

Audrey sniffed and nodded. Jack settled her on the little couch and lifted Margaret out of the pram and set her down on a thick woollen rug between them. He then poured tea into two mugs and handed one to Audrey. He sat in his rocking chair and they watched the baby playing.

After a while Jack said, "I heard about our Molly and Bill planning to move away."

Audrey looked up. "Oh…'

"And I know they want you and your baby to go with them.'

"But I can't Jack, it's not fair, not right." Audrey took a sip of her tea. "And not right for this little one either."

Jack frowned. "I think," he said slowly, "it has nothing to do with this little lady, and everything to do with you'"

"I don't know what you mean Jack." Audrey looked taken aback.

"Oh but I believe you do."' The old man's tone was kind yet incisive. "What our Molly said was right - you do think its charity she's offering you, and that's why you reject her kindness. You know, that must hurt her."

"Jack I never…"

"You being you – the way you were brought up and all, well, accepting what you think is charity - that would never do now would it."

"Jack, are you…are you suggesting I'm too proud to let Molly and Bill help me?"

To be judged like this by her dearest, oldest friend was too painful. Though her tone was indignant her eyes shimmered with gathering tears.

"Aye, too proud," said Jack unabashed. "That'd be the long and the short of it. We all have our pride Audrey. I'm finding no fault with you. I'm just stating the case plainly. There's no shame in feeling you way you do, you can't help it."

Audrey put her head down. She felt embarrassed, found out. Jack had seen right through her.

"But," he went on warming to his theme now, "neither is there shame in backing down, accepting Molly's help when she offers it. It can be as gracious to receive as to give."

"But I have accepted her help, lived under her roof for simply ages." she said. "I can't go on taking from her and Bill. Sometime I have to stand on my own two feet."

Jack smiled. "The good Lord didn't put us on this earth to see our neighbours starve and be lonely and go to the devil, though there's plenty of folk might behave like that. No, he put us here to help one another Audrey, and there's not a man or woman passes through this world that doesn't need it one time or another. You'll forgive my sermonizing, but the way I see it your pride's misplaced my dear. Molly and you have been friends since knee-high, against all odds. That's not something you want to throw away Audrey, not for pride. Don't go blaming our Molly for reaching out to you. I know the girl, if she didn't want you to go with them to Bristol, she wouldn't have asked."'

On the rug Margaret gave a sort of chortle and rolled over. Audrey's eyes were pendulous with tears now. "Oh dear...I just hope it's not too late to save our friendship."

Jack looked at her intently. "You come from money Audrey, class – a world apart from Molly and her kind. The way she sees it, by refusing to go with her and Bill, you're holding on to that world still, and turning away from hers."

"But I've never done that, never, my family turned me out, ever since then I've regarded Molly and the people of Jericho Road as my family..." blurted out Audrey.

"I know that, but now Molly might think you're having doubts about where you really belong. Perhaps you are. But don't you see – Moll's got used to you depending on her - she *wants* you to depend on her. It makes her feel special. The minute she thinks you can manage without her, she feels she don't matter no more. And against her better nature, she resents you for that."

Audrey's eyes widened. Her hand flew to her mouth,

"Oh my goodness, yes, of course." She moaned,

"Jack you've had hit the nail on the head."

Suddenly she understood, saw it all, the reason for Molly's hostility. She sat quietly for a moment absorbed, sifting her thoughts.

Then she said, "so what do I do then Jack, you seem to have summed up my situation."

"You're between two worlds, your heart cleft in twain. It's not so easy to cut ourselves off from our past."

"Don't I know it?" Audrey sighed heavily. "So you think I'm betwixt the devil and the deep blue sea?"

"Not exactly," said Jack. "But I sense your loyalties and sentiments are divided, and why wouldn't they be. Perhaps, if you're forced to make a choice it should be to go home, to your father and mother."

Audrey looked aghast. "Oh but Jack I couldn't..."

"Why not - they're rattling round at Crosslands in that rambling house, plenty of room for you and Margaret.'"

Audrey's face reddened. "I will never go back to them, never plead with them - never beg them to take me back. Not ever."

There was a pause then Jack said quietly. "Maybe you wouldn't have to."

"You think they'd even want me back?"

"You're their flesh and blood lass. Words uttered in haste and anger need not be set in stone forever. Molly's said her piece, and if you won't go with her, why not seek a way back to hearth and home. It's your decision of course, but you must remember you have your little one to take into account now." He stretched down and scooped up the smiling Margaret. "She needs a good home too."

Audrey looked at the two of them together, youth and age, wisdom and innocence, and was touched by the poignant beauty of the image. At the same time she shivered, gripped by a sudden intense awareness of the passage of time, the transience of human life. One day I will be old, as Jack is old now she thought, and Margaret will be a young woman. I cannot squander my time in idle indecision; I must do what is right here, but what is it? If she went with Molly and Bill they would always give Margaret their undivided, unqualified love, she would be safe with them, she knew that. Then she thought: but what about me?

"I don't think I can go with Molly and Bill," she said at last. "They are man and wife, and despite my friendship with Molly and all we have been through together, I fear that our lives, the balance, must now change – perhaps it has already changed." She paused. Jack gave a slow nod.

"As for my parents," she hesitated again, searching for the right words. "As for them – I will think about going to see them, just to talk to them, and...see. What more can I do?" She spread her hands imploringly.

"No more," concurred Jack. He smiled and brought Margaret to her. "If you do go then, depending on how things are and what they say, you make your choice girl. And who knows – you might find if you return home, you'll keep your friendship with Molly too."

"You really think I can have both?"

"There's a vast divide between your world and hers, and it would take a rare soul to bridge it, but..." Jack opened his arms meaningfully towards her. They sat in silence for a moment then Jack said, "Just one last word of advice - "

"What?'

"Don't dismiss your father. He's a changed man you know."

"Oh...?"

"Come," said the old man briskly, forestalling further enquiry. "Let's take Margaret along the seashore."

"Yes," Audrey's face was suddenly alive, vital. "Yes Jack - let's do that." She took Margaret to the door and stepped out of the hut. "Look the sun's setting!" Suddenly she remembered Jack's words to Martin:

"But young man, I must warn you that once you have looked upon the dying rays, it will burn deep within your memory, your soul and then, - it has you – it has captured your heart, and from that moment on, a little piece of you will always remain here, on these sands for all eternity"

Audrey looked at Margaret; Martin had left part of himself, here, on these sands with her to take care of forever.

Maybe she should visit her parents – though, if time had mellowed them, could she then swallow her own pride? If she went back to live at Crosslands how would Molly take it? Would she ever speak to her again?

She felt the divide Jack had spoken of opening up like a chasm beneath her: on one side Crosslands, and ancestry and memories and comfort and money, the ties of birth, kinship and upbringing.

On the other side was Molly, and a different, yet perhaps far stronger bond, of true friendship, and memories too, equally precious memories – yes, she and Molly were like sisters, would have been so if James had not been so suddenly taken from them both.

Somehow, she thought, however difficult it proves, I must be the bridge across the chasm. Her decision made she turned towards the setting sun and cried.

Audrey stared at the house. It looked exactly as before and all her remembrances came flooding back. It was as if time had stood still and she were a child again, just come home from school.
Steeling her nerves she opened the gate, pushed Margaret's pram up the path to the front door and rang the bell.
It was a full minute before the door opened to reveal Dorothy. Her face registered utmost surprise then fear.
"Oh! Miss Audrey – what…what are you doing here?"
Audrey felt a rush of happiness to see Dorothy, at the same time bridling at the question. Steadying her voice she said, "I've come to see my parents Dorothy - surely I am permitted to do so?"
Dorothy looked uneasy. "Oh Miss Audrey, are you sure this is right?"
"Who is there Dorothy?" a voice came from within. Audrey froze. It was Clarissa.
"It's me Mother." Audrey answered.
There was a chilling silence. Dorothy remained standing in the doorway.
"Kindly inform the young lady Dorothy that I do not have a daughter, and please close the door."
Dorothy shot Audrey a beseeching look.
"Oh dear -I'm so sorry Miss Audrey…I don't know what to say…"
Suddenly the door was wrenched open from behind and Dorothy was pushed aside. Clarissa stood there, her face a pale, emotionless mask. She looked at Audrey then the pram, then back at Audrey.
"Please let me come in Mother." Audrey said in quiet voice.
Within the blank face Clarissa's eyes registered nothing.
"You are not welcome here," she said flatly. "As I said, I have no daughter."
With that she stepped back into the hallway and closed the door.

CHAPTER FORTY-FOUR

March 1946

Desperation

It was now two months since Bill and Molly had left for Bristol. The whole of Jericho Road had turned out to see them off, Monty borrowing his brother's grocery van, still laden at the back with crates of vegetables to drive them to the station.

"You will be alright Aud, now promise me you will?" Molly's face was rueful and full of emotion as she leaned out of the window of the van for a final embrace.

"I'll manage somehow."

"I hope so, though I can't see how. For the life of me I still don't see what's keeping you here?"

"It was the sunset," said Audrey. "Jack showed me the sunset again. And Martin's there, there forever."

Molly looked at her, her expression a mixture of bewilderment and deep concern. She took her friend's hand.

"Listen Aud, if you need us, you always know where to find us. I'm so sorry I've been so grumpy with you these last few weeks –Bill says it's because I'm broody."

"I never put it quite like that," protested Bill, who was squeezed in between his wife, the driver and a stack of lettuces.

"You don't have to explain Moll." Audrey wiped away a tear.

"Sure you won't change your mind and come with us?'
Audrey shook her head. "But I will come down and visit, as soon as I can; both of us of course." She turned and picked up Margaret from her pram. "Say goodbye to Auntie Moll, Mags, and see you soon."

"Oh I'm going to miss you too little one." Molly planted a big kiss on the baby's cheek and squeezed her little hand.

"Hold tight all," cried Monty as he turned the starting handle. The engine growled into life and he jumped in. The van lurched suddenly forward, sending a crate load of cauliflowers cascading down from behind and into the passenger seats.

As the vehicle pulled away Molly threw a cauliflower from the window. Audrey caught it deftly and held it aloft, calling "Good Luck!" and waving till the van was out of sight.

Audrey had found it difficult to manage her job and care for Margaret since Molly and Bill had gone. She had known it would not be easy, but not feeling inclined to trust anyone to look after her child in quite the way she had trusted Molly – which was to say absolutely – the hours she had been putting in at the sewing factory were now few and far between.

On the days Mother Sarah was unable to mind Margaret Audrey simply stayed at home. Nonetheless, with careful managing of her outgoings, and making use of every scrap of food – she made potato peelings into soup and was now an adept at bread puddings – she was surviving.

Added to this Dorothy, when she could escape her duties at Crosslands and the eagle eye of Clarissa, often dropped by now and brought in half a loaf of bread and some cheese, together with milk and porridge for young Margaret, and loyal, thoughtful Monty was a steady supplier of all manner of tinned goods.

Dorothy also gave her regular news of Molly and Bill.

"Why don't you go and visit them Miss Audrey," she urged one morning as they drank tea together in the kitchen at Jericho Road. "I'm sure a little holiday down there in the West Country would do you and Margaret the world of good. Or I'll look after Margaret if you wanted to go on your own."

Audrey considered this for a moment. It would be difficult taking Margaret on a long train journey, even if she could afford the fare. Then a horrible possibility occurred to her: if she left Margaret with Dorothy, supposing her mother found out, and to spite her came to Jericho Road and tried to snatch the child? It did not bear thinking about.

"It's kind of you to offer Dorothy," she said, "I'll think about it."

"And Molly says in her letter that you're still most welcome to go down and live with them. She's worried about you, you know, and I can't say as I blame her. The rent on this place doesn't come cheap she told me, and you know what landlords are, if you can't pay you're out on the street, and then what are you going to do, what with little Margaret…"

"Dorothy!" Audrey snapped. Her face was livid. "I know you mean well, but I am an independent woman. I have a job, a wage. I am grateful for your help, but your advice I find impertinent in the extreme. I am quite capable of managing on my own."

Dorothy shot her a look. 'Ah well, I daresay you know best Miss Audrey.'

The next day, after leaving Margaret with Mother Sarah and reporting for work at the sewing factory, as she was about to clock in the foreman came up to her and told her not to bother. Her services were no longer required.

CHAPTER FORTY-FIVE

Dark Dilemma

Despite Audrey's pleading with the foreman to reconsider, he was adamant. There were plenty of girls, he pointed out, keen to come in full time, not "play around at working".
At half past twelve Audrey was on Mother Sarah's doorstep to collect Margaret.

"You're early Aud, everything all right?" Sarah had noticed her dejected expression.

"I've been asked to leave."

"Oh Aud," exclaimed Sarah sympathetically, "what you going to do? I can look after Margaret for longer if it helps."

"Thanks Ma, but I can't impose on you all the time you've your own family to see to. I'll have her at home. I've got all the time in the world now." She gave a joyless laugh.

Back at 112 Jericho Road Audrey went straight to the kitchen cupboard and surveyed the contents; there was one tin of apricots, some evaporated milk, a chunk of hard, stale cheese and a jar of baby food. Right at the back was a large cauliflower. It was the one Molly had tossed from the van the day she and Bill went away. The florets were still firm and crisp but needing using up quickly. And Audrey needed to eat. She diced the cauliflower, filled a pan with water and put it on to simmer. The cheese softened when grated over the warm cauliflower; and the bread, after dipping it for a few seconds in the vegetable water quite palatable.

She warmed the jar of baby food the same way and fed it to Margaret, who obliged with her customary gurgle of pleasure.
Looking at her daughter fondly Audrey thought: It's all the same to you little one, isn't it, so long as you have some nice food and you're nice and warm. Audrey felt a lump rising in her throat:
"Whatever happens little one," she whispered, "you shall never go hungry, you shall never be cold; you shall want for nothing, that is my solemn promise to you."

Even as she mouthed these words she shivered. The kitchen felt cold now the stove was off. She struck a match and lit the gas ring again. The flame purred for a few seconds then spluttered and went out.

"Oh bother, the meter must have gone again," Audrey exclaimed. She rummaged in her purse. "I'm sure I had a shilling here somewhere baby..."

She tipped the contents of the purse on to the table; a three-penny piece, two pennies and a farthing rolled out.

"Never mind," said Audrey to her self in a bright voice, "it'll soon be summer..."

Just then there was a knock at the door. A smile leapt immediately to Audrey's face. Perhaps that's Monty, she thought; I'll ask if he knows where I can find a lump or two of coal for the fire, we're right out. Then she remembered it was the afternoon, and Monty would be at work.

Opening the door cautiously she saw someone she did not recognise, a middle aged man in a crumpled grey overcoat and bowler hat. He looked equally surprised by Audrey. His lips parted in a thin smile as he tipped his hat in greeting.

"Afternoon madam, I don't believe we've met. I've come for the rent. You are the new tenant I take it?" He looked in his notebook. "That'll be twelve and ten pence please."

"Oh – I'm so sorry yes of course can I pay you next week? It's just that I'm..."

"Out of work are we? Oh dear, oh dear,"

"No, no, I'm between jobs."

"That's a good one I must say! You're already a month overdue." He looked Audrey up and down. "On your own then are you dear?"

Audrey looked down and nodded. "Yes, just me and my baby."

He smiled the thin, lascivious smile again. "Then we could always come to some other arrangement I'm sure."

"Other arrangement?" Audrey looked baffled; then to her horror he leaned towards her and stroked her face. She stepped quickly back into the hall.

"Now don't go all shy on me, a pretty girl like you, all alone with a kiddie deserves a helping hand..."

"I'll have the money for you next week," she interrupted and went to close the door. He blocked it quickly with his foot.

"Now don't be hasty my dear, no sense making a rod for your own back. You're a lady I can tell that. You deserve to be treated like one."

"But you are no gentleman!" retorted Audrey angrily, as with a swift kick his dislodged his foot from the door and slammed it shut. She jumped as the letterbox rattled open.

"I'll be round next week," he called. "I do hope we can be friends. It's no life for a girl walking the streets, not with a baby. I wouldn't want that to happen to you. Think on my dear, think on. There is always the air raid shelters you know."

The letterbox snapped shut again. He was gone; but he would be back again, Audrey didn't doubt that. Whatever was she to do, wherever was she to go? She knew of the air raid shelters, young men, women, families living in those abandon hovels. She'd quickly passed by those places, seen the people, their clothes dirty and bedraggled, seen their children, living in squalor, seen despair ingrained in their grimy faces, and hopelessness burning in their saddened eyes. And she like all the other passerby had hurried on. But what if she couldn't find the money and the landlord threw her out onto the streets.... He had as good as implied that. The realization of how close she was to joining those poor souls hit home. What if like them she was put in a position where she didn't have a choice…especially if she didn't comply with his disgusting lecherous suggestions. She shivered; it didn't bear thinking about.

With Molly and Bill hundreds of miles away she could hardly expect Dorothy's family to take her and Margaret in – for one thing they simply hadn't the space in their already overcrowded house.

Her mother's behaviour at Crosslands made it clear there was no going back there. If only she could get to see, or communicate with her father. What had Jack said – 'he's a changed man.' But where even was her father? Audrey had seen no sign of him that terrible day she had been turned away by her mother.

She tried desperately to weigh her options. She could try to find another job, but everyone was saying there was no work. She could capitulate and throw herself on the mercy of Molly and Bill to take her in down in Bristol, but some intractable knot of pride in her made this seem somehow impossible, more so than the appeal she had made to her mother.

Meanwhile the immediate, hand to mouth problem of keeping herself and Margaret alive seemed all-consuming; her mind whirling in ever decreasing circles like some hideous, sickening merry-go-round of indecision and despair. Audrey knew if she could not find the will or the means to get off this ride to hell then sooner or later, one way or another, she would be flung off.

The image of Elsie and the Magnet suddenly entered her head. *'I make more money in one night here than a week in the bakery...'* she had said. What led an otherwise decent woman like that to sell her body for money? Audrey gasped to herself. Of course, now she knew: desperation. Molly was right: people will do anything when they are desperate.

Dear Molly, she thought, my friend and saviour, if only I could find the humility to admit I'm in trouble and say I'm coming down to Bristol after all. What a strange, monstrous thing human pride was; for here am I, thinking I might almost rather do what Elsie did, than call on my best friend for help.

Almost - that was the crucial word. Perhaps she could at least try to get her old usherette job at the Magnet back. The money it paid would barely keep her alive.

Mother Sarah had told her of a rumour that the side door operations at the Magnet had been resumed, and that Aggie had taken Mrs Skillycorn's place. She remembered Elsie's words again: *'I make more in a night here than a week at the bakery...'* A desperate woman will do anything. I am that desperate woman, thought Audrey. She took Margaret upstairs, then lay down and tried to sleep, but the merry-go-round in her head would not stop spinning. An hour later she was awake again, and writing a letter, an apologetic, pleading letter to her Molly.

Four days later, a reply came back, welcoming her and Margaret down to Bristol with open arms, and enclosing a postal order with more than enough money for a train ticket to Bristol.
She had put her pride aside and appealed for help. And judging from the tone of the letter Molly was thrilled she was coming, and without a trace of I-told-you-so in her tone.

Audrey felt so happy now she wanted to burst into song. In fact she did. She and her dear, lifelong friend would be together again. It would be just like old times. There was such a thing as happiness after all, thought Audrey, and sometimes it's right under your nose if you only look for it.

CHAPTER FORTY- SIX

An Agonising Decision

Now that Audrey had resolved her dilemma and decided to join Bill and Molly, her fear of ending up destitute and on the streets was removed at a stroke.

It had however allowed another, somewhat disturbing matter to surface in her mind. It was an issue of responsibility, and now, as her escape to Bristol and the security and support of her dear old friend drew imminent, a certain dramatic chain of events she had recently set in motion - albeit from good intentions - tugged at her conscience.

It amounted to this; at the investigation into Mrs Skillycorn's violent death at the Magnet she had testified to the police that Elsie had been with her all evening. This had, as Audrey had intended, exonerated Elsie, whom she had regarded as the real victim. Of course, she had known that in doing so Maurice Pendleton would become the prime suspect in the case.

With all her other worries since, she had given that aspect of the affair little thought. Then one day she had overheard two women on the street corner saying, "Pendleton's going to swing for it."
Suddenly the full implications of her simple statement to the police became clear; Elsie, who by her own private admission to Audrey had, whether intentionally or not, killed Mrs Skillycorn, was walking free, while an innocent man, Maurice Pendleton was now likely to hang.

In the last few days the thought had haunted Audrey. One night she dreamt of a rope and saw Mr Pendleton's anguished terrified face, heard his fearful cries of innocence, his pleas for mercy as the hangman prepared...She had woken in a sweat, and with a desperate urge to go to the police and confess her lie.

Then she had hesitated. Firstly, if the police believed her now, it would spell doom for Elsie. Did she really want that? And what might be the consequences for her? She had withheld evidence, sought to pervert the course of justice; the police might arrest her, send her to prison. But if she stayed silent, an innocent man would die; could she live with that on her conscience, would she ever sleep soundly again?

She tried to convince herself of Mr Pendleton's wickedness, that in some way he must deserve this fate for condoning or turning a blind eye to the exploitation of vulnerable women at the Magnet.
She failed; instead she kept seeing Mr Pendleton's abject, terrified face, then she imagined his wife, his children – did he have any? It didn't matter she saw them anyway.

So was it to be Mr Pendleton, or Elsie who went to the gallows? It is my choice, thought Audrey in horror. The women's words echoed again and again through her head: Pendleton's going to swing…Never before had she faced such an ominous, world shattering decision. The trial would take some time she imagined. She decided to put the matter off, at least for now.

Audrey had decided to leave for Bristol early on the coming Saturday, before the landlord returned for the outstanding rent the following week; let him whistle for it she thought.
It was now late Friday afternoon, and having bought her train ticket, packed her suitcase for the morrow and said goodbye to Mother Sarah, she was setting out with Margaret for a last walk of the day.
As she approached the top of Jericho Road she heard the familiar cry of the newspaper seller. "All your local news…read all about it!" Then something in particular made her stand stock still and listen, "…Magnet killing, jury's verdict…read all about it…!"

Audrey pushed the pram faster, hurrying towards the corner. She saw the paper seller, his last copy sold, folding up his stand and getting on his bicycle. She called out, "Wait…" But he was already gone.

She hurried back the way she had come, the pram bouncing over the paving stones and Margaret giggling in delight. A minute or two later she reached the corner shop at the bottom but it was already shut, the newspaper billboard taken in for the night. Agitated she looked around; surely someone must be around, on the way home with a copy of the paper.
But the street was deserted, the light now fading, everyone indoors having tea. Audrey saw in her mind's eye the hangman's noose again, and Mr Pendleton's look of terror. Tomorrow morning she was going to Bristol, the ticket was bought.

She had to do something; she had to save an innocent man's life. Elsie would then be arrested, but she must plead it was accident - she had *said* it was an accident, she would be let off, she would *have* to be let off. I have to act now thought Audrey, if I leave it till I am in Bristol Mr Pendleton may be already dead.

Audrey crossed the road, and made her way quickly to the nearby police station. Breathless now she hauled Margaret's pram up the steps.

"Hello, hello, and what can we do for you Madam?" enquired a burly sergeant.

"I've come to make a confession," panted Audrey.
The sergeant looked at her quizzically. "Oh yes Madam? And to what crime precisely do you wish to confess?"

"Evening George, shame about that Pendleton wasn't it." Another policeman had just come in off duty.

"In a way I suppose," agreed his colleague. "But maybe he really didn't do it. If there wasn't enough evidence the jury could hardly convict him."

"Suppose not. Anyway he's a free man now. I wonder if they'll ever find out who really did old Skillycorn in." He turned back to Audrey. "I'm sorry Madam, now what was it you were wishing to confess to?"
Audrey had caught sight of a copy of that evening's local paper on the sergeant's desk. The headline on the front page read:

CINEMA MANAGER AQUITTED OF MURDER

"Well Madam?"
Audrey, her face already red from exertion, was now blushing furiously.

"I...I'm behind with my rent...and the landlord, has been making horrid advances..."

"Don't live in Jericho Road by any chance do you Madam?" Audrey nodded.

"I think I know which landlord you mean," said the sergeant sagely, "and not the first time we've had to have words about him pestering women. We'll send a man round to see him don't worry.

But if you can't pay your rent, he's every right to throw you out of course." He looked at Audrey's shabby coat, at little Margaret's thoughtful inquisitive face peering out from the pram.

"Your husband out of work is he?"

"He died," said Audrey quietly, "in the war."

The sergeant cast his eyes down. "I'm sorry," he murmured. He then dug in his pocket and pushed a silver shilling across the desk towards her. "You look as though you could do with a good meal love."

"I'm quite all right thank you," protested Audrey, "I couldn't possibly accept...."

"I hope you're not going to disobey an officer of the law," interrupted the sergeant sternly, "because that's a serious offence." Sheepishly Audrey took the coin. "Thank you...I needed a shilling for the meter as a matter of fact. I'll pay you back of course when my circumstances improve. I say, I couldn't perhaps take a look at your newspaper for a moment could I?"

The sergeant handed her the paper. "Take it home with you my dear. My boys spend far too much time reading the local scandal and gossip. And you keep warm now."

Back indoors Audrey read the article intently from start to finish.

Maurice Pendleton, manager of the Magnet Cinema in Liverpool has been found not guilty of the murder of Mrs Phyllis Skillycorn a cashier at the said premises by a jury at Liverpool Crown Court. Skillycorn, who was found dead in the cinema's pay office, was rumoured to be running a brothel in a concealed part of the building. Pendleton was arrested after the body was discovered and charged with murder.

Following the jury's decision Pendleton said, "I am naturally very relieved and can now get back to work and on with my life. The rumours of the brothel are unfounded, Mrs Skillycorn was a decent woman and a very good friend and she will be deeply missed by all at the Magnet. The cinema remains open, it is business as usual and I know the staff will join me in urging our loyal patrons in the area that we should all put this dreadful business behind us."

A police spokesman commented that the murder was possibly carried out in the course of a robbery, and that the case remains very much open.

Audrey felt as if a ton weight had been lifted from her, her sense of relief that an innocent man had been freed so immense. It was loathsome though to hear Mrs Skillycorn being described as 'decent'. Mr Pendleton could hardly believe this, and he had certainly known about the brothel, and no doubt profited from it in some way.

Still, hypocrisy was not a hanging offence; and, even though the police were keeping the case open, her alibi safeguarded Elsie. It was the best possible outcome.

She could leave for Bristol in the morning with a clear conscience, and look forward to a new life for her and Margaret with Molly and Bill. She would send the outstanding rent for Jericho Road on of course, that was a matter of principle, and she mustn't forget to send a shilling postal order to the kind sergeant at the police station. She smiled with satisfaction as she thought of the slimy landlord getting a good ticking off from the cops. That night she had the best night's sleep in months.

Next morning Audrey leapt out of bed with a spring in her step and a song in her heart. She washed, dressed and fed Margaret, and took her suitcase down to the front door.

She wrapped up the last of the stale bread and cheese, and some apples Mother Sarah had given her, and put them in the bottom of the Silver Cross pram for the journey.

This reminded her; she must send Monty a few shillings as soon as she was on her feet in Bristol, he had been so kind bringing the pram, not to mention all the food treats over the past few months. Then there was Mother Sarah of course, and Dorothy too – so many people had been so very good to her and Margaret. And now that she had decided to join her dear friend Molly, life was about to get a whole lot better. I don't deserve it, she said gaily to herself as she opened the front door and wheeled Margaret out onto the pavement, I really don't deserve it.

The postman was just coming along the road. Audrey gave him a broad smile. "Must be your birthday," he grinned back, and handed her two letters.

"Thanks," said Audrey.

Putting the brake on the pram she tore open the first envelope. It was an official looking missive, from a firm of solicitors, and read:

"Dear Miss Stephenson,

Mr & Mrs Marcus Stephenson wish you to be aware that you are not welcome at their home, the above address, and should you attempt to visit, or to contact them in any other way, they will take steps for legal proceedings for harassment to be instituted without notice against you.

Yours sincerely
Edward Carter
Carter, Simmons & Carter, Solicitors at Law

Audrey read the letter without much emotion. It bore all the hallmarks of her mother; pompous and cold, a piece of petty spite dressed up as high-minded legal nonsense. Her only surprise was why on earth, after her last humiliating visit to the house, Clarissa imagined she would ever dream of making any further attempt at a rapprochement.

Nothing now could dent her joie de" vivre; if anything the letter only reinforced the wisdom of her decision to go to live with Molly and Bill. She smiled, knowing the ridiculous letter would give Molly and Bill a good laugh. She stuffed it in her pocket and opened the other envelope. The communication within read:

Dear Miss Stephenson

You don't know me, I live next door to Molly and Bill and I found your address in their book. They were always talking about you and Margaret and were delighted that you had changed your mind to come and live with them. Molly was telling me only the other day that she missed you both and couldn't wait to see you again. But Miss, I'm so sorry to tell you this but Bill and Molly were killed two days ago. A bus over turned; they were on the lower deck, didn't really stand a chance. I don't know what else to say but I will inform Molly's mother. I'm so very sorry.

Yours sincerely
Dennis Stringer

CHAPTER FORTY-SEVEN

Sacrifice

Audrey stood on the doorstep. Silently her lips mouthed the stark, fragmented words: Bill and Molly...killed two days ago...bus overturned...didn't stand a chance...

The blank, chill statements reverberated in her ears like some booming proclamation in a vast court room, the judge donning the black cap, jurors bowing their heads, someone in the public gallery screaming: 'No, no, no...!' an awful, howling terrifying wail on and on and on...

The person screaming was Audrey. Except her scream, so deafening, so agonising, remained within; no audible voice could she summon.

"Bill and Molly are dead."

When finally she spoke the words they came out very quietly, almost with a sense of weird, fascinated absurdity that would not give them credence, such was the level of her horror. Five ridiculously ordinary words that when put together, smashed her world to pieces.

"How can this have happened?" she said out loud now, "how?"

Her mouth had begun twitching, but her eyes were dry, wide, and staring in disbelief into thin air. She pictured Molly, her lifelong friend, so bright, so warm - so alive. And Bill, the tough, stoic soldier, built like a lion with a heart to match – how could two such vital, solid, real people, going about their lives in the peace and quiet of Britain suddenly and so randomly cease to exist? It was impossible.

Audrey still could not weep. The shock had rendered her quite numb. Her face still jerking, she gripped the handle of the pram and began to walk slowly down Jericho Road.

As if wading through water, without being fully conscious of where her footsteps were taking her, she found herself following the route she had intended that morning: towards the railway station.

Ten minutes later she passed alongside the police station. She paused to peer in through the open doors at the clock on the wall. It was 8.30 am. The train she had planned to take was due in fifteen minutes. She must press on, she thought, must go to Bristol, of course she must, there would be things to do, to arrange, to help with...oh Moll...!

It was then she started crying, a sniffle at first, then, like a great storm that begins with a few drops of rain, her tears fell in abundance, her shoulders shaking uncontrollably, her body wracked with violent sobbing as she collapsed in a heap on the steps of the police station.

After a while she realised someone was bending down beside her. "Is there anything I can do Miss?"

She looked up and saw through her wet eyes the kindly, concerned face of the police sergeant from the previous evening. Audrey shook her head. "I'm sorry to make such a scene," she blubbered apologetically, "I've had some rather bad news today."

"I could see you were upset, here." He offered her a clean, folded handkerchief. "What's happened Miss?"

She blew her nose loudly. "My dear friend and her most wonderful husband...oh heavens...a frightful accident...I'm on my way to see them ... was on my way to...oh dear... I *have* to see them, except, oh; I can't ever see them again..." She broke off as a dreadful, suffocating wailing overcame her.

"I'm so very sorry." The sergeant's face was sombre, his eyes full of sympathy. He laid a hand on her shoulder. "You poor girl, where were you going to?"

"Bristol," said Audrey unsteadily. "They'd just moved down there, I was going to join them, to live with them, with my little girl here, they both loved her so much, and now..." She burst out crying again.

"Look, my dear," said the sergeant gently. "Go home. Postpone your journey, what good would it do? Remember them as they were. Does your friend have any family here?"

Audrey looked up. Of course, Molly's family. With a searing heart she thought: do they know? Most of all Molly's mother, Dorothy – did she even know yet? Yes of course, she must have been next of kin after Bill. She was probably even now on her way to Jericho Road to see her.

"You're right," she said quickly wiping her face. "I must go home at once, I must see Molly's family, thank you, thank you for your kindness…"

"You're from Jericho Road, the girl who reported the rent man."

Audrey nodded and looked at him, her eyes filling again, her lips trembling. "Molly took me in, and we lived there until she moved to Bristol. She was a dear soul - the dearest, sweetest, kindest soul imaginable."

The sergeant took her in his arms as she sobbed her heart out.

Audrey would not have imagined, when she had left 112 Jericho Road less than an hour previously that she would ever be returning, let alone so soon. As she let herself back in and eased Margaret's pram over the threshold she reflected grimly that it was a good job she had kept hold of the key.

Closing the door she noticed that two envelopes had since been dropped through the letterbox. Both were unstamped, one addressed simply, 'Audrey'. She tore it open and saw it was from Dorothy.

Dear Miss Audrey,

Please excuse my poor writing, but forgive me the news I have to give you. I got word yesterday our Molly, and Bill, have been killed in an accident down in Bristol.

It's a shock to all my family and I know you will feel the same. Our Molly said in her last letter that you were to go down to Bristol and join them. They were looking forward to you joining them and making a new life for yourself. Perhaps you will still decide to follow her example and set out for fresh fields and pastures new.

Charlie, me, and the family have decided to leave Liverpool for the countryside. We can't stay here, now Moll's dead, too many memories and Charlie's sister has a small farm there, she's been asking us to go and live with them and now I think is the time. There's a small cottage near by that we can make our home. Needs a bit of work but it will keep us all busy; take our mind off our dear sweet girl. I'm sure we can make ourselves useful in many small ways on the farm. The funeral is next Wednesday at St John's Church. I hope you can come. With God's Will, may we turn the dark shadows that now hang over us, to a time of sad but golden memories for us, and in time a joyful future for you and Margaret.

Look after yourself Miss Audrey.
Dorothy

She opened the second missive. It was from the landlord of the property. It was short and not at all sweet, warning her that if the rent arrears were not paid within ten days, bailiffs would be sent to evict her. She took the letters through to the kitchen and sat at the table. A renewed, more powerful wave of grief swept through her.

"It's not true, you can't be dead, Moll," she raged to the empty house. "You promised me if I should ever need you, you'd be there, and I need you more than ever now. Why you, why!"

She put her head in her hands. Her heart was racing uncontrollably – along with the grief, fear, desperation and panic was now fomenting within her. With no job, no money, and now no friends, the prospect of a new life for her and her daughter was dashed. Even Dorothy was running away, and who could blame her? "DAMN YOU MOLLY, DAMN YOU FOR LEAVING ME!" she screamed.

As if answering her despair the mood outside had also changed, the early promise of the fine spring morning now threatening, as ominous clouds gathered across the sky, filling the little kitchen with gloomy silhouettes as if nightfall were approaching.

Audrey shivered as the rain began to drum on the panes and she felt her own dark shadow steal menacingly over her. Molly was dead. It could not be altered. The world had changed forever, just as when Martin died.

As the storm intensified the kitchen grew even darker. Audrey got up and switched on the electric light. Why not she thought, while the meter held out. In the sudden brightness of the room she caught sight of herself in the mirror over the mantel. Was that really her reflection – that pale, unhealthy face, the lank, unkempt hair the faded dress? Oh what has happened to me, she thought with a sudden hopelessness, where, why, did my life go so terribly, irretrievably wrong?

Elsie's words echoed again in her mind: I make more money here in one night... She looked again at the letter from the landlord. She thought of Margaret, who would soon be hungry again.
She knew, oh yes she knew why Elsie had done what she had done. Now she, Audrey needed money, and going through the side door of the cinema was a way of getting it. One night, that's all she needed. She drew in a long, deep and painful breath.

At 6 pm Audrey left Margaret with Mother Sarah, telling her she was going to visit Mimsy at the hospital. Avoiding Sarah's inquisitive glance she hurried off to catch the bus. As it approached the Magnet cinema she rang the bell and got off. She waited by the steps and a few moments later saw Maurice Pendleton approaching.

"Hello Mr. Pendleton, do you remember me?"
Pendleton flinched slightly on seeing her. "Oh, yes, of course."

"I was so glad to hear of your...the trial...that things worked out well for you..."

"Yes, yes."
He seemed jumpy, nervous thought Audrey. It was understandable.

"I just wondered, if there were any vacancies at present...?"

"There's no job for you here."

"Oh please Mr. Pendleton, I need the money, you must have something."
Glancing quickly up and down the street he muttered quietly, 'Try the side door,' then brushed past her, went up the steps and into the cinema.

Audrey stood rigid for a moment. Then with a quickening pulse she turned and walked decisively to the corner of the building and turned smartly down the alley. The side entrance was shut.

Raising her knuckles slowly she then rapped boldly twice on the door. Then suddenly, behind her she heard someone calling her name.

"Audrey – Audrey wait for me…" She span round. It was Elsie, and she was running towards her.

"Elsie – what - what are you doing here?"

"I was about to ask you the same question." Elsie, who was looking smart and well dressed, was panting. "I just saw you, from the bus, and I jumped off – for god's sake Audrey don't do this."

"What on earth do you mean?" retorted Audrey indignantly, "don't do this. You've some room to talk, back here working again are we?"

Elsie took hold of Audrey's arm. "Listen to me, I heard about Molly, it upset me too, I know you were going down there to live with her and Bill, and I know you're hard up, but don't do this, please, there must be some other way."

"Nonsense!" Audrey spluttered. "I was just going to enquire about an usherette's job - I don't know what you're implying…"

Suddenly the side door swung open, and framed in the light stood Aggie.

"Well if it isn't Miss Posh Knickers!" she cackled. "Ma Skillycorn said you'd be back here one day, the devil rest her soul. Well don't just stand there, come on in."

"Don't do this Audrey,' Elsie pleaded. 'Don't go down that dark road."

"There's work for you too Else girl, if you're not too high and mighty now that is…."

Aggie's speech was abruptly cut short as Elsie slammed the side door smartly in her face. She rummaged in her handbag and produced two silver half crowns. She pressed them into Audrey's palm. "Take this, no, no take it, Harry's in work, got a good job now, we're doing all right."

"Elsie, I don't want your money – I don't need your money…"

"Listen," interrupted Elsie. "I'll never forget what you did for me, if it hadn't been for you I'd, well, we both know what. So take this, please." She closed Audrey's fingers over the coins. "And come with me – now!"

Audrey shook as Elsie tugged her back up the alley. A bus to Jericho Road was just coming along. Elsie flagged it down, shepherded Audrey aboard and watched till the bus was out of sight. Audrey, her face pale, her eyes vague and distant, began to shake even more.

CHAPTER FORTY-EIGHT

"I know you're in there, hey girl!" Mother Sarah shouted as she knocked again at the door of 112 Jericho Road. "Now open this door."

"What's up Mother?"

Sarah turned and saw the familiar tall, broad shouldered figure of Monty coming along the pavement.

"Oh, its Audrey," she said, "I've not seen her for days, and she won't answer." She knocked again. "I ran into Elsie who said she gave her a few bob a while back but since then there's not been hide not hair of her. She never turned up to Molly's funeral neither."

Monty joined her on the step and hammered loudly on the door with his huge fist.

"Come on love - let us in," he yelled. "Folk are worried about you." Still there was no answer.

"Last time I saw her she looked as if she'd been crying," said Sarah, her brow furrowed with anxiety. "What with losing her job, and then what happened to Molly - I'll never forgive myself if something's happened to her, god help me..."

"Stand aside Sarah," ordered Monty.

Stepping back a few paces he charged the door with his shoulder. With a splintering of wood it crashed off its hinges.

"Audrey love, it's us," Mother Sarah shouted as she and Monty almost fell into the house. "Where are you?" Monty bolted up the stairs and began searching the bedrooms.

"Oh love, sweetheart, there you are!" Sarah had gone into the kitchen. Audrey was sat in front of the cheerless kitchen range. She was shivering.

"Where's Margaret?" asked Sarah at once, looking around the room, which felt terribly cold.

On the table lay a piece of mouldy bread. Audrey lifted her arm and pointed to a couch. Sarah found the baby there wrapped in a blanket and fast asleep.

"There, there now." She put her coat around Audrey's shoulders.

"Molly's dead, and Bill," said Audrey blankly, her eyes staring straight ahead.

"We know love - we missed you at the funeral, that's why we came round."

"Oh my goodness, Molly's funeral, whatever's the matter with me, I didn't go, she deserved better of me, much better, she deserved to live, to be happy…" She began to weep bitterly.

", there." Sarah comforted her. "It's you we're worried about now."

"I spent the half crowns – Elsie gave me…. the other night, at the cinema… didn't know what else to do." Audrey mumbled. "I needed money, but the side door - I didn't do anything Sarah, honestly I didn't, Elsie stopped me." She began to sob.

"All right love, it's going to be all right. Monty!" She bellowed towards the hall where Monty was trying to wedge the front door back in place. "Go to my house and bring some coal and stoke a fire. And put this shilling in the meter. And bring milk for the baby and whatever food you can find."

"Right." Monty took the shilling and disappeared on his mission.

An hour later Audrey and Margaret had been fed and the house was feeling a little warmer. Monty, having temporarily stood the dismembered front door up, had gone off to look for tools to mend it properly.

"Right love," said Sarah, "now I want you to sit tight here and keep that blanket round the both of you, while I go off to find the doctor."

"Doctor? But I don't need a doctor,' protested Audrey. 'I've no money to pay him…"

"We'll cross that bridge when we come to it," said Sarah firmly, and patting her arm, hurried away.

Audrey sat on the couch, taking care not to wake Margaret. Staring blankly at the cold cheerless hearth, she heard nothing, felt nothing, cared for nothing. What happened to her now didn't matter, but what of Margaret? She watched her daughter sleeping blissfully unaware of the torment her mother was going through.

"My beautiful girl," she whispered, and gently kissed her child's forehead. "Your daddy would have loved you so."
A wave of sadness overwhelmed her and she began to cry bitterly.

"Miss Stevenson?"
Audrey jumped. It was the unmistakable, insinuating nasal voice of the landlord.

"What's been going on here then eh? Somebody take a dislike to my door? That's another thing to be paid for, one way or another. Miss Stevenson? Ah, so there you are."

Audrey froze as he entered the living room and leered at her.

"I've nothing for you," said Audrey quietly.

"I want what's owed to me, lady, and one way or another I'll get it. If not the bailiff will be calling. You'll not find him so tolerant, or charming as I am."

His hand grabbed her arm and twisted it. Audrey rose to her feet and screamed in pain. He pushed her hard against the wall and she smelt his foul breath as his mouth searched for hers.

"Get off me!" she pulled herself free but he grabbed her again, tighter this time.

"What's going' on?" shouted a voice. Monty had come back. He marched into the room and grabbed the landlord by the scruff of the neck.

"She owes me money," he whined.

"And she'll pay you," Monty growled. "But not like that. Now be off with you while you're still in one piece." He dragged the protesting figure to the door and threw him bodily down on the pavement.

With some difficulty the landlord picked himself up, brushed his coat down and glared at Monty. "I'll get what I'm owed," he said. "One way or another."

Ignoring him Monty went back in to Audrey. "Are you all right love?"

Audrey was shaking uncontrollably. He put his strong arm about her. "Come on," he said, "you can stay with Sarah tonight."

Audrey lay in the deep, enveloping feather bed in Mother Sarah's back room. Shafts of moonlight filtering through the threadbare curtains cast delicate patterns of light and shade on the faded wallpaper. She reflected on the day - and what a day it had been. The fact of Molly's death in itself still felt utterly devastating, and its practical implications for Audrey, poverty and destitution, were only getting worse. There seemed no way out.

Morbidly she cast her mind back once more, compelled to retread for the umpteenth time the path, which from her simple, comfortable, happy existence had led her to a place of such loneliness and horror.

Crosslands had been perfect, she had the best of everything and appreciated none of it, took it all for granted. Likewise Braeside –the old sepia photographs she had discovered by chance in her father's study. Oh, that immense, majestic house, enchanting as a fairy tale castle and hidden away, deep in the remote Highlands of Scotland, the lawns and terraces, the sprawling estate and the silent mysterious loch; these images, elusive, shimmering and magical, Audrey held in her memory like a precious picture book of her childhood.

She had never known exactly what had happened to Braeside. What *was* the real story there - how had her parents, who were so wealthy, so shrewd, so in control of everything, managed to lose such a place? There was something sinister, some dark unsolved riddle at the heart of it all, she felt sure of that. Would she ever find out the truth, especially now – would she even see her mother and father again? It seemed unlikely.

It was with the mysterious disappearance of Braeside, that the rot seemed to have started setting in for the whole family. The war began, and shortly after her adored brother James had been tragically lost at sea. Then of course Martin had come along. Audrey replayed the memories, the familiar, wonderful, intense and painful memories: how they had met, how they had loved at first sight and never stopped loving, and how by the cruellest measure of fate he had been snatched from her.

She recalled the night she had arrived at Jericho Road, and how Molly had taken her in, cared for her and asked nothing from her in return.

She had taken Molly for granted too, thought that their friendship would last forever. Now, in the blink of and eye, Molly was gone too. Now, even her parents might as well be dead.

"Nothing lasts forever," she whispered. "Nothing but the past - that can never change"

Audrey gazed at her sleeping daughter lying next to her, oblivious of the silent turmoil and desperation in her mother's mind. "Thank goodness you don't understand what's going on."

She kissed the child's forehead. Margaret stirred but did not wake. She is so beautiful thought Audrey, her dark hair like mine her violet blue eyes like Martin's.

"I love you so very much," she whispered, taking the child up and gently rocking her in her arms. "And I have to do what is best for you."

She decided she had to get away, leave Jericho Road and all its memories; make some kind of new life for herself - but what would that be like for Margaret?
With no family, money or prospects, it would be hard, impossible probably, for her to turn her own life around now.

As a poor, unconnected single mother, a grinding, shameful, hand to mouth existence, begging, borrowing or stealing to survive, was probably the best she could hope for now. But need Margaret suffer the same fate?

Perhaps not, maybe there was a solution, a way that would offer her child hope of a better future. Margaret would doubtless grow up to be beautiful; she might easily find a good, handsome man in years to come, a person of means. But till then she needed proper looking after, to be well fed, clothed, educated. "I want the best for you my darling, a life just like the one I had, but threw away."

The card the doctor had given her earlier lay on the chest of drawers. She squinted at the address. Turning to the window she looked out across the rooftops, the rows of chimney pots silhouetted against the night sky. As she lifted her face towards the moon, its ghostly light took her shadow, and cast it long, dark and obsidian across the room. Audrey gazed down once more at her daughter sleeping peacefully in her arms.

"My dear child," she breathed, tears now forming in her eyes, "I have to do what is right for you."

CHAPTER FORTY-NINE

Monty had repaired the door at 112 Jericho Road the previous evening and with a gentle creaking push it opened. Audrey carried Margaret in her arms to the bedroom.

The April sun streamed in through window, as Audrey dressed her little girl for the very last time.

"We'll put this lovely dress on today darling. It's the one Aunty Molly bought for you."

Margaret beamed her happy smile and jiggled her favourite teddy bear.

"We're going on a special outing today, and I want you to be a good girl for your Mummy and not cry," Audrey said brightly.

"Are you alright dear?" Mother Sarah had opened the bedroom door. Noticing the card on the bedside cupboard she looked at Audrey's face. Audrey said nothing, but nodded slowly.

"Oh love - you don't have to do this you know,' said Sarah. 'You could both stay with me."

"Thank you." Audrey made the semblance of a smile. "But I know what I have to do. There's no other way. Margaret needs a proper home, a proper family."

Sarah pulled the door halfway to and waited on the landing, occasionally glancing anxiously in. Audrey sat Margaret on her knee and began rocking her gently to and fro. Where I go after this, she thought, doesn't matter. But I will go in the knowledge that for once in my life at least, I will have done the right thing.

"Remember my darling," she whispered as her tears fell softly, "I will always, always love you, you're my best girl." She kissed the child tenderly. "Your daddy would have been so proud of you, you know, he'd have loved you and kissed you and watched you grow into a fine little girl and we would have been so happy together." She took the ring box from the bedside cupboard, opened it briefly then slipped it in her pocket. She was sobbing desperately now. Mother Sarah opened the door, took Margaret and went silently down the stairs.

Audrey contemplated what she about to do; her child would grow up with two loving parents and a better life than she could offer, but this knowledge did not, could not ease her pain. Sarah shook her head and waited quietly by the front door.

After a moment Audrey came slowly downstairs, suitcase in hand.

"You've made your mind up then?" Sarah said.

Audrey put the case down and nodded. She took Margaret and put her in her pram. "Too many memories here for one thing." She gave a deep, unsteady sigh.

"Here." Mother Sarah held out her hand to Audrey, and with it a ten-shilling note. "Take it, its from me and Monty."

Audrey hugged the old lady. "You've been a real friend," she said intensely. "Thank you."

"And you – where will you go?"

"I don't know." Audrey said. "But as soon as I get on my feet I will pay you both every penny of this money back."

"It's a gift dear. Gifts are for keeping, and some are more precious than others, the most precious things in the world."

She looked down at Margaret, then piercingly into Audrey's eyes as if she were about to say more. But she held her tongue. The next second she took Audrey tightly in her arms, "Oh you poor child." They stood locked in an embrace.

It was Audrey who moved away. "Please - Sarah, I have to go." She was choking back tears now.

"So you do love, so you do," Sarah murmured.

She opened the front door and helped Audrey ease the pram out onto the pavement. "You take care of yourself dear, Write to me you hear! Let me know you're all right."

"I will, and thanks for everything," Audrey waved a hand to the old woman and set off down Jericho Road with the pram, crying, and never once looking back.

It was a long way on foot to the city. Audrey could have caught the bus but she wanted to walk, to stretch out every last second of time she had left with her daughter. On reaching the High Street she headed straight for the pawnbrokers. Her heart was breaking. All the promises she had made, all the hopes and dreams she had cherished now lay shattered, her once beautiful life that had been filled with happiness, joy and laughter reduced to rubble by the ravages of war, misfortune, and her own foolish pride.

Passing the ring across the counter she envisaged Martin's handsome, smiling face. How brief their time together had been she reflected, but how utterly momentous and everlasting his imprint on her soul.

"Two pounds nine shillings." The jeweller said coldly. "Got a run on these since the Yanks left."

Audrey didn't reply. She had kept the ring through thick and thin, but now she had no choice but to surrender it, just as with Margaret. The band of gold that had bound them, and their daughter – in a few moments both would be gone forever. Her hand shook as she accepted the cash, folded the notes carefully and placed them in her purse. She still had the train ticket to Bristol and more than enough now to take her a long, long way away – Edinburgh, Dover or London…? Soon it would be over, Martin would be gone; a dream, a moment in time and all she had of him would vanish.

Tucking the blanket around her Margaret she took out the card the doctor had given her. Struggling to contain her raging emotions she made her way to the address. This was the hardest thing she would ever do. She could not bear it, could hardly breath….

The smoke-blackened Victorian building loomed up before her. With a nervous glance she read the inscription on the brass plaque: St Angelina's Adoption Agency.
Taking Margaret in her arms she climbed the steps to the huge oak front door and rang the bell.

"Forgive me Martin," she whispered in a trembling voice.
For the first time in a while, the usually happy Margaret, began to cry.

EPILOGUE

The grand Cunard Liner, in from America had just tied up. A tall imposing figure, dressed in a fine astrakhan coat and homburg hat strode slowly, imperiously, down the gangplank. Taking off a pair of kidskin gloves, he flicked them idly from hand to hand and looked around with a relaxed, though observant eye.

A man in chauffeur's uniform approached from the dockside. Doffing his cap he indicated a gleaming Rolls Royce. "Your car is waiting Mr Regent sir." He held open the rear door.

Oliver Regent took out a large cigar and climbed into the vehicle's sumptuous, leather-upholstered interior. On the adjacent seat there reclined a slim, elegantly dressed woman.

"You got my letter then?" murmured Regent.

His companion turned to him. It had been a good few years since he had seen her. He noticed threads of grey in her raven black hair, though her eyes, her dark eyes were exactly as he remembered them, a mirror image of his own.

"Oh yes," purred Clarissa taking his hand in hers. "Welcome home John. We've a lot to talk about."

Printed in Great Britain
by Amazon